BALCONY
OF
EUROPE

BAL

OF

EUR

Calder & Boyars

CONY

OPE

Aidan Higgins

First published in Great Britain in 1972
by Calder & Boyars Ltd
18 Brewer Street London W1

ISBN 0 7145 0102 6   Cloth Edition
ISBN 0 7145 0103 4   Paper Edition

Printed in Great Britain by
Ebenezer Baylis & Son Limited
The Trinity Press, Worcester, and London

For

RUTH

Este libro, esa casa, unos hijos: aquellos hombres.

And to the memory of Miguel Lopez Rojas, *camarero*, died December third 1964. Peace to his *manes*.

By the same author

Felo de Se

Langrishe Go Down

Images of Africa

The author would like to acknowledge with gratitude the assistance given to him personally by the Arts Council of Great Britain during the writing of this book.

DOJZŁOŚĆ

It's good what happened
it's good what's going to happen
even what's happening right now
it's o.k.

In a nest pleated from the flesh
there lived a bird
its wings beat about the heart
we mostly called it: unrest
and sometimes: love

evenings
we went along the rushing sorrow river
in the river one could see oneself
from head to toe

now
the bird has fallen to the bottom of the clouds
the river has sunk into the sand

Maturity
Zbigniew Herbert
(Tr. Czeslaw Milosz and Peter Dale Scott)

Traum: Ich finde mein Haus: leer, ausgetrunken den Wein, abgegraben den Strom, entwendet mein Nacktes, gelöscht die Grabschrift. Weiss in weiss. *

—*Tagebuch III,* 1914
(Studienreise nach Tunesien).
Paul Klee.

* Dream: I find my house: empty, the wine drunk, the river diverted, my naked one stolen, the epitaph erased. White on white. (Paul Klee, Tunisian Diary 1914)

It represents sensuality and lubricity behind which runs so many mortals that resemble beasts.

El Bosco: *El Jardin de las Delicias*
Prado catalogue: *Titulo ironico referido al mundo*
'*No pinto tan extranas pinturas Bosco como yo vi*'
(Quevedo)

They were as fed horses in the morning: everyone neighed after his neighbour's wife.

Jeremiah:v.8.

CONTENTS

Part I. Autumn 1961 Dun Laoghaire

Part II. Spring 1963 Andalusia

Part III. Winter 1962 Spain

Part IV. Summer 1963 Andalusia

PART I

Autumn 1961
Dun Laoghaire

1 THE GENTLEMAN RIDER: Flaking distemper fell from the ceiling and lay like snow, a greyish slush, on the damp linoleum that had buckled and perished here and there, by the door that would not close, under the draining-board, around the dinted and seldom disinfected bucket that had no handle, before the stove with its coating of thick grease, as Sharpe the taximan moved in the room above. He was their landlord, and the rent was low.

In the cold basement flat below, the old somnambulist, sodden with tea and porridge, stared out over the soiled half-curtain with its design of corn-stalks and sheaves of wheat. In the garden the finches moved among cabbage stumps, and valerian withered on the granite wall near the postern-gate. And then a tabby cat appeared on the path and birds flew out of the apple tree and the cistern upstairs began to choke and splutter.

My father heaved a sigh, turning away from the window, walked slowly on creaking cricket boots over the faded surface that sweated all winter, and entered the room off the kitchen where he slept. A barred window admitted some light. At one time it might have been a larder. He made up his bed. It had no sheets; a narrow bed covered in soiled and threadbare rugs. He put on his overcoat and muffler, prepared to go out.

My mother Dilly Ruttle was waking in the shadowy front room in stale air. A low table scattered with miscellaneous objects stood by the fireplace where she burned papers. A single uncomfortable armchair in leather, the last survivor of a suite from Sligo, was piled with newspapers. One of my early watercolours, *Cows in Clover, Dromore West*, exhibited in the Living Art show of 1952 but never sold, hung on the wall facing bed and window. The damp stain had come back on that wall. A ship's clock from *Irish Lights* (property of an uncle-in-law, a Belgian suicide) stood on the brown sideboard, bought second-hand in Cumberland Street from Andy Hand. It was Autumn 1961 and the clock hands were three-quarters of an hour slow.

Through the persistent drizzle of impressions and half-impressions filtering their way sluggishly through his morning brain, one effacing the other, interspersed with yawns, farts, belches, sighs, the sound of the hour came from the bell-tower of the church on Royal Marine Road. In Monkstown, Glasthule, Sallynoggin, Killiney, Dalkey, Kill o' the Grange and Cornelscourt it was nine o'clock, and nine o'clock where he stood, among fifty thousand others preparing to face the day in Dun Laoghaire, the old royal dun, now a place of church spires and dog turds.

My father crossed the dark hall to my mother's room. He needed money to fetch milk and bread for her breakfast. She brought out a purse from under the mound of pillows and from it took a half crown, which she handed across in such a way that her hand did not touch his, saying: And bring me back the change, mind. Not like last time.

Their roles were reversed. Now it was she who managed the money, such as it was, and issued the orders, such as they were, for him to obey. Whereas before it was she who had been the solicitous one, and he the strict one. Now she was strict and he solicitous. She had 'put her foot down' as to who should visit and who should not (I don't want that one in the place. Or: Don't talk to me about that fellow), Aunt Molly, but not Aunt Gerty. The flat was too shabby. It was a 'disgrace' and she had no heart to clean it, and would be just as pleased if no one came. So no one came. Corcoran, the publican who was interested in antiques, called and was turned away. My mother had never needed friends, and now towards the end of her life, she had none except Mrs. Bowden, a widow who worked in the Irish Sweepstake offices at Ballsbridge.

Are you finished with these? my father asked, pointing at the pile of newspapers on the armchair. My mother hid the purse under her pillows. Yes, she was finished with them. She watched him collecting them, folding one upon the other, pressing them down. He read nothing but newspapers and he read them thoroughly, omitting nothing, competitions in the London tabloids, sports items, lists of runners on race-tracks.

A languor and a weariness seeped up through the worn carpet, coming up out of the very floorboards. This had happened before, it would happen again, with modifications. The very air was tired. My mother turned her face to the wall.

Footsteps made a hollow sound passing on the pavement outside. A man and a woman shape passed. People were on their way to work. My father left the room.

What kind of a day would it turn out to be? Good or bad, wet or fine, ordinary or exceptional, a great sum won at long odds, a few hours of forgetfulness in the bars? Snuffling up his nose, my father went back to his room, piled the newspapers on another great pile already mounted there, hid the half crown in an empty Players packet, took out from its hiding place a florin, put it in his pocket, pulled on a pair of woollen gloves. There was hoarfrost on the window. News items of general interest were impaled on great nails, what he termed buck nails. A younger and more vulgar version of his younger son, myself with hair parted in the centre, arms folded, protuberant knees below white shorts, a small betasselled cap on the back of the head, posed in a school rugby XV. D. J. Ruttle, lock forward, brawler in the mud. The window gave on to a terrace that led to the Mariner's Church and the grey harbour, the mail boat docked at No. 2 berth. My father had been down that morning shortly after seven to watch passengers disembark. Three or four times a year he would see someone he knew. It made the day for him. The habit of going there had become a ritual. He had waved to Olivia and me when we had come back from Canada. A small indomitable man whose bowed back had surprised me, his vague eyes and Irish accent. Sharpe was there to drive us the few hundred yards to Haigh Terrace, and Olivia heard for the first time my mother's high sing-song voice.

But on that raw morning no one known to him had disembarked. Sharpe had a few fares. My father returned, lit the gas oven, left the oven door open, the only form of heating available. The kitchen warmed to a humid body-heat as he prepared the porridge. It was like attempting to warm an igloo. He ate his porridge, plugged in the electric kettle (a present from Olivia), went back to his room to change into his only good pair of shoes. Other figures passed the window, huddled against the cold wind blowing off the harbour. He changed out of his cricket boots. Now the passers-by were walking above his head. Above his bed the school group, purposeful young athletes, the crossword puzzle that almost won the prize, the charm contest ('Dalkey Man Wins £500'), spot-the-ball competitions.

If he won, he spent it immediately. Money burnt holes in his pockets. That was his nature: given a little he was a spend-thrift. He liked the open-air life, out in all weathers like a cab-horse. Once well-off, he had lived improvidently, and now he had nothing but the old-age pension and the rent that my brother paid. He collected the pension in Glasthule, where he was not well known, or not known at all. In Dun Laoghaire he was known. In winter, those interminable winters that he hated, a sack of low-grade turf came with the pension. He burnt it extravagantly and then went without heating. That was his way.

That bloody fool, my mother said, bitter as acid. The past and its retinue of cronies, good fellows, yachtsmen and ladies in white on the Shannon, brilliant days, waved to him from the white deck. My mother was there.

In return for light gardening duties in a Glenageary garden he had the price of a suit from one of his married sisters, one of thirteen, all married. He was the only son, the mollycoddled boy. My mother was the only girl in a family of seven boys.

Sister Molly bought him new shoes. His friend Corcoran put up £12 for a winter overcoat. So he was fitted out. He took charity, did not complain, wore the collars of one shirt, the cuffs of another, the body of a third (the tail of the latter cut up to make the former parts), wore another as an under-shirt, for he was thin and felt the cold. For the same reason he washed irregularly. The narrow bathroom with its flaking walls and lack of hot water was not inviting. He never took a bath. In the toilet the cistern was out of order, the chain wound about a wire scrubbing brush. You flushed with a handy chamber pot. It would do.

For most of his life my father had dressed casually, tight cord jackets with single or double vents (mark of a racing man or a bounder), thin-stripe good quality shirts, ties that stood out from the chest when secured by a tie pin, three inches of cuff on display, gold cuff links, a handkerchief up one sleeve, a display handkerchief in the breast pocket, highly polished tan brogues with pointed toes and perforated uppers, a centre parting in the hair, a dandy's socks, a whiff of eau-de-cologne. He never wore a hat. A short, nimble man with watery blue eyes who was sometimes mistaken in public for this or that professional jockey, Smirke or Quirke, which he accepted as a compliment. After all, he had ridden in his day, been a gentleman rider. Lifted his elbow at the Horse and Hound.

That bloody fool, my mother said. Oh that bloody fool! He had kept a race horse at Nullamore. A mare called One Down: aptly named, for she had never won a race. As a vet he had not been a success, playing golf at Rosses Point. He watched the Galway Plate from the roof of his car, saw One Down coming in well down the field, ridden by Grogan the stable boy. The going was too soft for her, my father said. It didn't suit her at all.

I had grown up with the horses. Grogan cleaning the stables, putting down new straw, watering and exercising, up by day-break. A racing horse needed more attention than a woman, Grogan said. A stunted youth with cruel hands, stretching the cat to see if it really had nine lives, lifting Wally and myself by the temples so that with slanted coolie eyes we could 'see Dublin'. Time stood still in the stable yard. Time stood still in the garden at Nullamore. The pediment of the sun-dial was cracked. I slammed the car door by mistake on father's fingers and he used atrocious language. One Down went on losing. Once she came in third.

Dr. O'Connor was a regular visitor. He wore a fur coat down to his ankles and was seldom sober. He liked my mother.

My father continued to play golf. We began to live in elegant poverty. My father remained calm. That bloody fool, my mother said. Oh that bloody fool. One night he woke her to say all the money was gone. Wally and I could not go to university after all.

Nullamore was sold and we moved to Dalkey outside Dublin, where we were not known at all. The actioneer's notice, discoloured with age, was impaled on one of his buck nails:

On the instructions of the owner

FOR AUCTION

NULLAMORE, SLIGO, PERIOD RESIDENCE

Suitable for Stud Farm
Ideal Hunting Box or Small Racing
Establishment
Inner yard with stabling for 9
Cattle yard with Dutch Barn &
ties for 40 Cattle. Attractive
flower and vegetable gardens.
Fee simple. Rateable Valuation
on Buildings.

SEEN ONLY BY PREVIOUS APPOINTMENT.

And a picture of the house, viewed from under the sycamore tree in the front meadow, with a work-horse grazing on a cloudless day. Only a fadograph of a yestern scene.

He spoke often of the great jocks of the 1930s: Joe Canty, Martin Quirke, Morney Wing, Dinnie Ward, Martin Maloney and Charlie Smirke ('a Jew-boy but a great jock'). For him they represented the golden age of racing, at a time when he himself had money, money to burn. These were the jockeys he watched going over the fences and on the flat. He saw Steve Donoghue win the Irish Derby at the Curragh in 1916. Donoghue and Smirke had each ridden three Epsom winners. They watched the Irish Grand National at Faerey House every Easter Monday. My mother in a cloche hat and fur coat, my father gazing through binoculars.

Grogan told me of the big stakes laid and won by the Aga Khan. He rolled in the hay with a local girl. Would you fight your match? Grogan said. He had bow legs and wore leather gaiters, hobnail boots. He went out with Lizzie Bolger, who wore powder and lipstick, frizzed out her hair.

In August they drove to Galway for the Galway Plate. They drank whiskey in the Great Southern Hotel and walked in Eyre Square. The Spanish Arch was named after the Spaniards from the old Armada who had been driven ashore. The living ones were hidden from the English and the dead ones were buried by the Irish. My father and mother drove home late, none too sober.

Uncle Jack bred and trained race horses and had more luck than my father, who played golf in preference to attending sick livestock. Dr. O'Connor drove a Rolls-Royce at ten-miles-an-hour about the country. My mother's gums were an odd colour, the colour of rubber. She drank a morning glass of lukewarm water and Epsom Salts. My uncle Jack sucked raw eggs, won the Liverpool Grand National of 1938 with a horse called Workman (Tim Hyde up). My mother's younger brother Jimmy Orr rode three times in the Liverpool National. Once he came second, the following year third. Wally and I sucked bulls-eyes, shot birds with Daisy air rifles. Plum puddings hung from bags suspended on hooks from the kitchen ceiling.

My father, who had once been an amateur rider, had always dressed like a swank. Nowadays, with the going a little harder, he still dressed like one. A dark suit with a display handerkchief in the breast pocket, patent leather shoes—relics from his dancing days. When the patent leathers wore out, he wore my old cricket boots, with wads of newspaper as under-soles. The paper came out in shreds. Walking about the flat he shed the stale old news that was just beginning to be forgotten, the stamp scandal, the fellow who abducted with the funds.

Another breeder, more methodical in his ways, took over the running of Nullamore, other race horses exercised in the seventy acres, Ringwood Son and Cabin Fire flew over the jumps where One Down had faltered and Grogan had come down.

I left home.

A Dublin insurance office claimed my time. I had some success in painting. My parents moved from Dalkey to Dun

Laoghaire. Fifteen years went by. I met Olivia, left the insurance office.

My father, grown old in the years I had been away, spent much of his time in the men's bathing place at Hawk Cliff in Dalkey, a good walk for an oldish man. He gossiped with the swimmers in the summer, kept his eye on Corcoran's clothes in the winter. Corcoran, a reformed alcoholic with ideas about physical fitness, swam in the icy winter sea, performing exercises in the buff on the cement ramp. He had a bald pate which he daubed with brown boot polish, bought my father an occasional packet of Players, taught him how to bid at auctions. He was shy (too damn cute, my father said), a silent man with a shaky hand (the jigs, my father said), a speech impediment. (That fellow would drive you mad, my father said. He's cracked himself. Who but a madman would want to jump into the sea? Do you know what temperature it is? Forty-two degrees. Corcoran's mad.)

The auctioneering was not done on a percentage basis, my father neither asked nor was offered remuneration except packets of Players. After a lay-off of about fifteen years he had begun to smoke again. (Corcoran's stingy, my father said, tight with his money. And he has pots of it.)

Keep it and you'll always have it, he said, hoping he might inherit some of it, my father who was at least ten years Corcoran's senior, and always spoke as though he would live to be old as Methuselah. His credulity was only matched by his ignorance, his faith had the naïve quality of primitive superstitions. What he believed had a charming inaccuracy about it, an arrested stage of knowledge of ignorance like the mythical basis of heavenly bodies as seen through pre-Copernican eyes. The Bug, my father said. I've got the Bug. It was 'going' in Dun Laoghaire. In due course he would catch a 'dose' of it. Pneumonia. About the workings of his own constitution (marvellously healthy considering how little he ate) he knew about as much as he knew of the language of the Copts.

He bought tickets in the Irish Sweepstakes, as he had done all his life, half shares once, now quarter shares. He lived in hope. Be the living Jaysus, Dan, this year my luck will change, I have the feeling, he said, staring at me with his weak blue eyes that were always watering now in the cold. *Arcus senilis* had spread, vague hopes swam there, prosperity at the eleventh hour, vague dreams, all addled together. Begod it can't get worse, he said laughing.

Mind your language, my mother said sharply. I'm sure Olivia isn't used to such language where she comes from.

Grow up, woman, my father said, endeavouring to make it sound as offensive as possible.

Very trying, my mother said when my father had left the room, that fellow is very trying.

She was jealous of his attentions to Olivia. Livvy, he called her. The girl's name is Olivia, my mother said. Will you listen to him, that fool of a man making a show of himself, at his age.

She mistook inbred courtesy for incipient senility; so in the ashes of their old love there was still a little fire. At all events she resented the gallantry displayed for my wife's benefit. Olivia was tall, if not outrightly beautiful then very close to it: a tall girl with a good figure who never put on 'side'. A sad clownish face, a good carriage, a certain grace and consideration in her manner. Olivia did not put herself out to please or impress, but she did put herself out to be kind, and to my father she was kind.

We called on them once or twice a month, hardly more than that, generally on Sundays. And at two and three in the afternoon we would find them still in bed, the shutters drawn, the light already beginning to wane, the fog-horn sounding mournfully out in the bay.

My father mentioned a new light-ship or floating light-house that was to be moored on the sand bank. Highly sceptical of this as he was of all services or improvements from any Fianna Fáil government (the new car ferry that would ruin the three yacht clubs). He had been to school with Eamonn de Valera, had beaten him in the 880 yards. A killer, my father said, that fellow's a killer. Talk about what you know, my mother said. My dear woman, my father said, my dear woman.

He had a prejudice against Jews. I know those bucks, he said, I know their sort. And yet Jack Ellis of the Grafton Cinema had been kind to him, lent him money when he needed it, sold him furniture at a discount; still he professed hatred and mistrust of Jews. 'The Chosen People!' he said, as he might have said 'Usurers!' It was an old attitude and nothing could change it. That man's a complete fool, my mother said. His best friend is Jack Ellis.

I had grown tired of these barbed exchanges and wished they would end (a fog-horn moaning out on the bay, the low kilowatt light already burning in the afternoon, the feet of people passing, my mother bringing out a Monument Creamery cake from the brown cupboard, my father in creaking cricket boots fetching a lemon for my tea). So was ending a long and latterly acrimonious association, at the beginning of which I stood in short trousers, a herring-bone suit with matching waistcoat, hobnail boots, vacant ways, standing with raw knees and red hands in a field at Nullamore. And in summer in shorts and sandals. I parted my greased hair in the centre like my father, whom I was named after, said to take after. Wally and I learnt our ABC with the nuns. We developed flat accents. Me ma, me da, dis an dat. My faw-dur. My mudder. Me brudder. Soft as the dunging of cows. We attended the National School and were strapped by nuns, caned by Christian Brothers.

So passed forty years. Kenelm's Tower of Howth Castle, George Collie's life classes, working under Delaney in the Irish Assurance Company in O'Connell Street, commuting from Amiens Street station to Howth.

From her lair my poor mother stared at me, as though I were already far away. The room stank of women's old stale things, cheap perfume, stale clothes. A stoop-shouldered man coughed in the vegetable garden that was as restricted as a prison exercise yard. He wore a cloth cap, a muffler about his throat, sallow like the consumptive Collins who had died in a sanatorium. Perhaps he was a war veteran, gassed or shell-shocked? He had a closed and miserable air about him, and no civil word for anyone. My mother said he watched her at her toilet behind the half-curtain, but that was impossible, for the half-curtain reached to the lintel. An apple tree with dark rain-saturated boughs kept out the light.

The garden was planted in cabbage. The apple tree yielded bitter cookers. The tall granite spire of the Mariners Church rose above the granite of the garden wall, which had a postern door in it, used by the surly fellow in the cloth cap. He was a roomer in the flat above Sharpe. The church had been built in the early 1700s by convicts, hauling the stone from Dalkey quarry.

The grounds of the Marine Hotel were infested with cats. They stared through the railings at the stout elderly lady with white hair walking painfully by. She had put on weight, her ankles were swollen; my mother advanced with a pronounced roll, uneasy on the slopes above Moran Park. There was the bowling green used by English visitors, there was the pond with its ducks and geese. My mother's health was poor, she did not look after herself, she drank. Injections for pernicious anaemia kept her alive. Without these lads, the doctor had warned her, without these, Mrs. Ruttle, you would not walk the length of this room. Sometimes the injections were painful, though she never complained. She drank JJ green label to put a little fire inside her, spent hours in Woolworth's in the winter, for the warmth.

She stood with her face close to the list of runners, the lenses of her spectacles criss-crossed with innumerable fine lines, an intricate spiderwork of fine white lines as the lines in Pavel Tchelitchew's *Inachevé*. It must have been like in a snowstorm; she was living in a twilit world at the end of her life. How could God be good if He overlooked what was happening to the Jews? she asked me. Wasn't He a Jew Himself? How could He let that happen, then? (She meant the concentration camps.) She felt the cold. For a while she blinded herself wearing her sister's castoff reading glasses, her eyes grown huge and froglike and confused.

Study the list of runners in the Turf Accountant's, fancy certain jockeys (Lester Piggott, Scobie Breasley, Joe Mercer), put a shilling on the Tote, win a bit, lose a bit, drink what you can, avoid people, endure life. Grief brought to numbers cannot be so fierce.

The fog-horn in the autumn, the leaves rotting off the trees, Cork Road, Tivoli Road, Ulverton Avenue, Corrig Road, Oliver Plunkett Road, the Orphanage, and one day like another, winter turning into spring and spring into summer, and that into autumn and then winter again, the delayed daylight shining on the Muglins, on deserted Bullock Harbour, filtering at last into Haigh Terrace and into her stale-smelling lair. A patch of white out at sea meant seagulls over sewage, 'stormwater'. One dark would be just as another dark, my father retiring at eight, rising at two in the morning to make himself a cup of tea, drinking it alone in that morgue of a kitchen, sleeping the thin sleep that the old sleep, awake at seven, and then down to the railway tracks, the barrier, like a crow in a cold field, watching the Irish with tired faces coming through with poor baggage.

Summer was worse: blunt-tongued Anglo-Saxons from the Midlands sucking HB ice creams on Marine Parade. And priests, gregarious novices or ruddy-faced curates, pale theologians, raw-heeled monks in brown habits up for the All-Ireland final at Croke Park. In ancient times herds of free-ranging swine travelled the forests and all Ireland was one great bullock-run. They walked on the pier, Christian Brothers with *fàinnes* in their buttonholes and simplicity in their hearts, self-effacing nuns moving at their peril in a high wind past the bandstand, their black habits streaming away from them.

So many ordained in Ireland, Olivia (the sceptic) said. So many nuns. What do they do?

Baptise Catholic infants, instruct the Catholic young, keep their Catholic parishioners up to scratch, marry the Catholic engaged, bless the betrothed, pray for the Catholic dying, shrive the Catholic dead.

Not all are priests, I said, some are novices, some will never be ordained, some go abroad. The Mission Fields, Uganda, Nigeria. There is a very old tradition going back to St Patrick, who converted Ireland from paganism not long after Socrates the stone cutter ended his life. And it's been going on ever since.

The penny Catechism, the 2d Catechism. A classroom that stank of wet clothing and a young piety as damp and green. Convent indoctrination like a damp turf fire in the schoolroom grate. Sister Rumold's class. What is sin, mortal or venial? A dark shaggy animal that gives off an overpowering smell. Chilblains and scrofula, the strap, my reddened hands before me on the desk scored with knife marks and inkstains. I sit in ignorance and hear Colfer's woeful stutter. The smell of the inkwell is like ether. Sister Rumold said we were the most stupid class she had ever tried to teach; she would prefer to be digging ditches, working for the Corporation.

I was confirmed by a Bishop, given the chrism. Theoretically I had become a strong and perfect Christian, but I knew otherwise: I was as hollow and imperfect a Christian as ever I had been. The old Bishop was deaf. You shouted out the answers. It was better to shout out the wrong answer than give none at all. Cotter shouted out the wrong answer and the old bemused Bishop placed a ringed hand on Cotter's shaven head.

We flung stones at the stuck-up Proddies walking on the Markievicz Road. Someone was hit, cried out, someone was bleeding. We ran behind a low wall, and stones rained down on the road. The Proddies were throwing stones.

Fake religious fervour, jingoism, chauvinism, that old paltroonery; the very ground I walked on was infected with it. The blood that flowed copiously from a gash made by a stone flung by a Proddy schoolboy was infected with it. A falling projectile that could have blinded. The local stigmatic.

Olivia, who had changed her religions as casually as she had changed her boy-friends in Auckland, remarked on the number of persons in Holy Orders entering and leaving good-class hotels in Dublin. Had they nothing better to do? Catholic cyclists, dare-devils with both hands off the handlebars, blessed themselves as they flew past Donnybrook Church. And a double-decker green bus full of commuters blessed themselves. Say the cyclist went under the bus—would his soul fly straight to heaven?

I don't know, I said.

The ghost of Pierre Teilhard de Chardin stalked along the Grand Canal and peered through the window of Parson's Book-shop near Baggot Street bridge, saw the reflection of his own austere countenance superimposed on many volumes of his own works.

On the pond below the Mariners Church leaves and scum had gathered, bloated white bread, geese, reflections of bare branches, iron railings, the trembling image of a granite wall.

A breeze passed over it, the images changed, the bowling green was deserted. Clouds were reflected in standing water, life was passing, opportunities wasted; a tracery of leaves and feathers, the hair of the dead drowning there.

My father passed down the dark hall, letting himself out with a yale key. Opposite was the Marine Hotel with its granite and gravel, its cat-infested grounds. He went on, huddled into his raincoat, resentful of the interminable winter that 'took it out' of him, made him anxious for his health. My mother had bronchitis. They stood on the pavement outside the Monument Creamery and called to us (standing on the platform of a No. 8 Dalkey bus) to come soon again. My father tapped the window, nodded, smiling, to come soon again. At Booterstown we saw the twenty-foot-high model of the TIME ale bottle, an illuminated beacon for thirsty travellers near the sloblands and the sign of Kinch. Córas Iompair Eireann had an advertisement on the lower deck for regular sailings to the Aran Isles, that *Tir na nÓg* occupied by the old, the embittered, the sea-enclosed. The *Naom Éanna* sailing to Inishere, Inishman, Inishmore.

My mother had herself photographed on a public bench at Salthill, that most miserable of seaside resorts, squinting into the sun, in a capacious handbag the letters addressed to her from cold and distant Montreal by her cold and distant son. The old *Dun Aengus* was beating out toward the islands, the last landfall before America.

From the draining board to the kitchen table, five anxious creaking paces, stare out through the half-curtains (yellowish flaw near the shocked blue of the iris), from there to the open bedroom door, five and a half slow, anxious creaking paces, snore through the nose.

I am at home on holiday, smoking in bed. He is breathing through his nose beyond the door. Almost I can follow the slow mundane thoughts drifting through his mind. The last chores of the day over, he needs an excuse to come in and gossip. You'll destroy your eyes reading, Dan.

It was the same every day, it is the same every day, he is the same. Snoring in his head, the last chores of the day over. Reading is bad for your eyes. You will destroy your eyes reading. Put away that book. Metaphysical thoughts were beyond him, he retired early. Before the light went in summer, before eight in winter, from draining board to kitchen window. At two in the morning he made himself a pot of weak tea ('Cat piss,' Olivia said) and drank it alone in the cold kitchen. Before seven he quit his bed, up with the birds. He had a beaked nose, ate like a bird, standing or sitting, his shoulders hunched, eating in a hurry (Don't bolt your food, my mother said, you will be killed with indigestion), a gull on the pier wall choking itself. Gull-eyed father. The door banged behind him, he was away to Hawk Cliff. Sun-up, sun-down, the regular aches and pains. Stoical, he took it all.

Green dishwater swirled down the drain, tea-leaves and cabbage, potato peels. The creaking of cricket boots and his patient sighs beyond the door, the light going at three in the afternoon, the shutters closed, fog on the terrace, the fog-horn mooing out on the bay. Summer and autumn, winter and spring, life going. I drank until I could not stand, I crawled back there, I could not sleep, the whole house was sweating; at six on a March morning down at the sea I threw off my clothes and swam out, saw the spires and the hills rising beyond the dingy town. The bells rang from all quarters. I swam back in the green waters of the bay.

Bad for your eyes, son. Draining eyes (five anxious creaking paces, sigh upon sigh). Sigh beyond the door. Excuse me, son, I'll go.

My gull-eyed father put down a sliced loaf and a pint of milk on the sideboard by the clock that was three-quarters of an hour slow and began slapping his pockets and frowning, saying (lying), You won't believe this, but that bloody bitch has given me the wrong change again.

He was a tanner short.

My father, a true stoic, accepted good or bad fortune in the same manner, like a gardener who instead of watering his plants, waits for rain, certain that it will come sooner or later. He read only newspapers, a lifelong and enormous consumption of newspapers. His an insidiously lazy mind.

Words and expressions used by my mother: Lug, sloshy, ructions, biddable, barging, farfetched, never-rains-but-it-pours, once-in-a-blue-moon, as bold as brass, as broad as it's long, as good as gold.

2 POMPEY: That year Father came not once but three or four times into the studio, ringing the bell below, offering me a listless handshake inside the door where a launch was hidden under tarpaulin covers, ready for the season. Turning his head, he gave me a look both chastened and aggrieved. I'm afraid poor old so-and-so (mentioning someone known to me slightly or not at all) is going. Meaning: dying. Or, more dramatically: Poor so-and-so is gone. Meaning: dead. Half of them were unknown to me.

He came one day, shaking his head, giving me a decidedly haggard look, saying, Poor Pompey is dead. More cemetery business; this time it was my younger cousin.

Willie Fay, long retired, who had in the old days been well-liked as a Sligo G.P., attending my mother at Nullamore, died after a protracted illness the exact nature of which was never satisfactorily explained to me. Something to do with the circulation, my father said. Dick Duggan followed him; mild-mannered, soft spoken, comfortably off, retired from business when the government bought his flour mill, with an invalid wife, semi-paralysed; he died with a nurse in attendance. And a well-to-do widowed sister who had lived the latter part of her life in the Shelbourne Hotel in Dublin, died there 'in comfort', as my father put it. He expected something from the will; but she left him nothing; he took it philosophically enough.

Others too, less close to him, but known to him, passed away. Three subjects, perhaps interrelated, recurred with monotonous regularity in his conversation: the weather (generally bad), his health (surprisingly good, considering the weather), the past— his own past, that is—and those who had occupied it. And now so many of them were dead. Still they had to play their set and unchangeable roles in his charades, and my father played in them too. The recurring visits to the graveyards left gaps; once that security was breached, the cold wind that had blown on them began to blow coldly on him too.

Dick Duggan had taken my father as a companion on vacation to Mulranny on a few occasions. He and my father and Eddie Spratt spent some time on the golf links there, but more time in the bar. My father wrote my mother without prefix, prenomen, or endearment, an undated letter:

**Great Southern Hotel,
Mulranny, Co. Mayo.**

Weather not very good. You get a bit fed up with the hotel, and Dick is a bit trying, he has his good and bad days, and had to have the doctor twice, young Dick came last night to drive us home. This hotel has changed a lot since you used to come here, a queer crowd here now, very common English sorry to have no dough to send you, if Eddie Spratt had come this year I would have some to spare, Dick gives me 10s. every day, its gone on two drinks. Love D.

Not the hotel we used to go to, not the hotel I took you to, not our hotel, but the hotel you used to go to, one of many. That's bad, towards the end of a life, on another's sufferance, and a woman's sufferance at that—a wife embittered. Mrs. S., as I recall, was majestic; a big spreading bosom on her like the chest of a drysdale.

Mulranny, Gweedore, Rosapenna, hiding in Port na Blagh and the Poisoned Glen, drinking sherry in the Royal Fort Hotel at Rathmullen, holidays in Donegal, My mother in a clinging '20s style bathing costume that reached midway down the thigh and exposed most of her back swimming in a cold and choppy sea at Gweebarra Bay. A local strumpet without panties sitting on a rock at Maas, showing me her secret hair and daring me to look again. One wet and interminable afternoon I walked the length of the main street at Glenties. My father played cricket with my brother Wally and me on Traloar strand. From Kilcar we walked two miles south to Muckross head, and in a cave there my mother's high birdlike voice was calling us back, as we walked deeper into the marine chambers cut out by the Atlantic.

I tried to visualize a face in one of the heavy family albums, pictures of a vanished time turning sepia on the thick pages; that one—was it he? was it she? My father, for a joke, dressed as a woman (too convincingly I thought) in a long white dress, holding a furled parasol standing beside a transvestite in bowler hat and tie, with female hips and a kissing mouth; and behind them in the shadows of a doorway, a wraithlike figure in a straw boater. Was Pompey that ghost? A stout English military man with a moustache, broadbeamed in knickerbockers, pushed a pretty girl (his niece?) on a bicycle on the gravel before Nullamore. Was that Major Duval-Smith? The *nice* Major. Or one among the couples playing croquet on a lawn backed by weeping willow trees. The downward curve of the hoops repeated in the downward droop of the branches; the players, dressed preposterously, were very seriously applying themselves to croquet. My father posed in twill riding breeches and a bowler hat at least two sizes too small for him, holding a couple of leashed black greyhounds with lolling tongues, and behind him, blending with the masonry, something or someone that must have moved as the shutter clicked, leaving an image blurred and undefined. Fading as the photographs of those who die are said to fade. Only fadograph. Yestern scene.

Who then? The man with pipe and blazer holding open the door of our Hillman-Coatalen, a parcel on the back seat, the hood down, my brother Wally and I in short trousers posed before the front door of the Great Southern Hotel at Bundoran. One of the two Russell girls, Maeve and Honor, one with her auburn hair in a bun, the other in spectacles and scandalously short pleated skirt, both leaning over a rustic bridge in Nullamore garden, staring into a pond of water lilies? Hardly. Who then? One of my cousins, the O'Donnells, in blazers and flannels, First Eleven colours, grouped about my father during visiting-day at Castleknock College, Vinnie and Sill pulling faces at the camera, and in the foreground, a stoop-shouldered shadow trying to get them into focus. Was it one of them? Or Stoop Shadow? I didn't know. What had become of them, what professions had they taken up, what women had they married? I didn't know. And there he was, isolated, very serious in mortar-board and gown, holding a scroll, looking as if he had known all along; there was Pompey.

I did not feel resentful; for, after all, what were they to him, at bottom, but distractions? And to me the same, a morning's safe distraction, a retelling of some old story I had heard before, listened to with no more enthusiasm than hitherto. He had little enough to occupy him, God knows, little enough to talk about, chew over, little enough to do; the weather, his past, his present health (not so good), his robust past, the weather in the old days, the past which I myself was after all part of, Daniel and Wally, now a balding bachelor, just another quantity surveyor in Wales. There was only this tenacious clinging on to the old useless things. There was nothing else to cling on to. Tenacious memory could not let go.

My mother, who had been glad enough to help him spend his money when he had it, saw her life with him as a long series of disappointments and frustrations, better alternatives neglected. She thought that she had married beneath her. She had married for money, and then he had lost it. Embittered by experience, by poverty, she came to unfavourable conclusions about people and their motives, their ability to please; and few people pleased her.

A bit trying was a phrase habitually employed by her, one of her barbed phrases, referring as often as not to my helpless father. He had nothing but his own good nature with which to defend himself; it was a poor defence against my mother. Is he popular? my father would ask, his head on one side like a hen, anxious, lacking prescience, intuition, knowledge of other's baseness. Is he well-liked? Is *she* well-liked? he asked. No, I said, not-well liked, hating his way of seeing others; not liked at all. Ah, my father said, sucking the air between his dentures. I don't think he's (she's) out of the top drawer.

By *queer* my father meant Public Bar people drinking in the Select Lounge; it meant ignorance if not exactly social climbing. Real bosthoons, my father said. Very Common (recognizably poor table manners) meant underbred. He thought of himself as a gentleman, yet made these opprobrious classifications; uneasy in

34

the presence of those whom he considered his social superiors, and positively uncomfortable in the presence of titled people—unless they were 'horsey'. He liked reckless individuals who drank, like Derek Graham, who had gambled his way through two fortunes (a coffee plantation in Brazil, a stable of race horses outside Sligo) 'without a worry on him'. A real gas artist altogether: meaning, an amusing fellow; or, no accounting for his follies. Anybody whom, he could not make out but to whom he was well disposed, he classified in this loose way. Wally, of all people, qualified as a gas artist. My brother, so reserved and silent.

The man's a fool, my mother said, and I wasn't sure whether she meant my father or the swashbuckling Derek Graham, or both.

Speak about what you know, my mother said sharply.

So he came ringing the studio bell and interrupting my morning's work. Telling me that someone whom I did not know had died. Until one day—it was May and the ground was hardening and the plane trees coming out in Lower Baggot Street—he came with a woebegone look, his eyes watering, all *arcus senilis* running into the faded blue, giving me an absentminded handshake at the door, telling me that poor Pompey was dead.

And again feet were pounding on the floorboards below, the feet of the dancers, the Sligo gentry heavy as horses, dancing two-steps, waltzes and foxtrots to the music of a gramophone. The mournful airs of a bygone time issuing from the whorled horn of a hand-cranked gramophone as the steel needle point bit into the grooves of the narrowing arc and a powerful baritone voice was declaring that he knew she liked him, because she said so, she was the Lily of Laguna, she was his Lily and his Rose. And then a reedy tenor, long dead, sang at a shaky seventy-eight-revolutions-per-minute, *Goodnight, Vienna*, city of a thousand melodies. And then another voice, a jocular fat voice, sang *Betty Co-ed* (with her eyes of navy blue), the tempo of the music slowing, as if the singer was sinking, sinking in the bathos of the lyrics, into the waves of the Danube, which had never been blue. And then the HMV record was revolving at a better speed, being wound up once more, the tune rising from the waves, from the ruins of the song. So the sounds of the dancers came up through the floorboards at Nullamore on the nights my brother Wally and I could not sleep; because the motor horns were sounding at the front gate, the hand-manipulated rubber horns and the klaxons, the Buicks and Citroens, Fiats and Rileys rolling up the drive, headlights splaying over the mouldings and ceiling, and then back into darkness and the ruby tail-lights flickering on and off, the silence after the motors were cut, and the port-wine-and-brandy voices, all conviviality, calling my father's name, my mother's name. Danny, Dilly. Cousin Pompey, precocious and indulged by his parents, was below drinking Bulmer's cider from a keg and making witty remarks, or what passed for wit in that solid company. Young Pompey is a scream, they said. He will go far (not specifying in what direction). But, offended by some of his sallies, they meant: Some day he will go too far. Or: Some day he will get his. Omitting to specify what. And, behind his back: Young Duggan is a right pup. Duggan is a rip. They are spoiling him, his critics said, making a right fool of him. Pompey's a brat, my father said. But my mother liked him: Pompey Duggan has *character*, she said.

I could not sleep, all the dancers were dancing through me, the sugary music, the saccharine pouring into me like adrenalin. So I stole out of bed and watched from the turn of the stairs, looking down into the hall flooded with light from the Aladdins, and I crept down the stairs and looked on surreptitiously.

Three buhl-inlaid fire-screens with complementary designs of peacocks and peahens in ivory bas-relief hid the big coal grate that in winter burned like a furnace all day and on into the night. The deep armchairs were pulled back against the walls and the carpet rolled up. The heavy records were stacked in a compartment in the body of the gramophone; it had a slatted door and was of dark-stained wood; it looked like a chiffonier and smelt like a sachet. Over the white marble mantelpiece in the oval mirror the dancers were reflected, the heavy Odlum boys dancing with the Orr sisters, my father talking seriously with a gentleman in one corner, and my powdered and scented mother in the arms of Eddie Spratt. My father wore evening clothes and was smoking a long cigar. My mother wore a revealing evening dress.

When a uniformed maid came out with a tray of empty champagne glasses, I went back to bed.

In bed again I still saw cousin Pompey's hand dipping into the chrome red cigarette box on the sideboard near a bowl of fruit. In the other hand he held what looked suspiciously like a glass of champagne. He wore his school blazer and was twelve years old. I was thirteen, a late riser and a slow developer. Wally was fifteen, still untroubled by pubescence.

Drifting away, in a state between sleeping and waking, hearing the drone of the music, the sound changing as a door opened or closed, a sudden gush of voices, the wind in the great beech tree outside, I had this waking dream or aural hallucination, that was to recur at widely spaced periods, years sometimes intervening, until I met and married Olivia Grieve of Range View Avenue and Konini Road, Auckland, New Zealand; and then once more, for the last time. The hallucination of being born: offered to me only the feelings, most uncomfortable ones to be sure, always to the sound of distant music or in dead silence that prolonged itself. A wind was flattening the rushes that grew above my head, and I, in the night apparently, in the grey-white murk of the caul, was being born or cast away in the rushes, like the infant Moses.

If I close my eyes I can remember that red cigarette box. The lid and sides were of a glowing crimson, the insides golden, as were its delicate hinges; and the honeycomb for the cigarettes— cylindrical recesses in a little tray which lifted the cigarettes as the lid was raised and caused them to subside as the lid was lowered—was also of this golden patina, so that you were offered twenty or so white discs in a gold surround. It was very pretty. Logically constructed as a theorem by Euclid, simple and complex as a honeycomb, ingenious as a mica box for looking into the centre of ant hills, mysterious as the curtained taber- nacle with its Host. In this bright box Pompey found not only Player's No. 3 and tipped Craven 'A', but his future academic success at Castleknock, his mortarboard and scroll from Trinity, first class honours in history, not only these, but his marriage certificate, the baptismal certificate of his son, the reviews of a book he would one day write (and live to see published) on a famous Munster Circuit Judge, as well as the notes for a book he would never finish on the southern canals, the weedy waterways of Ireland.

My mother, who understood him and liked him, and my father, who did not understand him but liked him, both mourned my young cousin Pompey Duggan, who at the age of thirty-eight had died of a heart-attack. Students and lecturers from Trinity College attended the short ceremony at Westland Row when the coffin came from Donnybrook. He had recently been appointed Professor of History, the youngest ever in the history of the university. My father said that he had died suddenly during a medical check-up at Donnybrook. The funeral was to take place at Sligo.

You and I must go, of course, my father said. I'll send a telegram to Wally. It's not necessary for him to come all that way. The Duggans wouldn't expect that.

So we went to the funeral, back to the place I had not visited since I was sixteen, the year we left. My mother, who suffered from claustrophobia, remained at home in Dun Laoghaire, resting.

I stood by my father in the church at Westland Row and watched the priest blessing the coffin, on the lid of which I could read the name DUGGAN on the brass plaque; so there it was, there stood the coffin, bigger than I had expected; Pompey was inside it. The next time I saw one the lid would be off and my mother would be lying in it.

The commemoration card had a black border. Below the photograph was inscribed: *O Immense Passion ! O Profound Wounds ! O Profusion of Blood ! O Sweetness above all Sweetness ! O Most Bitter Death ! Intercede, O Lord, for the soul of thy son, Vincent (Pompey) Duggan, departed this life January 17th, 1961. Grant him eternal rest.*

The pale face of the lover of Shannon jaunts, drinker of Shannon water, well-coloured (cowshit), in whiskey. Historian, good fellow, father, who had little expected that to be read over him so soon (the opening antiphon of the vespers for the dead), wore a bright expectant look. But all his jaunts were over. O Black Border!

O Angel of Time, you who have counted the sighs and the tears of mankind, forget them and hide them away!

Phrases associated with my father: 'Rip', 'dough', 'impudent bitch'. 'The wind always blows cold over graveyards'.

3 THE HOSPITAL BY THE SEA: That morning the bell had rung early, someone kept their finger on it. I dressed and went down and hammered open the stiff rainsoaked door. There was no one there. The lane was empty. I went back to bed again and must have dozed off. This strange dream came to me.

A Sunderland flying-boat of World War II was blundering slowly through clouds at no great altitude, and being fired at by citizens on the ground armed with antiquated rifles. I was discussing something with the coloured woman Guala Conroy in the studio. She was interested in one of my paintings and proposed hire purchase terms. There came a shout from the door: *Here it comes again!* I ran out and took up one of the heavy rifles, a Lee Enfield. I could see the shadowy bulk of it flying through clouds. It had a white fish-like belly. If I hit it I knew it would explode, a whale hit with a harpoon that carried a charge in its head. When I fired the dream ended. I didn't know whether I'd struck it or not, allowing for the altitude the dream-bullet had gone off on a trajectory well ahead of the flying-boat, passing high up through clouds, white as snow. I had certainly fired well ahead of the white belly; but it was me the bullet found—into me it struck.

When I woke again, there was the cold studio with its rafters and dirty sky-lights, the brown velvet curtains drawn; I had great difficulty in heating it. At one time it had been Dermot O'Brien's old studio.

Some warning there, a premonition, I felt uneasy, bad news was on the way. An hour later the studio bell rang again. I went down. In the open door a messenger in a crash helmet was taking a telegram from his leather satchel. He said, Ruttle? Yes, I replied, and took it from him. I read it inside, by the boat.

MA GONE TO HOSPITAL x COME OVER x DA. Dun Laoghaire.

The hospital was by the sea. It stood near the harbour and the yacht clubs, near the railway station. A bleak-looking edifice in grey stone.

The bus dropped me near the gate. Clouds hung low and I could see my breath in the air. Before midday it was already twilight. In the damp the snow had turned to slush and the slush to water soon after it reached the ground, forming irregular puddles in the hospital car-park. Nothing kept its shape. The name of the hospital was reflected upsidedown in pools of water. I saw the lame man going by and called to him but he did not hear me, chose not to hear me.

It was late autumn, in so far as there can be an autumn after no summer. For me it was already winter. Everything was grey, lead-coloured, not a stir of air, the low clouds releasing a drizzle of snow, the wettest autumn in those parts for seventeen years.

A doctor took me into a small well-heated room near the reception hall. He told me in effect that she was dying; her lungs were gone. We could but hope. (He meant there was no hope.) I could call him at any time. Any time, he repeated. We shook hands. He left. I went to her. She was in St Cecilia's, the female ward for the dying, near the service lift. I walked past the curtains for the last time.

Certainly she was dying. Her caved-in features and leaden colouring did not belong to the living. Her lower jaw had sunk. They had taken the bridge out. The flesh of her face had begun to collapse as the bones came through. If she lived through it, she would most likely be paralysed; opinion varied as to the severity of that paralysis, some holding out a little more hope than others, but none were sanguine. It was better, perhaps, that she should die knowing nothing and feeling nothing, go out in deep coma. The nuns were looking after her. They were dressed in white habits and moved about the ward, seldom speaking. In that hushed room the light was going. They moved past the windows, coifed and pale-faced sentinels of twilight, ghosts of this gloomy, fatal world. They did not represent the world, to be sure; they were the sexless gate-porters into the next. My mother was in good hands.

She, a great student of obituary notices, had feared death; first with religion, then without it, embracing it once more towards the end of her life. It's a strange Catholic fear, very Irish. A little light, a last feeble glow of intelligence about to be snuffed out, a little hard-won breath. It was hard-won all right, pulling her down. She was dying with each heart-beat; her sorrows and pleasures, shut up there for seventy-odd years would die with her. Something of me would die with her; I was watching part of my own death. It did not seem to belong to me, yet it was mine. Will my own death be like that, for another?

Now the long-brooded-upon, the long-feared, had caught up with her at last and soon there would be no more light, no more thought, no more pain, no more injections, no more breath. Knowing nothing of this, she was advancing step by step into darkness, going out in deep coma. She would know nothing of what had finished her—the cerebral haemorrhage, the night stroke. I took her hand. She was hardening already, tending towards the inertia of matter. I could not think of her dead, gone, no more, any more than I could think of myself dead. But nonetheless it was only too apparent that she was going.

Long ago, in the garden at Nullamore, she had sat on the rug and read Hans Andersen to Wally and myself. Red pulpy berries fell from the yew tree full of missel thrushes. She had been a beauty in her day. A local poet had composed a sonnet in her honour. The beauty sitting on the public bench by the Mall. Rhymester Jim McGinley had inscribed his little book of doggerel to her. Printed on poor quality paper, it had at one time been an object of wonder to me. Jim McGinley's verse was printed in the *Evening Mail*. The *Evening Mail* seemed to me a female newspaper, reserved and dull; it ran 'Mandrake the Magician'. The magician's cold, shaved features would never change, his coal-black hair and precise middle parting reminding me of my father. Cloaked, he was my father in tails. He had a gigantic Negro as body servant. The *Evening Herald* was masculine, with a red Crusader stamped as banner on the front page. It featured

Inspector Wade, who also had an eagle nose, hair parted in the centre, a quiff like bow waves. His Negro was a detective called Donovan. The *Herald* was hot bread; the *Mail* was a glass of cold milk.

All that seems to have happened, if it ever happened, long ago, belonging to someone else's past, not mine. We sat under the oldest tree in the garden. Yew berries fell about us; there were ants crawling in the recently mowed lawn. The smell of fresh grass, the smell of the lime going in straight lines and at orderly right angles on the tennis court, the odour of grass decomposing behind the bamboos, this belonged to my childhood, and my sweet-faced mother reading there in a voice that breaks my heart. The straight white guide lines were the life I would follow, out in the world. The bamboos whispered of the advantages and pleasures that awaited me there.

She had reared us gently. Taught us to like books and paintings and such, all the things that my father had no interest in; he had the horses and the farm—those other things were beyond him. My parents were kind. Putting our interests before their own they pinched and saved, and gave us a boarding school and a college education that they could not comfortably afford; an education that dropped off me like water off a duck's back, my mother said. I took only what I wanted, the residue of my own exasperation with it, the hard drupe, and myself in the toils of it, not wanting it. Boarding school in the country, the Jesuit fiction of the world's order and essential goodness, stretching out ahead like the white guide lines. No.

They were of the country and loved the country, as I do, the lake areas around Sligo, the eleven lakes. In summer we went to a hotel in Bundoran, on a golf links. Before we were born, my taciturn brother and I, our parents had gone to Mulranny, I imagine because of sentimental associations. Later in Dublin they took to drink and followed the horses; bad habits I too have acquired. For my brother I cannot speak; he went his own sweet way.

I looked at the caved-in eyes, the bad colouring, the white hair soaked in sweat, arranged in an unfamiliar way, and hoped that she would not survive it, not continue to suffer, but rather go in sleep. I wished this for her who so dreaded death. The previous year had been a year of deaths. Too many too near to her. She had lived with my father in the damp place below street level, poorly enough towards the end and victimized him. Everything he did (and he did little) and everything he said (and he said much) annoyed her, yes and beyond all endurance. She was dying, as women sometimes die, of their man's equanimity. The days that could not change, would not change, refused to change, going like the English visitors in droves in both directions; the dying dying and the living living, yet sick of life, this life which is not life at all. Weddings up and down Dun Laoghaire, in the suburbs, brides with rice on their shoulders, issue. Funerals in Glasthule. Slow-moving and complacent-looking hearses, fleets owned by Fanagan and Creegan and others, moving in the narrow way, pedestrians doffing their hats. Droves 'in all directions', my mother said. She meant the ceaseless activity of the living into apparent life, and the dead into the ground. The boat train drawing out for Westland Row, tired Irish passengers gaping from the carriage windows in winter, the level-crossing passed, rain on the tracks, the gate closing like the end of a yawn, my father huddled into his thin coat going home.

Your father, she said, as though disassociating herself from him. Your father, meaning: that abject fool. He went through a stage of dreaming winners, but it was too late. He still loved her in his way, but it was also too late. The life they had shared together had gone sour on them. Shortly before Christmas, her last Christmas in the year I am speaking of, my father won £24 with a tote treble on a shilling stake and bought himself a dark grey suit. My mother, knowing Olivia and I were going to Spain for a year or more, and feeling she would not survive another Irish winter, gave me, with a *contained* gesture, as a Christmas box, polaroid sunglasses. They were happy together for the last time. My father permitted himself, after a certain amount of Scotch, some broad but inoffensive jokes before Olivia. He was much taken with her. Crude, my mother sniffed, but Olivia laughed.

They had drifted apart over the years, as I from them, as my brother from them and me. We had never been what is called a united family, at least not since my childhood. My father, as a parent, had been anything any son could ever wish, and similarly my mother. My ever obliging father, none too astute in his dealings with people, particularly the fair sex, had given in to her too much and with predictable consequences. Each day more humiliations, which he pretended not to feel; she got in her digs, some sharp ones, *tela* followed by *estocada*, thrusts which he affected to turn aside, but which had, or should have hurt him deeply. Women were like that, tart, sharp-tongued, acid. Are they? Perhaps. At all events she lost any remaining respect she had for him; and, with that, restraint went too. She treated him like dirt. They disagreed, quarrelled incessantly; but it was all very one-sided.

She wiped the floor with him in company. It made any mutual assistance they might have given each other towards the end impossible. Each would die alone.

As a child I had a great fear of thunder, but never told my mother, who I think knew. Fear of thunderstorms around Sligo, apocalyptic lightning and the Garavogue gone green-grey, uncontrollable thunder crackling in the hills around Ben Bulben, my mother, pulling out more wool, looking over at me and saying, It's only God beating carpets in Heaven. Torrential rain fell, cutting small craters in the gravel. Seabirds flying inland, sign of a storm, my mother said, pointing with a knitting needle. Seagulls were floating in an air-current over Nullamore, staring down. I was nine. A pool, the colour of weak tea, was the gravel torn up. I sat on the window-seat looking out, feeling a sink of indescribable misery. I had no means to describe it, the world, myself, the world before myself. The world that would go on existing after myself, as if I had never been. I felt it all pouring out of me, this ignorance, the plug out and everything I had, which was precious little, running away. I was sitting in the window-seat and the rain was pouring down. And she whom I had come out of sat there knitting, saying without words, by her presence, by the way she yanked out the wool, *I am here, I am knitting, silly, don't you see? I am protecting you.* Perhaps she had an intuition of how awful I felt. Wait until you're forty, Dan.

You'll see. (I did not.) I see my white bedroom with nobody in it. Go back and draw the sea-green Venetian blinds. Go back to the timid puritan you were. When I go, my mother said, true to her obsession, when I go, no one will miss me. No one will grieve for me. I'll grieve for you, Ma, I said. And the upper part of a great elm, struck by lightning, fell into the swollen Garavogue.

At five that morning the tide began to go out for her, it was the turning point, entering the third day of deep coma. My father had been visiting her day and night, haunting the hospital. He had seen her at eight that morning, and was convinced she would not survive the day. It was her last day. Sunday in Ireland. The streets were virtually deserted, the sky grey and overcast by mid-morning, threatening snow. As I was shaving the studio bell sounded below.

My father came in to say she was sinking fast, not expected to last the day. Oh, she's very bad, he said, shaking his head. Very bad, Dan. I'm afraid she's going on us. Get over to her quick. I'll try and get the other fellow.

I told him to stay in the studio and rest. If anything happened I would phone. He needed rest. I built up the fire and he sat before it in his overcoat. Then I left. It had begun to snow. At the Circle I recognized a heavy figure coming out of a newsagent with English Sunday papers tucked under his arm. He pretended not to see me and turned quickly away, going by the wall with short, quick, fussy steps, a furled umbrella in one gloved hand. He would not go to the hospital, only near it, to feel he was somewhere near her, but not to see her dying. Some intuition had warned Wally she was dying that morning. I let him go. There's love for you. I too turned away. There were no radio taxis about. The streets were white. I stood at the Dalkey and Dun Laoghaire bus stop and waited.

I reached the hospital before eleven. The house surgeon told me what he had to tell me. I went upstairs to sit by her until she died. When I reached the curtained bed I did not know what awaited me—a death's head, my poor mother transformed into some kind of horror. A dull heavy breathing came from behind

46

the curtain; so she was still alive. I stood by the bed. A nurse came with a chair. I sat down. For two days death had been drawing closer and was now very near. It was doing terrible things to her; she was holding on with all her remaining strength, mumbling with pinched-in and discoloured lips, *For me? Is it for me this time?* Unmistakably it was for her. Death was already stirring in her. She had been relatively passive for two days, two days of more or less quiet dying; now giving way to this subdued turmoil. The weary breathing of a stubborn person ascending a hard hill. Her spirit was now engaged; before it was only her body fighting with the blow, the night stroke. A bird lost at a window. *For me? Is it this time for me?* The bridge of her nose was bruised on either side where the useless spectacles had pinched, or the mark of when she had fallen in George's Street. One windy night we had been out drinking hot toddies with the lame man. Now she was going up a steep hill, going on at all costs, puffing at it. It took all her strength and more, but she was obstinate, going at it, her nose pointed. My poor mother wearily persisting, her eyes sunk, her mouth collapsed, bitter and deprived, attempting the last impossible hill. Who may say what humiliations can be borne? What the body can endure? What the mind can stand? I sat by her, held her hand, called to her, felt her pulse where the feeblest lymph ebbed away, came fluttering back, uncertain, the blood that had given me life. I put into her hand her own rosary beads of mother-of-pearl, listening to her hard breathing, intermittent snoring, and wished her troubles ended. Her cheeks sagged and filled, loose on the bone, and a little white froth accumulated at the corner of her mouth. This sac wavered, agitated by the air brought up painfully from her lungs. It soon dried out and another began to form. Each breath dragged up with such painful and insistent effort disturbed the bedclothes where she lay on her side. Then another followed, hard as the preceding one, harsh as the one that followed, and the little scum wavered on the dry breath issuing from collapsed lungs, torn from deep inside her. All this interspersed with sighs such as a child might give, uncertain of what's happening. Then silence as though she were listening, harkening to something.

She had begun her death. I held her stiffening hand where *rigor*

47

mortis had already started. Her hair was damp. All about her the ghosts moved, whispering. A moth burning in God's unsupportable fire. It was quiet in the ward, a feeling of the Sabbath in Ireland. The minute hand moved around the dial of the ward clock and the hour hand dragged after it. Time went by sadly and slowly. The nurse on duty made an entry in the Day Book and went past, her starched uniform rustling. The ward was warm and full of nuns. On the table by her bed stood a bowl of water with a white towel over it, cotton wool, a glass tumbler, a black leather prayer book, a priest's crucifix. She had received Extreme Unction.

The thin snow blown against the long windows soon melted and ran down the panes of glass, but it was close and humid in the ward. My mother was the only one dying. The gob of spittle hovered in the corner of her mouth. An old arthritic nun with a mushroom complexion under her white coif came and laid a hand as white and speckled as another mushroom on my mother's forehead. Her fingers lifted up my mother's eyelid. *Leave me alone*, the hazel eye said: *I am soon leaving you*. That famous fixed stare. Her eyes were fixed on something moving within herself, something reflected there. World-weary flesh, unbend; eyes, look your last. I was offered rosary beads.

I took them in my hand, declined to kneel, for I wanted to watch her while she was still alive, so that if she opened her eyes it would be me she would first see, as she had been the first person I had seen with the light of intelligence in my life, looking down at me over the end of the cot and asking to be recognized. But her eyes would not open again, ever in this life. The dutiful nuns were kneeling around her saying a decade of the rosary.

They went at it sing-song, drifting with it. The termination of life, that bulk of sins at which their prayers were pointing, urging *Sanctify ! Sanctify !* a thurible swung to and fro by a server, his mind far away—more lullaby than dirge, pleading and lamenting in high sweet voices.

Now, thought I, if she who dreaded all this were to open her eyes! They wanted to hurry her away. No more sensual fret, they chanted, lost in their dream; relieve her of her hard cross, oh Lord!

But her eyes did not open. The hard breathing went on. Now it would pause, as if she were listening, before continuing as before. A heavy sigh, and then another breath, and then the rattling in the throat, a snore, then another breath, pushing out her cheeks, and the pitiful effort to live began anew. Ledge by ledge she was climbing, turret by turret, looking in all the windows.

Relieve her of her sad cross, the chorus of nuns chanted, staring at her, lead her to the light, take from her her hard burden. Let her have respite from her labour, oh Lord!

But she was still down at the foot of the hill. Grown cynical in the face of innumerable setbacks, a deeply disappointed woman, she would carry her cynicism and disappointments with her, into whatever region she was bound for, eyes tight shut (here the laboured breathing faltered).

It went on a little, faltered again, slower, and then, quite abruptly, stopped dead. 'She's going,' the old nun announced, falling forward on her knees and dashing holy water into my mother's face. They began the prayers for the dying.

The prayers were urgent now, the nuns' voices raised, the thurible swinging faster, sending up clouds of incense. They were hunting my mother's spirit hither and thither, trying to tell her that it was not like that, that it was not like that at all; but it was eluding them, rising through the smoke of the incense, the snow melting down all the long windows and the ward quiet. The nuns' breaths going together as if to help her on her way. It seemed like something I had witnessed before, though performed in a more accomplished manner. This was a botched rehearsal for what had never happened, would never happen.

And true enough the harsh and troubled breathing did begin again, hesitantly at first, uncertain of its welcome (her spirit had flown over the abyss), and then as determined and rasping as before—the obstinate effort to scale the impossible hill. The candle in her limp hand tilted at a dangerous angle, dripped candle grease on the sheet folded back, and holy water rolled down her cheeks like tears. Nonplussed by this turn of events, the old nun watched her, felt her pulse. The breathing was weaker but still persisting. The Superior made a sign and the other nuns left the bedside, went about their chores. Then she too followed.

I looked at my mother, who had been only pretending to die. Her humour had always tended to be on the grim side, rarely if ever directed against herself. This was another of her grim jokes, but one against herself. She was obstinate and set in her aversions, had not expected much; and now she was dying at her own pace and in her own way. The nuns' prayers had not touched or even reached her; they would never reach her. She had always scoffed at nuns—their dubious piety and questionable humility. Nuns and male hairdressers, barbers. Like slugs, she had said.

The plea of those who had turned away from the world in order to pray for it. Their lullaby could not touch her or reach her. Drops of holy water rolled unheeded from the cavities of her eyes. The candle had been snuffed out and taken from her. It would not be much longer now. This was the pause before the end.

Presently the old nun came back, watching her, felt her pulse. She whispered something to the young nun who had looked after my mother. Then she went to another part of the ward where a strong female voice was calling.

I held her hand. It lay limply in mine, life all but extinct there.

I liked the young nun, liked her calm face and unhurried movements (Sister Alphonsus Ligoura, Sister of Mercy). A different sensibility there. Nuns, with shorn hair and vanity gone, were different.

I had found a prayer for the dying by Cardinal Newman near the glass bowl, the wadding and heavy crucifix. I asked her to read this prayer. She knelt down and began to read it in her white voice. I knelt with her, my mother was a little above us.

And my Guardian Angel whisper peace to me, the nun read. She finished the prayer. Again please, I said. And my mother, her face discoloured, her breath going slower but resigned to it at last, down at the bottom of her hill, listened. I was handing her back the copy of Hans Andersen that she had read to me when I was ill; yew berries were falling all around us. Missel thrushes were moving in the branches. She took it in hands that were not discoloured, saying brightly, Enough for one day I think. It had a pale blue cover, no illustrations, the dust jacket lost. *Enough for one day*. The tormented breathing stopped, this time for good, and she had gone upwards out of her ailing body, past the falling snow, the unavailing prayers of the Sisters of Mercy, the accumulated slush. Slowly from the corner of her mouth some pale matter flowed.

And the nuns were back in a flurry of kneeling and re-lighting of the candle. The Prayers for the Dying set out after my mother, the candle lit and thrust into her dead hand. When they had finished they blessed themselves, rose up and moved away, the old Kerry nun and another nun hid the bed with screens. I could hear them whispering behind it. Church gossip. Inside the ward it was warm. Only my mother was cold. Outside the snow whirled away, over the pubs where she had liked to drink, out over the yacht basin and the harbour. Out over Ireland's Eye.

The old Kerry nun offered me a cup of tea. It seemed to be the custom. A strange custom. I did not want it but took it without milk or sugar and swallowed it scalding hot. She questioned me about my father and family. I told her I was married, had no children of my own. There was another unmarried son, not on the premises but in the vicinity. Tactfully she made no comment. Woeful human love—that bondage. She was small and bent, reached only to my shoulder, had rough manners (the way she had lifted my mother's eyelid), a broad Kerry accent and a kind heart. I've seen all classes go, she said, and no two go the same way. And was it your first? the old nun asked. Yes, I said, the tea scalding my insides. Ah that's hard then, she said; it's worse when it's your own poor mammy. But sure God is good and He will be good to her, poor soul.

Behind her, the nuns filed silently by; the curtains blew inwards, and I saw a darkness, a shape on the bed.

I had not been able to weep; not then; not now when I think back on it. I don't know why. Going, I looked for the last time at where she lay. Her mouth had fallen open and she was all dark and angular and stiff. When a thing lies still, it will be still for-ever, is a truth that no man can deny. Death had fixed her in this inimical pose—dark and punished; she no longer resembled my mother. The jaw had fallen, the brown stockings stuck out, this I saw before the curtains fell to. Go on now, the old nun said at my elbow, don't be needlessly troubling yourself. You can do nothing for us here.

I let the curtain drop, blotting out that face that was not my mother's known face; that dark and monumental figure. She had her wish anyway, I said. And what was that? the old nun in-quired, smelling of mould-mushroom. To die in Ireland, I said. The old Kerry nun gave me a sideways look, and the hand I held was almost as cold and unreceptive as my mother's. I thanked her and left.

Outside it was cold and overcast. The snow had stopped falling. I felt some relief. Pain and decay, pain and decay, something fishing just below the surface. It was like leaving the dentist's; decay in the system had to be removed; and now it was removed and one was glad to be rid of it. Something of myself had been removed with some pain and I was free to go on without it. The water in the harbour was the colour of lead. And there were the masts of the yachts, and there was the gutted church. I waited for a bus to take me back to the centre of town.

When I reached the studio my old man was sleeping in his overcoat, the sink blocked with his endless tea-leaves, the electric kettle out of order. No light. No fire. No matter. I made him tea and brought it to him, told him what had happened, that she was at peace. He sat wringing his hands and staring at me.

All had been done, everything was over. He had grown old in a few days. He lived in his overcoat, a gift, dreaming of summer like the flies, only emerging from a winter-long hibernation to lead a summer life hardly more purposeful than theirs, setting out each day for one or other of the bathing places. He expressed a wish to see her. Later, I told him—they said later; they are laying her out now. He stared at me. Drink your tea, Da, I said. He did so.

Later we would both go and see her; see how she was. A

death-blow is a life-blow to some who, till they died, did not
alive become; who, had they lived, had died, but when they
died, vitality began.

My peevish elder brother was nowhere to be seen.

4 MUSHROOM PICKING: My brother Wally was most retiring and reticent: one would hardly meet a quieter fellow outside an enclosed order of monks. We met for the first time in perhaps seventeen years on the occasion of my mother's death. He had not changed: merely grown into a shy and corpulent man awkward on his feet. He seemed to have convex soles like a penguin (the creature that flies only in its sleep) or a child learning to walk and was as addicted as ever to prolonged silences— that voice of his, when it came, shocked into reluctant speech, faint and mournful with neither lung-power nor will-power behind it. A strange fellow; he had grown fatter and older, wore good-quality clothes, with the same manner of walking (child, shackled somnambulist, or sleep-walking penguin on pool edge?), same irritating habit of manicuring his nails, same weak voice, same preoccupation with food, same indecisive manner, same long heavy silences interspersed at times with rather loaded sighs. He did not use tobacco and drank only in moderation (gin). His small and precise hand-writing had not changed since boarding school. For some it is the most real time in their lives, the first break with home, and for those days they retain a persistent nostalgia. For him, I believe, it was like that. At all events he kept meticulous records, subscribing to the college annual, an excessively dreary magazine that changed neither its format, contents nor policy over the years, as far as I could see. Year in, year out, the student body always looked the same, indoctrinated by the same teachers, lay and clerical. Prize-winners with bulging eyes, class leaders, scholarship pupils, Imperators of Syntax and Rhetoric, just the head and shoulders seen in formal poses (possibly taken by the same photographer): all studious eyeball, the anxious or complacent gaze fixed on some goal away ahead, out in the world. Perhaps that was the attraction: his own academic past preserved in aspic, and renewed annually.

It was characteristic of him, given that suspicious and evasive nature, that he did not subscribe openly to this magazine, but sent a postal order towards the end of each summer to my mother with instructions to buy it in a bookshop that specialized in Catholic literature. Webbs? Webbs-on-the-green.

In his youth he had a room set aside for newspapers and magazines, *Picture Posts*, *Lilliputs*, *Tatlers & Sketches*, *Illustrated London News*, the *Irish Times*; the shelves reached from floor to ceiling, the files went back ten years and more, yellowing with age, of mainly athletic and political interest. After the move from Sligo these records were dumped in tea-chests in my mother's basement flat where they accumulated damp and mould. The postal orders still came in. There were albums there too, sports photographs neatly tinted in watercolour. One day I took them into the garden and set fire to the lot. My mother protested feebly—for she feared his testy nature, his grim silences, his long intransigence.

A great Anglophile, he followed the cricket Tests and rugby internationals with the closest interest, keeping records, rugby programmes from Lansdowne Road, cricket score cards (the Gentlemen of Ireland XI playing in Dublin), Wisdens, following the fortunes of the Ashes and the Triple Crown. His heroes were Eugene Davy, the mauler Clinch, Bradman, slogger Walter Hammond. He filled diaries with notes, one of which I saved from the fire.

It was bound in leather cloth, bottle-green in colour, the dark green of the old corked Guinness bottles, with a loop supplied for a pencil which was missing—The School Boy's Note Book, 'Containing much useful information and many tables helpful for his work and play'; compiled by one Marc Ceppi (author of *French Lessons on the Direct Method*), for the year 1934. The useful information turned out to be a list of the sovereigns on the English throne from the first Windsor back to Norman times, a table of Latin, French and Greek verbs, some 'strong' German verbs, mensuration formulae, a table of logarithms and a list of possible careers in His Majesty's armed forces. The Colonial Service and Indian Police. Facing the title page he had written in pencil:

TO SEEK,

TO STRIVE,

TO GAIN,

AND NOT   *To end of June*

TO YIELD.

The motto of the school sodality. In this Charles Letts' diary I found predictable things. Predictable in a Roman Catholic boarding-school in the depths of the country—confessional material, half averred, half denied, already regretted, and at all times more *Schadenfreude* than *Schwärmerei*. Among other passing events he recorded the death of ancient Hindenburg, the assassination of Dolfuss, an Irish heatwave in July.

In that year General O'Duffy's Blueshirts ('a nice shade of blue') paraded in Dublin. Miss Paget's Golden Miller won the Grand National. De Valera informed the electorate and the Dail that the country was 'up against it', but did not specify what it was. His economic war. The Australians were in England, Bradman and Ponsford knocking up centuries with tireless proficiency. Our eyes were strained reading by Aladdin lamps. The Test results came in faintly or not at all from Trent Bridge and Leeds and the Kennington Oval as from a far remote country, crackling with static from the tall battery-fed radio in the hall. My brother kept his ear pressed to it, paring his finger nails, grimacing, swearing (Darling b Verity . . . 4. Chipperfield c Ames b Farnes . . . 99). He was perhaps twenty then, a slow developer, finickety, protected from corporal punishment at school, leading his class in subjects that interested him (history), coming last in subjects that bored him (Irish). Endlessly at his nails at home, a complacent nose-bleeder; never have I encountered anyone with so little to say for himself.

Or by this time he had left school. He did not go to university; he was learning the morse code at a technical institute.

My mother cooked for him (a faddy eater at the best of times), kept him on time (a slow riser), and for her pains was mercilessly bullied by him—a thankless sort of son. Perhaps she liked it. Who can say with women? She wore gardening gloves and chain-smoked—Gold Flake virginia tobacco, I remember the yellow and gold packet—bending with a trowel in her hand, cigarette smoke in her eyes, throwing out slugs and weeds on to the pathways. She raked the rockery paths and laid down orange peels for the giant black slugs that came out in the evenings. She worked there alone, content, in the falling darkness. A maid came out of the side door and rang a bell. Miss O'Brien, a licentious spinster lady, had called late with prohibited literature —*Flotsam*, a *Bildungsroman* done into English, in her carrier bag. My mother was in those days an omnivorous reader. She had known Crosby Garstin.

We went looking for mushrooms in the early morning, crossing an immense field bounded on all sides by granite walls, and collected on thrawneens the scarce white edible fungi that tastes of evening and decay. The field was still damp, sparkling with light. Among toadstools, thistles and cow manure, spider webs sagged on the grass, going with a checking motion, throwing off drops of moisture and light. White pupae were hidden in the still centre of grasshopper cocoons. Thistles, mushrooms, cowshit, hard and soft variety, counterfeit fairy rings, and the sun rising with difficulty over the hill. The resurrection of the body. It was six-thirty on the morning of the ninth of August, 1934, the twentieth anniversary of the Battle of Liège, and two days preceding the fortieth anniversary of the death of Cardinal John Henry Newman, according to useful information supplied in very small italics by the obliging Monsieur Marc Ceppi. We traversed the immense field, heads down, my mother, my taciturn brother and I, looking for mushrooms; but for him and his diary that day, as so many other days, would have passed into oblivion. The actual entry read: 'August 9, 1934. Thursday. Woke up at 6:30 & roused Ma and Dan & went to look for mushrooms in the field opposite. Got a good few at first. Got tin can from lodge people after. I brought some to Mrs. Coyle (in bed).

August 11. Saturday. Half Quarter Day. Cardinal Newman d. 1890. Hammond 302 not out. Very hot.'

But for that entry and Wally's patience that day would have disappeared from my memory. I remember the field and the sensation of looking for mushrooms (puffballs went sailing, spears of grass shone, we trod in liquid cowshit) but not the actual event and my mother there. It would have meant climbing either a wall or a five-barred gate. The days when she could do either are long past. Now that day has gone too, I have burnt the diary: and she is gone too.

5 MORTUARY CHAPEL: In a state bordering on intoxication my father and I visited the mortuary chapel after dark on the day she died. A young nurse led us to a wooden shed to the rear of the hospital. My father, grown old in a few days, went with bowed head; gallantry itself with the ladies, as a rule, he had nothing to say to the pretty nurse. She went ahead of us and unlocked the door and stood aside for us to enter. She had a small watch pinned on her chest. We went in.

An open coffin stood to one side of the altar. We stared at what was in it. My dead mother in her blue shroud. She was alone there, calm and composed; nothing would ever touch her and she would never come back, dressed in the cerements of the grave. She had been a beauty in her day and now that beauty had returned. I who have had a lifelong dread of touching a dead person, kissed her forehead. It was like stone. The Ice Queen received my homage coldly; she was as hard as stone, yet gentleness glowed from her. With her beauty, her good nature had returned. Her mouth was no longer bitter; the strained and worried look that she had worn for so long had gone. I had never known her, her expression, both disdainful, frigid and sweet, told me so. No one had ever known her. The petty annoyances of her life were over and done with—husband and sons who loved or didn't love, it was all the one to her. I had the feeling, looking at her there, so still and severe in mien, yet so sweet, that one is always observed, under constant surveillance, though not perhaps by God. Underlying theme of the overlying earth. Soon she would be as anonymous as it. As dull as earth. Now someone still watched and guarded her and from under her closed eyes she still watched me. We prepared to leave. My father hesitated between the coffin and the altar. Good-bye, Dilly, he said as though addressing a living person and not the stone corpse. He went out then, with bowed head, not looking at the nurse. She locked the door behind us. Crossing the moonlit yard we entered the hospital again.

He stopped in the corridor—the place was a warren of corridors—to say, I can't believe it, Dan. Fifty years married, and look at her there. His voice echoed in the corridor. An old nun dressed in white was coming towards us. She was a beauty in her day you know, he said. She's a beauty now, I said, watching the nun coming on. It would have been our Golden Jubilee this year, my father said. We'd have both our names in the papers. She said she'd never live to see it, but I don't think she meant it.

The old nun came up and spoke to us. They all agreed that my mother was a beauty. The Child of Mary blue suited her. The sisters would go down through the night and pray for her. Going out I tipped the doorman half a crown. I'm sorry for your trouble, he said.

It was freezing again, a cold night, the moon flying through clouds. The wind whistled down the hill from the direction of Dalkey. Across the narrow way lights shone in the shop selling funeral items. Behind blue stippled glass, wreaths and printed requiem cards; funeral hire purchase terms, artificial flowers in domes of glass, tributes to defunct near-and-dear-ones, the usual forlorn objects that one seldom notices, when passing by. Stained glass, blue shadows, arpeggios, church music, mental somnolence. Mother Dear, good-bye. One may hope: never again all this agony of life. Certainly it's not supportable, on a hedonistic basis. It is only supportable, if at all, when one digs down into oneself. And then? Soon for her, poor dear, would begin the barehead life under the grass. One more, I said, my insides burning, let us have one more.

The sad signs of approaching spring that my poor mother waited and watched for; the earth hardening in April, the birds building, soft days when her corns ached. She moved about more easily then, burdened with too many clothes, residue of winter.

Signs of summer in Nullamore. Corncrakes grating rustily in an upper field, cuckoos in the Crooked Meadow, a hare decomposing in the deep well and grass sprouting over the broken boards. Then the starling returned to build in the wall of the rockery between the limestone and corrugated iron. The only monogamous bird, feathers like fish scales.

I phoned Howth Castle. A maid answered. I waited while she delivered my message, hearing the voices behind me, recounting the old times. Presently I heard Olivia's voice, a sad English accent far away across the bay. I told her that my mother was dead. Could she come across?

Kick over a stone and out come familiar grubs. In the pub we met one of my father's erstwhile yachting cronies, an old acquaintance from Sligo now well on in drink. A man named Larry Ball. I bought a round of Scotch. He seemed unmoved by the news of my mother's death; perhaps he had not heard. Hearing from my proud father of my travels, he told me that he himself had sailed twice round the world. Bouncing Ball.

Ah, Larry, my father said, holding him with his blue stare, if she was here today the dear Lord knows she would be laughing with us now.

Stout, short of breath, with soiled protuberant boozer's eyes, Larry Ball was packed into a grey tweed suit with buttoned waistcoast from which a gold watch-chain hung; he had a blunt mottled face and clouded eyes like a gudgeon and sat with his stout legs apart, mopping his brow with a large linen handkerchief, staring at me with a troubled eye.

The big yachts, lit from behind, the prints magnified many times, ran before the wind before the harbour mouth. Howth, as always, lay in sunlight. The soiled eyes studied me (I could see a question formulating in that gudgeon's eye.) So this was the artist of the family. The mournful music was recorded from tapes in the office behind the bar: Sundays and Cybele. It had played while she was dying, while the snow was falling; now it played and she was dead; nothing had changed in the bar.

This is my son Dan. My son is an artist, my father said, hot and wild with mulled whiskey inside him. Begod, Larry, he's a better man than his father before him. I could only paint outhouses.

She had died on Sunday. But who was Cybele? She carried towers and temples in her head. The Jews of Thessalonika and Amsterdam kept the keys of their lost Spanish houses, the homes they would never return to. Was she a queen? Why towers and temples?

Ah God, Dan, the world is changed a hell of a lot since our days, Larry Ball said. Who is this fellow P. Kasso? (the soiled eyes were now looking at me with deep misgiving). Sure a child of four could paint better than that. What is your personal opinion of Mr. P. Kasso?

We left the gasbag Ball when the pub closed and took a bottle back to the cold studio. My father was by this time in a maudlin state, inundated by the past, and no one to share it with. I built up the fire, lit it, brought out the bottle. Olivia had gone home. My father sat before the blaze, his eyes watering, wringing his hands. I have his hands, these hands I paint with, he has mine, depending how you look at it. In the light from the unshaded bulb everything looked shabby. To die in Ireland—*A Bas in Erinn* —somehow the notion did not appeal to me. I had not wept. My elusive brother was not there. He was still circling the hospital, unaware that she was dead.

The broken-down small-holdings, the weedy fields confronting the winding road, the road going over the hill, and there the cottages with their windows broken and boarded up, grass and weeds sprouting on the roofs, weighing down the whole, pushing it back into the earth. The cottagers themselves, the stoics who lived there, were patiently waiting for the roof to fall in on them, saving them the expense and inconvenience of more orthodox burial, constituting as they did a kind of loam, human topsoil. From day to day, touch of clay; the most exiguous relief. I thought of Manormorehamilton and the lakes about there, where I had been on a painting trip the previous spring. The Western shielings.

On the morning of the funeral I lay in bed covered in coats, listening to my father snoring mournfully in the alcove. My brother was there too. The whole tribe. Rain had fallen or was still falling. I heard a car pass on the road. The sound came up clearly, as if we were on the ground floor—the slap of wetted tyres on wetted asphalt, changing gear at the corner and the pitch of the engine rising. It passed, and the sound died away.

Then I heard another coming, apparently driven by a maniac.

The sound of a car approaching at high speed, slamming into gear to take the corner, the driver impatient, taking it too fast, I felt it inside me, the wet tyres shuddering at it, the whine of the engine rising, ready to burst through the walls, scatter my thin morning sleep and all its borderline free-ranging associations, piercing my eardrums and penetrating into my skull, the fan-belt screeching: *Oxte! Oxte!* Awake! Awake!, a blast of sound. I was tightened up, waiting for the accident to happen. Then something immense and airborne took the roof off the house. I saw its shadow blunder across the wall, on to the cornice, and away. The whole house shuddered. It went on into silence. The roots of my hair stood up. It wasn't a car driven by a lunatic, not a jet airliner going through low cloud from Dublin Airport, no; it was her own unhappy spirit that had plunged past, looking for hell or purgatory, touching me one last time before disappearing for good and all, and I recalled the dream, the shooting, the spectral bomber.

My father had woken and was calling for us to rise. Quinn's black limousine was coming at nine sharp. My brother, true to form, had stood off to the bitter end. He had not visited her when she was dying and had seen her by accident when she was dead. He hadn't expected the lid to be off the coffin, and saw the occupant stiff and regal, unmistakably his mother again, surrounded by floral decorations, artificial roses in cellophane bags. Averting his eyes he had gone out into the yard and had taken a few turns there. The undertaker's men passed him. We followed the hearse to Glasthule Church; it was lowsprung, packed with flowers, and the lights on inside, looking almost gay, people stopped to stare at it going by. That was the evening before; now this would be her last journey.

After the requiem mass we rode in high style behind a liveried chauffeur to the cemetery. The hearse went before us. Out of the main traffic way, it picked up speed, threading its way through the lanes.

There were hearses before us at Dean's Grange Cemetery, and groups of people in mourning standing before plots or walking here and there in the barren fields. We were directed to the wrong grave, under a yew. Four rough fellows, grave-diggers in wellington boots, came across waving their hats and calling out Ruttle? Ruttle? So we walked behind the hearse for the last hundred yards. The opened grave was out on its own away from the congestion of headstones and crosses, and deep—eight foot of opened earth, livid clay, a plot in semi-perpetuity. The brand-new coffin would not be brand-new for long, down there in the damp. It was cold, a cold exposed place, with groups of dark figures gathered around open graves or moving away. There was snow on Three Rock Mountain. Few, as she had predicted, were there to mourn her. My brother was not present; Swift had not gone to Stella's funeral, the woman who may or may not have been his wife; Oscar Wilde refused to leave prison to see his dying mother. My mother's eldest son, true to his nature, had kept away. One may assume they had their different reasons. Fearing a nervous breakdown, he wrote, he had thought best to leave immediately after the requiem mass. I did not see him again.

A few months later he, who had been so considerate of his own feelings and comfort throughout the proceedings, emigrated to Australia, where the great cricketers come from, the heroes of the Ashes. Hammond driving among the oleanders in semi-tropical Natal. Leyland dead. Ponsford dead, Hobbs dead. Kippax dead. Iremonger dead. The Nawab of Pataudi dead. All the dead cricketers. My silent brother is there. Who is watering the wicket at Melbourne now?

The grave was left open, as is the custom now. As we walked away the grave-diggers began spitting on their hands. We left the cemetery, directing the liveried chauffeur to an out of the way pub in Dalkey. Bitterly we drank to her memory, my father and I.

6 EPISTOLARY (I):
Lista de Correos
Nerka, Andalusia
Spain

February 1962

Ruttle, what are you up to, lad?

I've a hell of a lot of projects swirling around in my head, a dirty eddy close to some sea-borne sewage pipe, and I can't get on with it until I've re-established contact wiv me foin Oirish friend.

True, amazingly, I wanted to come over and shake a bottle at you, but now that I've all the time in the world to do so, I feel compelled to stay where I am for a spell and work. I felt I just had to get something off to you. Probably to tell you that I've left the treadmill and am living in Spain as I've always wanted to. I've a million things to tell you about life here, but it'd take too damn long. Never in my life before have I barged into a set of circumstances, a way of life, that was more conducive to creation. In two words, I'm happy. And right now I don't care if I ever sell a line. I think this part of the world would be right for you too: If you want to know more write me and I'll tell you all. At this moment Fay and I are ensconced in a fine whitewashed shack by the sea. The place is expensive by Spanish standards. Friends, an Italian painter and his wife (Viennese) are renting a house with running water, five large living-rooms, big kitchen, garden, outhouse, bathroom, hunting quail in the corridors, for 1,000 pesetas a month! And there's no such thing as winter in the Costa del Sol! I read in my airmail edition of London *Daily Mail* that England is froze. Every time you buy a shot of vino in a bar in Spain they automatically hand you something to eat! A piece of calamare, an anchovy, a couple of olives and bread, octopus, clams, free! Some days, if we care to drink say half a dozen vinos we're too full for supper! Shit! Does it sound like Paradise? It is! It's a shame you Irish bums prefer the city! Now I've got it off my chest I can work. Forgive me if I've spoiled your day.

Right now the church bell is speaking with the voice of a well tuned garbage can beaten rhythmically with dry meat bone . . . *Santo Dios* goes the requiem . . . somebody died today. And it ain't me! Love to Olivia.

ROGER

P.S. the most expensive luxury around is a postage stamp! (hope I get out the screamer habit).

Cortijo de Maro
Andalusia

27.2.61

Dear Dan,

Thanks for your letter. You're thinking of coming here? Fine!

In my opinion there's nothing to beat it between Gibraltar (where the apes live) and windy Port Bou. Paloma, old Tarragona, Alicante, Almeria—you can have 'em. I hope to be able to work here. It's quiet.

Originally a Moorish town, I'm told. The name means fountains-in-abundance. There are fountains here, but who the hell wants water, and maybe a dose of the shits, when cognac is only 22 pesetas a litre, and you can buy a litre of wine in a bar for 7 pesetas, and a peseta is worth about $1\frac{1}{2}$d.

To give you some idea of the look of the place. It's built on a kind of tableland with its backside to the sea. From the main plaza you can throw stones down into the fishing boats. On the plaza there are a couple of bars and a double line of palm trees and crazy chestnuts like Japanese leechees that don't bear fruit, and a Town Hall with an anchor-and-chain emblem and a plaque that boasts in good capitalized Spanish that El Caudillo saved Catholic Spain from Communism. *Arriba España*!

When you enter the plaza—Plaza de Jose Antonio Primo de Rivera—from the narrow Puerta del Mar, the sea is slap before you. To your left, a low railing prevents drunks from falling into the halfmoonshaped and rather shitty beach below. There's a long building like a lock-up or calaboose and some poor cottages, a double tier of them, under an overhanging bluff.

Bare-assed bambinos from the cottages use this beach as an open-air shit-place. The tide rises and falls only a few metres and doesn't wash the *caca* away. The fishing boats are drawn up here by pulley and tackle around a winch. Above is Florian's Hotel, *muy tipico* Italiano. The beach is Playa de Calahonda. There's another one farther down, called Carabeo (meaning shit-strewn) and a big one beyond that—Burriana: a kilometre long.

Facing the Town Hall is the Marissal, bar and restaurant; half glass doors and wide windows looking into the plaza on one side and towards the Ciné Olympia and the church on the other. The summer residence of the Puerto Rican ambassador is in the church square. Next to the Marissal is a poorer bar which we prefer. Balcon de Europa, formerly Bar Alhambra—you can still decipher the old name over the door. A line of tables outside both. Prices at the former a little higher than at the latter, where the service is generally sharper. You will meet Miguel, a gentleman.

Every Thursday a *gitano* comes on a beat-up bicycle with a kid goat roped on. He cuts its throat in a cramped passage full of empty beer crates off the *retrete*. The carcass is hung near the kitchen door and used during the week for tapas, which you get free with the drinks. *Muy bueno*. The retrete smells bad. The whiff that comes out of it is lethal. How the women squat over it to pass water or anything else and manage to stand upright after, beats me.

Sitting at one of the Balcon de Europa tables you can see Maro up in the hills. The clouds over the sierras never come any closer. Rarely. Between the half dozen high palms on this side (I am writing this at one of the tables, getting into my fourth cognac) and the half dozen on the other side runs the promenade, broadwalk or *paseo*, where the entire population take their exercise in the evening. You can see for many kilometres down the coast. Very brown. Very wild.

King Victor Emmanuel named this *paseo* the 'Balcon de Europa' because of the view. During the Peninsular War it was a Limey gun-site. The Limeys, being no respectors of Catholic churches, knocked the top off a church that stood here formerly, to get a better field of fire. The church—most of it —fell into the sea. What was left was reconverted into a poor-class pension, with a colonnade (the old cloisters) for foundations, undermined by a colony of rats. *Su tropel de ratas.* Nowadays, what with the rats, rare tidal disturbances (it can blow here), sea erosion and general wear and tear, not much is left standing. One hears talk of a new luxury hotel to be erected on the spot. I'll believe it when I see it. There's always talk in Spain; talk of improvements, modernization, urbanization, *progreso*—nothing much comes of it, I'm glad to say.

The streets here are narrow and for the most part cobbled, without much motor traffic to speak of (most of this goes by on the *carretera*, slicing off a small section of the town to the north); what comes through is mainly of the mule and burro variety. Occasionally something on wheels. The houses are painted blanco-white, the doors generally open because of the heat—and in August it can be really hot here. You can see through into the patios, and even into the back gardens. The shutters are drawn to keep the rooms cool. *Nada mas.* Our love to Olivia and yourself. Write. Live soberly.

ROGER

Cortijo de Maro
Andalusia

18.3.62

Dear Ruttles,

I enclose a few photos of our shack. It's what the Spaniards call a *cortijo*, which corresponds to a-farm-with-a-farm-house-attached. It's never been rented before. Probably because of this, or perhaps because the owner is already pretty rich (he owns the town's olive factory), I'm only charged 1,000 pesetas a month, which is damned little. £6 English (or Irish). I've taken a lease for six months initially which takes me right through the summer traffic period, so I should have no difficulty in getting it for the same price next August.

The house is on top of a hill and has a full 360° view of the sea and the coast on one side and the sierras on the other. Between them is farm land, the campo; olive groves and almond. The land is uneven with a valley every half mile or so. The house is two-storey and painted blanco-white, with long windows and two terraces, as you'll see from the photos. *Muy tipico*. The kitchen's enormous, with a bank of three-tier wood burners which we don't use as we've had butane gas installed. There's no water or electric light. We have a butano lamp instead of the latter and for the former I go into the village every morning to pick up sixteen gallons of water from one of the fountains.

Fay's got the biggest studio in all Spain. Thirty-five feet long by twenty-five feet wide and a head clearance of at least sixteen. There's a grape-pressing area in the middle and a sump for catching the stuff. The bodega below her is as extensive as the studio. It should be full of bloodstuffs but aint, not yet. We'll kill a kid when you arrive.

The owner of the joint installed a loo for us. Before that we were commuting to the bushes and the countryside about was beginning to look as though a paperchase had just passed through. But it's all right now. In between buzzing around with water barrels, careering off to see if there's any mail, enjoying the luxury of a real stone shithouse, eating, drinking, sleeping, underwater fishing, hiking the countryside, going to the bullfights, getting locked up, sighing at the window, I write. It's nice. For the first time in my life I should be in no hurry, so I hurry. But that's nobody's fault but mine. The fever is on me. I'm often bad-tempered. I have a room set aside for it. You just take off the shutters and bung them in the bodega. The view is terrific.

I spent a night in jail here for a suspected drunk-while-speeding charge, with bail at ten thousand pesetas coming a bit high I thought—it's about £60. However, some of this I hope to retrieve. Fay, understandably enough, was riled with me. Enough of that.

As for the work itself, it's like walking into a treadmill. But once in and a rhythm established it's not so bad. I'll have something to show you. Fay's in the kitchen right now cooking supper. I see the lights of the village seven hundred metres below me, a mile away on the *carretera*. The lights moving out on the sea are the big fishing boats what went out earlier from Burriana. The butane lamp is hissing, my eyes are on a fresh glass of brandy at my elbow (the fifth since I started this letter), the door of the writing room is open behind me but I don't think I'll make it tonight.

Some days I pitch a rock at a passing cat; others I like what I'm doing so much that I can't write any more but have to go out for a walk. I could find you a place here without too much trouble. And you would both love it. Just let me know in time. I have made some inquiries. Christ there's a whole book of shit to write to you about, but soup's up.

Power to your elbow, my friends. And love from Fay and me.

ROGER

Cortijo de Maro

16.4.62

Dear Ruttles,

Look at this new postcard, a view from the air. The desolate part off to the right where the new concrete slab chalets and the parador are going up was once a forest of umbrella pines. Trees cut for lumber, stumps pulled for firewood, earth carted off for gardens. What's left looks like Miguel's face, maybe bleached. I sometimes think his face—and others as eroded—got that way from looking at what's left under the sun. Either way, it's what's left that won't get away.

We made a budget today and found we were almost broke. We left Canada with £1,400, but at the time of writing have only about £130. We spent £220 on the boat. I bought a motor-vehicle in Venice for £440, a DKW, and an excellent buy I think. We stayed a week there, another in Rome (hell to drive in), a few days in Florence, another few in Sienna, a week in Barcelona—the money runs away. To cap it all was thrown in jail and fined, as I think I told you. When do you think you will come?

Con abrazos muy fuerte.

ROGER

⬥

I received other letters from Amory in those miserable times preceding and following my mother's demise. All were on the same lines, all touched on the same theme, in all of them the promise (you won't regret it) and the refrain (when will you come?). We left in the spring of the year following my mother's death.

PART II

Spring 1963
Andalusia

7 THE PENSION ON CALLE DE LA CRUZ: From the street, you can see the brass bed-head in the bedroom on the first floor. He stays there alone, and goes about leaning heavily on a stick, speaks to no one—unless you count the Frenchman—and all avoid him. The company, the gregarious winter community of *extranjeros* who get together at the terrace tables, offer few attractions to the Dutchman; he keeps aloof, does not involve himself, preferring to play chess with the Frenchman in one of the two bars on the plaza or, weather permitting, under the trees there.

He drinks alone in the Marissal, staring out of the window; a region of dim illumination seems to please him better than strong sunlight such as you get here even in winter. He is to be seen in the daytime playing chess under the shade of the *castaña loca* trees, or drinking alone in the Marissal, or at night, again alone, in the ill-lit bar El Molino.

He has a bad limp and appears to be injured. The Frenchman reports that he stutters. Charlotte Bayless believes he is Dutch. He looks Dutch enough; a big-boned, lopsided *mijnheer* in non-descript loose-fitting clothes which he never changes out of, possibly his only clothes—spotted grey 'sponge-bag' flannels without a crease, black alpaca jacket such as Jesuits wear in winter—and so wrinkled that he might be in the habit of sleeping in them.

A big, pallid, frowning man with a pock-marked face (healed smallpox postules?), overweight and unhealthy in appearance, disgruntled, broad in the backside, with little covetous deep-set eyes and lobeless ears. A common enough type, but one you rarely see here on the Costa del Sol.

A limp, a speech impediment, not in the best of health, *and* Dutch. He has handicaps. For diversion he plays chess with the Frenchman: They play for the most part in silence, studying their respective moves; a mutual benefit arrangement. He volunteers no information whatsoever concerning himself; of the conditions of his own life past and present he remains silent (would that the loquacious Frenchman did the same). He is a mystery: a close-mouthed man.

His features are blunt and heavy, big bones, the eyes set deep, with wide simian shelf and massive brow-ridges. His complexion, as already mentioned, pale and unhealthy. An indoors man. Lobeless ears, sparse, muddy-coloured hair cropped close and plastered down with sweat from the exertions of walking with a limp, matted down on a forbidding dolichocephalic skull. He dresses drably and goes about apparently in pain, frowning, a black beret clamped over one ear. The slovenly head turns slowly to right or left, mistrustfully probing the area in advance of the trunk, and if an obstacle is encountered then, any hindrance, the body, bending acutely, turns aside to circumvent it— the ferrule of the walking-stick striking the ground the while— and with every appearance of ill-humour he passes, avoiding your eye. Impetuous Dutchman!

At first he played chess with the Frenchman exclusively on the plaza or in the bars; then he condescended to speak to me, whereupon I learnt that he wasn't Dutch at all. And, as for his injury, he had fought against the Russians and been wounded, semi-paralysed down one side. He offered to show me the wound.

The possible post-graduate student from The Hague or Utrecht, or the engineer on furlough from Rotterdam, makes way for this character, who has fluent German, French and English, and moderate Dutch and Spanish. Quite a linguist in fact; a gifted man. His name is Alex von Gerhar, Captain of the Reserve in the Finnish army.

Charlotte, inquisitive as a magpie, first noticed him about the place, drew our attention to him, and then discovered where he lived. In a pension on Calle de la Cruz.

I

The conduit pipeline, six feet or more in diameter, one hundred and fifty feet long and supported by heavy pillars, reinforced cement on a rock base, straddles the dried-up river beyond the factory. It serves the water supply of this village of ten thousand souls, the population of Guernica before the bombing. Discoloured and dripping in places as though exuding oil, like the drive shaft of a car, it stretches across the dry river-bed.

The Roman aqueducts are on the west side. On this side, the irrigation channels come down from Frigiliana, six miles away, up in the hills. Plantations of sugar cane, olives, carob, figs and almonds on the hills; sweet potato, tomato and sugar cane in the valleys.

The first poplar leaves and first almond blossoms appear in early March along the banks of the dry river of unknown name, where we go walking. Charlotte speaks a strange language. 'Got the hots', 'in back of', 'stroller', not 'attracted to', not 'in the rear', 'push-cart'.

Dredge, *Dreck, schmutzig*. And dill? A herb ('an 'erb', she says) that grows on the lips of gorges; a yellow wild flower blowing in the hot land wind, but not found here, where we go walking. She wears her hair in a long braid down her back, tied with a red elastic band bound in damask. It's sometimes sticky because of the salt in the air and her oily Jewish skin. Energy emanates from her, such truly grievous energy. I breathe her in, salty, sometimes bitter in her moods. Her husband calls her 'Dilly', a nickname from her childhood, her Lower East Side beginnings, because she was the 'toughest kid on the block', named after Dillinger the gangster (who was gunned down in a telephone booth, calling his mother). She comes from the dark plains of American sexual experience where the bison still roam.

It is the real smell of blonde pigment that I breathe, from her hair, her skin. She has high Slav cheekbones and a Byzantine nose that comes straight down from the brow. This beautiful young woman, carnal, individual, free with unforgettable eyes, and wide mouth—*pommes d'amour, Liebesapfel*—wears tight blue slacks under a white pullover and is rather undulant in her turning, in her leaning forward, pained by certain weights.

'Kilter', she says, 'a bout of the mean reds', 'a good lay', and 'butt', 'hung over', 'making it', 'drag'. She speaks from the back of the throat, the epiglottis, a complex human being's speech, made up of all her ancestors and past. Moisel Lipski. A petite woman with an exotic cast of features not uncommon in Eastern Europe, she goes before me, walking in that aura of decorum and modesty, and while her voice is pleasant enough, it can never be compared to the power of her appearance. We descend into a thyme and rosemary scented valley that gives off an odour of eucalyptus. Pretty natural walks come hereabouts, long grass good for bedding, rutted ways, *couloirs*, several landscapes in the sun. In the winter the women wash their clothes in the river. River of unknown name.

I, from my tired forty-six Christian Old World years, speak of an early love, telling it badly and break off, depressed. No, she tells me, beguiling me from her bright twenty-four Jewish New World years, it's not dull for me, urging me to go on, disposed to humour me (no Young Lochinvar), her teeth as white as dice (*la dentale d'Amérique*). Gana is the primitive need to take. So I take her there into the mint and thyme scented valley where there is no breath of air.

The American jets pass overhead, the sound rumbling in the cone-shaped mountains traversed by shadows of passing clouds, ridge-backed or fish-spined with a timberline of savin and cork trees, pines, a scruff of khaki. The absence of the old oak forests preventing evaporation, the clouds pass on grandly over Spain without releasing any moisture. High overhead the bombers go out of sight and hearing, crescendo and decrescendo. They refuel in flight from tanker planes, coupling and uncoupling like insects. Down in the riverbed under the cliffs that rise with rare acoustic potential, the jets sound loud and war-like. *Habet acht! Habet acht!* We get on to a powdery path where heavy trucks have gone before.

Her father, she tells me, made enough money to get her through college. Antioch, Ohio—'A very liberal college'. But disowned or at least disinherited her, for marrying a Goy. He later found himself in hospital in the company of Goys, and was surprised to find them human, like Jews. But although he liked Bob Bayless well enough, a principle was a principle; he disinherited the bad Jewish daughter who married the good Goy. Her sisters were Ann, Ruth, Estella, all of them married, one with a cancerous leg. Charlotte was the youngest and prettiest. Her father, bigoted old Orchard Street Jew, brought her up, taught her figures; until she could beat him at chess.

On the way back, below the Cortijo de Maro, we see birdcatchers staking down their long net. Trapped birds flutter in small wooden cages all around in the scrub. We separate outside the cemetery, go back by different ways.

II

Amory and I played billiards regularly in the hall next to the Marissal where the dances were held. Our respective characters showed in our styles: I was for coaxing the balls into the holes, the pockets, drop shots and soft cushions, whereas Amory would lay his champion's thigh on the side of the table, sight along his cue, a Celtas burning forgotten to one side. And then the violence of his desperate strokes. Illegal push shots interspersed with rough kisses and irresistible cannons, the balls jumping off the table and dropping with a horrid sound on the floor. Amory moved his ears (vestigial remnants), chalked his cue, sized up the game. He hated to be beaten.

My aunt in Constantinople, Amory said. And sometimes: That cunt in Constantinople. Once I banged into Margaret in the British Museum, Amory said. I was in a hurry. She's a better-looking filly than her sister. That awful smile—as if she'd just sucked off a horse. Game to me, I believe.

Sayings of Roger Amory: After the Lord Mayor's coach comes the shit cart. (From the bones of old horses rendered down is made the most beautiful Prussian blue.) Feeding your face. Talking up a storm. The only winds I know (farting like Pantagruel) are those that blow from below.

Four winds blow in these parts: Sud-Oeste, Terral, Poniente, Levante. The Terral is a strange wind. Hot at its source, it blows on the tourist ghettos of Marbella and Torremolinos. In summer it's like a furnace door opening. Rosa Munsinger said she could not sleep through it. It arrives in Nerka as a warm wind, its force weakened by the Malaga mountains and the Sierra Almijara. It blows leaves and papers about the patios and castor oil seeds burst and scatter, at night in the dark as in the day.

The Levante is an east wind. A destructive wind that wrecks the pergolas on the miradors and caña shades, it blasts the sugar cane and blackens the potato crop. (A fierce windstorm that comes to flatten everything in the fields. Farmers out next day look bewildered, not knowing where to begin picking it up. The lights off for two days and the water off for three. How can the wind effect the water supply? could it happen anywhere else?) It blows with great force, a day or night wind, depending when it starts, either beginning at sun-up and blowing all day, dying at sun-down, or beginning at sun-down and blowing all night, then dying in the early hours: it blows for three days or three nights. The full force of this wind is checked by the promontory Cerro Gordo three hundred metres above the sea. The force of the Terral comes diffused in over the Malaga Mountains and Sierra Almijara, arriving as a mild land wind.

The Poniente blows from the west and brings fine weather and fresh Atlantic breezes, coming low in over the sea, keeping Nerka cool in summer, while Frigiliana, in the foothills of the sierras, bakes. Seagulls arrive with the cold Atlantic currents from November onwards. They gather on Burriana. Daisy Bayless, a sprite in blue, likes to send them all into the sky at once.

A little shrine at La Cruz de Pinto near Frigiliana: wicks burning in oil and two little effigies inside the shrine, Archangel Gabriel waving *bon voyage* to the mad carpenter of Nazareth (sagging from his nails). Enough aceite inside and cached under heaps of stones to fry spuds for a long time. Summit levelled off with a whitewashed stone boundary around the perimeter. The

Sud-Oeste blows. One of the winds makes a high psychotic whine up in the air.

The winds blow. The palms and oriental planes turn up their pale undersides on the Plaza José Antonio Primo de Rivera and the drinkers move indoors. The Dutchman and the Frenchman take in their chess board. Bob Bayless is expected on the plaza. A big ponderous slow-spoken oxen-jawed good-natured capable American man given to nonsequitors. Also Olivia. Pseudo-sweethearts.

Nerka, ancient Nerika of the Moors, the coastal zone where life still keeps its flavour. Area of carob and oleander. Spain abounds with brackish streams: salt mines and saline deposits left behind after the evaporation of the Great Sea. The central soil is strongly impregnated with saltpetre, which is also common in northern graveyards.

> *Aqui, junto al mar latino*
> *digo la verdad:*
> *siento en roca, aceite y vino*
> *yo mi antiguedad.*

Latins: a nation of spitters. The women in purdah go by the wall. A *musée d'homme*. The littoral.

IV

Drunker than we knew and trying to sober up late one day of the previous summer, the summer Faulkner died and the girls ran at night on Torrecillas in bras and panties, watched by two indulgent Guardia Civil, Amory and I went for a swim on Carabeo. The beach was deserted in the late afternoon.

I was out of my clothes, into the water and well out before I discovered that the sea was dangerous. A strong current was heading off towards Burriana and I was in it, being carried along opposite the rocks. The way I was going I would end up out in the bay, would end up exhausted somewhere out there, before Cerro or Torre del Pino or Playa de la Herradura ten or more kilometres away. I could not swim it, not to Los Bereng, or Berenqueles, Punta de la Mena.

I turned and began to swim back as strongly as I could. I saw Amory ahead of me. I was the better swimmer, but he was stronger than I, and yet he was making no headway: head down he was flailing along with a powerful kick. I did not call to him, conserving my strength; he would not hear me; he would find out soon enough. I matched him stroke for stroke. Amory appeared briefly on the crest of an incoming wave and then disappeared down into the trough. He was like a big dog, an Alsatian, bitter about it, his head now well out of the water, breast-stroking and apparently making progress. Back! I shouted to him. Back! choking on it. I felt all the strength ebbing out of me and was too drunk to care. Out in the bay I would go down like a stone.

Previously there had always been a limit set, a little room for human error—my devious Da playing draughts with me, losing a piece, saying, No, wait, Dan, I didn't mean that, put that one back, in a game without rules, or arbitrary rules that could be altered at will, so there would always be a little room, for error as well as room to correct error; to be sure one knew reality was not like that, but unimaginably harder and stricter in what it could take, more punishing, leaving no margin for error. No, none. Reality was ferocious, was waiting, would tolerate no weakness; was unselective and most bitter. This, if I had not known it all along, I knew now. With all the strength and purpose I had in me, I began to swim for my life.

Now I felt the persistent outgoing pull and was in it and with the strength ebbing out of me, it was easy to give in. Drunk, I didn't care. As I was making no progress towards the beach, I stopped swimming, allowed myself to be carried along.

And now the rocks were passing in review again, my last sight of them, and I was being carried out towards Los Bereng and the old fire-towers on the headlands. I thought I heard Lenten music, far away. Albinoni's Adagio perhaps. The stream of the world. Very faint, distant but perfect. (The torso of a murdered woman, found in a waterlogged suitcase, was taken from the River Orne.) I turned about for the last time and saw Amory's drained face on the crest of a wave. He had made no headway, strong as he was, but was being carried along in my wake. We were both heading out for La Pina. I allowed myself to be carried along, conserving my strength for one last effort; at the point nearest to the rocks, against which the waves were breaking, I would make my play and take what chances were offered among the rocks.

And presently I began to swim. Ten strokes and I was in another current, not the slow and methodical one that had been pushing me out towards the bay, but a faster force pushing me in towards the rocks. I was to be saved from the bay only to be bashed to pieces among the rocks.

The undertow dragging me out had said, indicated so much, *I have you now, you bugger!* And this one pushing me in against the rocks said, in a strong Scots accent, *Where yesterday draun ae man, today I draun twa!* I felt too enfeebled to care, and looking back, saw again the white drained face on the top of an incoming wave, and then another coming suddenly behind me, took me with it, and I went under.

I was rolled along in it, borne along in it, buckled into its crest, and swept in between two spurs of rock. My feet touched solid ground, another wave broke over, I went under again. I hit nothing and went down. Then I surfaced.

Weak at the knees I stumbled out, Crusoe back from the disintegrating wreck. I sat on the beach and watched Amory come in. He came in as I had done, throwing up his head and then being swept forward, and another wave catching him from behind, and going under, defending his face with outstretched hands; and then the wave broke, spent itself, retreated, fetching him up on the beach, only to his waist in water, as if the sea had merely been playing pranks all along, with no serious intention of drowning either of us.

He tottered out, all bursting virilia and pallor. I made no comment. In silence we began to dress. Amory untrussed himself, the sopping black trunks fell to the sand exposing his thickset, crestfallen member in its black bush. *La plante qui fait les yeux émerveilles.* His *Wunderhorn.* Hob and nob; hab and nab. That he had the physique and the parts cannot be doubted. The Dong with the luminous nose. Red mullet from the Bay of Cadiz. Sardine become shark. *Cazon.* Amory's member was thick as a dibber, purposeful as a Dyak's. There was nobody about but ourselves. Amory stared at the sea, putting on his red bikini briefs and when he stood upright the lingum bulge at his crotch was worthy of the Lord Siva himself. Siva, whose function it is to dismantle the fabric of existence. A lover set out with all his equipage and appurtenances. Boneless meat-dagger he called it. The Spanish bride with the down-turned mouth had never had one in her mouth, he said. And Doña Inez there at the wedding party. He'd like her to 'drop her drawers'. Really ravening.

Se greata mann thone hwitan se greata folgode, Folgode thone hund hwitan se greata mann, Thone hwitan hund folgode se greata mann.

Invocation of the wand and elevation of air dagger. Dominion over women—*dominio, descabello, estacada honda.* Play it by ear, Amory would say. A passionate irrational man. Women liked him and he knew it. The sexual aspect, the troubled presence, Liebig's extract of beef.

He kept looking at me and I at him. There was something odd and disturbing about his stare. He had peculiar amber eyes, tawny, like an animal's; the expression one sees in a zoo, the gaze directed from behind bars. What life did he bear secretly within him? I took him for an animal metamorphosed into a man. He had the sad air of a beast. Somewhere in the maze of his life there were lions. The big cats: their cataracts of eyes that seem to weep for what they will never have, on a wet weekend in the Dublin Zoo. Keeper Flood. The smell of excreta and the smell of the cages. Amber's deceptive, everyone knows that.

A waterhole trembling in the mirage, an afternoon kill. He was the explorer Robert O'Hara Burke as Nolan saw him: the flat head, the beard shaping the oval face, a suggestion of horns above the Toby Jug ears, the eye of the impulse-driven wanderer. A drained look. Look of Pan, god of priaps. A woman-chaser. Woman-killer.

Amory was putting on his string vest and getting into his fancy shirt. Not a vicious man, only a little callous, though kindlier than most, as such men go. And now he was dressed in his worn bush-boots, and his damp trunks rolled up neatly in the towel and his bullybag covered.

Let's get the hell out of here, Amory said.

I followed him up the path. The top of his head was certainly rather flat. His broad cranium or Celtic bean. The cranium of a skull perhaps Neanderthal. He had odd mannerisms, peculiar tics, and the broad back of ex-miner and world heavyweight contender Tommy Farr. Farr fighting the Brown Bomber, the Manassa Mauler. Amory never got into fights, for if he fought he thought he might kill his opponent. A prizefighter's shifting shoulders, shrugging. He seemed uncomfortable in modern clothes and compromised by wearing suede jackets, coloured shirts, bush-boots, missing slashed sleeves, ruff, cod-piece and hose. He walked, when I first knew him in cold Montreal, touching his right thigh at every second stride with the first two fingers of his right hand, as if lacking *arme blanche*, the sword pommel. Now he had other tics.

He had worked for Cockfield & Brown the big national agency, tried to get me to take on commercial work, and even persuaded some firm to reproduce a painting of mine for their annual calendar. At the Montreal Forum, the ice stadium, Amory had cheered the Montreal Canadiens with fourteen thousand others. At Blue Bonnets and Richelieu on the edge of the city we had lost and won. I saw the dome of a cathedral where lay the bones of holy Brother André whose heart was pickled. Mat Talbot had lived piously in chains. Pilgrims went up the steps on their knees. We had celebrated a win in Chez Clairette, a *boîte* at Au Soleil de Marseilles which we frequented, because the woman from Marseilles sang Edith Piaf songs. Amory came from the bar, weaving to the table in a suede jacket, dark shirt, suede tie, tan boots; and Milly Mayne sitting there watching him.

He lived with her in a stone house near McGill University, a street of rather classical architecture and sweeping iron railings in a relatively inexpensive area. A few steps up and you pulled the bell that hung out from the wall like the tongue of a hanged (or drowned) person, and then Milly Mayne, three or more months pregnant, frail, a semi-invalid looking more and more like Christina Rossetti, was standing there watching me. And Amory, before him a night of Bloody Marys.

He ran a Combi, painted battleship grey and already somewhat battered, the engine had some defect and the silencer did not work. Every second week he was fined for speeding or traffic infringements. I remember their bedroom door, which was next to the lavatory, hanging off its hinges and Amory smiling one lunchtime at Chez Pierre. Why such high spirits? I asked. He exposed his dog's tooth. Why not? He'd had relations with Milly that morning. She was a semi-invalid and I presumed it happened infrequently, not frequently enough for Amory at least. He had other women in Montreal. On Thursdays he lunched alone at Au Pierre Gourmet on two dozen oysters and half a dozen Guinnesses. He dined grandly like that; the last man in the world in need of aphrodisiacs.

Milly Mayne lost the child.

What do you say to making a hole in a bottle of Fundador? Amory said, putting his head to one side and causing his eyes to roll back until nothing but the whites were showing (man drowning), then closing, then opening them again: gink. A fowl with the gapes.

Good idea, I said. I have a bottle up in the studio.

So we went back to the studio. After a few drinks the colour returned to his face. He despised those weaker than himself. It's a poor basis for friendship. He thought I had talent because some critics had said so, knowing next to nothing about painting himself but talking a great deal of frothy stuff about it. He spoke more of writing, but did little of it himself. Some of it he showed me. Frothy stuff. Bob Bayless would not show me any of *his* lucubrations.

Suerte! Amory said, rolling the cognac on his tongue. Bottoms up! No heeltaps.

He looked out cheerfully at the sea where we had all but drowned, assenting, for that was his way. You could not keep his buoyant spirits down. A type (although I have never met any-one like him) conscious of sensation but largely without thought; an unencumbered spirit that took whatever came his way, good fortune, money, women, a hedonist who did not suffer from remorse. I thought: You have come a long way for an ambitious milk-roundsman. That was how he had begun, in Hounslow

West. And even then he had cornered too fast on his pedal bicycle. Cranford Co-op Dairy on Martindale Road and Amory seized with his first creative fever: the imminence of power and speed and precision (but he came down) on self-propelled road vehicles. An internal combustion engine was an inspiration to greater freedom, to an emancipation which bound him to the earth. Pegasus on a push-bike. He *flew*.

The lizards jerking in and out of hiding places, living on the sunny walls, freezing when a shadow moved, flicking away quicker than sight could catch them—his nerves and quick responses were like that, eager, acquisitive.

Once in Cumberland an enraged forester had flung an axe at his head, but he had one of his intuitions and ducked in time. The axe flew harmlessly over his head. Once he swam out to the reef off Torrecillas with the skin-diving major in the Spanish army and had come back blue with cold.

There is a sort of vitality that makes the heart rejoice, and Roger Amory had it. It was impossible not to like him—this man now turning on me his humid gaze. Once at Cockfield & Brown a colleague of his, a Scotsman, had felt Amory's demented gaze fixed on *him*, and looking up had seen Amory massaging his chest in a particular way (one of his earlier tics), and next day the Scotsman had developed inexplicable shooting pains in that area of his own chest. He said that Amory was gifted with diabolic powers.

Do you know Juan de Fuca? Amory asked, staring at me with his animal eyes. (Island of Scoria where the amber grows.) Jan de Fouw yes, I said. Dutch graphic artist who lives in Dublin. De Fuca, no. The Spanish Ambassador at Helsinki in *Kaputt*?

Kaputt my arse, Amory said, the strait that separates Vancouver Island from the mainland. A very rough stretch of water that baffles most of the idiots who go in for marathon swimming, on account of its tricky tides.

Never been on that side of the coast, I said. Never been further west than Portage La Prairie. I knew someone in Souris but never went there. No inclination to go further west.

Amory told me that he had gone skin-diving with an Australian. They had gone off for a long week-end skin-diving. For two days

87

they drank, not attempting any skin-diving because the water was wrong. Then, on the evening of their third and last day, with the tide turning, Amory suggested they give it a try.

Amory found himself on a spur of rock, saw the Australian swimming back. He was diving off the rock and going down after the fish he could see below, coming back to the rock to re-load. He was using a long cruelly barbed spear-gun; the twin of this would later require a special licence from the Guardia Civil.

When he had finished killing fish he strung them on a line at his belt, and dived in on the other side of the rock to swim across the strait—a matter of a couple of hundred yards. There he found himself in a regular millrace between the rock and the mainland. Swept down into a little bay with not much stir in the centre, he stayed there trying to decide what best to do. The Australian was drinking in the tent. They had to start that night to get back to the agency in time.

Amory got rid of the spear-gun and the fish and his lead weights, swam out into the millrace again, dived. He dived to the bottom and crawled along like a murex, holding on to rocks, surfacing, going down again, holding on to the rocks and clawing along the sea-bed. Five, ten yards at a time, and then up again. And then down, fifteen, twenty yards at a time. And in this way across the tricky patch of water, getting out more dead than alive.

Anon the pennies drop, anon we smile. Nature that old spendthrift, a cut-and-patch, fit-and-start now-and-then thing. Chambers accepts all.

The Australian in the tent had noticed nothing. They arrived back in Montreal a day late. There had been a board meeting. The Australian was fired. Some time later Amory was promoted. That was how it went for Roger Amory. He had more than average luck, and insuppressible springs of energy. A marine bachelor, hard as a rock.

8 THE BARON FROM BALTICUM: Journalism? the so-called Dutchman hazarded, staring at me, with his vitreous no-coloured (goat's) eyes. You are a journalist?

No, I said.

You write fiction?

No, I said, I don't.

What then?

The last of the sun shone like a fire beacon from a window in Maro. The tall, limber, lantern-jawed *gitano* was stepping into the Marissal.

Is this an interview? I said.

No, no—I am merely interested.

The sun shone from the Maro window up near the caves, the *gitano* had disappeared. What kind of work? Fiction? Journalism? He was merely interested.

Tush, I said, there is no such thing in me. I paint.

I did not know there were Irish painters, the Dutchman said.

Be that as it may, I said, you find yourself sitting opposite one.

Ach so—this in a bleak and toneless voice as non-committal as the look in his eye.

And how long had I been in Nerka he wanted to know; he had seen Olivia about the place and knew she was my wife.

We've been here eleven months and expect to stay another few. I have a commission of sorts that holds me here.

Ach so.

And had I profited from my stay? Was I working well? Did I find the place conducive to work? And did I by any chance know the rascal Behan (pronounced Be-*han*) whom he had met in Stockholm, stone drunk and singing rebel songs?

Yes, I know Behan, I said. He speaks Gaelic, like the poet-patriot from Rosmuck. *Labhar Gaelige.* He finished a translation of Merriman's *Midnight Court*—a much-translated work in our country—from the Irish, and lost the manuscript in Paddington Station. Or so he said. Sounds apocryphal, like most of his yarns.

He is a man of great heart, the Dutchman said.

He is a man of great capacity, at all events, I said, and it's capacity that will ruin him. You don't require a fortune-teller or a physician to tell you that. He said to me once in a rare moment of self-illumination 'As I grow older my hopes get less and less. Like rotting fruit, we rot down to a hard stone.' He was about twenty-eight at the time.

In Anglesea Street, in Shackleton's studio, under the skylight, with the table between us.

They deported him from Inishere for his atrocious blasphemy. A God-fearing, rosary-reciting island like that—Medieval Ireland. He goes to the States now and is well paid to make a fool of himself—a sort of latter-day Brendan the Navigator. Except he travels by jet.

Are all the Irish like that, drunk all the time?

No, I said, not all the time, not as a general rule. Can't afford it.

⸎

It was one of those brave white sunlit days in the Andalusian spring that comes early here. Olivia had gone to the beach on the west side of the village. I was alone on the plaza. It was deserted at that hour and flooded with early afternoon light. Already it was ending. I felt tired; my work had not been going well, nothing would work out and I felt depressed. Too many people had been talking; I was tired of company. Miguel had pulled a table for me into the sun and I sat there reading, with a glass of cognac and a couple of cigars from the kiosk. The idle forenoon lay behind me, the idle afternoon before me. But it can never be expected that things should be in all respects agreeable; I was to have company. The Dutchman, emerging from the dark interior of the Balcon de Europa bar, shielding his eyes against the outer glare, saw me sitting there alone, decided there and then to join me, and came limping across. All the other tables were unoccupied, even those outside the Marissal, so I kept my head down and went on reading, hoping that he would pass, take the hint. But he came

90

stumping up to the table and asked, civilly enough, if he might sit down.

As you wish, I said without enthusiasm, not offering to rise, but indicating a chair.

He took the chair facing the plaza and, dispensing with the civil formality of introduction or handshake, hooked his stick over the back of it and began to lower himself down.

You are English? he began. *Habla español?*

English-speaking, I said, I'm Irish. I believe I've seen you playing chess with the Frenchman.

Czech, the so-called Dutchman said.

Check? I said.

I understand the man is a Czech, he said, from Czechoslovakia.

And in these chess-games, who won? He did; it became somewhat tedious. Did I play? (He would pay me that compliment: I looked like a chess player; but I was to disappoint him.) I did not.

A pity—you miss something.

So I'm told. I regret it myself.

He nodded, satisfied with this answer. Silence.

You should ask the big American, I said. He's a chess player. The one with the attractive wife.

Robert Thirwell Bayless of New York, formerly of San Francisco, husband of Charlotte Bayless (née Harlan, changed legally from Lipski) of New York and San Francisco, second generation American, of Polish-Jewish background, my heart's victim and its torturer.

I do not know this person, the Dutchman said.

A big solemn man whose thoughts were buried deeply, deeply hidden, of the America of Thoreau and Emerson, Henry Adams, Henry James, illustrious representatives of the exhausted puritan conscience.

You'll see him about the place, I said.

You speak Arse? the false Dutchman asked with his head on one side.

I had it regularly beaten into me in school but have since managed to forget most of it, I said. Geometry, algebra, physics, Gaelic, all lost. Erse or worse, all lost.

Fr Brendan Diffely S.J. with his revolutionary fervour in 'extra'

Irish class. Hot-head, Gaelic revivalist. Pearse. The impalpable dimensions of the elusive Irish mind.

It has an alphabet of special characters and an antiquity of nearly three thousand years. Someone Yeats knew studied it because it brought him in contact with a civilization 'immediately behind that of Homer,' I said.

What does it sound like? This old Gaelic, the Baron said.

On modra eh shuh? I said. *Taw, iss madra eh shuh. Arr-a-naher a-taw-awr Naave.*

Interesting, the Baron said. What does it mean?

The beginning of the Lord's Prayer, I said.

Our Father who art not in Heaven, hollow be thy name.

The Dutchman grunted, then stared around as if on a swivel-chair, looking for service and making a grimace (scrofula? crab lice? collar chafe?). Me to command; you to obey. Catching sight of Miguel, he clapped his hands for service. Here, *hombre*, and *muy rapido*. Miguel came with a grave face, received an order for one *vino tinto grande*, and went away to execute the order with a face just as grave.

Cuando viene a Nerka bebe vino . . . The so-called Dutchman sat at my table and did not think to offer me a drink. He had given the order in abrupt, convincing Spanish. Now he inquired what I was reading.

Animal Form and Function ('An Introduction to College Zoology') and *Pale Horse, Pale Rider*. He examined the fiction suspiciously with his colourless eyes pale washed-out lime-blue pigmentation, red-rimmed, no eyelashes to speak of, suspicious pin-points for pupils, their oily sheen, fishy, dull and vacant-looking and his gaze, somnolent and guarded, took in title and author: from this he would learn something of me.

Light holiday reading, he said, dismissing it and me, handing it back.

What were you expecting, I asked, nettled—*Liber Amoris*? Besides, I am not on holiday. I came here to work.

Ach so (this again in the same bleak and toneless voice).

Arrogant and self-opinionated, he reminded me of a Teuton I had known; they had unpleasant features in common. *Ach so* thine self.

A black tank-corps beret was down over one ear, fitting like a clamp, biting into his temples where splotches of eczema showed. There were food stains on his shirt over a pronounced paunch, and cigarette ash on his crumpled alpaca jacket; below baggy grey flannels, broad at the turn-ups, he wore wide broken-down shoes in need of polish. Did he sleep in his clothes? He had a puffy look about him—the look of a man not long out of a sick-bed—and his complexion was bad.

A long silence followed. We drank in silence. Were all the Irish like that? Were all the Dutch like this? Or what nationality was he? I heard the noise we had grown accustomed to and looked up. Two bombers of the US Strategic Air Command, Kennedy's vigilantes, were passing punctually on the hour. At the wing-tips and at a point in the head, the nose-bulb, points of scarlet showed like drops of blood. They bored into space, devouring it, creating a great turbulence in the air, their body-shape worm-like and tubular, their excretory products sensational: like the monsters of antiquity, constantly ejecting a thick white wake all of forty kilometres long. It seemed to pull them back, it was so thick and dense. *Hydra* and *Dugusia* the jet bombers, archangels of destruction, with flame bulbs and excretory tubules in their buccal cavities secreting the nuclear bombs, levellers of cities, patrolled in pairs, day and night, like the Guardia Civil with automatic rifles on the ground. Half the American air-strike was airborne, following the events of the Bay of Pigs. This was the Gibraltar–Cyprus run. 'Cuber', Kennedy said; 'Cuber' (to rhyme with tuber, invoking his Irish ancestry). According to Sonny Hool, ex-*Time Life* staffer and expert on political economy. The arrogant supersonic boom and rumble came down, rolling in the hills. Alone above a lawless world they flew to kill time.

The fleeing shadow of the second jet followed, like a fly on glass, in the dense wake of the first, and was reflected there, one wing disappearing into it. They passed down a sky the colour of gun metal. Always they appeared to be going down the sky, following the curvature of space, falling a long way from simple-minded Immelmann turns. I watched part of the world air blockade go out of sight; *Langue d'oc, langue d'oil*. The wake remained behind, drifting slowly inland.

93

I too, the Dutchman said—I too am engaged on a novel. An autobiography really. However, I do not anticipate finishing it.

You are not alone, I said. There are five or six of them here, all writing, in varying degrees of sobriety and application.

We spoke of Hamsun. He too admired Knut Hamsun, knew where he had farmed in Norway, had read all his books, all twenty of them. I contradicted him—no, at the most, Hamsun had written nine or ten. The false Dutchman compressed his thin lips; he would not argue with me. No.

The jets had passed from sight, through the intricacies of the palm fronds, over the roofs, they were over Catalonia now. All that remained was a sensation in the eardrums, and a pastel smear turning red in the sky. I was talking to an arrogant man and could not get away. The orbitals very deep, wide and of rectangular shape. A tall man with a stoop, pale, big-boned.

Why will you not finish it? I asked at last. Unfinished work— I know what it's like. But one goes back to it. Flog yourself to your desk.

Yeats' advice. I ordered another cognac.

The Dutchman was staring up at the fading sky-lanes of the bombers. Why not? . . . because, plainly speaking, there was not sufficient time, two years at the most, nuclear war was imminent, a final holocaust, an annihilating blast would flatten the Iberian peninsula and Spain would be wiped out together with the American air-bases. He knew the Russians, had fought against them. They were men of iron, obstinate and set in their ways. They wanted world conquest, nothing less would satisfy them. And the Americans, out of confusion, in their stupidity, were capable of matching them, starting another war over Cuba. Or, if not over Cuba, then over somewhere else. One half of the world would destroy the other half. Two embattled world powers were preparing to pound each other to pieces. Two great world powers in collision. The magnetic attraction of iron to iron. Two embattled demi-urges at each other's throats. It was our misfortune to be born in this time. After that, all would be over; the world would be depopulated, as at the beginning. Life perhaps would begin all over again, in the caves

It would be something like that. Who could say with certainty?

Not a true *Fin du Monde*, in the accepted Biblical sense . . . an apocalypse, a violent and total wiping out. *Hochwasser*, an act of God, where nothing would remain. Nothing living except some marine life and possibly some animals. Perhaps some human life too would survive the bombs. Little pockets here and there, one not knowing of the other's existence, deformed and maimed certainly. Over the years perhaps they would come into contact, see each other's fires; out of fear would attack each other, club each other down. Then would begin real and everlasting peace, the only peace one could hope for, humanity wiped out; all vice and corruption disappearing with them—twenty centuries of progress, a progress towards destructive possibilities that eventually got out of hand; and as many centuries as that and more of pre-history, when bear- and wolf-like man first emerged out of the caves, sharpening his claws.

And if the few survivors didn't kill each other with clubs, they would eat the poisoned crops or drink the contaminated water or be torn to pieces by wild beasts even more ravenous than they. After the slaughter on a grand scale there would come the slaughter on a very modest scale, Cain and Abel all over again, and then silence. There would remain only the inarticulate murmurings of Mother Nature at her ramblings; and humanity, the little that was left of it, dead and rotting back into the ground. Good riddance to it.

This would happen within two years, that was all the time left. No time to write books—a supremely futile occupation, in view of the circumstances. The cities would be in ruins, waiting for the moss to grow over them. There would be no sounds, no movement of ground or air traffic. In time perhaps rational creatures from another planet would land on the earth, and be puzzled as to what had happened; for nobody would be buried— the entire population of the world, Adam's billions, not to mention farm stocks and zoos, would be there on view. It would be like dating the great explosion that made Oregon's Crater Lake. By analysing the wood in the trees, the trees destroyed in the explosion, the time of its formation could be guessed—something in the nature of four or five thousand years back. Yes?

But here the fires would hardly be out, their smoke might

still hang in the air: the bodies radioactive, clothing still intact, and all looking in one direction, towards the blast.

Here would be something infinitely strange, immense and complex cities full of corpses and cars, airports jammed with grounded airliners, some blown into the city; ports full of shipping, and all the world's shipping being blown about by movements of wind and tide. Arterial roads stretching across continents, leading from one dead city to another, over and under by-passes, with line upon line of stationary cars, some blown up into the mountains. Long lines of dead traffic halted at closed toll-gates, bridges blown in two and the rivers full of cars and corpses, and all radioactive. That was to say, unless a great period of time elapsed; and then an even stranger sight would be presented. A Moss World in full bloom.

Better that way, the alleged Dutchman affirmed. Let the Russians start their war.

Fatum; Imperium romanum. For himself, he intended staying on in Spain, drifting with it, drinking wine on the Costa del Sol while his health lasted.

I drink to drown my sorrows and to forget.

You are not married, then? I asked him.

Married, yes; and with two children—a boy and a girl.

And your wife, your children, have you abandoned them?

Breadwinner. *Schmerz.* This was a strange one. I encountered his vapoury blue stare.

Abandoned them? No. They are comfortable enough in northern Finland. I have a house there. We live on Russia's doorstep.

From the port, you could see the mushroom clouds from the testing grounds out beyond the Barents Sea, where the Russians were exploding their nuclear bombs. *Oceano Glacial* Artico.

You are Finnish, then?

Yes. His family might just as well stay in Finland, as come to Spain, and be blown sky-high with the gum-chewing idiots stationed at Moron de la Fontera (a most appropriately named place for an American air-base).

Nothing, nobody, was ever left, abandoned, in my sense. No, but moved on of its own accord, going nowhere in particular, the Finn, erstwhile Lowlander, erstwhile democrat, believed. He himself drank to drown his sorrows, five or six litres of red wine a day. His appetite was negligible, but his capacity for drink, unretarded.

Impetuous *Schmerz*! Five litres. Enough to kill a bull, if a bull drank wine.

We spoke of other things. Had I been in the war? No, I told him, Eire being one of the non-aligned nations, neutral in two world wars. England's misfortune being Ireland's gain, I said, or so the legend runs. De Valera carried his neutrality far, even had his government send a message of sympathy to the German government on the death of Hitler. Dev and Hirohito sent messages of sympathy when Odin died to the strains of Bruckner and Wagner's *Liebestod*.

The Finn himself had been called to the colours to fight on the worst front of all, the snow-bound Russian front. It had been a bad war. As a member of the Hitler Jugend he had served and seen brave comrades fall. But for what could one hope? Then, as now, the world was an atrocious place, run for the most part by gorillas.

And yet, when one fought in defence of one's homeland, there was a glory for a time, and one lived. That brief glory was all that mattered—the best philosophy of all—the rest did not count for very much; family ties, home, one's own petty and conflicting ambitions—these were nothing. He had no use for effete people, people with too much water in their faces; one was strong, acquired strength to defend what one had, clung to it with tooth and nail, with all one's strength. Or took what one needed, by force if necessary, and hung on to it. Wasn't that the rule in politics, as in life?

Perhaps, I said, lacking the incentive to restrain him; perhaps not. Looking into his baleful, washed-out eyes, I saw little hope there.

Now, shifting his posterior on the chair and perspiring freely, he brought out a knife from a sheath around his waist and gave it to me, handle foremost, across the table. I held it, not knowing what to say. It was heavy, well-balanced, with an inscription cut into the blade above the outline of a running deer. '*Uti possidetis.*'

I am a *von*, he said haughtily, a baron. I come from Balticum—a very old and highly respected line, I assure you.

He stared at me, his head wobbling on its base, amused, considering something. Then from an inside pocket he drew out a leather wallet, took out a card, glanced at it, handed it across. It said:

Baron Alex Leopold von Gerhar

Where is Balticum? I asked, displaying my ignorance (he would expect that).

Baron von Gerhar described where Balticum was. He was a baron, then, unless he carried forged papers. I felt suspicious of him: his injuries, after all, could have resulted from a car crash. Had he been in the war at all? I handed back card and knife without comment. I was tired of encountering his watery stare, tired of his patronizing manner, and wished he would leave.

He turned with some difficulty, his mouth embittered, and clapped his hands again, a flabby sound. Miguel came at the double, took his order, went away. The Baron thrust out his stiff leg and looked across at me. I stared at his gudgeon's pale, undershot lips, more cannibal pike then gudgeon. He would go on drinking and talking at his own sweet will; I was tolerable company until he found better.

You are a true-born Irish Catholic?

Yes, I said, in a way. Yes.

He too was Catholic born, now turned apostate. I must, he assumed, be an apostate. Yes? His own belief in human goodness (not to speak of the divine variety), in the perfectability of life, was shaken; indeed had perished with his brave comrades in the snow. And what remained? Zero. *Nada*.

And now my children . . . another mistake, I'm afraid.

Baron Alex Leopold von Gerhar thrust one fat, almost female thigh majestically out. The airy qualities of physical force in repose. He had a look of someone I had seen in a painting. An Iron Guardsman. Berruguete. The great *condottiere* reading at a lectern. To those who yet hope to live a while.

Now labourers in red helmets were pushing wheelbarrows along the narrow catwalk that led between mounds of gravel where the new hotel was going up. On the rear window in the dust of the architect's car an unpractised finger had scrawled AMOR A MARI.

The drinks I had taken were beginning to have effect—a suggestion of codeine injection about the lips. I had matched the hard-drinking Baron round for round, neither one of us offering to pay for the other, he on vino tinto and I on cognac. He now launched into a long peroration, the gist of which was this: a distinction would have to be drawn between those things that ought to be preserved and those that should be destroyed.

Over-tender humanistic feelings, he argued suavely, would not get one very far. We were on the threshold of the next stage in human evolution. A point had been reached at which physiological processes were disrupted, and we would have to make physical and functional adjustments, as the animals had already been taught to do; it was at this stage that selection operated. The philosophy of 'Survival of the Fittest', if applied with sufficient resolution and force, would result in the creation of a new species—this was what National Socialism had understood. In one bold stroke the cancer could be removed, and one would breathe a clearer air. The actual squashing process might not appeal to the squeamish, but it could be carried out with only slightly deleterious effects.

Wait, the Baron said, bringing up his pink palms, please do not misunderstand me—a feature of evolutionary progress, nothing more (wiping his brow). To introduce sentiment into it was misleading and certainly wrong.

The bladder worm, the Baron said, only two or more inches in diameter, yet lodged in the brain, liver or abdomen it produces death. The practice of letting the pet dog kiss the baby is not to be recommended. Not in the best families, nor in the best zoological circles.

And you don't need a zoologist to tell you about the habits of roundworms—Ascaris, man's faithful and constant companion, and its hardly beneficial association with us since ancient times.

Bad as the Wandering Jew, the Baron said.

I felt a hot stab at the heart.

The disease trichinosis may have brought about the Jewish

ban on pork, the Baron continued suavely, but National Socialism would have resulted in the eradication of a far worse disease— International Jewry.

Oh they were wily, wily, had connections everywhere, and used those connections well; had dug themselves into the fat of the life they affected to despise, the very odour of which offended them—Goyisher life. Inherent in those creatures were destructive tendencies, or, one might say with more accuracy, self-destructive tendencies. Because in the long run their war against the community betrayed their own best interests, like bluebottles on raw meat; and the community rose up against them and destroyed them.

About their fate, one might as well have feelings about the fate of lemmings, or locusts. Or weasels or rats. But one man, a great and inspired man who had read deeply into history and knew the extent of their infiltration, had led the march against them. Those little animals. Vermin.

AMOR A MARI, I read. Holy Mother!

At present his reputation was low, but that would change, no doubt of that. In time he would be splendidly exonerated; people would come to see what he had done in its true perspective. Not now perhaps, but soon. And he would have a proud and blameless place in the roster not only of German history but world history. Who could doubt that, after an impartial examination of the facts? He had decided to rid his country of them for Germany's sake, for Europe's sake. Promethean labours, too much perhaps for one man, even a great man as dedicated as he. And how weary he had looked, towards the end! In Berlin in '44 Hitler had looked 'weary to death'.

The Jews had no one to blame but themselves; they had brought this terrible wrath down on their own selfish caftans. It had been an evolutionary step, and a gigantic one, the application of Mendelian laws. But the Jews, almost the acme in parasitic adaptations, had been expecting it, and could adapt themselves to any contingency: their own history of oppression had taught them that; to be shrewd and calculating, to go underground, to wait; only a wholesale burning and fumigation would serve. They had the numerical strength, and the tenacity, of roundworms in their victim; but in Hitler they had met their match. He had laid his soft negligent hand on them.

The actual squashing process, admittedly, had been painful. A certain 'Germanic' thoroughness in the execution had aroused the antagonism of the so-called free world, and the liberal press of the decadent democracies had been in uproar, and the world had turned against him. The West, itself more and more touched by death and turned towards it, had been revolted.

If the worms are irritated, the Baron said grimly (raising an admonitory finger), look out! Nothing will impede the progress inwards—the instinctive response. After a while a certain smell from their victims gives them away.

I had a moment of fear for my own welfare, then it passed and the emptiness came back, the void I occupy, this air I breathe, as if not breathing, not living.

The drive and energy of one undisputably great man, the Baron went on, laying a soft negligent hand on his thigh. Germany and its people had let him down, but the world's accolade awaited him, this (striking the table softly with his palm) the Baron firmly believed.

Long live the white race, I said. Long live the spirit of Hitler.

You joke a little, the Baron said amiably. I encountered his vapoury blue eye again. He wasn't really listening, lost in a daydream, standing submissive again before the luminous blue eyes that saw right through you, a stare of pure reason from the dreamer of Berchtesgaden. Taking up his card and knife he stowed them safely away.

'*I go the way that destiny dictates with the assurance of a sleepwalker*', he had said of himself. He was sleepwalking over Europe, ancient bone-heap, where every grain of earth has passed through innumerable bodies.

What do you mean? the Baron asked in a whisper. He meant what he said.

I answered, *Nada mas*.

No, the Baron said calmly, coming out of his dream, neither the *Wehrmacht* nor the German people were able to keep up with him. They had failed him, I promise you.

Fuddled with alcohol, I tried without success to recall another

(Jewish) Leopold's defence of his race. What Jew had said of his people that for them Judaism was not a religion but a misfortune, a plague trailing along the valley of the Nile, the sickly beliefs of the ancient Egyptians—Heine?

None left in Yugoslavia, I said, if that's any consolation to you. He succeeded there anyway, or Himmler did. The SS set the dogs on them, desecrated their cemeteries, pillaged Jewish shops, removed the synagogue roof. They were banished from Yugoslavia as successfully as St Patrick of immortal memory banished the serpents from Ireland. I've been there—not a semite in sight.

Towards the end the days and nights had run together into one continuous nightmare, and he in the centre dreaming it, his arm stiff, the bad taste of metal in his mouth (the taste with which the Fatherland had become all-too familiar), the small revolver that he'd carried since the *Putsch* grown heavier and heavier, the troops of the war-monger Churchill and Morgenthau's armed Jews on German soil, the Rhine crossed, the Mongolians pushing in from the east, his putative son mad in Scotland, the crashed Messerschmidt ME 10 already a museum-piece, Spandau empty. He felt ill, slept badly, his short sleeps tormented, his past no longer belonged to him. Must not his last days have been as tormented as the last days of the last Aztec Emperors, knowing that the palace stank of blood, that the country was rotten and had turned against him? (Ten soothsayers were flayed alive, an enchanted crane flew in broad daylight, the mirror in its beak reflecting a night sky full of stars.) The sky over Germany was full of stars, the white stars of the Boeings. Red-starred Soviet tanks were blowing the leaves off the *linden* in Potsdamer Platz. The Tiergarten was bare as a blasted heath. Lightning struck from the sky, the Americans by day and British by night, every day and every night. The Flying Fortresses soaring out of sight, dropping bombs as heavy as pillarboxes on Munich, setting the Ruhr on fire. In Unter den Linden the spirit of Queen Louise walked daily, following the ghost of Heine. They heard Paul Lincke's music, the 'Berliner Luft'. Those who wanted to betray him were considering how it could best be accomplished, the rats were studying the escape routes, the

Gestapo burning secret files near at hand in their HQ at Prinz-Albrecht-Strasse, a mountainous accumulation of evidence saturated in Jewish blood. The death camps had been discovered, full of the walking dead. Primo Levi was leaving the Lager at Buna-Monowitz, Dr. Schuschnigg preparing to leave Dachau, Russian artillery shelled the Kaiser Wilhelm Kirche on the Kurfürstendamn. The Reichskanzlei, former palace Radziwill of the Prussian-Polish nobility, was surrounded by a wall, fifty feet underground was the Bunker. The underground wedding was informal, no flowers. They would take poison, Kempte set the fire, Gunsche lit the funeral pyre. The two bodies burned as Russian T34s were firing from the Tiergarten and the Potsdamer Platz, only a block away. Cuckolded by one chauffeur at the beginning of his career (another suicide there in Prinzregentenplatz in Munich where Geli Raubal swallowed veronal), his suicided remains burnt by another at the end.

Time to go home, Hänslein klein! Time to go home! Lippa Horenstein, Hans Leopold Weissich, Israelites known to me in cold Montreal. All good Jews from the Land of Dan.

9 MARTIN BORMANN, FRIEND OF THE DARKNESS: The Baron had seen Hitler and Goering, the former twice, the last time in Berlin in '44. He had piercing blue eyes. The jovial *Reichsmarschall*, togged out in full regalia, was in boisterous spirits.

In Berlin, I said in '44—before or after the July plot?

After.

He had marks?

No; ill and over-worked, yes that was apparent; one of his arms hung by his side; that was all.

He had walked, dog-tired, along the line of last defence, boy-soldiers in sagging uniforms cut for men, defenders of Berlin and their Fuehrer. A wan smile for the boy-soldiers who had knocked out Russian tanks.

Napoleon, after all, eagle that he was, would swoop down on one of his Old Guard standing in the line and pinch a loyal ear. No sign of favour for the eaglet Finn?

That Field Marshal, whose name I forget, received special treatment, I said. Accused of High Treason without belt or suspenders, collar or tie, not to mention legal aid, while Goering raved at him—a *von* like yourself, stripped of rank and decorations, humiliated. He and eleven of his friends were strangled with piano wires.

Rottger the horse-butcher did the job. Trial and execution were filmed by the Gestapo and shown to Hitler that same evening at the Chancellery. How could he keep his dinner down? The Gestapo destroyed all the prints before the Russians could get their hands on them.

And the *Reichsmarschall* himself?

Phenomenal! High-fed and in good humour. The representative of Berlin and Potsdam in the *Reichstag* would need to be an exceptional man, and Field Marshal Goering had been that. An iron fist in a chamois glove, a latter-day Roman Consul.

Banqueting would be part of his official duties, and one that he greatly enjoyed.

On the same principle that morticians became drunkards, out of sympathy for their clients? I said.

I thought of Goering towards the end, smiling villain, heroin addict, acting mad at Nuremberg, knowing he could still escape, the *Reichsgeist* capsule, the silver object, deeply hidden between his ponderous buttocks. And unable to sleep, watched by fidgety American guards, questioned by Colonel Andrus, hemmed in the lavatory (*para las necesidades fisiologicas*) with his mouth full of broken glass, tasting blood, dying in distress amid his own unwholesomely rising fumes. *Nux vomica.*

Tyrant Hermann Goering, flabby as an old tyre, all the wind gone out of him, finally deflated. Humpty Dumpty fallen from his wall.

Suicidarse. Revolutionaries break the shell of being; the yolk flows everywhere.

Schleswig-Holstein; Bavaria, brimming *Steins* and Friesian cattle knee-deep in lush grass, guns or butter.

Was Hess mad? I asked the Baron. Like Swift, half-mad at the top. All those years in . . .

Berlin-Spandau, he said. Von Schirach our youth leader is there, Baldur von Schirach, with Speer the Arms Minister.

Still I could see the face of Rudolf Hess in that rogues' gallery before the International Military Tribunal at Nuremberg. A tree struck by a lightning bolt. That fixed and frozen stare. Silent throughout the proceedings. Jodl, Kaltenbrunner, Streicher, Sauckel, Funk, Raeder, Seyss-Inquart. Some turned renegade and some wept.

Why was Hess silent? Was he thinking of the effects of Zyklon-B. Wasn't that his brainwave?

No, the Baron said. You are confusing him with Rudolf Hoss, Commander of Auschwitz. A different man. He used the gas first.

Genocide, suicide, cyanide, Zyklon-B. Goering overflowing from the lavatory, his face gone blue. Then laid out on the small bed where he had not slept, dressed in an open-neck white shirt and the bottom-half of black silk pyjamas, bare-footed. Roman

Law. Retribution. Ides of March, a month dear to the Fuehrer's superstitions. He had in his possession the secrets of initiation with a divinatory voice. Der *Gröfaz*.

And how did Hitler strike you? I asked.

Had I taken leave of my senses? *Strike!* The Baron favoured me with another of his sunken smiles.

I mean as a man. Your Nietzschean *Übermensch* who loved cream cakes. The shit-brown riding breeches and high boots, the obligatory *Mensch* stance, even for un-*Mensch*-like upstart Goebbels and sow pale Ley. How did it happen? The whole *Volk* going over the cliff like Gaderene swine.

Bland manner, a tapas eater; that light red sausage that tastes of soap and gives you diarrhoea, *Blutwurst*. The fingers that held the wine glass trembled.

An old ram going slowly in, I promise you.

Strong, the Baron replied, *fuerte*. (An aggressive thrust of the shoulders.) A seer, deeply committed (this with much solemnity).

His colourless eyes, pupils just pinpricks, observed me coldly, indicated that he was not a man to be joked with about his convictions. This time we will get even with our enemies in a way that we National Socialists are accustomed to, I promise you.

AMOR A MARI, I read, feeling solid ground giving way under my chair. ROMA A IRAM.

That historic moment when he stepped before the whole *Volk* in his old military cloak of army grey. Do what is asked of you. Give gladly. Give all. *Heil Volk! Heil Vaterland! Heil Hitler! Sieg Heil!*

The ego feeds on established facts; the super-ego on dreams and hallucinations. The symptoms spring from the dream.

You have not told me your name, the Baron said.

Ruttle, I told him. Dan Ruttle.

A strange name, he mused. Is that a typical Irish name?

Telephone directory full of them, I said. It's common enough.

Pollexfen (the last one died in 1938: the man who did so well at Zeebrugge), Ewing, Swann, Yeats, all Sligo names. Daniel John, son of Daniel James Ruttle, scion of an illustrious house, late of Nullamore, in the grand old kingdom of Munster.

The hard Dan!

Ah, the hard man yourself! On the bridge over the Garavogue. We are of Ireland, the holy land of Ireland. Come dance with us in Ireland. Come booze with me in Ireland.

We could be friends, the Baron said. You must call me Leo.

Half-way through his fifth or sixth vino tinto grande I had finished my seventh or eighth small cognac; a quarter way through my eighth or ninth cognac the Baron had drained his wine to the last drop and was calling imperiously for more. There was no keeping up with him.

I'd like to say something in confidence, he said. An unwell face drew close to mine. I lent an unwilling ear.

He ordered me to kill all his enemies, the voice from Finland whispered in my ear, and I inhaled an odour of brimstone, cold drops of sweat moving at a glacier's pace down my spine.

I was seated opposite a maniac, close enough to touch. I decided then and there that if he became dangerous I'd ram the table into him, catch him off balance, and lay him out with his own stick. There was a silence.

Where will you find enemies of Hitler to kill so long after the war? I asked drily as possible.

The Baron made a wide depreciating gesture, none too sober. I was not well informed, far from it. In Tunisia. Algeria—he had fought against the Arabs there.

In Poland, Algeria, Tunisia, in Israel, the struggle goes on. No end to it, no option but to fight. *En Brerah!* Ben-Gurion's white patriarchal head. When Jewish blood spurts from the knife (*caesura*), then things go right again. The abominable Horst Wessel. Wälsung: no Nieblung. (Dr. Geobbels made a funeral oration under a dripping umbrella, puffing out his cheeks like a frog.) This hero, this German!

We are back where we started, I said, talking about the Jews.

The Baron raised his glass again and smilingly studied the sun, or what was left of it, through glass, as though examining a phial of bad Jewish blood. *Blut*. I looked down, opening a page at random, and read:

> if a planarian is split lengthwise from the head end to about half-way down the body length, and if the two pieces are kept apart for a period of twenty-four hours, each split will regenerate as a portion of a head, with the result that a two-headed animal develops. An interesting extension of this experiment is possible by splitting each of the two heads and as a consquence a four-headed animal can be formed. The experiment has been carried much further . . .

I looked across at the Baron, who with closed eyes was complacently now drinking his red wine.

> Similarly (*I read*) if an electric device which shocks the animal is inserted in the dark regions where it moves, then it may be taught to avoid the dark. This avoidance response will . . .

The Baron sighed, breaking the silence to inquire whether I knew the name Martin Bormann.

Yes, I said, Hitler's aide.

The future Fuehrer, the Baron sternly corrected, appointed by Hitler himself in the bunker at the eleventh hour.

I had the honour to be chosen, I, von Gerhar, of all the Hitler Jugend, to accompany Martin Bormann when he flew to Sweden to negotiate peace terms. But nothing could be achieved.

The decadent democracies had decided to fight on.

I looked into the washed-out eyes, the same that had gazed sternly into Bormann's, and submissively into Hitler's frozen eyes (full of dead people's eyes). And how did you kill? I asked. With the family carving knife you have there?

Nein, he answered, indulgent with me but inviting further provocation. Not exactly so. (My cognac glass had a thick rim, it held only dregs.) What then?

Other weapons, he said.

Other weapons; other ways. I tried to calculate his age: if his present age was, as he had said, thirty-six, how could he have been more than sixteen in '44, and hardly pubescent at the time of the Russo-Finnish fracas in the snow? He could not have been more than twelve when war broke out, and scarcely of military age when it ended. Was it all lies he was telling, was he a Nazi at all? The black tank-corps beret rested on one lobeless ear, perspiration trickled down his face, entering deep furrows about his mouth. When he turned, the light in his eyes had gone dead, I looked away. I wished to be somewhere else, with someone else, but could not move to save my life. I asked him whether he believed Hitler dead, since he believed that Bormann, for one, was alive.

Does it matter? he answered me. Dead or alive, nothing can alter what he has achieved.

True, I said. (After a long questing and beating for small game, six million dead. And if a planarian be split lengthwise?) At this point the Baron rose with some difficulty, grasped his stick and went stumping off to pass water. I watched him as he moved awkwardly between the drinkers. Did it matter? There was cold philosophy. Anna Hansen (who was Dutch) had sworn that all the Finns were mad. The sun never penetrated into some of the deep valleys of the north. Like the Cimmerians, the Finns never saw the sun. Perhaps this one had emerged, full of wind and piss and deplorable ideas, out of one such sunless valley?

Going again over the grey northern sea to Turku with the sun going down and remaining there and sunset all night, while on the starboard side a full moon came up to shine on the wake and in a terrific freezing wind on interminable rock and forest, whereupon the sunset turned itself into a sunrise and a hot sun. Helsinki and breakfast at the Olympic Stadium, familiar from postage stamps, Paavo Nurmi in bronze transfixed in one of his gigantic strides that looked like a miscalculation on the sculptor's part. A granite city of wide cobbled streets with uniform five-storey blocks in the socialist-realist manner. Behind the stadium purple-faced meths drinkers in a park. In the back streets more drunks, male and female together supporting each other as they staggered along. A hard land. Sharp distinctions. Night or day, or both together, no half measures. Straight from architectural neo-classical to twentieth century. Finland.

The Baron came back mopping his brow and sat down again opposite me.

I inquired whether he knew the Frenchman's—or rather Czech's—Finnish wife, who had two novels published and was working on a third, shut up in Sanchez's hotel and rarely venturing out. A Spanish nanny looked after the two children. She resembled Michele Morgan in *Quai des Brumes*, except she wore a black macintosh.

She seldom goes out, I said, speaks only to locals, in Spanish, and avoids the foreign *canaille*. The Baron said that he had not noticed her about. He seemed to be turning something over in his mind. And presently, fixing me with his red-rimmed killer's eyes, he put it point-blank.

I may assume that you do not share my feelings about Hitler?

Assume anything you like, I said.

Nor about National Socialism? the Baron asked.

Echo answers: *Ja wohl.*

Nor about the Jews, he pursued.

A long silence.

I doubt, Baron, whether I share your feelings about anything, I said, and least of all about the Jews.

Leaning back, one hand masterfully gripping his glass, he considered me at full length; this was capital entertainment.

A number of *extranjeros* here are Jewish, I said, and a concentration camp Kommandant was recently run out of Torremolinos. He was running a bar. You are in a minority here.

Charlotte Bayless, Jewish. Sonya and Sonny Hool. Lily and Tommy Lowen. Salina Biez.

The Baron, not impressed, was clapping his hands for more drink. Miguel, who had been keeping an eye on him, came briskly and stood in good soldierly fashion by his chair. The Baron, not looking at him and consulting neither me nor the table (where his full glass stood untouched) with an imperious gesture ordered the same again.

Señor? Miguel said, leaning forward from the hips and narrowing his eyes.

The Baron stared at Miguel, who looked pointedly at the full glass.

Ah si, eso es, the Baron said. He raised the glass and began to swallow down the corriente wine as if it were a good brimming *Stein*.

Miguel with a flourish removed the empty glass on his tray. Wiping himself where he had spilled wine on his chin and shirtfront, the Baron watched Miguel go. From the set of the latter's shoulders it was apparent to me that Miguel did not care too much for the Baron's table manners. However, he had two unmarried daughters to consider, was a good father to them, a good husband to his wife, and courteous, hard-working, even indulgent with lunatics who drank corriente wine as if it were *cerveza*. Cruz Campo for warriors. He mocked in dumbshow, pointing his chin in our direction, for the benefit of his employer Antonio terció who was standing in a slothful manner in the doorway of the Balcon de Europa bar, considering the evening. Charlie Vine and Salina Biez, in the act of sitting down at one of the terrace tables, were looking over at the Baron, as though it was the Tower of Pisa sitting there.

Above Maro the shadows were lengthening along the middle ranges of the sierras, the pale *arete* (fire breaks) showing up on the nearer spines. Another air-patrol was coming up from Gibraltar, laying a fierce white condensation trail. I looked into my glass, again full of cognac, with increasing apathy, and burning lips. No matter, I played the part assigned to me. This obscure and decidedly *louche* personage who sits before you, merely to challenge belief.

Do I disgust you? does my being a Nazi disgust you? the Baron asked.

The sun had begun to leave the plaza. Hours had passed. It seemed to me that I had been sitting for an inconsiderable length of time with this Baron, and would have to go on sitting with him. I missed Charlotte.

Disgust is a big word, I said.

I think so, the Baron said. Perhaps a little.

Two fishermen went past Antonio into the bar. Casting a look of sour aspersion in our direction, he followed them in. As the lights went on in the Marissal the foliage outside turned a poisonous green.

Yes, I think perhaps a little, the subdued voice said, as though somehow I had wronged him.

No, I lied.

The Baron favoured me with a serpent's smile and the look that accompanied it said that we were, if not true comrades-in-arms, at least had some understanding of each other. Eyeing me with a moist eye he drank again, finishing off what remained in his glass. Miguel was coming towards us with another loaded tray, the paper napkins fluttering like pennants. His movements had become surer, more ballad-like and stagey, as his animosity grew, moving with much dignity between bar and table, table and bar, more and more enigmatic, for he did not care for the Baron at all. He would serve him, yes, but there it ended. He set down the drinks on the table that was already covered in saucers. The saucers stayed. Illiterate himself, he used this old-fashioned system of notation. Not subservient but correct, *muy correcto* in white jacket, bow-tie, black trousers with knife-edge crease, he put down a plate of tapas within the Baron's reach. Wine for von Gerhar, cognac for me.

Gracias, Miguel, I said.

De nada, Señor (baring his brown stumps of teeth).

His neck was weatherbeaten, creased like a tree-trunk, scraggy, a turtle's head emerging from its carapace; his teeth were wood colour, the canines inclined at an angle, pit-props, the two lower incisors missing. He took up the tray and went away holding it poised level with his shoulders. The Baron lifted his wine glass, brought it with care to his puckered lips and, closing his eyes, drank again. A long draught. AMOR A MARI I read off the grime of the Volkswagen window near which a weasel-faced labourer was tipping out a wheelbarrow load of debris.

I received a sidelong and hopeless look from soiled hopeless eyes. Voices of the dead: something like a door slamming, a rope breaking, a box being shut. *L'ange et la bête*. Walking forward, advancing rapidly, checked, repulsed, retreating slowly. The eyes stared at me with a lingering, piteous look, and then the head disappeared. The sound of the jets came belligerently down: there was no shutting that propulsion out, that combativeness, even the deaf would hear it; enough to bring the dead back to life. *Habet acht! Habet acht!* Something reached for, torn at, breaking, like secateurs among roses, inaccessible roses. These aggressive destroyers of peace set up disturbances in the head. Then another sound close at hand. I looked, and the Baron had disappeared. Then his bowed back appeared above table level, the paper napkins fluttering merrily in the breeze now blowing across the plaza. I looked over at Salina and encountered her bold mascaraed Jewish eye. She held her nose. Your roses fall. Your stars fall. I saw a semi-digested pool spreading on the ground. The Baron was vomiting. Groaning, he was letting go everything he had, the full contents of his uneasy stomach. In the pool of disgorged stuff I saw nothing more substantial than floating grape skins and the shards of recently ejected tapas (goat, *Blutwurst*), which bore out his claim to a poor appetite. The mixture was mostly wine, thin, and mercifully, odourless.

Adieu, adieu, *Judenhetze!* Reader of Nietzsche, Schopenhauer, superman, admirer of anti-British Hamsun and Jew-baiter Rosenberg, protector of Martin Bormann. *Ach, du!*

The church bell began to ring; the Baron went on vomiting. He had to get rid of up to five and a half litres. *Que hora es?* I listened to the hour striking: loud ding-dong of doom and time. A last tremulous vibration in the air and it was finished. Time to go in. The Baron, who had incautiously begun to lift his head, went down again, groaning and besplattering his shoes. Feeling something akin to pity, I turned myself sideways on to him and stared at the sierras, the sky-lanes of the jets. He who was quite beyond humiliation needed a little time to pull himself together.

Lifting his head with the utmost circumspection, beret half off, the soiled and bloodshot eyes took in the table top, the fluttering paper, the mis-arrangement of saucers testifying to his thirst, then up at the volcanic-looking mountains, the eyes turned on me. Perspiration trickled down cheeks that had gone the colour of putty, glistening like cheese going off; *Understand me, comrade*, the soiled eyes appealed, *understand me well*. And: *Forgive me, forgive all*. The chin rested on the table, the eyes closed. Then he put his head into his cupped hands and began to take in air, murmuring *Ja, ja, ja, ja* many times, as if breathing into an oxygen mask. He was through now; he wanted to leave. Taking a fistful of paper napkins he began wiping himself. He got to his feet unsteadily, took the cane. He faced me and announced: I am the Fuehrer's soldier still! (raising his right arm in a limp and drunken version of the famous salute). Unsure on his feet, column wobbling on its base, and choking with emotion, he called out in a high mordant voice, *Heil Hitler!* and stood there, drunk, and as if anticipating applause.

Charlie and Salina, struck dumb, had thin smiles frozen on their faces. I studied a concavity on the toe of my left shoe. The Baron's flabby hand was clutching the back of the chair. He was either going to topple over on to the table or sit down and begin all over again. He was like a force of nature; one could do nothing but wait and hope that it would either end or improve. In silence he accepted the stricken smiles of Charlie and Salina, in silence felt my no-response. Without a word he pushed himself off from the chair, his feet moving in the direction of the Puerta del Mar. The evening crowd parted to make way for him, and he went through like a battering ram, striking the ground with his stick.

❦

Now it was windy on the plaza and the sun had gone down. I felt empty. Charlie and Salina waved to me. I went across to their table. Charlie was huddled up in his chair, knees level with his chin, the collar of his reefer jacket about his ears, his hooked Rabbinical nose stuck out. They sat close together, the whites of their eyes enhanced by the darkness of their skin, a couple of Red Indians.

Evening all, I said.

Hi, they said.

Cold? I asked.

Cold! Charlie Vine said, looking down his discoloured nose. Jesus my ass is frozen off.

And how's yours? I asked Salina.

Get along with you now, Salina said.

Sit down on the parliamentary side of your own, *hombre*, Vine said. Take a drink.

Shouldn't we go inside? I said. Unless you're paralysed.

We went in and sat at the bar. A mauve light spilled down the stairway up which Antonio's paternal grandmother, aged one hundred and two, had toiled with a bottle of anis seco in her hand. Vine was 'off liqueur' on Dr Jorge del Bosque's orders, but, in view of the circumstances, the hour, the chill in the air, the agreeable company, thought that a cognac would do him no harm. From the poster at the turn of the stairs a mute procession of *penitentes*, robed and hooded in white and bearing croziers, were attempting to march downstairs. The mauve light, broken up by the shadows of the banisters, splayed over them, their long pointed scaral hoods seemed to move. We had nothing better than the tawny tennis girl on the Pepsi advertisement below. The smile that volleyed from her wide mouth was a smile of white fatuity. *Dentale d'Amérique*. Pida Pepsi. Keep-smiling Californian teeth.

She's warm anyway, Vine said.

Miguel set up three cognac glasses with a professional flourish.

Who was that *Schwab* we saw you with outside? Salina asked, poking me with her elbow. Sacher-Masoch?

Yeah, where did you pick him up? Charlie asked, eyeing the drinks that were being poured by Miguel, wouldn't trust that bastard no more than I'd trust a vinegar eel.

He says he's a Baron, I said, a neo-Nazi. They're emerging from their holes again.

That *Schmutz*! Salina said, baring her white teeth. That *schmutzig* . . . !

He is sickened with humanity, I said. Sickened by the brute world that we are smiling with. Saving your presence, Salina, he thinks the entire Jewish race should be wiped out.

Sounds like a proper shite to me, Salina said pleasantly.

Miguel put three coffees before us.

He's all that, I said. *Muy duro*. An iron man. He mistrusts domestic happiness. Some far-fetched near-relation of Himmler's. I didn't inquire too particularly. He was pig-drunk, as you may possibly have noticed. Did you catch the salute?

We did, Vine said with his long nose down near the cognac. We surely did. We caught more than the salute. (Raising his glass.) *Suerte!*

We smelt a bad smell, Salina said.

10 GUNNERY PRACTICE: The day following my meeting with the Baron, I was waiting for Charlotte on the plaza, by Calahonda beach wall. During the winter we had been meeting at ten in the morning, but now there were more people about and we were meeting an hour earlier. Still there were difficulties. Their house-guests.

Spring had come around again: the sun had a real sting in it at last. Work was progressing on the new luxury hotel next to the old Balcon de Europa bar. Construction workers in red helmets moved about on the roof.

I sat on the low wall that was warm as flesh, watching the archway of the Puerta del Mar. Early English tourists were breakfasting on the terrace of the Hotel Florian. On the bedroom balcony above a scorched septuagenarian appeared, exposing his drooping coarse-haired pink stomach to the sun. Waiters moved between the tables, observing the manners of polite society, manners half disguised and masked by bigotry. The sun-terrace overlooked the poverty trapped below, the poor cottages of the fishermen under the cliff, where convolvuli drooped from the overhang in long festoons. The long double-storey building which I had thought of as the municipal calaboose or jailhouse, had turned out to be an infirmary for an epidemic of typhus that never came.

Dressed only in pyjamas trousers, the septuagenarian held on to the balcony rail, drawing in lungful after lungful of sea air, gazing with complacency about him. Below on the horse-shoe-shaped beach, fishermen tired out after a night's work sprawled asleep in the shade of the boats, their faded cotton pants with big patches of darker cloth at the seat and knees. Sleep the slain white bull. The jackets which they had thrown over their heads were washed and rewashed to a greyish shade; darker hexagonal patches gave them a festive, musical comedy look: the elegant poverty of the Mediterranean fishermen. They lay prone, arms and heels crossed, with jackets thrown over their heads. I recognized the barrel-shaped torso of one, the half-demented Lobo del Mar. Of a free and easy disposition, he gave away any pesetas he had to the scrofulous children of Calle Italia. They came in early with their catch and were drunk in the tabernas before mid-morning. In the bar Barilles in Calle de la Cruz and in the bars on the *carretera*.

Two lay prone, brown bare heels touching, in the shade of the heavy truss of butano lamps rigged on the stern of the *Aux Carmelina*. The boats that had been out the previous night were drawn up by the wooden winch above the wet rim of the virtually non-existent tide. The bigger boats were over with *La Purísima* on Burriana. And was it true that in the olden days white bulls, bred specially for the purpose, pulled the boats up there? Not the white bull mentioned in the Apocalypse, nor the black bull of the D'Arcys, descendants of Charlemagne. Probably just bullshit.

At that hour the plaza on which I paraded was deserted, except for myself and the owner of the kiosk, who in tinted spectacles behind his geraniums, with crumbs on his lips, was drinking coffee. He owned a terrier that could do tricks. Balance balloons on its nose, walk on two legs. The owner of the kiosk was thought to be an informer. His sweet-faced wife was said to follow an even older profession in Malaga. Perform other tricks. Lies probably. Who could say?

A woman came out of one of the poor cottages with a basin of dishwater, walked across the flat roof and threw it over. The lean cats, foraging among the fish heads, scattered. The woman went in again. Now a tribe of mongrels were moving along the shore-line. One of the older fishermen had woken and was mending a net. Patriarch Noah among his beasts. Apostles snoring in Gethsemane. Mantegna's glassy cliff of shelving rock, and above it the marvellous city. And in my mind's eye a heron, symbol of longevity, reminder of Yeats, and therefore Sligo. Nullamore. *On the Boiler?*

The plaza was damp; it had been hosed down like a ship's deck. And I was engaged in a shipboard romance with a young married woman from another class, from another continent. I walked there with a void in my stomach, as on the mornings after breakfast on the Cunarder *Sylvania* ploughing back from Canada. Mind not poor lovers who walk above the decks of the world in storms of love. I longed for her; looking through the archway of the Puerta del Mar, hoping to see her pass, rounding the Town Hall in a blue suit with black stockings, walking towards me with that gravity which was so much part of her character. Strange to feel so much for another fellow-creature; the heart feels as if it is being drawn out of its socket, and one can't tell whether it's pain or pleasure. Strange that one human being can do that to another. I walked up and down in the shade of the palms, crossing from one side of the plaza to the other, keeping the archway under observation.

The sun stung my shoulders when I left the shade. The kiosk owner had left his kiosk and was watering his geraniums, not looking in my direction, as a good informer should. This place, this time; I was in a state bordering on happiness. What's it like, happiness? I felt so strange. I thought: It must be that; this must be happiness.

Then it struck me, stuck in my throat: she had forgotten we were to meet an hour earlier. Or, worse again, forgotten we were supposed to meet that day. Assignations were made hurriedly, and if for any reason she could not come there was no means of telling me. Or, in the reverse case, of me telling her. No means of stopping Bob if he wanted to accompany her. No means of stopping Olivia if she wanted to accompany me. Charlotte's excuse was that she was going to the market (she went every day). My excuse was that I needed exercise before starting work. How would I know if she could not come? Or had forgotten? We had been intimate and technically were lovers. There should have been trust, understanding, some intuition, even of a non-verbal nature, but there was not, only this difficulty of going on. Each time we had to begin over. She had to re-present herself to me, I had to re-seduce her. Intimacy had not produced trust, but almost the contrary; between us there was not only Bob, but Olivia. It was a wearing business, producing as much antagonism as it produced love.

Love, even the word for it is strange. *Amo. Odi et amo.* Sometimes I hated her, with a particular kind of hatred, hated her because I could not have her, as she in turn must have hated me, to judge from her occasional venom.

What is the chief and first requirement in love? asks Montaigne. It is to know how to take fit time. And the second requirement? The same. And the third? The same. Watched by both Bob, the most uxorious of husbands, and Olivia, the most jealous of wives—not to mention the house-guests, and leaving out the native population of arch-gossips—we had trouble with our fit times. So there and then the morning began to go sour on me.

I sat on the low wall, beginning to feel already the mono-tonous gloom of a day without her lying ahead of me. A day without seeing her, speaking to her, was indeed empty for me. As the hour advanced, I longed for it to end, so that another could begin, perhaps more hopefully, bringing her closer to me. It too would end, after an interminable period, and another would begin as leadenly, pass as slowly, and still she would not come. Restless and nervous I sat on the wall, watching the archway of the Puerta del Mar.

Nothing passed; then a mule laden down with sugar-cane went by, the muleteer pacing directly behind, clinging on to the animal's tail and being pulled along. They disappeared behind the kiosk, reappeared before the Ciné Olympia where *Lo que el Viento se llevo* was showing for one night, *con* Clark Gable *y* Vivian Leigh, Leslie Howard *y* Olivia de Havilland. I'd seen the billboard. The coarse face of Gable; behind him a con-flagration, Atlanta in flames and Sherman riding away. Years before I had seen it in the Regal Rooms in Dublin. Two dead actors, a cinema that no longer existed in a narrow street so changed I hardly knew it, as dead and non-existent as my own youth. Non-existent as any touch I ever had with her, any claims on her, as I sat on the wall, watching the archway of the Puerta del Mar, my harried feelings of frustration went out towards her, reaching blindly for her. I was a bridge of suffering that only she could cross, her face still marked by sleep, despoiled by the intimacy she claimed she now performed in a per-functory manner with her loving husband, while thinking of me. And then, instead of Charlotte, came prudent Charlie Vine, pigeon-toed, his shoulders hunched, heading for morning coffee in the Marissal. He took his coffee at ten o'clock before beginning a day's work. I moved behind one of the palm trees. Looking neither to right nor left Charlie Vine stepped into the Marissal. His sight was poor. I crossed to the low wall again, more hopefully now. Here was a good omen.

The sun had burnt away the clouds. There was a shimmer of light over the water, with little wisps of cloud down near the horizon and the air without strength to scatter them. The septuagenarian now reappeared on the little balcony accompanied by a gross female with raw shoulders, dressed in a black kimono that did not altogether conceal her heavy figure. She wore curlers. They stood there looking down into the beach, tufted armpits perspiring verdigris. Mustard weed grew in the waste ground before Florian's. Charlock. A rowing boat was putting out from one of the little coves. Three men were in her, two rowing, one standing and preparing to let down the net; drops fell from the oars—the image looked burnished. The *chop-chop* of the oars following after the image. The couple on the balcony watched with their stomachs pressed against the iron grid. Pale hairless torsos, a sense of stale embraces, their sluggish senses hardly aspiring to contact. Sometimes this company, sometimes that, both to dine and sup. The woman turned heavily, leaning on the rail.

When I first my wedded mistress saw bestride my threshold. They watched as the figure in the stern began to let down the net. A closed sea, in the middle of the land, the old centre of the earth. On its shores Noah's children, Shem, Ham and Japheth, and their sons, have worked since the Flood. Touch beauty on the one hand, human misery on the other. You can't have one without the other. Over the sea-wall and into the dreaming town.

The English breakfasters were rising, throwing down their napkins. Waiters in navy-blue with white anchors emblazoned on their chests began clearing up. The couple retreated into the bedroom above. The waiters went in. The sun terrace lay deserted. *Parade des Anglais.*

A freshening offshore breeze made a kind of inditing on the surface of the water, innumerable diamond-shaped points of light glittered over a wide area, leaving the rest serene. The Mediterranean and its little mirrors. The dance of the little mirrors of the Mediterranean, with everything trembling, constant little tremblings, junctions, disjunctions, nothing still, no, never for a moment still. A calm day out at sea. Two boats were fishing far out, working well apart, half lost in the haze. On the horizon three or four bigger vessels were hull-down into the glare. I watched the archway—more than my eyes watched it—but there was no sign of her. Instead of Charlotte came now a rumble like thunder, but unmistakably not thunder, a long shudder from over the water I felt now under my feet, hard as iron. It passed through the palms, the plaza, on through the village, a pulse, a gust in from the sea. Among the wisps of cloud over the ships a puffball of flak appeared. It was lead-coloured in the centre, turning septic yellow, spreading out innocently enough, as a small white cloud. I looked up, listening for the sound of aircraft, but there were none flying over the area. Nothing in sight at all events, nothing had banged through the sound barrier. Were the ships shelling the clouds to try and disperse them? Was it firing practice? Or had war started? I listened, with more than my ears. Nothing.

Nothing. Only a stirring in the palms, a faint breeze on my face, a voice murmuring, You are done for; and a few small dun-coloured birds flew away.

Then a second flakball joined the first at precisely the same altitude. The reverberation rolled in thick and dull, and from over the horizon—a chain reaction—came the heavy spreading rumble of answering fire. Heavy calibre naval guns were letting go their salvoes down near Gibraltar. The Baron's grim prediction came to mind. Had a world war started? The last. How could we get back to Ireland, or back to Aran, and would we be safe there? Or, if it came to that, could I give Olivia the sodium amytals, take them myself, or a 'massive overdose' of sleeping pills? Or would Charlotte come to me and say, If I have only one more day, one more hour to live, I want to spend it with you. As I knew I wanted to die embracing her. Doubtful.

Charlie Vine was leaving the Marissal in a hurry. I watched the hunched up figure rapidly cross the plaza, his hands deep in his pockets. Caught up in the ardour of narrative construction, Vine was going back to his typewriter. No sooner had he left the plaza when a third flakball appeared alongside the other two. White at first, then turning septic yellow—and the third ponderous detonation followed. The stiff palm fronds above my head shivered and the last of the dun-coloured birds flew away. A triple blast of destruction had blown in from the sea. Above me among the palm fronds outstretched like arms, skeleton features grimaced, announcing the opening movements of another war. World War III had started on the site of the old Peninsular War.

The bell of San Salvador at this precise moment sounded the half hour: sounded ten-thirty. I had not heard the hour strike. The single stroke hung in the hot and luminous air. You go, the bell said sweetly; I stay. Half past the hour. A slick of heat on my back. Nothing stirred. The white puffball with its sickly centre, human pus on cotton wool, hung like a sign in the sky over the motionless ships. I waited for the blast to blow me off the plaza, off the face of the earth. The informer was going back into his kiosk, shaking the last drops from the neck of his watering can. Then, always taking me by surprise, *nur schlecht aneinander gewöhnen*, the second stroke, like an overtone, sounded calmly from the church. Or from another belfry? But there was only one belfry, one church, one God, one true religion, one winter cinema (but two summer ones to make up a trinity), and fifty tavernas for a population of ten thousand souls, the population of Guernica before the bombing. Iron on iron, hammer on anvil, one questioned, the other replied, and real life was over. A lick of heat. A tongue of flame.

I thought: She isn't coming. She: meaning Charlotte Bayless. The archway of the Puerta del Mar offered me nothing but its blank wall-eyed stare, and a tall red-headed fellow was advancing towards me from the Plaza de la Iglesia, followed by a woman pushing a go-cart (Charlotte called it a stroller). Honeymooners off the early bus looking for a place to stay? The man was tall, with foxy hair, and probably American, judging from the way he dressed. The woman, leaving the stroller and the child it held, ran to the wall, looked down, called, very excited, for him to look. He went across to her, put his bush-boot on the wall, stared down at the dirt, the sleeping fishermen, the false calaboose, the untangled nets. He was a giant, perhaps six feet six, very lethargic in manner. They stood there talking in low voices, looking at me out of the corner of their eyes. He intended to speak to me; I knew that. I kept my eyes on the archway. I only wanted to see and speak to Charlotte. He knew Herbert (*Nickel Giseries*) Gold.

Sure enough, after a moment's deliberation he turned to me. Did I speak English? How long had I been here? Were there Americans? He had heard of a Writers Colony, was that true? Where did they go during the day? The tone of the voice, the presumptions, the long serious face, the engaging brown eyes, these were hard to take, and my answers were not encouraging. I disliked being questioned in this downright way. He was American all right.

Come here about midday, I said, you should find some of them sitting at the tables over there.

Suddenly I saw behind him Charlotte's brown face and brown neck. She looked at me, smiling. I left him without a word, crossed with Charlotte to one of the terrace tables and sat down.

How are you? I asked (meaning so much more). I thought you weren't coming.

My house-guest, Charlotte said. Michèle wanted to come to the market with me. I had to shake her off. We had a late night last night.

Miguel came. I ordered two coffees, for myself a cognac. Swallows were squirting about the sky. The new couple were staring into Calahonda beach, the woman, who might have been German, holding the child against the rail. The war receded. Charlotte removed her sunglasses and looked at me with those unforgettable eyes.

Who were you talking to?

One of your fellow-countrymen lost without compatriots. She's German I think. They're looking for a place to stay.

Immediately she wanted to help them, and knew of a place that was vacant. I stared at her, speechless. Did she know what she was doing? She had helped Charlie Vine to find a place, and now she wanted to help total strangers. I said nothing to that suggestion. My love, my crying need for her, was of such a nature, selfish because deprived, precarious and hard-won, attentive to its needs, threatened from inside (her husband) and outside (incoming strangers), that any overt act of kindness or generosity for others, offered by her and carried through, tended to alienate her from me. I wanted the *status quo* to remain, however miserable: I felt I had a chance only if everything stayed the same, the *status quo* being the four of us, Bob attracted to Olivia, I to Charlotte; inside of that all was uncertain, but to a limited and bearable degree; outside of that all was uncertain, but to an unlimited and unbearable degree. And similarly in a limited circle of friends and acquaintances my love had some chance, however slight; whereas if more pseudo-intimates came in, under obligation to her at that, well soon it would be impossible to sit alone with her for any length of time at any table, however discreet, at no matter what hour we went there, someone would always be butting in, sitting down without a by-your-leave, pushing in, the Hools, the Loewens, the Summerbees. Lecher Lar Summerbee puffing out his cheeks, staring at us, stuck on her himself, coming to his own conclusions about what was going on between us, estimating his chances with her; with his Volkswagen and his yacht: If you let *him* have you, why not let me have you too, a fellow-American after all. Soon it would become impossible to stand alone with her at any bar or be anywhere alone with her, but always under observation, the subject of comment and gossip that invariably would get back to Bob and then to Olivia, and the *status quo*, the very delicate balance of power (You-take-what-you-want-provided-I-can-take-what-I-want) would make way for something else, something I did not want. And could she not see this? Charlie and Salina watching us through powerful binoculars from their flat roof, Charlotte and I embracing three or four kilometres away near a cane plantation; Charlotte and I imagining ourselves alone in the Balcon de Europa bar on a cold day, and the Summerbees and the Loewens heading towards that very bar, down for the day from Torrox. And more and more Americans coming in, with their damned gregariousness, their mutual crying need for an amicable social life at all costs. Community of interests, New York, certain bars, Rumpelmeyer's. Charlotte as a person in a given society, a society I did not know or want to know, irritated me; before, that side of her had enchanted me, but now it only irritated me. I wanted her alone, to be my Albertine.

Why act as an unpaid travel agent encouraging *extranjeros* to settle here? I said testily, when we have too many already.

You may be right, she said, although it was apparent that she did not think so, and in fact had already decided to help them.

Let them try further along the coast, I said, if it's company they're after.

She was in a hurry to get to the market. Bob might come to the plaza for cigarettes. I said I'd go with her as far as the post office. Waiting for Miguel to bring the change, I described the shelling. She had heard nothing from Calle Pintada. I tipped Miguel and Charlotte stood up. She suggested going on to Vine's roof to look through his binoculars. I said I might do that. As we left the plaza I felt the new couple staring after us. We passed through the church square and entered Plaza de los Martires, a small square planted with *castaña loca* trees and a black Cross. We turned into the Calle Granada. Near the far end, opposite the post office, hard by the grocery store run by Los Hermanos Iranzo, stood Vine's rooftop flat.

Being with her, I felt lifted out of my lethargy and sloth, from the banality that encumbered my life; this small bright-faced person had that effect on me.

I never see you alone these days, I said.

I know. I feel it too, she said, touching my arm. Almost six of the nine months we were to spend together had passed; we were seeing each other every other day but never spending a night together; and she had kept me out of my mind all that time.

But she, whose amatory comprehension was matchless, must have felt something of what I felt for her that morning, with the sound of big guns and all known security blowing away, for she said, touching me again on the arm:

Can you wait until I get back from the market? I must make Daisy's lunch, and Bob's working all day. Can you meet me on the bridge in say two hours? . . . Daisy will be sleeping then.

Yes, I said.

Charlotte went into the post office to inquire for mail and I, feeling like a prisoner who has been given a last-minute reprieve, went across to Vine's flat to pass the time. The outer door on to the street was open. I went up the stairs. It was cooler there. The door to his flat was closed, with a facetious notice tacked up, pedlars and beggars referred to the back way. I knocked. No answer. I tried the handle; the door was open; I put my head in and called out *Vine*!

Hey, wait a minute! (Salina's voice), I've nothing on.

If that girl in *Gatsby* had the sound of money in her voice, what sound had Salina? A promise of something. Venery? Back and sides go bare, go bare.

I'm not waiting, I said. I'm coming up.

I heard her laugh, and bare feet above my head as she ran into the bathroom. I went up the last steep flight of stairs that gave directly on to their living-room. The high-ceilinged room where he worked, down a step directly opposite, was empty. A small table, a typewriter, a ream of yellow copy paper, a blown-up print of Salina on the wall, very grainy—a hostile Iroquois queen. Salina's darkness, the petals of a full-grown peony.

Where is the bastard? I said. Dead? . . . working?

Working my ass, her high excited voice called from behind the door. He's asleep on the roof.

Asleep, I said. Now do you mind that.

A copy of *Time* lay face down on the table alongside an Olympia Press *Molloy*. I stepped into the white glare, and saw Vine's small Oriental feet. Looking very jaundiced he lay sleeping on a mattress in the sun, in black trousers and black aertex shirt. His bare feet stuck out in a defenceless way.

Will you look at that now, I said, but Vine did not move. The swarthy meagre countenance of this man for whom it would never be hot enough looked none too good; throughout the winter he had complained bitterly of the cold, had lived in dread of contracting hepatitis, managed to avoid it when the Summerbees and then the Hools had gone down with it, and yet now looked as jaundiced and worn-out as they. Lazarus, or a haggard El Greco Christ? Hardly. When he had first come to Nerka he had looked like a love-sick Saint Loup pining for the actress and whore Rachel; now, bearded and thinner, he resembled nothing so much as their creator, the dead and disdainful Monsieur Proust, his labours over, laid out on his death-bed.

Salina came out on to the roof, her arms up arranging something at her neck, exposing her armpits' *ferea naturae*. She wore a sack dress with a design of russet and brown squares and rectangles, purple and dull red lozenges, caught up about the neck, a Mojave maiden padding on bare feet, saying Hi! She had been sunbathing in the nude alongside Charlie. Her tan had gone a shade darker, brazilnut turning into hazelnut, the whites of her eyes most pronounced. A quite savage-looking beauty, with widely separated toes. Her pupils were darkly flashing stars. Eula Varner.

Will you look at that slob sleeping, she said.

Let him sleep, I said. He looks done-in. You must have had a hard night. I won't stay long. Just came for a look through the old spyglass, *por favor*.

Salina said that they had heard the firing but had not noticed the flak-bursts.

I was on the *paseo*, I said. They seemed to be firing from the ships.

Hearing our voices, Vine stirred, threw out one arm, mumbled Bastards!, opened a jaundiced eye and saw me.

Where in hell's name did you spring from? Charlie asked, sitting up stiffly, groaning.

Vouchsafe good-morrow from a feeble tongue, I said. You look bad, Vine.

Feel bad too, Charlie said. Not too good anyway. He removed his dark spectacles to massage his eyes. About the eyes his skin had the paleness of winter.

Take a cold shower, Vine, Salina said. That'll wake you up.

Vine looked at her, yawning.

Think I will, he said. I feel pooped out. Won't be long . . .
Give the gombeen man a drink.

He went in, followed by Salina. I heard the clink of glass
on glass, a door closed. Presently the shower started. *Mamma,
mamma!* Christ, it burns like fire!

Salina was Charlie's occasional girl. Penrose, lecturer in
philosophy at Liverpool University, reputedly preparing a
thesis on Ludwig Wittgenstein, and given to quoting from the
Tractatus Logico-Philosophicus when in his cups, which was fairly
often, had taken her from a friend called Ned Jarvis, one of the
clique Vine was forever going on about, and Charlie had taken
her from Penrose. Salina loved neither Penrose nor Vine, but
another, an oboe player in another country; but although she
didn't love Vine, she was willing to accommodate him.

Charlie Vine walked like a plainsman, pigeon-toed (sign of a
reserved and cautious nature), unlike Charlotte Bayless, who
walked with her toes turned out (sign of a liberal outgoing
nature?); a small neat man so broad in the shoulder that you
would suppose he had left the clothes-hanger in by mistake,
with hips tapering away to nothing below the knees. He had
the strong delicate fingers of a plainsman who braids leather,
an urbane manner and the vocabulary of a buck private. Ass and
shit, he said often, shit and ass, meaning Soul and filthy Cir-
cumstance and not much more than that. Just a kind of brown
man—this sometime United Press correspondent—now groaning under the pitiless needles of the shower.

Salina carried out a tray of drinks and set it on the low white
wall and went in again for the binoculars which Vine had bought
cheaply in Gibraltar with an umbrella that opened when you
pressed a button. She handed the binoculars to me through the
bedroom window, saying, There, sir. The double bed was
made, with an Indian blanket spread. As I turned back to the
wall, I saw below, among the levels, a couple of houses away, a
glassed-in patio partly covered in creeper, and in this a stout
old woman in a rocker knitting peacefully among sleeping cats
and pots of geranium. The flat roof and whitewashed walls
reeled in the sun, and all that remained of the flak was a single
wisp indistinguishable from cirrocumulus.

The binoculars drew the ships into closer range, but still it was impossible to determine what type of vessel they were, whether destroyers or not, lying-to out there on the hazy morning sea. They were disposed in a triangle, the nearest with radar-like superstructure veering this way and that, while the others stood-to further out. I felt a twinge of fear, recalling the Baron's gloomy and prophetic words. Let be; let be, let no one see. Go on.

Vine reappeared tucking his shirt into his pants, his beard and hair wet from the shower, followed by Salina with a jar of ice cubes and some packets of cigarettes. I accepted a Montilla from her hand.

She took a vino tinto and poured Charlie a beer. They studied the vessels in turn but without coming to any conclusion about them. They were not fishing boats, no more could be said of them; whether they were armed naval craft was another matter. They looked peaceable enough. I pointed out the remains of the flak. Vine turned his binoculars away from the sea and studied the sierras and the pylons marching down the valley from Murcia. Then, leaning his elbows on the wall, showing his long back, he studied the street below where it joined the carretera a hundred yards away. He had dried himself in a hurry, the shirt stuck to his spine.

Here she comes, he said.

Who? Salina said. Who comes?

Fred C. Dobbs, Charlie said, in person. (This was his nickname for Charlotte.)

Ask her up, Salina said.

Okay. Wait until I get her into focus. I crossed to the parapet and watched her approaching. She came strutting below, walking from the hips, as she would walk with her eyes open into trouble. Helen walks in light. Long ash-blonde hair hung down her back, she came on grandly, picking her way with swaying tarty steps, leading with the pudenda: a strutter, a gripper-of-the-earth, a neat mover. Knowing herself under observation she was puffing out her lips and going *Chuff, chuff*, walking down the lane of shade carrying a shopping basket of provisions. She came swaggering below and looked up, sunglasses as blank and noncommittal as her smile was broad and engaging.

Hi there, Charlie said. Hold it. Come up for a drink.

Okay, Charlotte answered from below.

Vine rarely raised his voice or became worked-up about anything. He turned away from the parapet.

She's coming up, he informed us, as if it were a matter of complete indifference to him whether she came up or not.

He trained his binoculars again on the pylons. I had been wrong about this sagacious Charlie. Presently out on to the roof came Charlotte. Hi, she said. Charlie and Salina said Hi. Taking up the binoculars I sat on the low wall.

A cold beer for the memsahib? Charlie said.

All right, Charlotte said, a quinto. She brought her drink over and sat next to me, crossing one dark knee over another. Well, then, she said.

Puked his goddamn guts out, Charlie said. Damn fool Finn.

He went on to describe for their amusement the Baron haranguing and damning the Jews, incurring Miguel's disfavour, giving the Hitler salute, tottering home across the plaza. The girls laughed, showing their fine white teeth.

And looking into it, I said, as if he could divine his future there.

The sun shone on the low white walls, on the glasses and bottles, on the sea beyond. Charlotte held a cigarette level with her mouth, a quick puff, then between her knees, looking at it. All her quick movements touched me, the way she smoked, the way she drank, the hands she felt self-conscious of picking at food, pilfering cutlery from the Granada bars, knives and forks spirited away into her handbag. Surely some atavistic racial trait there. The art of survival. Her gestures became her. She wore a heavy gold ring to match Bob's, who had bought both in Sausalito. I dimly connected distance with the shine of gold. Yet I felt her near me, and wasn't that enough?

A thin gold chain, a sad half smile, a bit of gold, maybe a bit of flecked gold in the aqueous humour of the eyes that seemed to reflect another seascape even brighter than the existing one.

The eyes that were sending glances in my direction. *Compelle intrare*. Later I would take her into the *campo*, even that was possible. Oceanic eyes. *Flora de California*. *Fruta-oro-vinos*. A wave, a glow. Her whole world was coming to meet me in a wave.

She and Salina were talking. Well, Salina certainly *talked*. The sweet and civil contention of two amorous ladies. The ladies closed their musing eyes, their thoughts were but a pool. Two Jewish beauties, dark Deborah and blonde Queen Esther, two beings from a lost civilization standing apart remote in their burning elegance. Their clothes hardly seemed to cover them. Coastal sirens from the New World.

Laughing indulgently now, they were showing their dice-like white teeth, amused at something Charlie had said, as the heat settled on the walls.

In profile Charlotte had Renaissance eyeballs and a Byzantine nose; it came straight down from the brow. The flesh on her face, the round modelling of the cheeks, her healthy colouring, all delighted me. She was the famous actress waiting for a train at a suburban halt, a small station (Windsor? Howth?) that could hardly accommodate such grandness. She had a kind of beauty that is not usual in an age like this. She spoke, thrusting her lips out in a kind of pout: it was her cheating voice. Her features seen close were not quite perfect but had a coarseness that made her beauty all the more touching and unforgettable. Beauty was in the strong arabesque of her spine, in her sad half-smile; she represented the opposite to cowering, old age and bodily decrepitude (Sleep with a Jewess and you'll never feel the same about another woman again). Seeing her there, walking up and down, it seemed impossible that she would ever wilt or age. She had Sylvie Selig's purposeful jaw and smile, wore black leather shoes with low heels, cuffed in suede, with buttons like garnets at the instep. Now looking at me. You to move, shift yourself, sir. With her it was the skin, some colouring and warmth that belongs essentially to her, emanating from her. *Blandus lascivius*.

Walking proudly on Bob's arm that first day, down Calle Pintada, proudly about the narrow streets of Nerka, her face bronzed by the sun had the foreign look which travellers bring back from another hemisphere: an ineffable air of gaiety, pride and daring. It was her first time in Europe, that ancient bone-heap and the event was reflected in her face. Her impatience was surely indicative of breeding. Full of life she made everything look bright when she came and had no use for bores. Charlotte seemed to have oil in her veins, as well as blood, a young beauty made up of glands and oil. If not a Cleopatra, she was at least a Charmian, a soldier's girl. When she entered a room she made an impression. I thought (watching her laughing on the roof): I should like you to ruin me.

She was the representative of a type I could not resist, although I had never met anyone else like her. (One says too little or too much) I was entering another world, moving in another time, another forenoon without time or name.

Charlotte Bayless, holding in one hand a glass of beer and in the other a tipped cigarette, crossed one dark knee over the other.

You and I are alike, she had said, accusing me of her own faults. We are from different countries, different backgrounds, we were the same. I had met her and been drawn to her, experiencing it with a completeness that left nothing to be desired, in any old ground. I only want to kiss you, I had said; and at this bold admission she had turned on me a long challenging stare. Her eyes read me up and down; then: You don't have to apologize for what you want to do.

And now it was out in the open for the first time. Her dreadful boldness. That boldness without which there is no beauty. Olivia had retired early, Bob said he didn't want to go, and why not take Charlotte? But we left the Western before it was half-way through. Oh God, she said, I can't sit through all this horseshit, and we left the Ciné Olympia and went to the bar El Cruzero, round the corner in Puerta del Mar. We sat by the window with our cognacs, three-quarters of an hour at our disposal that need never be accounted for, and I said, I only want to kiss you. Her eyes were blue as the sky.

I had touched her, this woman from a lost civilization, so close to me. Wait, she said, staring at me with her unforgettable eyes, portfires burning, pupils black as obsidian—Now what's so difficult about it? We left the bar El Cruzero.

The rim was thick and uneven, the contents tepid. I wanted to leave, feeling superfluous or worse, my head thick, my tongue too, my presence amorphous, able to contribute nothing. Not that it mattered, for as usual Salina was talking enough for two. An ear-bender; you can do nothing about it. The sun shone on my head, on the shining glass—an object radiating heat, pulsating and shifting convulsed by intensity of light; perspiration trickled down my sides.

And Bob? Charlie asked.

Working, Charlotte said, looking quickly at me. He had grown mistrustful of me, I could see it in his honest-to-goodness blue eyes. The closed door, the scattered papers, *la vie de l'étude*. His dinted yachting cap, Cruz de Mar cigars, the tapping of the trusty portable. When he worked, she escaped. He had to go on working, so that they could go on living in Andalusia, and he could keep her in the comfort she was accustomed to, for she was a woman who expected and received attention. Bob treated her like a queen, his Jewish queen. Tracey Weddick, perhaps jealous, had said that in New York, in the States, it was a joke—all those Jewish queens. Quite ordinary girls, Tracey said, with a trace of bitterness, what makes them queens?

Charlie took the Montilla bottle from the tray, held it up to indicate it was half full. *Otra vez?* Charlie asked me.

Para mi, no gracias, I said. (Charlotte had declined a second small beer.) I have work to do, unlike you idle bums.

Idle bums, Vine said. Get that, Salina. And me with boils on my ass from sitting in there, my fingers worn to the bone from typing (stretching his olive-coloured simian fingers). Hell!

Must be getting along too, Charlotte said. We left as though going out together were an accident, Charlotte saying to Salina, I have to fix Daisy's lunch.

Down on the mezzanine I opened the door for her. She brushed past me and I closed the door, read the notice where pedlars and beggars were referred to the back way, feeling her closeness. She had a perfume all her own, an odour of the sea perhaps, brine and salt, where her body opened there, Eve's fig-leaf; something of her internal secret life, the woman's life she carried in her body, some sweetness of Charlotte. That was her sun-bathing, sea-bathing, oily Jewish skin and below that her sun-pervaded body gave off something of the musty scent of hay in rain. She smelled of honeysuckle and clover and other fragrances of the field—jasmin, horsemint, hornbeam trees, herbal whiff of something wild; orchards, sage, dry hay, youth's permissiveness. A being trapped in that perfume and that sun. I put my hands to her narrow waist, then over her breasts. *Un cher image.* For the old Greeks the brain was in the waist. Staring at me with her famished tigress eyes, she said, I feel your hands on my breasts even when they aren't there—offering me her moist Lipski lips, and all of her honey thickness, as I pushed her against the door.

Now I smelled the honeysuckle and touched the rose. Her face, so tanned, so close to mine, showed traces of the weather, like a Greek sea-captain's. Her Cointreau breath. I breathed her in at my nose and mouth. A sort of fluid glow emanated from her skin. Everything about her disturbed me, everything, inside, outside. Her mouth, her unfathomable Nile-blue eyes, the weight of her sorrowful eyelids, her quickened respiration (as now), the scent of her Sabine-rape hair. I was holding another woman in my arms and touching a forbidden body. Now I heard voices through the door but could not make out the words. Vine and Salina on the roof above. Clinging vine. Mimosa spray.

She broke away from our long embrace as if caught up by the wind, ran quickly down with a light step. Someone was coming through the open doorway below, perhaps Bob or Olivia. But no one was coming up. She smiled at me from below. I went down to embrace her again. We went out into the sun then. Charlotte to Calle de la Cruz to fix their lunches. I out the other way, towards the bridge. She was to meet me there in an hour's time. Faith, unfaithful wife kept him falsely true.

Bob Bayless sprawled in an easy chair on the mezzanine at

No. 12, smoking a black cigar. Bare shins showed between worn canvas sneakers and rumpled cotton pants, tight about the crotch, his shirt was open to the navel and he was unshaven— all ponderous head, Negroid upper lip and lobeless ears. I sat on the red divan and Charlotte stood facing us, her skirt raised to expose a discoloured bruise the size of a fifty peseta piece high up on her brown thigh, the mark less obvious because of the brown skin.

See here, messmates, she said.

I looked at my darling's wounded flank but out of motives of prudence offered no comment. Bob stared at the bruise and then at her face, drawing on his cigar.

Are not health and corruption said to be incompatible, by the Ancient Rhetoreticians? She glowed with health and well-being, a ripe-thighed temple dancer. Who then had done this thing to her? what ape's paw had marked her? Her pose was a cajoling one. One of her most endearing and characteristic movements began as a shudder in those ardent hips. A beautiful gentleness glowed from the skin there. She dropped her skirt, watching her husband.

What do you make of that? she asked him.

Bob tilted back his head to allow cigar smoke to issue from his nostrils.

On a streetcar in Hode, Arkansas, he said in a preacher's voice, I glimpsed the exhausted. Anything is permissible and possible in a world in which no one any longer believes in anything. But don't despair. Study-groups among the Pennsylvanian Elks, after extensive Bible porings, revealed that the Second Coming had in fact already occurred, unnoticed by anybody, in or around 1870, with the Kingdom of God established 'invisibly' a few years later—let's say around the time Queen Victoria made herself Empress of India.

Charlotte sailed across the room, very well gathered-up, as the Spaniards say of their horses: *muy recogida* (especially tearing along at full speed). Going downstairs with only the upper part of her body showing, she called back brightly: Okay, I'll let both you guys do it into my behind!

Rare, rare, her pierced beauty. The heavy musk of falling

hair. In a field of force, the coiling honeycomb of forms, the golden wheel of love.

I was with Charlie Vine in the small bar on Calle Cristo on Good Friday, during a power failure. Candles were burning along the bar counter and the place was deserted. I heard a scratching sound outside and stood at the door to watch a silent company file past, carrying the figure on the Cross, covered in veils. The silent company of mourners filed silently by like ghosts, and as though ashamed. We went back to our drinks. What do you make of that? I said.

Vine looked at me with his afflicted Jewish eyes. That guy wasn't carrying no Cross, he said. He was trying to hold it down.

La Sangre. Las Cinco Llagas. Christ's five bleeding wounds sculptured over church portals like bunches of grapes. Jarry has written somewhere that God is infinitely small. (*xpi*). God's honour. St. Paul writes somewhere in his Epistles of Jesus as the image of the invisible God.

> *The wonder of the Jew*
> *Is the world of the Jew*
> *And yet*
> *And yet*

☙❦❧

Sayings of Charlie Vine: The old UP, stick it up your ass, old Salina would talk the scrotum off the statue of David, cold as a gravedigger's ass.

11 ILLYRICUM: I returned to the flat later that afternoon. The place was empty, the kitchen full of flies.

Following intimacy under a carob tree (she had changed into black slacks that unzipped at the back), we had separated and returned by roundabout ways, she by the Plaza de Cantarara and its white roses, sunflowers ten feet high, dried mule-shit on a blancoed wall, wasps over a puddle, I for a swim on Burriana, to have the lie that I'd been swimming, as in a sense I had, for I was ringed and anointed with her person.

Olivia had closed up the place and left. The house-flies swarmed in the kitchen, the bathroom, where the window was broken, the cardboard fallen out. I took a Cruz Campo beer. It was tepid. We had no cooling system, so the beer stayed tepid and the milk went off. There was a letter from the gallery on the table. I drank the beer. The house-flies were sinking and rising, going at odd tangents, and a blue-bottle banged against the walls like a charge of electricity. I too felt charged and heated. On the draining-board a halved lemon was decomposing, full of fruit flies. Ants made their way across the stove, over the white tiles. They were into some damp granulated sugar spilled there, carrying it off in their pincers. I undressed. Her skin scent pervaded my senses. The knees of my bags were stained green and I dropped them into the wash-basket. I took the letter out on to the balcony to read it. It was brief enough. The paintings had been received, one sold already, he liked them, he said, owed me some money. How were the Stations progressing?

The sky was teeming with feeding swallows. *Golandrinas*. A line of pylons marching down the valley with power from Alicante. Outlines of houses against a tinted sky, the swallows flying over the telegraph wires, no television masts in Spain. Swifts were dive-bombing the roofs. I heard the sow and her

litter moving in the outhouse next door. In a mood of subdued elation I went back in. Faint dizziness, senses stirred
(*chusem*, life's anguish, *zaar ba'ale chayim*, a kid, a kid!), my tepid
blood still heated by contact with her, how could it be otherwise? Under the cold shower another resurrection of the flesh;
An after-image in the retina. I dressed and powdered using
Olivia's powder, and had the remainder of the beer. It was flat.
I sat there, drank flat beer and felt elated. I read the letter
again. He wanted to see more work. I threw it into the basuro-
bucket and the spoilt lemon after it. It was like being in a wood
with all the flies, my skin air-scorched. *Son du cor, le soir, au
fond des bois.* Lapidary fingers.

And where was Olivia? Guardian of the tomb. As for me,
dear, I am no more yours. Nor you mine.

Now the late Andalusian afternoon had a bitter taste, the
taste of a weariness that not even love consummated could
quite dispel. Was it the famous post coitum ennui? Hollow feeling of betrayal and guilt. I went to the room where I worked
but the sight of the uncompleted canvas on the easel stank of
unfinished things. Because of Charlotte I could not work in an
orderly way. My thoughts were with her. More unfinished
business. Love requited demands more. I crossed to Olivia's
room.

Her underclothes were scattered on the bed. Why a shift
in such heat? She was untidy. I threw these on the floor and
lay on the bed. I heard the fountain, and the swifts going under
the clouds, their airy high-pitched screeching. Go to, go to.
Schnell. The gauze or muslin hung limply down. No breath of
air stirred it. There were fewer flies. I felt less elated. Conscience began to bother me lying there. The tearing cries of the
swifts over the roofs. Split the eardrums. In the open window a
reflection of grass and weeds growing on the opposite roof
where a black cat crouched on the tiles.

The whole world knows what a beating is, but no one has
yet made out what is love. Some natural philosophers have
affirmed that it is a sort of electricity, an out-streaming fluidum
from a person or a thing. Unter den Linden: the scent of
honey from the pods, a studio near the Opera.

A line of swifts shot by the window. They copulate in mid-air, the females opening their feathers. Ah free-born nature, nothing like it. In Bavaria they come in May and depart three months later, last seen down the streams in the English Garden in Munich, the heat and the long African days calling them back. A lighter atmosphere, land the colour of buck (turds, Amory claimed) and ochre. Back after the worst European winter since 1740, was it? Coming and going, their existence was short and sweet. *Schnelligkeit.*

The black cat was watching something. What is it a sign of, when you see a black cat or a chimneysweep? All depends what happens after. In some German villages a cat crossing the road from right to left is considered a bad omen. I thought of Bob, working, sweating. Are the horns of cuckoldry ever silent? *Dieu! que le son du cor est triste au fond des bois!* She would be there with her lies. How would he take them. We had arranged to meet on the plaza at eight as if by accident. I could not keep away from her now. Soon the day would draw to a close and I who had invested in it all my hopes, the last of my strength, longed for it to end. The day was ebbing away. I was ebbing with it.

I woke again when the door opened below. Olivia. She had an abrupt way of opening doors. The street lights were on; perhaps an hour had passed while I slept. It was now seven or half past. I heard the cries of children playing in the street and Olivia's resolute step on the stairs.

Anyone in? she called out. Anyone at home?

No, I lied.

I

Is it part of the natural perversity of things and of choice that I should associate in my mind Charlotte, who is warm-natured, with that high, silent and cold city—La Paz, where I have never been; and Olivia, who is if anything rather cold and reserved by nature (her Scots Presbyterian background), with

Cavtat in Dalmatia, where we spent three weeks in stewing high summer heat? There was the scent of pine and eucalyptus, a small amphitheatre where an English company gave a marionette show, and Mestrovic's mausoleum, a white dome showing on the hill. Olivia opened her packet of cigarettes in a special hasty way, the tobacco shredded. We swam on Cavtat and Mlini beaches, walked up three hundred or more stone steps through sub-tropical vegetation to visit the Puppet Master on the high road. He had rented a room for working and stood there in the wood shavings, wearing dirty white shorts, labouring on the torso of a female puppet in the clamp. It was the barber's home.

Olivia, by permission of the Supervisor, took to showering in Mlini Power House. The houses were reflected on the surface of the water in the little harbour. Below that, in a mirror image, the shallow bed of the saline Adriatic. Olivia walked naked through the bedroom in Hotel Supetor, the fierce glare coming through the wooden lattices stippled her with light and shade. Her figure was so suntanned that she seemed to be wearing a white bikini. I worked like one condemned to it, renting a studio from Karlovic-Maria down on the beach, and swam every morning shortly after sun up.

It was summer. Let it always be summer there. The beer tasted of lead and slate, brought up out of a well in a bucket. Kulinjic, the producer from Sarajevo recited *Hamlet*. To pee-or-not-to-pee, death-ease-the-question. His English sounded like Crusoe's parrot. An affable man. He spoke of Tito.

Understand, Mr. Ruttle, I am not . . . ah (coughing discreetly behind his hand) attempting to make a Communist of you. No.

The tall palms in the garden by the sea were fidgeting in the breeze. Their fronds.

We took a bath together in the hotel and the water ran out correctly enough when the plug was lifted, but came up unexpectedly through a drain in the centre of the floor and flooded the bathroom. Olivia went to the fruit market, bought eggs, prepared lists of words.

She wrote: Today when I tell—*Danas kad ja recin*. Every

next day I find—*Svaki drugi dan ja nagin*—Your round eggs—
Tvoje oblo jaje (formal), *Vase oblo jaje* (familiar).
Today when I tell—*Danas kad ti recis* (formal).
Danas ka vi rečite (familiar).

> *Dobro vecer !*
> *Dobro jutro !*
> *Lako noč !*
> *Dobro dan !*

She swam nude at night under a translucent moon down in a translucent sea.

We saw the lights of Dubrovnik, jewel of the Adriatic, the southern Venice. Ragusa, Epidaurus. And behind a spit of land, a copse of pine, opposite the German youth camp which was at that hour (two a.m.) mercifully quiet, Yugoslav naval ratings, dressed in white on the deck of a white corvette, serenaded her (splashing unseen, stark naked) on their mandolins. One night there was a spectacular summer storm, with sheet lightning. Next morning the corvette had gone.

I showed my work to Olivia and she said it meant nothing to her but hoped it was good, and did I like *Soutine*? I said no, not all that much. But later made an even worse admission, as far as Olivia was concerned, I did not know Derain.

Side by side on that narrow path going between the groves of grey-green pines and eucalyptus, my shoulder touches her shoulder. And if I try to see her before me, no, whereas I think, now, I do not know her, but I go after her. What I think includes the delirium which we have shared and in which every word unfurls like her own desire. And just at that moment she pulls back her hair, her eyes close, wincing (the blare of the bugles from the German youth camp), and then the torso and legs, and the shadows of leaves, pine branches, on her bare brown shoulders.

When we come out of the grove of pines, the walk by the sea, the rock is below us. Olivia steps down on to the rock, begins to undress, arrange her hair. The heat is excessive, the white egg-like dome of Mestrovic's temple is cracking. The heat is such that you imagine, on the hills the air seems to become fire, the fire sinking into the air.

I look at her wide hips as she goes in. Her hair comes undone in the water. She swims, a leisurely breast-stroke, her dark hair spread wide, one shoulder strap slipping off, a well-built female. I dive; I can see her shape under the surface. I follow her; it's deep, dark, one cannot see the bottom.

At night she swims in the nude below the house of Madame Olga, who played with Garbo in *Panama Nights*. Directed by Francis X. Bushman in the old days in Hollywood, when stars were stars. Madame Olga is as old as the hills. Again her hair comes undone in the water. Some way out, we see the bejewelled lights of Dubrovnik down on the horizon; Olivia rises a little out of the water, revealing her shoulders, bust, nipples, and with a quick movement of her arm tries to point out to me the white egg-like dome on the hill, in the moonlight, laughing at the iced cake perched on the hill, Mestrovic's prize cake, there, there, and then falling back, laughing, her hair like sea-fronds all about her.

There at night, her eyes shining in the dark that isn't a darkness but a white light, swimming in a buoyant sea, and leaving a phosphorescent wake breaking up, forming and going out from her, Olivia is slippery under the surface where I touch her, her responsive regions in the depths of which I am. And then her body opens there from within in a nocturnal confusion, and her eyes close, wincing, no doubt thinking that other tideless too saline sea is withdrawing, driven away by those words, as I advance a little further, and there is the white corvette against the wharf and the music of the mandolins.

I watched her sleeping in the airless bedroom in the Hotel Supetor, her face damp with perspiration.

I thought, She is beautiful. From her there emanated the true and basic sense of the life of the viscera, of hunger, and of animal warmth. The idea proper to stables, to haystacks, and from all lowly pragmatic sanctions. Her gem-like eyes, a child's, enunciated the name of a happiness that was still possible.

The hotel was Government-owned, the fan not working. It was inconvenient, possibly dangerous, to draw a bath. We ate out.

We saw Trebinje, Cetinje, Lake Scutari. The service in the Government-owned hotels was bad. The hoteliers were not interested in quick service. The rooms were ovens, the days hot and airless, the beaches a scourge of heat. Serbs the colour of teak sat at ten in the morning under small pines, with a cask of wine. The sea was transparent blue and very saline. There was a rumour of a shark in the Adriatic. Olivia did not become pregnant.

Since I saw it first in summer, for me it will always be high summer there. Odours of pine and eucalyptus and the beer tasting mineral, cooled in a basket let down into a well, and Kulinjic reciting 'To-pee-or-not-to-pee' with much feeling under the palm trees in the garden of the bar there near the square. And the musical comedy sailors dressed in white uniforms stood on the deck of the spotless white corvette of the Yugoslav navy, now playing mouth organs and staring after Olivia.

I was on the plaza at eight. Not long after, Charlotte came down and sat with me. She told me that an immense hound had followed her all the way home, and telling of this outsize stray had made it easier to face Bob, who had chased this veritable Hound of the Baskervilles away. This animal would not be seen again.

I felt myself perceptibly changed, charged by renewed relations with her, my senses alerted and profoundly stirred. He was not obtuse, far from it—this big seriously disposed man with the dinted yachting cap and Cruz de Mar cigars—he would smell incontinence from afar, and was probably truculent when aroused. No joke to be caught fooling about with his hot young wife.

I have no hound to distract him, I told her, and to tell you the truth I cannot face him at this particular minute.

I got up to leave, putting some money under the cup. She stared at me and her eyes had the bluish tinge which appeared behind the dark lashes like the Mediterranean behind a curtain of pines.

I want you to know that this winter meant something to me, she said, as if threatening me with her fidelity. That terrible thing: returned yet unrequited love.

And for me too, I said. (Words that are held to be binding).

I went by Calle Granada and Calle de las Animas to the bar El Molino in the Calle de San José.

II

Bob Bayless watched his cube of sugar dissolve slowly in a glass of coffee. A geographer's image of erosion. Knuckling one eye fiercely, affecting not to notice what was going on more or less in front of his nose; he stopped and glared at me with a very bloodshot eye.

Once, when I was sixteen and more gullible than I am now, he said, I went to Hollywood with a car-load of young rake-hells. I got out at the gates of one of the great studios and offered my services to the industry. They missed a chance. Coming out of the cafeteria I encountered Anne Blythe in pancake make-up—a skinny little thing with a face the size of (a vague gesture)—well, it looked too big for the rest of her. A perpetual close-up. I stood for five minutes only a few feet away from her, absolutely paralysed. She was alone, pointing my way, but she didn't see me. She looked but she didn't see. And when she walked by, she was close enough for me to smell the make-up. It was the happiest moment of my life. And if Anne—I always call her Anne—if Anne walked up to me today in her high heels and offered herself to me, I'd thrust myself upon her.

The table-cloth, a white check on a red ground, secured by steel clamps, was stained by chicken paella and Valdepeñas; Charlotte and I had shared two different courses. The Baylesses had insisted on standing us dinner at La Luna to celebrate the sale of one small oil painting (£25 less commission) in Dublin, where they had never been.

Two packets of Celtas cigarettes (a thick-set Viking brandishing a short sword), four glasses of coffee, four of cognac, a blue yachting cap dinted at the crown, were arranged in no particular order on the table. The valley, open for ribbon development, stood out in the moonlight, the olive groves below the Cortijo de Maro on the hill. A local real estate agency had put up a notice.

FOR SALE MIHS LIGLIT & WATER
Terrains a Vedrelleau Electricite

Vento de Paracelass con luz y agua
LIGCT WASSER ANCHLUSS!

The village was in sight, seven hundred metres below, a mile away on the *carretera*. The tree near the church on Plaza de las Iglesias was higher than the church itself. Gingko or Aleppo pine. The ancient Greek triremes, before the Phoenicians come to Malaga. Light streamed from the church door, a festive and holy light, but far away.

I'm talking of drive-ins, seductions in parked cars, Bob said. I have gone in for this pursuit myself as a young shaver. Sure I have. If the girl consents to go with you alone it can hardly fail. Though a seduction in a parked car requires a special sort of approach. Problems with gearshifts, steering wheels—buttocks striking or, worse again, pressed against the cold instrument panel. But what could be better after all, than turning around for a breather and finding the ripe charms of let us say Betty Grable stretched twenty-five feet across the screen, smack before your eyes? A smoochy kiss, distorted thus, has the impact of a train collision and the sound jars like a rifle-shot. Of course you can always bring booze along, boxes of tissues, lubricants (glaring at me with an infuriated eye.) And there is the hideous pleasure of publicity. Even while smoking and to all appearances gazing at the screen, your true lover has one hand applied persuasively. The ruin of it comes with the intermission. Suddenly lights go on, and they are the sort of lights that illuminate fields for night baseball—but blue-white. So the girl turns blue. And out of the loudspeakers comes wretched unromantic music. You have to walk half a mile for coffee, and stand there with men whose lips are bruised, and trousers bothering them. Still, there is a sort of comradeship that develops. Nods, inquisitive greetings; a victor says 'Guess I better wash up'—can't be too delicate. A loser complains that he has been cut out by the moon. Or Betty Grable. Might as well be in a theatre. They sip their coffee, smoke, gaze out over the cars wherein passion has flared and abated. The refreshment stands are always sideless shacks, cheerless places. The girl's coffee cools. Then the music stops and the lights go out; the men wink at one another and depart. Soon crushed paper cups are dropped from half-closed windows, and automobile springs begin to groan in chorus. My California.

⚶

Sayings of Bob Bayless: Good Faulkner gets better with time, bad Faulkner worse. Stick with me, honey, and in a couple of years you'll be farting through silk. Lace-curtain Irish.

III

Returning late one night from the taberna that stank right royally of lavatory, I climbed the stairs, none too sober now, saw the light shining under Olivia's door, knocked and she said to come in. I entered and found her lying naked on the covers, reading a book and smoking a Celtas through a long amber holder, her bison-brown hair confined in two braids, *liga de goma*, as the Andalusian girls wear it. Her dimpled back, the braids tied with rubber bands, her bare backside, conferred a look of innocence that her posture (Gauguin's Spirit Watching) and physical development denied; for if there was something

147

of little girl innocence about the braids and bottom, whiter than the rest of her, the tendresse and division of the back, the broadness of the hips were adult woman. An inviting behind, a promising bottom, wide target-practice area: Olivia's *Ars Amatoria*. Calmly positioned, patiently waiting, true femininity. The pelvis girdle fitted suavely into the vertebral column; then the arched globes—shutters and screens of secret lusts. *En prise* on the sheets, in a good position to be taken. Gauguin's dark temptress or Boucher's famous erotic sprawl of Mlle O'Morphy's elegant backside? At all events a poured voluptuousness hardly to be contained in one poor room. The calmly fixed gaze of her tawny eyes were fixed on a text that seemed about to burst into flames. *Ruhendes Mädchen!*

I felt myself swayed, awaited by a pair of appeals, or (as one might say) suggestive matter. The antagonistic thrust of those well-muscled layers, moving away from me, had caused me, in my time, some anxious pain and sorrow. *Nec tecum*; *sine nec te*: our life together, where had it gone wrong?

Globes of fire turned in the mirrors, encircled by rings of smoke. Olivia said nothing, her eyes fixed steadfastly on the text. I recalled another time when she had lain on her then scarless stomach in a train travelling to Ljubjana, groaning and complaining of 'apricot sickness'. In the Mater Hospital in Dublin surgeon Burke had removed gallstones the size of olives. Olivia's hard drupe. Now she lay on that long scar, and on an appendicitis scar, but her true nature belonged more properly to her back and behind, the back she never saw, her *dos*, beautiful, smooth, intelligent—if one can say that of the back. She was divided in two by her spine.

She said the heat was 'killing' her, as an explanation of her nudity. Light is the body's life. Pregnant hills. Olivia Grieve *passim*.

I'm sweating like a bull, Olivia said.

I felt the weight of my eyelids, my time, remorse for the happiness I could not give her. This darkly blooming secret flower, the pull of darkness, sadness. The sheet was doubled carelessly under her, a defenceless hind showing her *hartbeest* flanks. Warm and sedate, her breasts crushed together, the hard nipples of a childless woman. *Potentilla nitida*. Her scent: marzipan, kissing comfits, fruit preserved in syrup. I sat on the edge of the bed. At the *feria*, with bare arms and backs, the girls in their traditional Flamenco costumes rode the swings. Young pullets with sharp shoulder-blades, the satiny backs of the mature girls. Do they not wear bras? I asked Olivia, referring to the pullets. I'm sure Charlotte didn't at their age, she had said sourly.

I asked her what she was reading. *Middlemarch*. Restless and not sober I sat there and the fan turned languidly in the warm night air and the flies hovered. The hourly air-patrol was passing above the house, US bombers growling in the darkness. Olivia sighed and closed her book. The bedsprings groaned as I moved.

It's been so long, Olivia murmured, I feel like a war widow.

Middlemarch fell to the floor. The jets passed away into silence.

IV

At the top of the flight of stairs Amory and I came out on to an empty terrace. Weeds sprouted there. A narrow flight of broken steps went on a little way and then stopped, fell away into nothing, air. *Je regrette l'Europe aux anciens parapets.* A medley of voices coming from below indicated where children were playing in some playground. The cries came faintly or not at all. Busts of Romans heavy on their pedestals stood among the weeds: coarse-featured men with bloated eyes, though perhaps the several likenesses of true Emperors. Ivy grew among the stone. Amory turned to me and said, That's it. Not perhaps as fine as the Villa d'Este in autumn. I prefer it to the Villa d'Este in autumn.

We stood in the Generalife gardens above the main building where the white faces of German tourists stared from windows. We were on a hillside to the east. Charlotte said that the hedges stank of tom-cat. We stood in a group around Amory, our Alhambran guide. What now? Bob asked. Where now? *Nada mas*, Amory said, *Finito, amigo*. That'll be 75 pesetas each. He held out his hand, looking pleased. Well, he had after all been a good guide. What do you want to do next, Amory asked. I'm at your disposal. He kept looking at Charlotte. She had a smile for him.

Now my love caused me extreme anguish. I felt out of sight and far way, although I was near her. I had watched them and it seemed to me that they had been up to something. My jealousy now fastened onto Amory as a magnet drags at iron filings. He was running away with her and I could do nothing about it.

My insides were scalding, entrails falling out, and although I was standing there, rooted to the spot, my craven spirit fled away at top speed. Ashamed, I could not look at her.

There's a sign for you in the sky, Charlotte told me (behind her a kind of grotto, dark with ferns, the sound of water falling). I looked up at the white jet trail stretching from zenith to zenith cut short by the Generalife walls. The sky sign seemed to indicate that I was finished.

They had hurried away from me. In some hidden place they had come together. Guides in green Forest Ranger caps, hidden here and there and waiting for just this, watched them kissing. I came upon Amory looking smutty-faced and mighty pleased with himself, his legs stretched out. He stared at her, but she would not look at him. Bob trailed behind, pale and constipated.

Amory's DKW had a flat back tyre. Fuck that, Amory said, I'll take it to a garage. Nonsense, Olivia said, there are two men here. Did she mean I was no man because I could not drive a car nor mend a flat, whereas Amory drove like the wind. Amory left the car in a garage. We walked among the trees and she saw it. You could leave it there, Charlotte said. I went back to tell Amory that a garage was there at the bottom of the hill. We coasted down with the engine off. Did you try her? I asked. Amory looked at me strangely. Why, yes, he said. what do you want now?

I want my love to die.

But instead we went to a small bar below the gypsy quarter, where between them they completed my defeat and humiliation.

They revealed themselves as adepts. We had booked into a hotel where Charlotte took the best double room. Nothing unusual in that. We went out. Olivia slept. Amory took on Charlotte at pin-ball. Amory lifted the machine up, coloured lights flashed, padded American footballers with degenerate faces from strip cartoon crouched motionless on a blazingly verdant field. Was it perhaps Kezer Stadium? It rattles your kidneys, Amory said. Bob had gone out to buy a present for Daisy. I stood mortified at the bar and watched them. I had seen them playing on the beach 'horsing about', Amory (tuft-tailed Pan in rut) whinnying, Charlotte screeching, her costume torn off her, falling on the sand, Amory with an erection.

Generalife, Charlotte said. I used to think it meant General Life. An insurance company.

You're getting education, Amory said.

Bob came into the bar with a parcel under his arm. Charlotte wanted to see it. He took out of the cardboard box a small white wooden horse. I want a present too, Amory said. You can have this fine pin-ball machine, Charlotte said, if it doesn't rattle your kidneys too much. I suspected that she was inferring something else, less innocent than what she actually said. She seemed to be saying, I am your present. And you can engage in foul and endless copulation with this girl ('rattle her kidneys'), because I'd like nothing better.

All right, Amory said.

Charlotte laughed gaily. Bob looked a trifle mystified. I looked into my glass and saw only dregs. Olivia was in the hotel off Plaza de Bibarrambla, sleeping. She was always sleeping. Amory went to the garage at the time the man had told him to come. He came back in the DKW and we climbed in, the Baylesses in the back and I in the front with Amory.

Hey! Charlotte said, what's this? She had sat on a bar of chocolate. It's soft, she said, it's melting. It's yours, she said, giving it to Amory. Give it to Sandy at midnight, she said. (I'm soft, I'm melting. Give it to me at midnight.)

All right, Amory said.

I saw Bob's face in the little mirror. I saw grottoes, a hedge in a courtyard cut as the Star of David, a flight of broken steps leading nowhere, a distant blackened rail terminal, the baked brown vega, yellow mustard weed on the roofs of Granada, an inscription cut into stone.

DALE LIMOSNA, MUJER,
Que no hay en la Vida
nada como la pena de ser
ciego en Granada

The wedging action of dust was forcing apart the cracks in the reddish walls of the old fortress. Imperceptibly yet irresibly dust trickled down the superficies, moving massive stones apart.

The most beautiful flight of steps in the whole world, Olivia said, but when you get up close, quite shabby and nothing much at all. (*Todo su historia es mentira.*)

I wanted you to see it, Amory said.

Charlotte at another time had said to me: Marriage seems to me like some out-moded mystery. And: Once you've had a love affair, it's difficult to go back to the old stuff.

The confidences of one sensual woman: oldest sound to reach the porches of man's ear.

I had waited in the Orangery near the municipal market. It was almost midday. I had been to Vine's flat with a note but had not delivered it. I had waited in the Orangery since before eleven, trying to decide how I would ask Vine for the loan of his key. He was going to Torremolinos with Sally Lester, who had been invited on board HMS *Ark Royal* at Gibraltar.

The midday bus left for Malaga without them aboard. As I walked away someone called my name. Olivia had been hiding in the Orangery, spying. She was jealous of Sally Lester. We went down towards the plaza together, I marvelling at Olivia.

One afternoon I was painting in the front room, Olivia's bedroom, when I heard someone coming upstairs, and in walked Sally Lester. She was dressed in extremely close-fitting silk slacks, black under a white shirt open generously, and Cuban boots. She came over to the table and put down an outsize pot of Marmite, a present from Gibraltar. Without saying a word she left again. Charlie Vine had perhaps instructed her not to interrupt my work.

It was a wooden bridge. The arms came down to reach the spans. The river was brown. The bridge was unlit. I walked over the bridge where a young couple were standing and looking into the water. I bought a cigar in a kiosk, lit it and walked back towards the bridge. The cigar began to come to pieces in my mouth.

Now the bridge was unlit. Evening had come down. The lovers were embracing. *Aranjuez!* The royal flower beds. The King of Spain's court. The Queen's tantrums. Plaza de las Armas. Carlist wars, pretenders to the throne, foreign marriages. A royal breast on the wooden parapet, royal arms on polished wood, a tired royal smile down in the water. The river kept its counsel, its secrets. The evening was marvellous. The Rio Tajo flowed under the bridge where the lovers were embracing as if in the depth of a wood.

Six rivers flow through Spain. They are the arteries which run between the seven mountain chains, the vertebrae of the geological skeleton.

12 SHE PRAISES MY COURTESY: I'd seen her from Burriana, a small neat figure in a broad brim straw hat with a wide blue ribbon waving down to me (putting on trousers, preparing to go up). I had been longing for her to come. I climbed the path to meet her.

She stayed where the waterfall came down—dry now— explaining that she couldn't come as she had promised, because her husband was restless, and spoke of going out and working somewhere in the shade. She didn't want him to see us together, she said, smiling down at me. Crouching there on the slope of rock, heels under her haunches so that her hips bulged out on either side, her knees together, she was open to me like a flower. Her inviting posture said: Have me. Her eyes: Yes, I want you. She said: No woman would have done that, come all the way up.

Her posture and willing eyes looking fixedly at me, her young sensuality much suppressed, subtle preparatory moves, on the brink of something. She had given the *visu*: that notorious first look which transfixes and inflames, in Antonio Cerezo's dim bar. You, looking fixedly up at me, I perceive you there standing below me.

Leaning forward until her brown knees were level with my chest, her shaded face drawn down to mine (she had removed her sunhat), her lips above my lips. Intense feeling flooded into me. I was held bound within the aura of her charms, about to penetrate one of her adopted disguises. She had revealed something secretly to me, something intensely private (she, the youngest of three daughters of Yiddish-speaking parents, immigrants from Eastern Europe, running a corner grocery store on the Lower East Side, a Jewish store that stayed open until the last customer left at night, who had served behind the counter), a Jewish girl with brilliant eyes, all her future reflected there, the colour of her special being, innocent of any moral sense, a valour that required protection. Bob, her husband and protector (sweating and typing through the afternoon), had said: She thinks she can handle anything. I thought: Yes, anything but failure.

I don't want him to see us together, she said. But her bold eyes had already said: *Take me if you want me, as I perceive you do.* She would not have minded what my instincts prompted me to do, her eyes affirmed. There was something about the day. She was smiling down at me, her whitening knees above my eye level. Crouching there on the warm slab of rock, she had said: See us together; not catch us together, and I liked her directness.

All right, I said. Can we meet later? What beach will you go to?

She thought Torrecillas after lunch.

I'll be there, I said. We'll go there about three.

She went back the way she had come, a small neat person, a strutter, a gripper-of-the-earth; her scholar husband restless, possibly suspicious, had spoken of coming out and sitting somewhere in the shade. She told me, her head and shoulders against the sun, arch of the eyebrows, nose, mouth, a high-liner, a skin-scent like candy. Her Cointreau breath; hers the privileged body on which the light fell to perfection. I was deep within her affections and held secret riot there.

⁂

One overcast afternoon we sat under an umbrella outside Miguel's bar. She had her back to the plaza and faced the open door of the bar. I watched the light going off the sierras above Maro.

It was one of those grey overcast Maine days, Charlotte said, when the sun goes in and out and I didn't mind it. We had a clambake and then began drinking beer. I never drank so much beer or enjoyed drinking it so much. Never got so tight on beer.

I asked her what was a clambake: She told me and explained where Bar Harbour was situated and what it was like there.

She nibbled food (a Jewish trait, according to the Chameleon) and was very fond of fruit. 'That small woman.' That Jewy woman. I asked her to explain *schlemiel*. Why was Saul Bellow a *schlemiel*? She spoke of her childhood and her first boyfriend, an athlete, a swimmer. She had dragged the telephone into a cubbyhole filled with junk for a marathon four-hour gab with him. He was a 'great swimmer'; they went spear-fishing at night. Her married sister had long, tedious conversations on the telephone. Charlotte said: Why do people who lead the most humdrum lives have to talk about it? Their perceptions dulled, they spoke only of their boredom.

Charlotte had felt ashamed of being Jewish until she came to Europe. It had taken Christians talking of Jews to make her feel proud of being one. I thought she meant me, talking of Nathaniel West and Babel and Primo Levi; but she did not mean me. Bloom, she said. The invention of a Christian, I said.

I told her that I'd watched her through Vine's binoculars at the corrida in Malaga. She had been sitting on *tenido*, six rows above the barrier on the *sol* side. The sun was hot in April, in Malaga.

Yeah, she said, we were sitting right on the bullgate.

Dolphins jump in the Mediterreanean in April: sign of settled weather.

PART III

Winter 1962

Spain

13 CAVE: The cave is entered by descending to a depth of some five metres by a stairway which leads into a hall under the roof, fourteen metres in diameter and five or six high. This vestibule opens into a winding corridor of white calcite; half-way along the corridor an opening on the right leads into a small chamber at a slightly higher level—a small room like an entrance hall, used as a store-room and called the *Oficina*. This hall is triangular in shape, orientated more or less east–west, with some forty metres along its greater side, and ten along the shorter; at the bottom there are various hollow spaces.

A staircase built on to the rock descends to the Sala de la Cascada, so called because of a fanciful resemblance to a petrified waterfall. From its balcony you can see the Sala del Cataclismo some two hundred metres forward in the illuminated depths of the cavern. The hall is roughly triangular in shape, the longer side measuring some fifty metres; the roof is twenty-five metres high and about thirty wide. Archaeological specimens include vessels of different kinds, neolithic implements and human remains.

The geological original of the cave goes back to the Miocene period of the Upper Tertiary, the period immediately before the Quaternary; the Quaternary being the last of the four main geological periods into which the history of the earth has been divided.

All prehistory, all the darkly entwined ancient world, world of boulders and animal skins and mankind's first formless and uncoordinated thought, must have been permeated by an immense sexual reverie and longing (heart-beat of lion, brawl of beast, dark and primitive loves, thick hair standing on end on the short bully neck, testicles of goat, tyranny of lust): passion coming from such deep sources.

The rotting humus in the lawnmower's catch had a damp and sweetish smell of warmth and cyclical corruption (germination). Humus disturbs me and stimulates my imagination as the smell of rotten apples stimulated Schiller's imagination. (He kept some rotting away in a drawer of his writing desk.) Whereas Amory's imagination was fired by the smell of excrement. (Nine million tons of crude excrement—he said 'ecrement'—poured daily into the Hudson River, he told me. These statistics made his brain reel.) The exuberance of the eternal lymph.

The chemical composition of skatal, the volatile aromatic portion of human faeces, is very close to jasmine. These two odours have a common root. The smell of the lawnmower's catch at Howth Castle. The smell of Malaga after rain. A brown ligneous aroma. Like brown standing-water in the boles of partly rotted trees. Maja-odour, scent of leaves. Maja-scented evenings, Andalusian summer night, dry earth, magnolia, vapoury sky. Ambergris. Thermal evenings.

That which is past is past; that which is wished for may not (cannot) come again. Certain scents imply: *a longing for what cannot come again.* Charlotte assenting.

(A mossy path by the Garavogue, an abstracted temptress sauntering there. A tank of well-water, its sides coated with green moss. My seed floating there like frogspawn in Sligo long ago.)

14 DUENDE: Days begin with cold *anis* and hot coffee. From my window I see the drenched mountains. A pair of dampened turkeys scratch about in the sodden yard below. The half-completed Saviour stares at me from the easel. Finish me, says Christ before Pilate. Details should be many or none.

Morning downpours of heavy rain, leakings into all the rooms, some watercolours spoiled, and rainwater spewing from the mouths of the dog-headed gargoyles. Calle de las Angustias, numero 16. Gushings and splashings all around our new home. The catch-basins on Calle Pintada choked, a shallow river runs into the Puerta del Mar. Tertullian comes to the window of Heaven to rejoice in the sight of the damned.

The turkeys are stalking each other, their crests puffed out like shields. Clouds are forming over the sierras. A damp, depressing day. Which Felipe had left money for one hundred thousand masses to be offered for the repose of his royal soul?

Daylight begins to go in the late afternoon. The half-finished Station on the easel starts to loose its forms, inundated with Nature's version of Matisse's 'black light'. Finish me, implored the eyes of the man about to be flogged, for God's sake, I am the Poor-Mouth-Jesus. I leave the room.

Antonio Cerezo's bar is empty, not even a barman in sight. At the head of Calle Italia a niche now illuminated shows a foolish-looking Saviour rolling His eyes heavenwards and holding in His limp hands some long-stemmed flowers. Looking along Calle Cristo to a cramped view of the sierras (cumin seeds), wherever I look there are mountains and impossible Saviours. A tall man in a loose overcoat comes into the bar. He says *buenas tardes* and goes behind the counter and lifts the lids from the arrangement of *tapas* put there by Antonio's spinster sister. A man in his seventies, prosperous-looking with a long cigar, he puts the *puro* in his mouth and goes out without a word, as Antonio comes with more *tapas* from the kitchen.

Duende! Antonio says, pointing with his chin after the departing one, and raising one sceptical, circumflex eyebrow. Antonio Cerezo Criado has the longest and curliest eyelashes in all Andalusia and at one time captained a Malaga soccer team. Now he ran the bar for his father, who was ailing. *Duende!* Antonio repeats in a stage whisper. He makes a face; his moist brown eyes bulge. Yes, Dan? he scuffles his shoes on the boards, nodding at me. Aye, Dan? He takes a few dance steps on the catwalk, laughing silently. Few patronized his bar, but it did not seem to worry him. His heavy mahogany-coloured brother collected bad debts and acted as pot-boy on Sunday nights when the bar was full, and for his pains was treated like dirt. Antonio took a day off twice a year and then his brother managed the bar.

I walk through the bar past the poster of an antique cognac-drinker. The patriarchal greybeard's lips are pressed together in a severe straight line, dark as the slit of a letter-box. He holds in his wormy-veined hands an inferior brand of cognac. Antonio's sister Carme is in the kitchen, standing on a chair by the window with one finger to her lips, holding a glass of water in her free hand. Then she flings the contents out and bangs the window down. It's the *Duende*, the tapas-taster, snooping in the yard. He lives next door. *Un hombre muy malo*, she says, rolling her eyes just like her elder brother. *Poco loco!*

She is strongly-built, perhaps thirty years old. Both her parents suffered strokes and now she looks after them. She made fiery *tapas*, looked out the small porthole in the room above the bar door, rather tied down, with little liberty, no free life at all. She passes in and out through the door with her hair in curlers like the Gorgon Medusa, a resentful force. Her colouring is high, a toned-down version of her mahogany-coloured brother. She is sad, terribly caught (*Strašné šmutné*). She speaks to Olivia and Charlotte, to Tracey Weddick, a free lady. Laura looking for Petrach. Her life is all old flesh, stale old flesh, bedpans. Even the fishermen, whom her brother despises, has more of a life than she; even the *campo* workers, whom Antonio puts a little above the fishermen in his scale of values. Meagre values. The *campo* workers would not work on the sea and the fishermen refused to work on the land, but Carme is tied to old stale flesh and bedpans, a view of the Puerta del Mar through the little porthole above the bar door —and what kind of life is that? Carme had eyes like Melmoth's, which no one wants to see, for once seen, they are impossible to forget. Carme Cerezo Criado dreamed of love.

From the *retrete* at the rear, trying to be quiet, I hear her banging pots and pans together out of delicacy. When I return to the bar some locals have come in, not *campo* workers or fishermen (for Antonio would not serve them, or served them with such discourtesy that they would not come again), but a shopkeeper and a clerical worker. The latter might have been Irish, a grey-haired gregarious man with a breast pocket full of pens and pencils, to indicate his social status. A great spitter. The other was a tall man with a long nose, he had dusty skin and had lost most of his hair, owned a hardware establishment that sold sanitary equipment. They are drinking small vino tintos and listening to Antonio lay down the law.

The dear normality of contingency, the healthy ingenuousness of custom.

15 AN OLD BREADWOMAN: The days are cold, often wet. A freezing wind blows off the sierras and sets its teeth into those who walk out early. The fishermen go hunched up in their thin clothes; the older women cover the lower part of their faces and go in purdah close to the wall. The cold eats into the arthritic bones of the old breadwoman who suffers from hardening of the arteries and rheumatism, her eyes and nose perpetually running. Painfully, bent double with hardship and age, she creeps up the stairs, too steep for her, croaking, at the limit of her strength *Pan! Pan!*

Her voice disturbs my sleep, rouses me, I smell rain. I quit my bed, collect some money. She stands at the head of the stairs trying to catch her breath, weeping cataracts of eyes dimly focus on me, dimly perceive me. I pay her, take the fresh bread, thank her. She goes away. I go back to bed. The freezing wind blows over the snow mountains that cuts off the town from the interior, as all Spain is cut off from Europe by the Pyrenees. Even worse weather rages beyond.

A day passes.

The old rheumy-eyed breadwoman stands stupefied with cold at the foot of the stairs that I have forbidden her to climb. She waits at the foot of the glacier, calling up *Pan!* drawing a deep shuddering breath, wheezing again *Pan!* Her voice summons me from deep sleep. I put on a raincoat and go down. Her gnarled hands and wrists are knotted like wood, the knuckles shiny; long arms deformed with age, thin and scraggy as branches, hair the colour of sea-grass. Her hooded eyes are filmy like a bird's, the *arcus senilus* has spread; she speaks close to my face, and from her breath I smell decay. She touches my hand, trusts me, her semi-paralysed hands fumble at the purse and presents me with bent *centimos* deformed as her own extremities. She persists in trying to find the correct change although she can hardly see, the sums clog in her bothered mind. She doles single pesetas into my hand, fifty-centavo pieces, a few silver five-peseta pieces. *Un duro!* she says. For her it's still *duro*, an extinct currency, although stamped with the choleric features of the Generalissimo. In another year there will be twenty-five years of peace in the land. The old breadwoman was already over sixty when peace broke out. Now she tries to add and subtract an extinct currency in her mind. *Un duro*, she says, pressing it into my hand, but a little later takes it from me again, begins a long tot on the table, using her fingers to count. Maravedos issued by Alfonso the Wise at Burgos; ducados worth about six pesetas in the sixteenth century. The cramped fingers press a silver *duro* stamped with the suffused features of the little pop-eyed (mark of intelligence, ambition, vision, will-power) Generalissimo and some bent and useless *centimos* into my numb hand. *Señor*, the expiring voice whispers, *Senor . . . Es correcto?* The gnarled fingers push the sea-grass from her eyes, the troubled eyes observe me. The heavy basket packed with bread lies at her feet. *Si, si, perfectamento, Madre*, I say. She sighs, bends for it, with surprising strength lifts it. Take up thy bread and walk. I go back up the stairs, stand at the window of the little balcony and watch her go. A little old woman bent with age carrying a heavy bread basket. I think of James Clarence Mangan walking along the dark Dublin quays, a man of the night, and the half-blind and irascible Degas towards the end of his life, walking the streets of Paris in an Inverness cape, tapping his way, always alone. He had no use for cant, flowers, humbug, fools and Jews. A true Frenchman, anti-Dreyfusard like Forain. A lover of horses and ballet girls. Old age, old age, that uncomfortable time.

I dressed, made a pot of coffee. Olivia was not yet stirring. A book by her bed; she was into *Middlemarch*. The thin sunlight had already entered her room. I left the coffee for her and went out.

On the Plaza José Antonio Primo de Rivera the thinly slanting sunlight moved, seemed to stir the surface that I walked on, crossed with the shadows of the palms. The *paseo* was the tilted

deck of a liner ploughing through heavy seas. I took a few turns
up and down. Rough seas to port and starboard, whirling guts.
I do not care for sea-travel. I saw shovels, bundles of reinforc-
ing bars gone rusty in the rain, a cement mixer, bags of the
stuff, a mound of sand, but no workers. I entered the Balcon
de Europa bar. The woman gave me coffee and cognac. Miguel
had not yet come from his home at the end of Calle de los
Huertos. From where I sat, waiting for the coffee, I saw sierras
capped in snow, palm trees and a window shining in Maro.
Outside the plaza moved, seemed to move.

My queasy stomach.

I swallowed the hot coffee and observed the sacral hoods of the
penitentes. Soon it would be *Festividad de Todos los Santos*, and
then *Commemoracion de los Fieles Difuntos*, and then *Santa Silvia*
on November 3, and a week from that would be Polish Inde-
pendence Day. *Los Fieles Difuntos*, the feast-day of all massacred
ones flung into mass-graves and also the feast of those who
passed away peacefully in bed. *Funes accensi* with garlands of
flowers. Richard Ford had called it the region of hot passions,
land of carob and oleander, but it was cold enough in the bar.
He had written that Jews stink. A perfect Englishman of his
time. The masked *penitentes* came on towards me, brandishing
huge maces. The hooded Brethren of the Misericordia—
delectatio morosa attempting to translate itself into reality, force
itself into life. After the Black Death no Jew was safe in Europe;
in the reign of the bigoted Catholic Queen a million of them
had been deported from the *tierra caliente*. I thought of the
Jews of Thessalonika and Amsterdam and how they kept the
keys of their lost Spanish houses as icons. I was attempting to
paint one of their race with a conspicuous lack of success, not
once but many times. One cannot say his name with too much
familiarity (except in times of distress) or see his face, and for
convenience sake we call him Saviour. Who had ever rendered
his human image convincingly? El Bosco in his tropical animal-
infested Eden? He stood between Eve and Adam, God as
Referee. A shadowy God that you could hardly perceive in full
sunlight. To seek to paint that which cannot be painted—the
Deity's human form—was considered by the wise Ancients

to be human imbecility. Pliny's thought. I stared at the *penitentes*. They came bearing down on me with their maces, but told me nothing. Someone touched my shoulder. I turned about. Miguel stood there. The day had begun.

16 ROSA MUNSINGER'S SINGULAR STOOLS: Rosa Munsinger told Tracey Weddick that she was collecting old newspapers as a 'kind of therapy'. When she felt one of her depressions coming on (and she felt one coming along already) she was going to take the papers and stuff her poof. Rosa's secret life, Tracey said. The daily ABC, the unique Monarchist rag.

I told Charlotte, who laughed. *Her* frailty and moods only made her more beautiful: her low blood pressure and tendency to fainting fits. I saw her sometimes as a child, not the lower East Side Jewish tough kid but that other less favoured shadow —the Polish Jewess Gittle Mosca. Still a child, an innocent, thin and sad, she did not weep, could scarcely smile; more a flower than a beast. But feminine, always that, incorrigibly so; and therefore prone to change; already practising the art. Lotte Lipski.

Her eyes, those swimming, imagining eyes, were Nile-blue. The long neck gave a certain delicate balance to the head, snake on the end of a stick, poised to strike. Something of that, a threat. The heavy braid of hair kept the small striking head upright on her shoulders, causing her eyes to protrude a little (Ingres' *Baigneuse*) the effort of being beautiful was a positive strain. Nefertiti's head. Was it the Egyptian sculptors who incised a thin line at the base of the neck where age begins to attack and deface with lines that are coarser, the change of life? I could not think of Charlotte defaced by age; that long column of the neck, almost disdainful, and the classical ophthalmic stare, a certain aura about forehead and temples. Her cheeks had the perfect oval form that belongs to the young. Did it matter if she had monkey paws, quite simian? It did not matter. The contour and skin texture of her bare brown arms were extremely shapely in contrast to their extremities; she was round and ripened. Do with your hands what you can do with your hands, Charlotte.

The broadening and coarsening that alters a woman past a certain age, the putting on of flesh, had begun and was proceeding along orthodox lines in the person of Rosa Munsinger. Her dressmaker in Frigiliana had remarked jocosely on her broad beam, what she termed *pompi*, and very down to earth Rosa called 'my ass'. What matter? Rosa was proud of it, good substantial matter after all.

She spoke to Bob Bayless of trouble of a more intimate nature, and what she had done to overcome it. Now she was having odourless stools. A noiseless inoffensive vent, Bob Bayless told me.

Rosa, a heavy smoker of Celtas (she bought packs of five at a time from the consumptive tobacconist on Calle Pintada), showed at times small brown shreds of black tobacco on her heavy smoker's lips. She talked and talked, the themes always revolving about herself, fat self-smelling appreciation, and I watched and listened.

A lubricious Spanish lady, all décolletée stood in the tobacconist's shop, bending and addressing a small pampered dog, ordered an American brand. I and the consumptive tobacconist stared down the front of her tight dress. She had adhesive tape on her ripened lower lip, where a bee had stung her.

Rosa had small brown spots of tobacco on her smoker's lips, like the spots on the spines of certain books. *Mosca caca*. Flyshit on *The Golden Bowl* and *What Maisie Knew*. I had never observed very carefully Rosa Munsinger's hands or any other part of her extremities. That broad quivering calf, that tumultuous butt, that foot set down on the middle of the roadway with such resolution. She advised me not to overdo the red wine as vino tinto discoloured your teeth. It hardly matters, I said, mine are in ruins as it is. No, Rosa said, very solemn (very Jewish in this), you must hold on to your teeth. While you have them.

She advised me to drink lots of local water, as its calcium content was exceptionally high. I said that I never drank water. Oh, but you get it all the same, Rosa assured me, in soups and coffee.

Save me, Rosa said (serious as sin), from my soft heart and good nature. I am too kind, it was implied (the inference reinforced by a brown glance from her snaky eyes, to see how this pabulum was going down, for we mistrusted each other and always had). Teach me to say no, Rosa said, looking at me around her nose. I laughed in her face. This was splendid duplicity and no mistake; she was fishing for compliments again, and yet vain of her sagacity (and what was that but more self-interest? vanity was a circle she would not break out of). Once more the incense was rising on the altar Rosa had erected to herself, to Rosálba de Pudica.

Certainly, I said. Count on me.

She looked at me quickly and then laughed. Behind the more or less constant self-seeking, what formidable will-power was there! And all directed towards her own interests: self-aggrandizement, the inveterate disease of self-love. It may be affirmed that she was prone to spasms of self-complacency, very open to the sin of self-esteem, often surveying with some complacency the field of her own ineffable nature, and in the habit of taking for granted, on poor evidence, that *she* was always perfectly in the right. She treated herself to occasions of homage.

Forgetfulness of self, the most primitive source of courtesy, was unknown to Rosa Munsinger. She was still giving me a suspicious eye, around the corner of her nose.

I'll never do it again, Rosa said, never. People took advantage of kindness and good-heartedness, yes. One put oneself out to oblige, and you got only more trouble and no thanks.

I tried to recall genuine acts of disinterested charity performed by Rosa. Certainly she had given No. 12 rent-free to the Bayless family. But they were nice Americans. And Charlotte was Jewish like herself. Was not that perfect Christian charity? It only looked like it, Lady Bountiful. If Rosa performed a generous act, it was to profit from it—if only to the extent of hearing someone say that she was generous. She was not. And if she was charming and amusing (and she could be both, when she forgot her persona for a time), it was only so that others could say of her that Rosa was both charming and amusing and the best possible company (which she could be at times). There was an unpleasant side to those 'generous' acts: a self-promotional basis for what she did, asking no thanks but begging for something else. She did all for an effect, attempting feminine airs and graces, sweeping bows as one came in at the door, her exquisite sketches of ballet steps, pointed; her proficiency in Twist, Hully Gully amazed her New York dancing teachers. All this was wily, a beck and a nod towards a past about which she would very soon begin to bore me. When Rosa as a young thing danced in old Vienna. Look at this! Look at me! bowing, dancing, laughing, having 'fun'. Am I not admirable in every imaginable way? She had never grown up, she was still a bright little girl unable to stop conniving. In this world everybody gets what he helps himself to, and no more, and this is particularly the case with women, who have much more reason than men to make good use of their time while they may. For when they grow old neither their husbands nor anyone else will look at them, and they are sent into the kitchen to talk to the cat and count the pots and pans.

Rosa Munsinger had a theory that, given the existing rate of development, carbon monoxide fumes from traffic would make the planet uninhabitable by the first quarter of the next century. No lung-breathing creature would survive into the second half of the twenty-first century, Rosa believed. She had heavy haunches, her thighs quivered, she rolled along monumentally —self-obsessed to an Addinsonian degree.

She said: *My* algarroba tree . . .

It was a gnarled old algarroba tree that grew in a siding by the bridge near La Luna. *My* algarroba tree. She had sat under it, surprising a pack-rat in the act of moving a sardine tin into the tree. She threw a stone and it disappeared. I said that I had never heard of a rat living in a tree. Rosa assured me that she had seen the pack-rat pushing the tin into the tree.

Was Munsinger a Viennese name? It was her maiden name? No, it was her married name. Her maiden name was awkward to spell, difficult to pronounce, and impossible to remember. She spoke of Klaus Munsinger, who lived in New York and was in the 'art racket'. He blackened his face at parties, spoke like Henry Fonda.

When Rosa went to London on a business trip she ran into Fay Blair, Amory's discarded Canadian girlfriend. She was going about with lesbians in Chalk Farm. Rosa spoke warmly of

Fay's 'warm', 'out-going' nature. Rosa herself was immediately accepted by all Fay's friends. Indeed she felt that by accepting luncheon engagements, she was conferring a favour on *them*. Rosa here laughed down her nose; *I* was neither warm nor outgoing, that much was certain. She had an absolutely insatiable appetite for flattery, and I could give her none.

She had danced the Twist in front of Bob Bayless at Los Vientos. Brodey turned off Bach or Brahms, and Rosa got up and started wagging her behind in Bob's face. I couldn't very well ask them to turn it off, he said. Embarrassing.

Still, she has her moments, he admitted. But it's dangerous to believe in what she seems to be. One often has the impression that there is another desperate woman underneath.

I imagine she is hardly more than she seems, I said.

No Gittel Mosca. Once, perhaps, she had been that in gay Vienna. She and her parents had left Nazi Austria, moving to a new life in America. Rosa's past had drowned on the convoy going over.

Brodey, whose company I did not seek, danced attention. She was never on her own, Brodey tagged along, carrying ice. Wherever Rosa was, there too was her Moose Jaw. He had a born grafter's deep voice, confounding the Spaniards by slapping them on the back, declaiming into their faces *Que pasa, hombre?* He worked on popularity like a politician seeking rural votes; distributing largesse in the form of benevolence, high-handed patronage—stump speeches delivered *con moto*. They had lived together for eleven years in Torremolinos, watched it change from fishing village to the Sodom and Gomorrah of the Costa del Sol. He knew the Spaniards, he said.

Brodey, the best the coast could offer in the way of bronzed self-assured American male heel, was a crafty mixture of New World bounce and Old World charm. Boaster and bester among equals, King amid loyal subjects (Brodey with Spaniards); did the latter detect the high patronage of his manner, the back-thumping? I think so. Brodey was admired because he had *muchas mujeres*; he was not popular. Both Con and Rosa set themselves out to be rather pleasing; they both worked at it; it made me nervous. If you had the one, you had to have the other, like some night-club act.

Brodey, of course, was a congenital liar. I would not have trusted him with the spoons. Women liked him. He had a daughter. About your age, girl, he told Charlotte. To Olivia he said: I've made many mistakes in my time. But I love this place—and here I'm not going to make any mistakes. His flattery was gross. Rosa swallowed it. Brodey worked on her vanity: The authoress, some homage was anticipated. Brodey was loyal to Rosa, in his own way. Rosa was open to all the flattery she could get (little girl conniving still), and Con gave her plenty. In company he steered his questions around towards Rosa's main interest: herself. Rosa doing things, not doing things, being witty or cutting. Her life in New York, her published work, her married years, time in Torremolinos, girlhood in Vienna ('She pulled and twisted her long legs along the bar. The dancer was literally stripping the muscles of her thighs'). Rosa would come up to me with a fixed smile, gliding along the bar counter as though it were the dancer's bar she had left long ago. Can you see the halo about my head? Rosa asked, standing close to me. She hadn't been to the beach. She had been making out income tax returns at home. And now the sun was going down, *and here I am*! Rosa said dramatically. She had mentioned herself in the first ten words spoken. She would like a glass of Montilla and some tapas. Antonio came forward rolling his eyes like a bull, and Rosa started in straight away on her act. She had an act for everyone. Anaesthetized to the world that was there in flagrant opposition to her way of looking at it (not even seeing it, but reading into it only what she intended to read into it) and to everything that was continually filling it, she stood there laughing too easily, chatting to Antonio.

One day I had come into the bar and found her sitting subdued with Brodey. She had received a cable from New York saying that her mother was dead. But she had made it abundantly clear that her mother meant little or nothing to her. She and Brodey sat near the door, considering the future. She had now inherited a business; her father was dead already. She was going to give up writing: fortunes were to be made in real estate. Brodey looked suitably grave.

Shortly afterwards they left Nerka. Brodey flew to New York, leaving behind him a dishonoured cheque in the Banco de Credito. Rosa followed after Brodey, apprehensive of what he might be writing in cheque-books in New York. They passed in mid-air: for the next thing she heard was that Brodey was in London 'on business'. That meant only one thing: doubtful cheques, double-dealing. Rosa flew to London; but Con had fled again. In a sub-office of the Banco de Credito the Fernandez brothers waited. Was this how business was conducted in America? By this time, Rosa and Con had parted company.

Rosa in New York wrote to her new tenants in Spain, referred less and less to Brodey, more and more to her ex-husband. He was really a 'nice guy,' she had misjudged him. She was seriously reconsidering a second marriage, if he would have her. Brodey was not to be traced: he was back in New York, said to be working as a butler somewhere, and wanted by the FBI.

There's old Con polishing some poor rich guy's silverware, Bob said. Would you trust Brodey with silverware?

If I ever had any, I said, no.

No by God, Bob said, and neither would I. That chiseller. A real genius at the great democratic art of gum-shoeing.

In subsequent letters, Rosa scarcely referred to Con Brodey. The Fernandez brothers held on to their dud cheque, hopefully, but Brodey did not return.

Rosa Munsinger had a flat in New York. She wrote pulp fiction. Soft-core pornography, Bob said. As a girl she had lived in Vienna, her parents were Viennese Jews with an unpronounceable name. After the *Anschluss* an understanding German officer, a stormtrooper, had helped them to escape from Austria. The price was high: her father's business. They sailed in convoy to South America; began again in New York. She married but was soon divorced. She decided to return to Europe. Her mother told her she was unwise to go. In Torremolinos she met Con Brodey. They lived together. Before that she had been in Paris. Detailed description of how she had a bath in a bidet.

She visited Vienna once. The ex-stormtrooper had expanded the business. He took her out for coffee. They exchanged civilities. He asked her if she liked New York. She said, yes, she did. She left Vienna.

How was it? I said.

The Danube is nice, and the woods, but I'm afraid nothing much can be done with the inhabitants. The Austrians are a sadly provincial and intimidated people. In spite of their lovely land and charming city, they insist on making life difficult for themselves and one another. The authoritarian perversion prevails (here Rosa smiled a wintry smile, thinking of the xenophobic people) and the conservatism is rather suffocating. The much praised *Gemütlichkeit* amounts to nothing more than wearing *Lederhosen* and *Dirndlen*, eating cakes and listening to operettas almost as sickly. Strauss, Skat and Salzburger Nockerln. They make a high ceremony out of those *idyllischen alt-Wiener Frühlingsgefühlen*. You can have it, Rosa said.

Rosa sang rounds, played the spinet. She sang:

> I lay with an old man all the night
> He did not do as well as he might . . .

She drinks a fair amount in private, I think, Bob Bayless said. And something stronger than Montilla. Alcohol, a triumph of the thermogenetic activity of human thought.

Rosa sang:

> He tried and tried,
> But it would not be . . .

17 IN THE OPEN RIGHT UP AGAINST THE WALLS OF THE FACULTY BUILDING: For her last year at university she worked outside, collecting case histories for a remedial clinic in a Connecticut mental institute. Dressed in a white uniform, holding her notebooks, she walked through the corridors, like Chateaubriand's Lucile wandering through the complexes of Combourg. She left Antioch with a degree in mathematics (she said 'Maff'—I gotta degree in maff.), worked at Bill Harrah's Club at Lake Tahoe, carried change in some kind of satchel ('Bad for the ovaries'), Sacramento, Charlotte said, gold-panning. Hoffer country. He walked there. Ever hear of him—Eric Hoffer?

All spoke the same language, all thought the same thoughts, expressed in almost the same words. Pride in New York, pride in the Big Time. Tracey Weddick praised the New York fire brigade, the best in the world. Her method was heavily freighted: a very trying laudatory effusion.

On the freeways! On to the great freeways! The automobiles were travelling east and west, the jets were circling over La Guardia, Newark jets dipping their wings over Ellis Island. Idlewild had not yet become J. F. Kennedy Airport. Jets were circling over La Guardia, one landing or taking off every thirty seconds. And so looking back towards Manhattan with Brooklyn slipping by on the port side, you see the Green Lady rising aloft behind the derelict military base, giving the good old democratic fuck-you finger sign all day long, Charlotte said.

For a time she worked in Chicago, shared an office with a Chinese girl. The Chinese girl was 'well-stacked', all the men (Charlotte said guys) were 'crazy' about her. She handled a lot of attention in a very accomplished way. Three men were phoning her, and then came a fourth. Their boss was over seventy, but still interested. He played patience when he came into the office to calm his nerves before making decisions. No. 2 phoned, he said. He lifted a card. How do you manage? he asked. The Chinese girl smiled an inscrutable smile.

What was her name? Nancy Yin? Betty Yang? Charlotte noticed how she changed her clothes. Arriving in the morning in a sweater and skirt and returning from the lunch-break in a blue two-piece suit. She was having it in the lunch-break. The men kept phoning. If those jokers are getting it, you gotta give it to me too, the boss said.

I'm kinda tired of it, the Chinese girl told Charlotte. It's getting to be boring.

They were walking in the street. The wind blew off Lake Eyrie. The Chinese girl's face was greenish in the cold. (Gangbangs? Fancy oriental positions? Kama Sutra stuff? Charlotte wondered.) You know, kiddo, the Chinese girl said, you know what I mean. It's always the same. It's getting to be a drag. She had wonderful eyes. She was older than Charlotte. If a thing is boring, keep repeating it. The Noh-play principle.

A neat bit of goods, Charlotte said, with her big knockers. Boring? Charlotte said. Drip, drip, the Chinese girl said.

Stage by stage she had shown herself to me, revealed herself to me, then offered (and given) herself to me. She told me of her past, her university days, her first admirers, loves, the maple walks of Antioch University. The co-educational college that went bankrupt, put back on its feet in the nineteen-forties by millionaire Morgan, the inventor of the self-starter, friend of Berenson. She attended classes with the son of Jascha Heifetz. The creek feeding the little artificial lake that had become stagnant, the Dutch elms dying in the grounds, the tomb of the donor in the glen, Birch Track and all the great walks there, the rotting grove. She suffered from low blood pressure and was prone to blackouts. She went with the grand-daughter of Karen Horney, going about bare-footed, her virginity lost two years previously. The cicadas drowning out the lines of Shakespeare spoken in the open right up against the walls of the faculty building. 'You put your hand against the trunk of the elm tree and the cicadas stopped yakking.' She heard aircraft coming and going from Wright Field twelve miles away. Then the cicadas began shrilling again, drowning out the lines of Shakespeare. Some breed of predatory insect slaughtered them in hundreds of thousands every summer. They died in their millions, their chances of survival small. The town of Yellow Springs received endowments for development from millionaire Morgan. Charlotte walked there, carried text books. She went into town, into Yellow Springs. An athlete accompanied her, carried her things for her, they walked by a lake stocked with fish. He said he wanted to know everything about her, the colour of her hair before touching it up, the way she might sit up suddenly or slowly, stretch out in bed, the curve of her back in the morning.

I saw her rising in the middle of the night, summoned out of sleep by the thin crying of the infant, or rising in the early morning light when nobody was about, taking the bottle from the ice-box, warming it, finding the sterilized teats.

It's the course of life, Charlotte said.

Young children, Charlotte said, the one-year-olds, they must cry. All the time—like birds. Daisy was like that. It's hard on the poor parents at first, but they get used to it. Have to.

18 THE SPOILS OF EXETER: We had met him first during the August feria. Olivia and I were eating *pinchetas*. An Arab in a fez cooked the garnished meat over a charcoal fire. We were eating pinchetas and drinking beer and minding our own business when he came up to our table in a rush— small, impetuous and sweating, tow-coloured sandy hair standing on end—asking obliquely: My wife wonders what you do? looking at Olivia but the question was addressed evasively to me. I suppose what he really meant was: Are you queer? Or: Are you as queer as me? Olivia invited him to join us. It was a mistake. I bought a bottle of cognac. An hour later Olivia had excused herself and Eddy Finch was drunk.

He was not the sort of homosexual you would meet every day, nor would want to meet, if it comes to that; he told *everything*. He was a London queer, with all the vanity, the fussiness, the unreality peculiar to the breed; had strong Dominican affinities, spoke of Savonarola, St Thomas Aquinas. Converted to Catholicism he was a daily massgoer, referred to confessors in Farm Street and Brompton Oratory. He arranged children's programmes on the BBC, he said, contributed to the *Cornhill Magazine*; was married and had a daughter whom he dearly loved. The Finches lived in Friern Barnet.

About us were the stalls, the tombola prizes, green plastic tubs and buckets, hideous mauve dolls, little bulls with synthetic black hides, bottles of Montilla and cheap cigars. And the orchestra played as a high female voice repeated over and over, *Otra muñeca! Otra muñeca!* Pink plastic dolls were passed from hand to hand as the orchestra played and Eddy Finch took me into his devious confidence.

How strange is the homo-fire! He said it was rather loud there and what about going back to his place where it was quiet. They had a flat near the Hotel Sanchez. We went there.

He produced a bottle of Gordon's gin and began telling me the story of his life. He was most indiscreet. His complexion was bad. I hardly knew him and had to listen to impassioned anti-feminist diatribes. His wife's flesh and womanly odours repelled him. When he was drunk he slept with her, had to satisfy her natural needs otherwise she became intolerable, though it gave him little pleasure. Have another gin? Someone coughed in another room, called his name. He went to her; I heard the voices murmuring, then he was back again. She could not sleep, had asked for a glass of water; it was her way of saying she had heard every word. It did not seem to concern him.

Jennifer Finch, née Bode, was a stuffed doll. I met her the following day. She seemed to be immune to his insults; and he could be caustic, with a mixture of the greyhound and the ferret in his nature—his eyes red-rimmed; fidgety, sniffing, never easy, seldom sober; eager, too eager. Like Wilde, though for a different reason, he had served time.

He coveted jewellery, precious stones; with another quick-fingered like-minded lad had planned and executed a daring night robbery at Exeter; drove with the spoils to Lymington Spa; £800 worth of stuff lifted from a display window. Masked and gloved they had approached the jewellers; innocent-looking, laughing immoderately, had driven away. They had trouble disposing of the stuff, the profit was small. Rashly, not leaving well alone, they had decided to try again. They decided to rob on a grander scale, empty a big window. They had seen the display at Exeter, lit up, there to be taken.

But this time they were caught.

Halted (a cardinal error) before traffic lights in empty Exeter, they waited for the red to turn orange, when another car drew up alongside them. Finch lost his head, began laughing hysterically, pointed at the other driver, laughing. We're spluched . . . *Do* something! The other gave them a sour look and took their number. At the next town—it might have been Lyme Bay—the police were waiting. Grim-faced constables waited, threw up their hands; Finch (the world's worst driver) swerved away, crashed through a picket fence. He was sentenced to twelve months. In jail he performed fellatio on an Irish gypsy, a handsome and greasy lad, most unwashed. It was like 'sucking off a dirty steam engine'. Later they shared a cell, a flowery dell, but the gypsy would not consent that Finch touch him and called him a terrible name. When he came out he was conscripted into the British Army. From one grand English institution into another, he said.

He found, after a few months in the Army, that of the two institutions he preferred prison, and decided to get out. A friend in Prague sent him Communist literature and this he left lying about, 'planted' in the officer's quarters when he was cleaning there. He was summoned before his superiors and failed to make a good impression. A month later he was back in Civvy Street.

All this and more he told me that night. Jittery, a thirsty drinker, at first a plausible and then a most implausible liar (he could embellish his stories too well to bother about the literal truth), five feet two inches of queer aggressiveness and spite. He prized (coveted) what others had according to the value they set upon them; itched to steal what others owned. This was also true of his homosexual loves. He drank gin, smoked long cigars, liked to impress, lied. Like all undersized people he was ambitious, there was a considerable feminine streak in him; he was seldom calm. The hidden wife stayed out of sight in the bedroom, let him rage on.

Jinny Finch was calmness itself, never losing her even temper or raising her voice; her colour didn't change. He was very high-handed with her. She wore spectacles, patiently endured his frequent outbursts and tantrums. She concentrated on her knitting. Her knowledge of the ways of the world was limited. Walking on Burriana beach her wide pale thighs shook. The child followed.

They had met at the Pushkin Club in London. Jinny undertook translations from the Russian and her publisher sent cheques. She cycled about the city; together they visited the grave of Karl Marx at Highgate cemetery. He discovered that she was to inherit money. Eddy's origins were lowly, working class, which he attempted to conceal (not that he had ever worked manually); it showed sometimes in his dirty diphthongs. Despite his diminutive size he picked up trade around London —lonesome Paddies in Kilburn, inverts from Camden Town, lost souls near the Craven 'A' factory, exotic gentlemen in South Kensington, rough night trade off the Edgware Road. He pulled the chain as a signal, followed a passage of notes in Belsize Park Underground station, the deepest and dirtiest in London surely, half-opened the door of his stall and, with the noise of a waterfall off, confronted, in puny disarray, an old man short-taken who thereupon attempted to force an entry, while with the most perfect sang-froid an elusive and lovely youth waved and went. Love and its inevitable setbacks amid the rank reek of male piss and chlorine, love flowering in such ordure, its mansion pitched in the place of excrement— *Brutalität des Lebens!*

He went to daily mass, twice- or thrice-weekly confession, confessing hastily, sometimes turned away by Iberian priests astute enough to recognize that the penitent was not repenting but boasting. He liked to speak of sin and redemption, carried his missal about with him, attended mass at Nerka and Malaga, the cathedral near the port.

It means so much to you, then? I asked him once.

Oh, but it means everything to me, my love, he said. Sometimes I don't go on purpose, just to punish myself.

You can cut out the 'my love', I said.

He spoke of Eugenio Pacelli, Pius XII, who had an Allee named after him in West Berlin, the Pope with the Latin profile who levitated about the Vatican Gardens as six million Jews went up in smoke. His Oiliness. White puffs of smoke over St. Peter's, the great crowd of the faithful packed into the square below. *Habemus Papam!* The thin hands over their heads, *Caelo supinas manus.* The last Pius, the charmer.

He really used the confessional; some of his accounts of sins committed sounded like tales from *The Decameron.* Once he had made a trip to Moscow, once to a film festival at Pula. He travelled around. Strange is the homo-fire, the glow of inversion, like the fire of a cat on heat, the thin and anxious thread of need stretched to the limit, the membrane wrung. Something of the blind blood-lust of the ferret there, the blind animal with its curiously reddened eyes that hunts and kills its victims underground and in the darkness, taking them from behind against the burrow's end wall. Or the edginess of greyhound or whippet, highly strung and chronically constipated, that senses more than sees the lure, the false hares careering by. He had qualities of those creatures in him, predator and sporting; and something in his eyes moistly appealing behind heavy-rim spectacles, recalled the novice in the seminary or the saint in the sentimental print. He tittered worse than Fay Blair, an uneasy tittering that hardly cleared the breast and lungs, the most innocuous of all diuretics. With Brillopad hair, dusty sideburns and bad complexion (the seminary again), pock-marked face, he stank worse than Colfer of old. Was it the salve he put on his face under the make-up, the infected flesh, or a sad mixture of all three? Those nervous hands, big-veined and moist, were never still, hands that never tired of probing and never gave up, that urged 'Feel and escape!' Hallucinations.

He spread his spiderweb carefully, notecase abulge with hundred and thousand denomination peseta notes, laid on the table by the *Continental Daily Mail* and open cigar box, bait for the local unsophisticates, the handsome young men who were sauntering from Marissal to Bastion and back again, with *gitano* and even Moorish blood in their veins, holding themselves like *toreros*, glancing his way, both polite and curious. Feel and escape. His Spanish was adequate: *Comprende mucho!* his ways devious (still spider in sagging web), fast with chairs, quick with offer of cognac and coffee, reckless where his passions were involved (and that was most of the time) as a suddenly risen wind blew peseta notes and pages of the *Continental Daily Mail* across the plaza. And some honest fellow would give chase, catch and bring it all back to him there rising, sweating, profuse in his apologies, reddening with pleasure, knocking over his cold coffee and gesticulating at the empty chair. He loved them all.

Finch spent many hours alone outside the Marissal, a small patient spider in its web. It needed much patience to go on sitting there, pretending to read the newspaper as if he hadn't a care in the world or a lewd thought in his head. I sat with him there a few times, or outside the Balcon de Europa, and watched the youths whom on previous occasions he had taken into the Ciné Olympia, bought them popcorn and perhaps pawed them in the dark, now going by, nudging each other, laughing at him. I marvelled at this persistence. He really lived for it.

So that was inversion, perversity: a kind of willed daydream that went on all day. He lost his unstable heart regularly every month, this small voracious and unsated lover; for him it was the rutting season all summer and all winter long. (Would the ancient Greeks have sympathized with such a state of mind?)

The local boys laughed, but went with him. He found a small beach beyond Burriana and took to spending the day there, waited, nude. And there was always Malaga. The soft evenings were for mass, the nights for the Ciné Olympia. The interior of the cinema was curious, the walls decorated with what looked like a mixture of porridge and pubic hair. Amid the stink of collective farting, popcorn and *sotol*, Finch sat pink as a rose with the dream-boy Mariposa. Pepito Corelli. He sat outside the Marissal and complained of the service. I told him to try Miguel's bar, where the coffee was cheaper and better and the service faster. But you quite misunderstand me, he said, it's not the poor service I complain of—indeed I quite enjoy the waiting—it's not the conventional service I want. I want to be *serviced*. He looked at me with his gooseberry-coloured eyes, the pockmarked face touched up, the green pork-pie hat with its sporty pheasant feather on the table by the sun-glasses and cigar box. He sat amid his props and frustrations, as the lovely boys walked up and down. He closed his eyes, sighing. Pardon me for bringing up something so delicate, I said, but you must have a tiny crack. How do they manage?

Finch opened his eyes. Tiny! he squeaked. Absolutely. Small as a mouse's ear-hole. But they manage all right. Where there's a will there's a way. Love will find a way. I lost my cherry young, dear.

Jinny was to be seen pushing her daughter in a pram down the Puerta del Mar, heading in our direction and smiling sweetly. Here comes my dull wife, Finch said.

He gave English lessons for very nominal fees. The blonde ephebe who worked as courier in the caves was one of Finch's two students. The Cave Man, Finch called him, being both Cupid and psyche, both the curved bow and the butterfly wings, all tensed calf, curly hair and virilia. Finch 'rotated' him with a pale-faced young Guardia Civil who was anxious to better himself by learning a little English. Finch referred to him as the Young Officer; the other he called the Cave Man. The latter had a tricky smile and used it a lot, the former never smiled at all. The Cave Man wore tight Levis, he had a blond quiff like a bow-wave. The Young Officer was *muy serioso*.

All that winter in Andalusia, in Spain, which is not part of Europe, during the worst winter in living memory, the worst in two hundred years, the lights failed with even more regularity than in less bitter winters and the village disappeared in Stygean darkness. The bars laid in stocks of candles. The effect was pretty when they were lit. Finch sat alone with the winged messenger of Love from the Underground, sweating with desire and embarrassment as the lights went down.

It was a room absolutely made for love, he told me, and there was I blushing like a traffic sign. It's a wonder he didn't notice me, glowing there in the dark.

I asked him what was homosexual love. He gave me a considered stare but did not answer. Was it, I suggested, going to bed with dray-men and coal-heavers? No, he said, not exactly; he was attracted only to boys and young men, and handsome ones at that.

In Mother Russia I was hot all the time, he admitted. He laughed with his bad teeth, the laughter wrung out of him. It never stopped snowing, he said, can you imagine that? I travelled into Russia by train. Russian trains are wonderful.

The Ost-West Express. Bruges (Thomas Hardy liked the design of the railway station there), Brussels, Liège, stations named after famous battles. Cologne half asleep, Hamm, Helmstedt, Marienborn, the Saxon accents of the East German frontier guards (Vopos), Berlin. Stations after the DDR: Poznan, Kutno, Warsaw in Central European Time. Brest,

Minsk, Orsza in Moscow Time, Smolensk, Moscow in the afternoon, one thousand eight hundred and eighty miles in twenty-
nine hours of travelling. The railway gauge changes at Brest
Litovsk over the Polish border when a different set of wheels
are under you, and the ride through Warsaw to Moscow is
fast and smooth. Lemon tea available at all hours. A decent
man sits by a brazier dispensing it. The atmosphere is friendly.
All types travel. Nigerian girls studying medicine on Russian
scholarships. Six different nationalities travelling with me.
One worried English schoolteacher and family bound for Japan
via Siberia.

The approaches to the city are poor—wooden houses,
most of them abandoned and lousy, set among trees. The skies
over the city very high, limitless grey. I stayed at the Hotel
Moskja or Wockba on the Prospect Marx just opposite the
Kremlin. They said the Moscow summers are very close and
hot, but when I was there the water came out of the taps just
above freezing point. Maybe that's the Russian sense of humour.
The citizens have slug-white faces, the sort of complexion that
goes peony pink in summer. And mountains of snow on the
streets. Summers said to be hotter than Nigerian summers.

The people I found very suspicious. They watch you. During
the day the houses are deserted, the owners out at work. A
disciplined people, though many drunks at night, staggering
about. The old ones like going for walks in the daytime. You
see them in the big stores and markets, just staring, keeping
warm. They like playing *Moscow Nights*.

The great axles groaned over the frozen tracks, the snow
flew by in an agreeable manner, all the carriages were heated
and the windows coated with ice. Finch felt at the opposite
end of the world and could do anything. And yet and yet,
he felt like a child, the tears came welling from his inmost
heart, thinking of *him* of whom he would always think with the
most tender love.

I knew to whom he referred: Lothar. A perfect name for a
brute. Lothar Ebbinghaus, the spotty art student, whom he had
accosted one wet afternoon in the National Gallery standing
between Veronese's *Unfaithfulness* and *Scorn*. What can you do in

the National Gallery on a wet afternoon? What do you make of the Mona Lisa's smirk? The Italian Method? What do you think of our English school? What do you say to coffee together in the Strand?

Lothar allowed himself to be picked up, pretending to believe that his host was an amateur jockey. So small and neat. Flat or steeplechase?

They lived together. Lothar was Alcibiades. When Eddy Finch married Jinny Bode, he was Best Man. The wedding was high comedy, a sofa farce by Labiche. He told me about it, laughing as though it were someone else's affair. Before the nuptials the prospective father-in-law surprised groom and best man making up their faces, the best man naked and Finch dressed only in Jinny's panties and in a manifest state of tumescence. Both were evidently drunk. But the wedding itself went off without a hitch. Well-primed with rum the nervous bridegroom kissed the composed bride. The reception was rather grand, the house full of the most proper people. Later that night the mother-in-law discovered the groom under the best man on the grassy verge of the front drive. Nothing was said, but eyebrows were raised. The guests left. The day had not been unfree of incident.

He told Jinny that he wanted to 'go away somewhere' in order to 'be quiet', and write 'seriously'. She believed him. He found a house in the Highlands that had possibilities, set between two small lochs. From tall elms crows squirted their droppings against the long windows. It was perfect, he said, and his wife agreed. They rented it. A fire was kept burning all day in the big grate of the Round Room, and there Finch worked with his feet up, smoking cigars and drinking gin, reading, making notes. His stories, when he began to compose them, were thinly disguised homosexual exploits of his own. Jinny praised his inventiveness. He would do well, she thought. Tell the truth, but tell it slant.

The Round Room with its lime-green walls was like a Beaton set for a Wilde play. The house was extensive and old, with many bedrooms: it would take time and work to get it into shape, not having been lived in for years. The owner was dead.

A local woman, a Methodist with a cleft palate, Mrs. Mac, looked after it. She lived in a room off the kitchen, feeding the pigs that wandered through the plantation. Finch walked around the estate in the evening, smoking a long cigar, a sulky country squire looking over his property, Flaubert at Croisset, immersed in the land, his writing, the past. Congreve the gentleman farmer.

The neighbours were impossible. The crows dirtied the windows, a nest fell into the fire. Nobody ever called. Finch stared up at the moulding of the white ceiling. He lived for the post.

When Jinny became pregnant, she still worked at her Russian translations. Her husband praised her to the skies, genuinely proud of her. Publishers wrote her, sent her cheques, she met her deadlines, she was wonderful. They kept in touch with the Pushkin Club but rarely visited London. The black Plymouth had taken a beating. Once it had run into a tractor, once into a wall, almost every outing left a mark, a bent bumper or scraped door. Jinny's translation fees kept the anxious husband in cigars and alcohol. He spent a certain amount of each day poring over his papers. The in-laws were informed that he was steadying himself for some concentrated creative effort. A baby was on the way. He could not be all bad.

⟨●⟩

He became bored with the country. It didn't really suit his temperament and he needed stimulating company. Then Lothar, the bad angel, found his good angel out, phoning from London to say he was destitute, could he come for a short visit? He arrived looking pale and sick.

Jinny had had her child. In the huge house the baby cried in a great empty room. Eddy Finch took his daughter in his arms, showed her the perfect view, the elms full of evening crows, the lochs, Mrs. Mac beating the undergrowth for straying pigs.

Stippled with white emulsion, the men painted part of one of the bedrooms, as a preliminary exercise to painting the entire upper floor. Finch ran laughing upstairs with beer. The painting did not progress very far. Lothar wore gloves to protect his hands. They sat around the log fire in the Round

188

Room at night and smoked cigars, spoke of creative projects. Finch admitted to Lothar that he had succumbed to a labourer while putting up fences. He visited the cottage, drove him to local pubs. Lothar made a wry mouth but said nothing. Yesterday I met a dear farmer in a cornfield. Poor Monsieur Melmoth rode the lame horse Madrone. Jinny smiled, went on knitting. She felt well-disposed towards Eddy's Continental friend, so quiet, so serious, so German. They drove in the battered Plymouth to country pubs where Lothar made eyes at the men. They drove back. The long windows were splattered with crow shit. Wild words were uttered. Keep off you! Oh I hate you! Stay out of my life! Lothar left. It was very dramatic, melodramatic; Jinny said they were being silly. The absent lover was reviled before the wife, knitting a green pullover by the fire. Eddy, his hands shaking, held the wool, stood to be measured.

Then he relented, drove to London, where something far worse than a rebuff awaited him. Lothar was living with a woman whom he wanted to marry. A woman! Would his old *Freund* be Best Man? Are you serious? Eddy asked. He drove back to the Highlands. Jinny had to listen to more abuse of the absent one: his sullen ways, his many crudities of thought, his deplorable manners; *not* the most diplomatic person alive. Jinny was ordered to pack. They were leaving the Highlands, flying from Gatwick to Malaga.

Love, the imminence of love, and intolerable remembering.

19 MOSKWA! MOSKWA! (When I first saw her.) With my eyes closed, Finch said (closing them the better to savour the memory), I'd recognize any country in the world where I've ever been by its smell. And with my eyes closed now, were he to enter this bar, I'd know *he* was here.

People are what they are, they have no other choice. Every man's opinions go in accordance with his permanent hidden prejudices. I yawned. Finch opened his mole's eyes. We were standing in Antonio Cerezo Criado's dim bar, deserted at that hour. Antonio was brewing up coffee in the kitchen.

Would you? I said, bored by his persistence, for surely he did go on about his amours. The pockmarked face showed avidity; tenacious memory would not let go. Although he had not specified an individual by name, I guessed to whom he was referring: Spotty Ebbinghaus. Mountaineers speak of the mountains they have climbed or want to climb. Eddy spoke of Lothar.

Who contends that love melts in only pleasure, that there must be set-backs before the arrows and the fire? Lothar was married to an unknown woman, living in London. Finch, relenting a little (could he do otherwise?), bought an expensive wedding present, wishing the faithless one a long and happy life. Lothar, true to form, had not replied. Finch would not see him again, but could not forget him, that sour-faced German with the bad complexion and the mouth made more for sauerkraut than for the 'madness of kisses'.

I stood there drinking London gin wishing I was alone. Finch had an importunate way of filling one up with his past. Standing by the high bar counter, he could not rest his arms on it. It was the day of his departure for London. Memory glowed in him, a real homo-glow, his face lit from within like a Bellini angel. That strange Italian painter Bellini, all his Saviours resembled women wearing false beards. I bent to light a cigarette and Finch kissed me quickly on the cheek. Take care, he said, and stumbled out of the bar. I stayed where I was. Never hit a queer, Boss Hemingway advises, they scream.

I thought he had gone. But in a few minutes he was back again with four packets of cigarettes from the kiosk. He gave me two. Antonio brought in his coffee as though bearing a holy chalice. I asked for more gin and tonic.

I never told you of my trip to Moscow, Finch said, blowing Celtas smoke out of his nose. He laughed his wild laugh. Russia, he said, a red duster on a pole down a narrow road in a green pine forest. The customs shed back a couple of kilometres on a plain of rich grass and wild strawberries. Picture the waiting room! On the table a game of chess set out, indicative of monstrous bureaucratic delays to be expected. Above the desk and the po-faced Soviet official hang matching pictures in faded monochrome of two bushy-bearded sombre-eyed men of destiny in loose tunics—Marx and Engels.

A land where time and space have a different scale to what one has been accustomed. Leningrad in the rain—and what rain! Black bile discharged from the clouds dragging their bases on the broad Neva. A river like a sea. I visited the Winter Palace and Hermitage and left the others alone, they can wait —Summer Palace, Admiralty, Exchange, Academy, Stroganoff Palace, Smolny Convent, Fortress. Façades thousands of metres long of coloured colonnades and sculptures set against the sky and against walls coloured ochre, eau-de-nil, maroon, cobalt. Architectural spaces to the scale of open landscape calling on an architecture of movement, scale, depth and relief, colour and sculpture to stand up to it. When I got back I could follow John Reed's blow-by-blow account step by step, so to speak. In the Hermitage gallery I looked for the rarely seen Impressionists and very early Cubists and after about an hour found them up under the roof. Monet water-lilies and rather uncertain Picassos straight from the Bateau Lavoir. Just in time. Looking down on the Place of Mars I got a blinding attack of migraine and was uncertain myself what century I was in. One day was enough to shake me. Far away in the distance a white church with a gold onion dome.

The ruined churches, roofs gone in and vegetation springing up, might have been expected yet stop one short, stopped me anyway. The queue for Lenin's mausoleum is seen by some as apotheosis, evidence of necessity to take account of more than the passing. That queue certainly requires some explaining, a larger than life arrangement of a crowd by Eisenstein. Inside no cameras or hands in pockets enhance the illusion that one is in a kind of cathedral. One chap's hands dragged out of his pockets by the guards, producing the air of a holy place, but perhaps by coincidence, through fear of bombs. It is a fine country, that's all I can say. In Russia the ways are still very long and things distant and remote. The sun barely rises above the horizon during a Moscow winter. Even at noon it hangs low in the southern sky, casting a yellow light and long shadows. The air is filled with fine white snow, a 'real Moscow frost' as the natives say. In the evening rush-hour the tramcars rattle along with frosted windows. You cannot see in or out. Didn't your man Yeats write somewhere that there may be a landscape equivalent to certain spiritual conditions and awaken hunger such as cats feel for valarian? That was Russia for me. There is the sense of limitless land and limitless time, and I suppose the constant possibility of violence.

He went off to pass water, leaving me thinking of what he had said. The Beateau Lavoir. Impressionism: the lost dream, the one that took such a long time to get accepted. The lost paradise, the undemanding dream of oneness with Nature, oneness with other people, oneness with ourselves. Monet's water-lilies, the 'lavendered limbs' of Madame Bonnard.

He came back grinning, wiping his face with a paper tissue. I had ordered another round of Booth's London Gin, for he seemed in inspired form. He took up the long glass. Bums up! he said, winking at me.

Strange times, he said. One must cross the wide square by subway. The surface is only for traffic. The penalty for walking there is instant fine, as I soon discovered. The population is practically underground, great hordes shambling along in subterranean conditions where black marketeers sell fashion journals from the West and you can buy the most delicious ice-cream I have ever tasted. The standard of clothing for sale in the stores is approximately that of the Age of Steam.

In the corridor of a train travelling at high speed towards Moscow, Eddy Finch stood with all his papers in order, trying not to look too often at a handsome youth who was putting his fair head out of the window. He was ripe for an affair, and already in his mind's eye could see many young handsome Soviet males walking about in fur-lined boots, slapping gloved hands together, puffing out their reddened cheeks and saluting each other in a language as difficult as it was melodious, a beautiful but incomprehensible tongue. They were tall and straight as spruce or pine trees, laughing into each other's flushed faces; big glowing males would have him under fleecy eider-downs; a regular stud farm, a collective, blood brotherhood! blood brotherhood! Unwise. The tongueless vigil, the foreign faces, and all the pain.

Avid for new love, he was throwing caution to the winds, casting nervous glances through his blue shades at the lovely lad who, for his part, was moving his weight from one foot to the other, sighing, darting the most pleading looks, while Finch in turn was praying for an endless tunnel to swallow the train and the lights to fail and never come on again and the journey never to end. Oh the hot unambiguous stares! Love, Russian-style, was the sound of huge greased wheels grinding over the frozen railbed, the windows latticed with ice, a blindingly white horizon with onion-shaped domes advancing towards them, madness howling in the belly of the locomotive and an unknown destination rising slowly before them in a screen of blown snow. The utmost grace the Greeks could show would scarce compare to this. They were entering Moscow hand-in-hand; the city beloved of arsonists and pyromaniacs lay before them, the wheels sending out sparks, the brake mechanism giving sudden spurts of smoke, and in the overheated corridor the long madness of hot returned stares, preceded by uncertain looks, fidgetings, sighings. In ancient Greece, in days of yore . . . Love, awaiting him in Moscow, had sent forth this pretty knight errant, this lovely page. Fucksters (you that would be happy), for standing tarses we kind nature thank.

The young man standing in the corridor was bony, fair-complexioned, with an intelligent face. I could have jagged myself to death on him, Finch admitted. And he wouldn't have minded, from the look of him. (This candour was engaging, Finch at dalliance.) Then the long train started into a curve, blowing its whistle, running mad. The faun was looking out of the window at white domes and minarets in a pearl sky. Moscow! Russia! Land of horses. Land of bells and bass voices.

I wanted to offer him roubles, wanted to grope him, offer him all I had in the world, Finch admitted. But I kept my hands to myself and was a good boy. Then the floor of the train began curving into the gradient and I was carried across into his arms. He literally lifted me off my feet and kissed me. I smelt garlic and vodka and fur. Do you suppose it was love at first sight? or just pity because he saw I was an English midget?

Love at first sight undoubtedly, I said.

Oh you are nice, said Finch, touching my arm and blushing, then burying his nose in the gin.

With much shuddering down all its length the train began drawing into the terminus and a stout uniformed station guard appeared at the window, calling something and pointing before disappearing, and the train, letting off a great deal of brake smoke, began drawing up alongside the main platform, and the doors were banging open and the faun stepped down, going backwards, his breath steaming in the air. He waved and began walking quickly out of the station and out of Finch's life.

He was glowing now, absolutely, and looked quite beautiful. It is something that I have observed in homos, how even the plainest ones become radiant and glow at times. Love has a spider's eye to find out each particular pain. Is it pain, Florentine sodomy, Cellini's 'Italian method'? To tell the sober truth, I was good and tired of his false boys.

All the carriage doors were banging open all down the long train and he heard loud martial music blaring out from loudspeakers and saw a printed incomprehensible Russian name with some of the letters reversed. Then he left the train and began looking for a cab, a hotel.

Moscow was like nothing on earth, said Finch. Soviet sailors walked about hand in hand with the names of their ships emblazoned on their caps and wearing the *tightest* trousers. With all the church bells pealing, huge hairy fellows had him; and he could neither repent nor confess and be absolved, due (first) to the variety of the temptations offered and (secondly) to language difficulties and barriers; the young men were angels playing dirty games. The Russian earth was frozen under a blanket of snow and his British reserve (of which, to give him his due, he had very little) melted like snow under a hot sun. He was shown all that was beautiful and best by kind-hearted Soviet men. The angels were most obliging and the young men were beautiful.

He showed them the Tube map of London-under-the-ground and photographs of Jinny and Kitty, his small and adored daughter, and made a show of himself in the bars. Moscow was teeming with handsome soldiers, sailors, flyers, and in the morning when he came out of his hotel, hoar-frost formed on his eyebrows. The walls of the Kremlin faced a square where nobody walked, the bones of Gorky, the traveller, were immured there; Finch stood at the crossroads of his life.

You asked me once what is homosexual love, he said. It's the same as any other love, a strange city where you've never been before. That at least was Moscow for me—the *terrain inconnu*. His voice trembled with the eternal chronic anxiety that sounds so querulously in the voices of all queers. I thought of Beyle in Milan and love in the air (the tang of horse manure).

Soviet-samovar-and-vodka-style love is very heating on the system, he admitted. It was just as well that I left when I did, I was like an athlete overdoing it.

At night, alone or not as might be, be heard the trains screeching, leaving the seven great terminals for points beyond the Urals; Siberia. He looked out of his hotel window one morning and saw a ruddy-faced Red Army major dressing down a group of privates, all of them heavy as tuns, with small little suspicious eyes, their breaths steaming in the air like horses. The major was in a tearing rage. Their tracks in the snow made pretty patterns over the empty square. The sun rose late over the honey-coloured churches and the guards with sullen manners admitted a large car, with pennants flying, into the Kremlin. A strapping young fellow marched up and down with an inverted, automatic rifle. Finch, full of *bonhomie* and alcohol, attempted to speak to him and was coldly rebuffed. I was really philandering, he admitted, I hardly knew which way my sitting parts hung.

The really big studs had knocked the stuffing out of him; they seemed to enjoy themselves. He was laid by brawny he-men who came puffing in giving off a heady reek of barracks and gymnasium, drank great quantities of vodka in quick time and began throwing off enough winter clothes to cover the backs of four or five needy British families. I'll not conceal it from you, dear friend, Finch said, I was fucked silly.

And Pula? I asked, trying to distract him from his fancies. Pula was different: he brought back a great sun-tan, a holy icon and a dose of the clap, which he had picked up from some casual young thing, Soviet or Serb. It was inconvenient, particularly when he returned home to Jinny. He attended a VD clinic in London and was cured after a humiliating experience. The holy icon was something to see.

Can I see it? I said.

Unfortunately not, he said.

He had grown tired of it and resold it to a London dealer at considerable loss, having paid fifty pounds for it, a most exquisite thing. I believed him; he had good taste. It was Jinny's money, but his loss. Jinny, who had no opinion or taste of her own, 'forgave' him. It was all she could do. She rarely reproached him; for, accused of anything, he flew into a tantrum, screaming like a hysterical woman and made the wildest counter-accusations, very Russian in this, so it was best to remain calm and say nothing, and this Jinny did as a rule.

We had now drunk three-quarters of a bottle of Antonio's alleged London gin and were hardly sober, for though Finch was undersized he had a giant's thirst.

Then who should round the corner of the Calle Pintada at that moment but Rosa Munsinger and Con Brodey with three strangers, laughing immoderately, a young couple about Finch's age (mid-twenties) and an elderly man in a suit and a green pork-pie hat. The younger man was big-boned and fair-haired, wearing sun-glasses and limping on a stick, looking like the Polish film actor Cybulski. The young woman was small and neatly made. They were American friends of Rosa and Con: poseurs, fools, imposters (the limp and the stick). They came into the bar with a great show of conviviality and sat around the table near the door away from us.

Who are these people? Finch asked rather too loudly. Are they interesting? Rosa and Con, I told him, with American friends, strangers to me. Brodey ordered a round of drinks. Rosa and he did not stay long; after half an hour they stood up, said so long and went out. I stood there with Finch, not listening to him now, hearing the voices of the Americans, the three of them there talking together. It was late October.

20 EL MUDO: There's the doctor's friend from the caves, Charlotte said. What about buying him a drink?

All right, I said. Wait until he comes over. A party of rowdy Spaniards had come into the El Molino back bar, all undersized and arguing loudly, a hobgoblin company of warty Latins pushing their way in through the bead curtains, among them the amiable mute. There was a cellarish smell: wood, sawdust, *sotol*.

But he had seen us already and came over, nodding and grinning from ear to ear, the rings on his fingers flashing in a barbarous way. The El Molino was crowded, both bars. We sat opposite the service hatch, Bob and Olivia opposite us, their heads together in private conversation. The crack-pated Flamenco record was playing, the voice of Marcheno singing under the waves. The voice, all gravel, sang of deepest despair, incorrigible hope. In dumbshow the mute asked permission to sit down. He had warts, a certain sign of sexual prowess. He sat by Charlotte.

She offered him one of her filtered cigarettes. Nodding and smiling he accepted, thrusting out his jaw as though his collar irked, and flashed a lighter (a cartridge case). A small weatherbeaten man, deaf as Beethoven. An illusionist, finder of secret exits and hidden entrances, a bearer of impossible burdens. He could lip-read, his eyes half-closed, blowing smoke through his nostrils, keeping an eye on Charlotte's lips. I asked him what he would prefer—anis, beer, gin, vino, cognac. Cognac. José took the order. And the same again for *La Señora* and myself.

Another Marcheno number began. Bob was still holding Olivia's interest and not paying too much attention to the mute or to us. I had a whiff of drains: someone had opened the door of the *retrete* in the first bar. Tobacco smoke trailed from the mute's nostrils. He smiled at me, nodding vigorously, revealing copper fillings. He wore a cheap wristwatch, had many rings, and warts even on his nose. Charlotte was deploying all her charms. The mute responded in emphatic dumbshow, nodding and hissing, opening his eyes wide (astonishment), narrowing them (grave doubts), closing them (the bliss of total agreement with her); his hands were never still, the rings catching the light. He laughed silently, cat-like, showing her his shaven neck and hairy nostrils. Wolfing smoke down into his lungs, he stared at Charlotte's lips, nodding, smoke trickling from cavernous nostrils. He and she were about the same age and weight. He could not agree more, no, impossible. He and she were in full accord.

He took up the small glass of cognac, dipped his head and shot it back. A wiry little man with warts on his face, hair on the backs of his hands, good hands, artist's hands with long fingers. The delicate bone structure of a hand. Hands are the things that best show the march of time, that never tire of probing and never give up, says Aranas. Mute's hands. Charlotte's brown American hands holding a deck of Spanish playing cards, a glass of cognac, a Bisonte. Charlotte asking: What games do you play—stud or strip? She liked the games men played between her feet. She seemed to like the mute, cleft chin, warts, rings and all. Above her reckless head on a small block of wood was printed, burnt out with a poker, the legend:

> Miguel Baez
> Litro. Corbacho
> Jerezano Finoquinto
> OSBORNE
> *Al mal tiempo buena cara*

Charlotte crossed her knees and the mute looked away. She wore her black leather shoes with low heels, cuffed in suede, with a garnet button at the instep. Garnet or agate, this red eye winked at me. She wore an orange dress, which gave to her skin an ineffable glow, a nutrition-blaze of well-being. The mute's tongue flicked in and out like the old Finn's; they both had lizard tongues. Again he closed his eyes in passionate agreement with something she had said, tilted his chair back on two legs, hissing. And then she was laughing at something conveyed in clever dumbshow, concerning the doctor. Whereupon Charlotte bent forward, tapped his knee and spoke to his face.

He narrowed his eyes, observing her closely, very serious now. Then Bob said something loud and exclamatory behind the mute, who was leaning back in his chair and likely to topple off, pointing a long mock-accusing finger at his own mute breast, making a woeful face, the corners of his mouth drawn down. And then his long brown fingers were going like a metronome before her amused face; he was robustly denying it all, every word, stretching out his neck and hissing into her face. Then Olivia left to ask the boy Miguel (they were all Miguels) for the key of the *retrete*, and a door opened and an overpowering stench of human urine blew sourly through the serving hatch. Bob said something sarcastic, and Charlotte was leaning forward, showing me the strong line of her back.

The mute now took up his second glass of cognac, which he had not touched since José had put it there ten minutes before; crooking his little finger, he shot it back just like the first. Light glinted on the mute's rings as he put down the glass. I ordered another, motioning to José who was trudging between the tables with his lounging Spanish walk (Seneca has written somewhere that Cicero progressed in that way—the otiose saunter of an oriental), as though he were advancing through a ploughed field, with a fixed grin on his face, the world's slowest waiter. But, after all, where was the hurry?

The mute moistened his lips with his lizard's tongue, darting it in and out as alcoholics tend to do, not in the least constrained in her company. And it suited her to be there with the little mute, playing up, a Big City girl who knew a thing or two; she carried it off well. Other American girls, once they set foot in Spain, fell ill, went down with unspecified ailments. The food did not suit them, dug out of the ground, and the climate bothered them. And then there were too many idle days, dreary rehearsals for unperformed acts of revenge; one sort of freedom, unhappily, not breeding another. Leisure is the loveliest thing in the world, once one doesn't suffer from it. Charlotte Bayless thrived on it.

She had come from Bill Harrah's club on Lake Tahoe, my change-girl. She carried a satchel of change, dollars and dimes. (Bad for the ovaries, she said.) The club was in the Sierra Nevadas. *Al mal tiempo*, I read.

Wonder what he'd be like in bed, Charlotte asked me in English, smiling mostly sweetly at the mute, who nodded in a sage manner to encourage further indiscretions. Everything about him was quick and darting; he had come up from a hole in the ground to meet her. She could without offence use indecent words charged with sexuality. It was part of her style, it became her, she could carry it off. Not all women can, but she could.

Probably very good, I said. Read you like Braille.

Charlotte laughed. *Fingerspitzengefühl.* Warty hands of such callosity, elegantly breaking bread, raising a glass to the lips, gutting a fish, opening his fly buttons, shaking hands, endowed with all the natural good manners of an Andalusian, an out-of-doors man, deft with manual operations, mute as a bat. The language of hands and eyes, a gently stealing influence. Neat-handed, a coxcomb flashing his rings, a speechless lover with a delicate exploring touch. Constraint vanishes with the dark. I signalled to Cicero.

You think so? she asked, amused. Then buy him another drink.

The mute, watching Charlotte closely, noticed the drink being put before him and thanked me in dumbshow. He was deaf and dumb but *muy valiente*, on his back had carried the stout Dr. Jorge del Bosque out of the pitch-black caves. Pointing with an Ideales packet in his brown fingers, he curled his wicked tongue, taking with it into his mouth the last half-inch of cigarette, raised the glass of cognac, threw us a look of dark complexity, tossed back the drink with the light firing on all his finger-rings, and made a great show of swallowing. Then he laid down the glass, and without more ado brought forth the cigarette again on the tip of his tongue, took it with his lips and closed his eyes, inhaling smoke. It was Antonio Anejo's favourite trick. I expected to see smoke issue from his ears, if not his arse; but only black hair sprouted from his ears. He could carry heavy amateur archaeologists out of impenetrably dark prehistoric caves, and perform clever legerdemain; though dumb, could divert Charlotte Bayless; it was more than I could do, generally speaking.

The mute, who had been screwing his head around, now very lightly touched the *muy simpatico Señora's* wrist, using only the tips of his fingers, the spot that is swollen with a tiny sensitive bump, by means of which the blind read, to draw her attention to a newcomer who had just walked into the bar. Holding in one hand his small black medical hold-all, Dr Jorge del Bosque was speaking to some Spaniards near the door. On Pepe's *poco disco* Juanito Valderrama had sung *El Minerico* and now began waveringly on *Baladilla de los Tres Rios*. Charlotte's Spanish teacher was standing near the exit.

Pepe Gomez now put his head through the serving hatch and nodded to us like Punchinello, indicating in sign-language that a round on the house was on the way. And Charlotte, who had her back to the serving hatch and exit and had therefore seen nothing, was smiling into the mute's face and as good as telling him that he would be a considerable success in bed. *Loco en la cama.* And he was nodding in a very downright manner, his eyes mere slits. He would indeed. He would not mind at all, provided he could perform with someone as beautiful and *simpatico* as the *Señora* herself.

The doctor, spectacles pushed on to his head like goggles, continued to engage the Spaniards near the door. The mute, light flashing on his rings, was attempting to explain something about the doctor to Charlotte. The other side of the story no doubt, how the doctor had fallen and twisted his ankle and how he (El Mudo) had borne him out. He was pointing now to his ankle and making a grimace to indicate anguished pain: thus had the good medico been stricken. And now young Miguel had changed the record and Marcheno was singing again, deeper under the surface, in among grit and gravel Marcheno was singing, and it was almost impossible to understand the words. The cognac was beginning to take effect.

Then the doctor caught sight of Bob Bayless, who was in the act of turning to thank Pepe (a fixed but receding smile in the act of disappearing back through the service hatch) and waved across, looking mighty pleased, no doubt anticipating another agreeable night of discussion with the *muy serioso* American, on subjects dear to his heart. He had seen Olivia, who was smiling at him, but he had not seen Charlotte, because the mute, standing and looking towards the doctor, had his back in the way. And then Dr Jorge del Bosque was taking ceremonious leave of the Spaniards and making his way across the bar.

Charlotte recrossed her knees, and again the mute tactfully pretended not to see, while Cicero, smiling a fixed smile, was pouring overflowing libations of Fundador and murmuring (genii summoned by a ring) *Invitación de Pepe Gomez*. And Charlotte my restless love was changing again—for she had seen the doctor—no longer the lady who could amuse a mute with good Spanish, and low innuendos in English, innuendos that even a Spanish deaf mute could understand (particularly one so well endowed with warts), changing again: soon she would be discussing points of grammar and pronunciation with her educated Spanish admirer. The doctor murmuring lines of Frederico Garcia Lorca into her ear, the poetry of Machado, of Lope de Vega; and all I knew of these was that the first had been shot, the second had died on or near the sea-shore (according to Regler) and the last-named had a cinema called after him on the outskirts of Malaga near the Jardins de Puerta a Oscura, the Gardens of the Dark Door or English cemetery, which was also a nursery garden.

So she would always escape me, changing shapes, changing clothes as she changed her lovers, changing her style as she changed admirers; no longer Mistinguette or Tamara Karasavina or Sylvie Selig or Marcia Paz-Pero or even Charlotte Bayless; all that remained, like the lees of cognac in the heel of my glass, was a pale little girl with a plain Polish face, wearing lost spectacles several sizes too large, with red rims and no lenses, standing with raw chapped hands in the freezing school yard of Samuel Gompers High on Lower Manhattan

Island on the lower East Side, shouting at the top of her lungs: *Fornicate! Fornicate!*

Obras, fin, oscura: change for the next world. *Todo cambia, y el amor no menos. Somos vencidos o vencedores. Asi es en todo, en al amor tambien.* All things change, and one's love not the least; we are victorious or defeated—so it goes in love, The doctor came up at this particular moment and smote me a genial blow on the shoulders, saying *Einhorabuena!*

⁕

'Their language (Andalusian) sounds like heavy raindrops falling down,' said Charlotte.

21 BAR EL CRUZERO: She wants you to come for supper, Bob said, putting a hand on my shoulder. She told me to say a place is laid for you. Will you come?

She wants you to come to Dolores Street.

The window of the bar El Cruzero was open. Outside it was blowing. Dilly was buying salted peanuts and *Bisonte con filtro* from the informer in the kiosk. Bob Bayless was regaling me with stories of young love, early connections.

The window was open. Outside lay Kezer Field (a wide field, a strong light etc.). The terraces were crowded. Sporadic cheering.

This, then: the rim of the great stadium. The triumphant cheer caught in the light. The sophomores wildly signalling. The girl cheer-leaders waving their arms. The drum majorettes lifting brown knees, twirling batons. The defiant roar of victory (a field goal). We had a lovely view, said Charlotte.

They went on with what they had begun. It was the first time. Bob was sunk. His great fear was not to succeed, to be 'out-fucked', nothing for him was easy. *Quinque linea sunt amoris: scilcet, visus, allocutio, tacitus, osculium, coitus.* They were reviving a sacred custom of remote origin: the semi-public nuptial bed, an odd custom still practised in France up to the middle of the seventeenth century. Bedding the bride. He had gone too far to go back. The window was wide open. The bed was in the sun, against the wall. The crowd was cheering. From the stand or some high terrace they could see into the room. The cheering was becoming louder, more ribald the shouted remarks. They heard only buzzing in the background, out of doors where the game was in progress. Odeardilly darling! Ohboblove! Ohcharlottehoneyyou'resosweet! Oboblov! Oh-honey! like the famous duet in which Tristan and Isolde mingle their names, deny their names, sing of surpassing the separate self, and time and space, and earthly calamity. And then a great cheer almost lifted the roof off the covered stand. That was the Forty Niners scoring. We could be seen, Bob Bayless said. But at the same time they had gone rather too far to draw back.

The cohesive principle; the annoyances that love sometimes meets. (Her whsipering Go on! Oh go on! Oh Dilly darling, Oh Bob sweetest, Oh honey. Oh you're so sweet, and so on. Her groans of pleasure are lost in the stirrings and murmurings of the football crowd. The drum majorettes twirling their batons and lifting their knees, the wind thudding at the microphones.)

Isn't it silly? she said, I can only come by thinking of you. In bed with Bob, he found her all ardour. She was all ardour in order to hide where her true feelings lay. She wanted to satisfy him, pacify him. Her ardour in bed had the opposite effect: it first aroused and then confirmed his suspicions. She was having it with Ruttle.

I was going to Olivia. She was taking Charlotte's place. Perhaps Olivia was dreaming of Bob. Imagined herself in his arms, receiving his kisses, his ardour, his love. He worried about being 'out-fucked'. I had marked her the first time. Her bitten lower lip swelled up. She was like a boxer after punishment. She said: You make love like he does. (Was that a compliment or a reproach?) The rhythm changes subtly with different partners. He had sensed her infidelity, her fourth adultery. She went on with it anyway. She was covering her tracks. A cat covering its excrement. Now I looked for the marks of his passion, looked and found nothing. Jealousy is another form of mistrust. The four of us were united in intricate connivance. Cuckolds all awry. I was Bonnard in the bathroom at La Cannet, painting his ageing wife in the bath. I was Rubens painting Ellen Fourment, his cousin, his young second wife—in the process of forgetting his first, Elizabeth Brandt, whose fading memory he preserved in his Dutch heart with mingled grief and resentment.

You and I are alike, she said, looking at me with her extraordinary eyes.

We were meeting on the Plaza Canterero beyond the Guardia Civil station, there by the cemetery, past the lime-kiln, and going out on the Maro road. It was the way to La Luna. We went on to the *tablazo*, a giant's causeway of rock deposits, past a brickworks and rows of bricks drying in the sunny yard. Black smoke issued from the brickworks' chimney. We followed a goat path on the rocks of the table-land to where it stopped, and below was the river taking its last bend by an empty factory before going out into the sea. The river was just a shallow stream flowing fast by the far bank. Sugar-cane grew there, beyond were cultivated fields with men labouring, and then a sable hill with olive trees. We could not go there, but went the other way into walled upland fields where the pylons came marching over the sierras with power from Alicante or Almeria. We climbed down to the riverbed, followed the path through cane until it joined another below the plateau. From there we made our way into the walled fields. This was the uninhabited campo where no one worked. Mule trains came up by the river-bed laden with tomato crates. Later on it would be sugar-cane for the gin factory at Maro. Under the shade of a carob tree she lay down. We lay there together in the shade.

I listened to the sound of a mattock breaking hard earth in an upland field and I heard what Charlotte was saying to me. So long, she said. It's been so long. Was it long for you?

We went on to La Luna, after. In the dining-room the lady archaeologist from Madrid was dining with a child younger than Daisy. *Señorita* Ana Mariá de la Quadra Salcedo wore a blue dress and had put up her hair. I hardly recognized her out of slacks and mountain boots. She was from the Beaux Arts, Madrid. She was as attractive as her name. (Mme Laurette Séjourné in Teotihucan.)

She was finishing a late lunch. Then she came over to speak to us. Charlotte asked her was the little girl her daughter. Oh no, she said smiling, I am not married. She was going back to the diggings.

22 A CHILD'S FUNERAL: A funeral was passing along Calle Pintada (Calle Generalissimo Franco), the coffin lid not in place, a little corpse being carried away in flowers by young boys. I stood on the balcony of No. 12 with Charlotte and looked down into the open coffin, and there in the middle of the flowers was the infant's peaceful face, a little girl, with that slightly asymmetrical stare peculiar to the very young: an unfocused look directed past us and the wrought-iron dog-heads along the roof, at a remote heaven. Hardly into life before she was being ushered out of it again. The colour of the dead face was the colour of my mother's face on the third day of her death. Off-white clay gone back to rock and returned with thanks to the hands of the Maker.

The small white coffin was bedecked with flowers, exposing only a section of the *caja-fuerte*. Covered in flowers with the lid off to the dead eyes open in the waxen face. The boys bore it along at a brisk pace. It was followed by a smaller object that was also covered in flowers, carried by two other boys. The coffin-lid. In among the flowers a small chromium-plated Saviour braced His chest. Between the snow (winter) and the flowers (spring) they buried Him. A single adult walked behind: this was the stricken father, walking with eyes lowered, hands clasped behind his back, wrapped in thought. He was followed by a cortège of little girls dressed in their finery. And behind them again came a young priest reading from a breviary. This small woeful procession passed below us.

From her altered breathing I knew that it had affected Charlotte. She had a daughter. It had affected me. Suffer not to perish us and our offspring. The father would bring back the crucifix to the bereaved mother who had mourned at home, as is the custom in this sunlit corner of the Mediterranean. Nobody wept; the young coffin-bearers held the *caja-fuerte* low, and all along the route to the *cemetario* the women with folded arms stood in the doorways and said *Que guapa!* Which was indeed true: she was beautiful. The cemetery was outside the town, near the brickworks on the Maro road.

An odd place, an odd home for the dead: 'Deadsville,' Amory called it. 'Endsville.' He liked to walk about there, near the grassless soccer field, to the sound of cheering, the sight of a black-and-white object rising above the dead wall.

A narrow short avenue of cypress gives on to a high white-washed wall into which is set a black wrought-iron gate. In the first part of the cemetery lie the well-to-do defunct in ostentatious family vaults with heavy embossed iron double-doors sunk into a cement bed. This leads into a larger enclosed area beyond the mortuary chapel where banks of coffins rest in a columbarium. There are no cypress trees here. The effect is not sombre but functional, on the lines of bakery furnaces, the inscriptions for the rich dead engraved on marble or stone by Carlos Clu & Co of Malaga, while the common dead have their names and dates cut by inexpert hands on cheap material —slate. But, rich or poor, the pleas addressed to our Maker are modest and restrained.

The best flowers of the year bloom in October and throughout November, as though specially for the dead ones, and during these months the cemetery is full of flowers and presents a festive appearance, with chrysanthemums in the niches; and above the walls the sierras white with snow, in the distance, over the river. The sierras are the washed-out blue of distemper, a whey-blue haze, Mary's colour. Children are buried in the centre plot, without headstones. There are no grave-diggers as such, the caretaker digs the children's graves, breaks open the ossuaries to admit adult corpses, looks after the place. I walked about there unmolested, addressing wordless prayers to my departed mother. At a Spanish internment there is always the merry sound of hammering and breaking of walls, a last look at the petrified dead person behind a porthole of glass, then more hammering as the coffin-lid is nailed down.

On All Souls night candles of remembrance burn in the *cemetario* and visitors behave quite informally, the men smoking and walking, hands in pockets, the women calling out to each other; no kneeling or ostentatious prayer (the lips moving: a most disgusting sight) or telling of beads, but loud gossiping and emptying out of dead flowers; not the deep infestive gloom of damp cypress ride and Celtic cross and mossy ways, matching the hushed and reverent tones of my fellow countrymen, the women adopting the soothing and mollifying cadence of priests and nuns, going about the execution of their sad duties; quite unlike those megoliths of the dead at Dean's Grange (my mother one of its more recent citizens) or Prospect lying between the canal and the Botanic Gardens at Glasnevin, where I liked to walk in the glasshouses, in the heat.

Here visitors called informally on old friends. Outside the walls on the riverside there was a dump for the bones of those whose term of tenancy had ended, *rejecta membra*. It was all on a very decent human scale.

I stood with Charlotte on the little wrought-iron balcony and watched the funeral cortège go on up the hill. A fat woman standing in the doorway opposite stared after the priest. Presently rain began to fall. Bob was out in espadrilles, going for *Bisonte con filtro*. He was coming down the hill in the rain, with his shoulders up, whistling. Sometimes he acted like the narrator in *Our Town*.

They seem to love the dead here, Charlotte said. One does of course.

I said nothing to that.

Threads flex, hues meeting, parting in whey-blue haze.

23 THE SIGN ON THE WALL SAID LOS CONVALECIENTES: The bar Pombo, a miniature Alhambra. I was in great turmoil of spirit watching an old man retiring to his lodgings. He was loath to go in, posing in his doorway with a latchkey in his hand, a rolled newspaper under one arm, the day's news already stale, stale ABC news, already consigned to the past; examining the four quarters of the sky, feeling himself observed, or wishing-longing to be seen by the young people in the little square sitting about the tables. I watched him but my whole being was concentrated on her to whom I could say nothing, once more. I'll drug mine, she had said, earlier in the day, but you must drug yours too. You can come into my bed.

The old man shifted about from one leg to the other, looking up at the sky, held the key in his hand, looked, yes it was the key all right, not wanting to go in, wanting to astonish them by turning into a goat before their eyes, or to fly over the roofs of the houses, stalk through the door itself, become young again. He wanted to achieve the impossible, but not to vanish. Circumstances were forcing him to do just that. Once the yale was into the lock, he'd have to turn the key, and the door yield and he disappear. I sensed his discomfort; he did not want ot go in, though by staying out he could not alter anything. He looked for neither truth nor likelihood, stood there play-acting, making me feel uncomfortable. How well I understood how he felt, deforming himself, deforming habit and custom. But nothing would change.

Lonely old man of Malaga, lonely old bachelor, widower, show-off, recluse, old sleep-alone, I see you. He wanted to transform the night. It was, in fact, a lovely night in Andalusia. The desire was growing in him to make grand operatic gestures, unnoticed by all save me. To a casual observer he seemed to be just fidgeting on the doorstep.

We were having a last drink near the Bar Pombo, under an awning at the bar Hijo de Matias, near Los Convalecientes. Why should a Malaga bar on the fringe of the red-light district be named after an African beer, and also a village in Peru?

The Pombo river flows out of the valley and one branch runs very calm and deep.

24 DR. VUC EISEN: She came down on to the *paseo*, some mornings, straight from bed, wearing her morning face. Or she had overslept the hour we had agreed to meet, and came straight out, her face still marred by sleep, by the sheet, by strands of hair. She came straight to me in this manner, from the most distant country there is, her brightness unimpaired. Her voice was slurred. She brought some of her sleep with her. The brown hand with the symbolic ring made its intensely private gesture, my heart turned with the movement. She touched her hair. I must look awful, Charlotte said.

She sat on the high bar stool and asked for coffee, crossed one leg over another. She spoke of her past. She was travelling towards me now.

They came east on Route 66, from the bottom of California, the legendary coast. At night, tired travelling, they came to an Indian town. Perhaps it was Winslow in Arizona. Charlotte wanted to spend the night there. But Bob, the cautious young husband, was having none of that. He said: These are mean bastards, Dilly. You don't fuck around with Indians.

They drove on. She stared with a vatic glare through the windscreen all smeared with squashed bugs. They sailed out of New York harbour on the SS *Klek*, a Yugoslav freighter bound for Tangier, saw the jets circling, going down every three minutes.

Dr. Vuc Eisen was the ship's doctor. He spoke of Yugoslavia, his home town, he was home-sick. They walked the decks at night. He was very handsome, Charlotte said, I think he liked me. Bob spent most of the voyage below-decks, puking his way across the Atlantic.

Did he try anything, I said, this Eisen?

Sure, Charlotte said. We were on the high seas. Every licence allowed.

Manchmal! Manchmal!
With long travel, girls suffer changes of heart.

The great romances in life, and in literature imitating life,
as you probably know, Bob Bayless said, have never been
between husbands and wives but between husbands and other
people's wives. Look at Irish and English history from the time
of the Norman invasion up to Edward and Mrs. Simpson. Consider the known high content of adultery in world literature.
Madame Bovary, Anna Karenina, that game-keeper and Lady
Con.

What he meant was: I know what you're up to, Jack. And
(progressively): This I'll tolerate, up to a point. Or: You are,
after all, old enough to be her father. (Ilium had to burn to
create the *Iliad*.) And: *Don't touch her, she's mine!*

I lifted the knocker and let it fall. The sound reverberated in
the house. I waited, lifted the knocker again, let it fall. The
sound reverberated in the house. I waited, lifted the knocker
again, let it fall. I pushed the door; it gave. I entered. Ferns
hung from wire baskets supported by chains, a nondescript
chandelier with branched fruit of light bulbs. A heavy maroon
cover on the table. And in the centre of this an airletter addressed
to Mr. & Mrs. R. T. Bayless, 12 Calle Pintada, brought to
No. 26 Calle de la Cruz by the postman. Strange stamps. I
turned it over: Miss Mimi Fagg, The Museum, Nigeria.

An empty hallway led to empty stairs, their empty flat.
I knocked on their door. No one answered. They were out.
I was alone. Solitude—one knows intuitively it has benefits
that must be more deeply satisfying than other conditions.
I let the knocker fall again in case the old woman was there.
Oyenos! it said. Quite empty. I walked towards the *paseo*,
carried that empty feeling away with me.

25 BATH NIGHT: I sat on a rock above Burriana, watching the antics of the seagulls. They were behaving most strangely. The evening sun lit them from below, their wings scarcely moved, drifting up and then around in the air currents, like leaves or confetti. What pressure or compulsion stirred them? Their underbodies and outspread wings turned grey, then pink, then white again, meeting and turning from the sun now going down somewhere behind the Torrox lighthouse. They were several hundred strong; a third of this number would take it into their heads to part from the main flock, and drift about on their own. And then the whole body would be united again, flying strongly after one leader, following the course of one of the two valleys that opened on to the beach. They would be drifting on the upper levels of the air, aimless, circling, silent, without purpose; and then losing height and racing in a confused mass away from Burriana, over the Cortijo de Maro (boarded up and Amory working in London) and Los Vientos (closed up too and Rosa Munsinger and that slippery customer Con Brodey living independently somewhere in New York), and then going down among the olive plantations with a peculiar clattering like hundreds of secateurs cutting. But no sooner down than up again, flying at full tilt away, as if their going down had been a mistake. And then up again, until there was a funnel of them, circling, hardly stirring their wings, just drifting up there. Until the need to come down again overtook them; and then down again with their harsh cries into the olive groves across from La Luna. Rooks play in the air, I thought the only birds who play in the air; I had watched rooks play in air currents around Knocknarae and in Howth Castle demesne; but never gulls playing. And then who should come walking there but Mrs. Bayless and her daughter, going by the sea, singing, Charlotte with a stick.

They began sailing pieces of driftwood in the stream. I called to them but they did not hear me. I went down, following the path, and then the stream out to the beach. As I came out I heard them singing. They sang: 'And she waded in the water. And she got her (something) wet. But she didn't get her (clap-clap) wet, yet.'

I surprised them there, coming on to the beach. Daisy, a small glowing version of her mamma, ran up to be embraced. We all dancin', she announced. I heard you, I said. I went back with them. When I linked with Charlotte, Daisy stopped her chattering to watch us, and then manœuvred until she had my hand and her mother's hand, so that we could not link.

You'll come to supper? Charlotte asked. Ask Olivia. I said yes. Good, Charlotte said—about nine then. Come early for a drink if you like. All right, I said. I left them at the door of numero 68 Calle Italia and went on to Calle de la Angustias. Olivia was not at home. I went down to the plaza and found her drinking coffee with Charlie Vine in the Marissal.

⊙

Charlotte's way of bathing the child touched me, as did her manner of doing a number of mundane things. A long braid of fair hair hung down her back, her beautiful, valorous womanly back, Juno's love-back and mesial groove. Her skin had a glow from walking on the beach. I watched her moving there, soaping the child. We localize in the body of another all the potentialities of that other life, until it becomes dearer to us than our own. So many ways, so many places, so many seldom different degrees of giving and taking. I'd known exaltation with her, misery too, a depression of spirit new to me; she half giving and I half taking.

I had found, and was already in the process of losing, all that I'd ever wanted, as one unpropitious day followed another, then weeks, and the circumstances that I had no control over not yielding. *Je ne sais quoi.* My sluggish senses (seemingly more so than most) hardly aspiring to such turbulent contact. They'll go away, I told Olivia. I'll forget this. We'll find each other again. Is it likely? Olivia said bitterly. I assume from the ridi-

216

culous way you carry on that this is your first experience of the really hot stuff. Do you expect me to believe that you'll ever forget her? Hardly.

I recognized the truth of that: I couldn't change.

Charlotte wore a white linen housecoat and white cord slacks, very tight when she bent over the bath, putting a drop of oil in the water, soaping the child, the image of herself as an innocent. That odd small face, those knowing eyes. *Tu* one says to beloved and child. *Tu. Du.* A mistress and a child.

Daisy made an island of her stomach for the little plastic yacht with its red sail to run aground. In the silence then I heard the rain falling. It seemed to be coming straight down from a great height. All through that month it had been pouring. Uncle Dan, Daisy said. Yes, my love, I said.

Did God draw us first and then turn us into real people? she asked.

I thought about it. I don't know, I said. Perhaps. Her mother came in with a warm bath towel. I could hear Bob typing in his study upstairs. I watched her drying the child, powdering her, putting her into the night things, brushing her hair. She taught her how to behave, to wash her hands and brush her teeth and other basics of hygiene, and she told her fairy-tales, a young mother putting the final touches to her daughter before the night came down.

I was Bonnard in the bathroom at Le Cannet. I had heard the front door slam. Olivia and Charlie Vine had gone out for mulling wine. It was raining hard now, spewing from the open mouths of the dog-heads. The street lights were out and a stream was pouring down the hill from the upper reaches of Calle Pintada into the darkness of the Puerta del Mar, where Vine and Olivia were drinking in Antonio's bar. The sound of rain falling at night: the oldest sound to reach the porches of man's ear. To say that I felt happiness would be an understatement. Alone in the house with her there with the child. Alone but for the husband, involved with his work, Shelley drowning, Harriet drowned. Madame Magritte drowned.

Late love has this in common with early love—it is again involuntary. A legacy. Love, the cruel fabled bird that pinches like a crab, had pinched, found me. I heard the American bombers going punctually on the hour, flying above the rain, moving on their radar-path. Hank from Ohio and Herb from Brownsville, Texas, The Macy's Kid. The Moron air-crews (*zopilotes*) who await only the ratification of death.

Vultures are said by ornithologists to be the first of birds, and will probably be the last of birds. The sound of a type-writer in the upstairs room, the noise of rain falling, water seepage, the hiss of butane gas, the sounds Charlotte made preparing salad, and in the candle-lit bar the others drinking, waiting for the downpour to end. No doubt they were as pleased as we were, that it did not abate, and showed no signs of doing so; it was in for the night. Charlotte's spoon struck against the side of the salad bowl. She was droning some wordless song that made little headway. A Jewish drone that went on a little way, hesitated, broke off, only to begin again. *Yiskaddal yiskaddish.* When Bob worked at night or retired early, as he sometimes did, Charlotte would go out to the bars and find me there. Daisy woke at night, because a wolf was 'chewing her lips'; she had gone to their room and found her father snoring and her mother gone. Where were you, mammy? Under the bed, Charlotte lied, and the child believed her. It was a German fairy-tale. Drop oil in the water, soft-soap the innocent, close your eyes, tell the most likely lie.

Charlotte had stopped dicing salad. The typing upstairs stopped. I tasted *tequila* while the rain poured down. The vultures were over Catalonia.

The tapping began again upstairs. Charlotte went on droning. I watched her. The butane lamp was giving out its white light.

Charlotte was smiling, thinking her own thoughts, prepar-ing some potion or aphrodisiac. Her salads were exceptional. That smile of hers, it might have meant anything. Daisy was in bed.

Some of Bob's papers were scattered on the table. Smoking one of his black cigars and drinking his *tequila* there with his wife, I read the papers surreptitiously, upside down, my eyes lowered, my heart quaking, for what might I not find? A sheet of quarto on which a line of type was struck through with a pen, held to other pages with a clip. I read:

> The idealization of an identical woman through various incarnations.
>
> *The Court of Love:*
> Elizabeth Hitchner ('The Brown Demon')
> Emilia Viviani
> Teresa Guiccioli
> Harriet Shelley
> Mary Shelley
> Jane Williams ('The Magnetic Lady')
> His cruelty to H.

The Court of Love. The loves of Percy Bysshe Shelley, drowned and then burnt on the seashore. His friend Byron removed the heart. An Aztec ceremony on an Italian beach. Leigh Hunt's bust of a fallen angel.

Daisy came trailing downstairs again in her blue dressing-gown. Do a bird for me, Uncle Dan! she pleaded, giving me an eye just like her mother's. Oh please do a bird for me! I might, I said, looking at the titles of Bob's books. New ones were being added all the time, mailed from the States. Helen Wadell's book on Abélard, Auden's *Letter to Lord Byron*, Harold Nicolson's *Byron: The Last Phase*. Harriet Martineau's *Society in America*. Kissinger's *The Necessity of Choice*. Hegel on Tragedy.

Go on, do a nice bird for me, Uncle Dan! the child persisted. I tasted the lemon. What class of bird? I said. Any class, Daisy said. Right, I said, give me something to do it on. She brought me a block of paper and a Bic ballpoint. *Naranja Fina Bola Carburo*. In the street outside the rainwater was splashing from the open mouths of the dog-headed gargoyles. Streams of water were falling from either side of the narrow street and overflowing the catch-basins below. There were no drain pipes. The pen made an evenly severe sound on the paper. Charlotte went on singing, droning away. She had not noticed Daisy's reappearance. I finished the sketch. The child examined it critically, a strand of fair hair down over her forehead, a diminutive version of her fractious mamma.

Nice, the child said, nice (flapping her arms like wings). Do me a one feeding now, Uncle Dan. I watched her, and it seemed to me there in that warm room with them, hearing the butane hissing and the rain falling outside—that the long, rebellious and self-willed jaw, combined with those ophthalmic eyes, made for judging distances, belonged also to one of the heroines of my youth, Amy Johnson. I took the sketch and began to draw a gull feeding.

One gull airborne, one gull on the ground. I gave them back to her and she compared one against the other, a blue-eyed child curling a strand of fine hair about one finger, her pinky. The result seemed to please her.

You do nice birds, she said, real nice birds. She wished to kiss me. I bent to take her peck on my cheek. She had her mother's nasal delivery and lingering vowels. Deya wanna? Deya? I closed the sketchbook, pushed Bob's papers away. Charlotte touched my arm, offering me another *tequila*. I had a plate of salt and sliced lemon before me. What are you doing here, imp? she said, you should be in bed. Okay, the child said, okay. She kissed me again and went back upstairs with the sketchbook under her arm.

Will we ever have any time alone? Charlotte asked. Doesn't look like it, I said. What time does your man finish work for the day? About now, Charlotte said. He has to get something off for tomorrow's mail.

A hard worker, your husband, I said. Yes, she said indifferently, he applies himself. I put my arm about her waist. She liked to be touched, liked the sensation of me touching her. One blonde touch to set us both on fire. In the silence, embracing her, I heard the rain pouring down (someone was hammering on the front door).

Charlotte moved away from me, giving me a look that might have meant anything. Late again, Porpoise. As she moved to the door the lights in the house came on. And in the street outside. I heard Vine say Hi! And in came Olivia.

Charlie came forward with his shoulders hunched up, less

Hasidic, more damp crow, struggling with a drenched umbrella, a crow attending to its bedraggled feathers. They had a carafe of red wine and two full bottles.

Fucking awful weather, what? Vine said. The suspicious eyes behind the beaked nose studied us. Had we been necking? *Wet!* Vine said. Christ! I'll say. Get your husband off his ass. We're here for some serious drinking.

26 RED POPPIES: Daisy Bayless had a combination of her parents' features, though by nature and in appearance she more closely resembled her mother. She had something of Charlotte's eyes, her ways and something too of her deviousness, though naturally on a more restricted scale. The rather long face and big mouth were her mother's in embryo. She might grow up to be another Charlotte.

Once she was in a rage with me and ran like a hare. I caught up with her to have it 'out', trapped her in a doorway on Calle Pintada. I'd given her some pesetas at the kiosk. In the middle of buying something she had changed her mind and I was left holding some ice-cream.

I knelt in the doorway facing her. Her furious eyes were level with my eyes. Her eyes were all pupil, in a tearing rage. The mother's eyes glared out of her child's eyes. I recognized the obstinate turn of will. We made it up. She took my hand and told me that I didn't understand her and, furthermore, sometimes annoyed her. But only sometimes. Uncle Dan, she said, coaxing me. She could get around me, just like her mother.

She sang, listened to music a lot, seemed to enjoy drawing and looking through books. She was by nature an adult-pleaser; at all events she pleased me, probably because she resembled her fractious mamma. Bob complained that she had a sense of humour. She laughs off discipline, he said. When I beat her she grins. I cannot but grin back, though I continue to cudgel. And the beating is rendered meaningless. A difficult girl, I fear. What do you do in such cases?

Stop beating, I said.

One day I was sketching in the open near the Cortijo de Maro where the ground slopes away. Red poppies were blowing in the Poniente. I was sketching there when Charlotte and

Daisy came walking up the path. They came with me, and watched me working. They had been at La Luna and had seen me against the hill. I saw you, Uncle Dan, Daisy said gaily. We saw you.

The brown hand with the symbolic ring made an intensely private gesture, the wind blew hair across her eyes and mouth. While the child was looking for grasshoppers I wondered whether I could steal the mother away from her, disappear into the long grass.

If she was delicate in all her movements, she was indelicate in much of her talk. It was part of her charm and a very potent part. Not many women can talk bawdy, let alone carry it off even tolerably well. She had an incessant propensity to indecent allusion. As a rule she was gentle and generous. But she could turn into a vixen, could be a right bitch at times. She changed from day to day, from hour to hour if necessary.

She confessed to me once that there were times when she felt 'heavy with remorse'—not specifying why she felt remorse— the mother to whom she had given a hard time, or her later adultery with me. Would she feel remorse for that? I doubted it. She wanted to be punished, beaten. She set her honest husband on to beat her. He beat her, not knowing why; in this way she 'punished' herself.

We came in once in the middle of one of these 'beatings'. They were half-way down the stairs, out of sight. I had hammered on the door but they had not heard us. Bob was beating his wife, on her instigation. She was asking for it. *Pegame! Pegame!* He had a chair in his hand. What's all this? I said, like Nastagio in the pine wood. Bob had been belabouring her about the thighs and hips, the deep fat. They came down laughing. Bob set the chair down. I sure as hell beat the shit out of her, he said, blowing out his cheeks. How pleasant to be taken seriously, even if only for a while, Charlotte said pleasantly.

I watched her bending forward now with hair in her eyes, her knees were in the grass, and below her and behind her, outlining her, that rareness, the multiple image of redness blowing—the poppies. Watching her, being with her, made me disconsolate. Daisy was nowhere to be seen.

Children? (she had said once)—I haven't yet discovered

their point. They seem an uninteresting disorder. They waste your time. Why waste one's time to make a contact that is no sooner established than it's lost anyway? They soon change.

Was she then a 'bad' mother, in the accepted sense?

It seemed a cold way of looking at human progeny, particularly one's own. I don't know, since I have none myself. Her child touched me. Her flesh and blood. Charlotte said: One cannot imagine an intelligent little girl, only a pretty one. I said: I think she's intelligent. She looks like you.

Oh you are nice, Charlotte said.

I just counted a million grasshoppers, Daisy said, reappearing with pollen in her socks and hair.

27 CANTO HONDA: Antonio Molinos Campos was delivering his dire stuff at point-blank range into my face. I was exquisitely embarrassed. Was he drunk? No, just drunk on *canto honda*, deep song. It was something about undying friendship but the only word I could understand was '*crucifixíon*'. Did he mean to convey that he found my company intolerably boring? Why not, sweet Christ. We were standing at Antonio's bar and Antonio Molinos Campos, grasping my upper arm, was employing his free hand in a pumping gesture. He sang in his ruined voice:

> *Este querer*
> *dime dónde va a llegar*

with eyes shut tight, he drew a breath, his fingers shifted their uncertain grip. He sang into my face:

> *tu tratas de aborrecerme*
> *yo vez te quiero*

at which I broke out in a sweat. Olé! I said. *Bueno* Antonio!

> *este querer tuyo y mío*
> *dime donde va a llegar*

(deep shuddering breath here) his eyes opened, he fixed me with:

> *tu tratas de aborrecerme*
> *yo cada vez te quiero mas*

(he was digging deep indeed for the ending now, sweat running down his face, his fingers pinching):

> *que Dios me mande la muerte !*

I bought him a drink. Behind the bar Antonio Cerezo, the sceptic, was rolling his eyes. He had heard better songs sung in Spain, in his time. A *Malagueña*.

Antonio Molinos Campos' song:

> This love of yours and mine,
> Tell me where it is leading?
> You try to abhor me;
> I, every time, love you more.
> May God send me death!

28 CAN AFTER CAN, CAN AFTER CAN: She sure was white, Bob Bayless said. The winches white, the anchor chains white, the covers on the lifeboats, the plates, the hatch covers. Peer into a vent and the shadow was white. The sand in the fire-buckets was as white as the steam from the stacks. Everything white. Look into the paint locker: can-after-can-after-can of white paint. Sailors in white singlets and officers in white uniforms walk the white decks. It was the whitest, brightest small freighter in maritime history. The SS *Klek* of Yugoslavia. We crossed in her.

I saw Charlotte walking the decks at night in the company of the ship's doctor. She looked quite brilliant, a mixture of honey and sun, matt skin and burning lips.

Sunrise following sunset following sunset, Bob Bayless said, the boredom was absolute. Changes of current, tidal shifts, the wake of passing vessels, the islands. I can't remember which ones we stopped at. They all looked the same to me. The sweet winds blowing from the horse latitudes to the doldrums.

And Dr. Vuc Eisen, I said.

He sure enough charmed the pants off her, Bob said. Once in our cabin he gave her an injection right up the ass.

I said nothing, seeing her face down on her bunk, and the handsome ship's doctor preparing the hypodermic. This may hurt, he said, but she was ready for it, her skirt up, smiling.

Walter Pater spoke of two things which penetrated Leonardo's art and imagination beyond the depth of other impressions: the smiling of women and the motion of great waters.

We cut loose, Bob said.

29 NEWS OF SHELLEY: Bob Bayless liked to take a final turn on the *paseo* with a cigar (the perfect antidote to restore exhausted nature) before turning in for the night. He was sorting out the following day's work in his head, separating the wheat from the chaff. I went down for a last drink and found him marching up and down there, wreathed in cigar smoke. He invited me to join him. I had arranged to meet Charlotte in the same place on the following morning, if she could get away. She had complained, I'm surrounded by house-guests like a warden with madmen. I'll come if I can make it. She who prided herself on keeping promises made to her lovers would come if she could, if that was good enough for them it was good enough for me; in the meantime I marched up and down with her husband, neither of us saying a word. The *paseo* was deserted. A harvest moon was rising behind the palms. The Balcon de Europa bar had reverted to its old name, and was now Café-Bar Alhambra, as of old. The new hotel was ready to receive guests. The name was up—an effect like stencilling light through rolled copper: BALCOᴎ DE EUROPA it said in white light. Miguel was watching us. The Marissal was quiet, a few figures stood at the bar. We marched up and down in silence. The light spilled from the new sign. BALCOᴎ.

Feeling depressed as hell, Bob said after a while.

I offered no comment, wondering what was coming. Gettin kinda *mannish* around here. Would you just lay offa my wife, buddy. To betray, get between man and wife, is to make a second fall of cursed man, already cursed enough by God. What was he leading up to?

Can do nothing, Bob said. Feel tired as hell all the time. Did you ever get that way?

Yes, I said, often.

We marched up and down in silence. The sallow invert,

who had once been offered to Olivia, came sauntering alone on the *paseo*. The treacle moon was turning pale behind the palms.

Drowsiness assails me, Bob said, a hummy feeling all through my body, the way certain grass fields tickle. *Les incertitudes de la mémoire*. Do you know the Yankee euphemism 'retiring room'? In head first and the attendant pulls the chain. Shades of Murphy. An honourable end!

You need a drink, I said.

Certainly I do, Bob said. Was there e'er a time when a man didn't? Let's have one. But not there (BALCOИ EUROPA it said, the preposition had disappeared, there was a black gap where the DE had been) and not the Marissal—that's a bloody place. All glass. Let's sit out here.

As soon as we sat Miguel came. What will it be? Bob said. Vino blanco, I said. Be your age, Bob said. What pap is this? All right, I said, give me sack. Gin's right, Bob said. I'll have one too. Miguel took the order.

Have you ever thought about time? Bob said. I mean sat down on a chair somewhere and gave it all your attention. Not space. Not space-time either. I don't mean space-time at all. Fuck space-time. I mean just time, all by itself. Just try it some day. Find a comfortable chair, bring along cigarettes, matches, an ashtray, clear your head, relieve your bladder, and think about time. How long it is.

The sallow invert, using his hands like paddles, sauntered up and down. The moon was over the palm trees, travelling serenely through space, its natural home. A full moon over Spain.

I merely ask, he said, not that I expect an answer. The events in the thing I am supposed to be working on took place just fifty years ago. In Geneva, of all places. Ever been there?

No, I said.

Don't, Bob said, it's a bloody place. All water and well-fed Swiss bankers. When the diarist John Evelyn visited the place in 1648, he saw a crocodile hanging in chains outside the Town Hall, and seven judges without hands painted on one of the walls . . . and it doesn't surprise me in the least.

I said nothing, watching the invert sauntering up and down, and the moon over the palms. Miguel came back with our tall drinks and set them down. Two inches of ginebra to four of tonic.

Byron had just read some God-awful German ghost-stories and invited his buddies to write one of their own. Bob said, each to have a stab at it, try their hands. Mrs. Shelley got going straight away at *Frankenstein*—that was easy, no problem there. The pale student was Percy Bysshe, part of him anyway. And part of the monster was him too. The good Dr. Polidori got out his quill and began scratching away at *his* Vampire. And Byron himself penned a tale of terror.

And Shelley? I said.

Shelley had other things on his mind, Bob said, offering me a very sour look, with a dead cigar in his mouth.

The side-long glance of a jealous husband.

30 EVENTS ON THE FEAST DAY OF ST. QUIRICO: El Caudillo's name-day. On Radio Malaga a priest is speaking. (Who was San Quirico? a nobody.) His words pour out. *España—Iglesia—Dios—El Mundo.* On this overcast day I go out to find uniformed Falange youths walking about the town. Three thousand of them have come in coaches from Ronda, Bilbao and towns about, tassels on their red caps, very short pants, budding militia men. It begins to rain. An impassioned speech is delivered from a rostrum by a dedicated-looking man to rounds of applause. They have taken over the Plaza de José Antonio Primo de Rivera, where an inscription on the wall of the Town Hall reads:

PLAZA DE JOSÉ ANTONIO PRIMO DE RIVERA
ESPAÑA VENCEDORA DEL COMUNISMO
EN LA CRUZADA QUE LEVANTO ESTE DIA
BUSCO LA PAZ DEL IMPERIO POR LA UNIDAD,
POR LA GRANDEZA, POR LA LIBERTAD EN EL SIGNO DE
FRANCO EL CAUDILLO
ARRIBA ESPAÑA
XVII-XVIII JULIO MCMXXVI

paseos and plazas are named after the handsome hard-faced founder of the Falange. All over the Iberian peninsula and in Republican Malaga, capital of sorrow. A picture of the dictator's head decorates the plaza wall at Competa and a plaque commemorating dark doings, shootings. A naked priest with flowers attached to his member, a present from the women, with his back to his church, falls before the firing-squad. Blood and flowers. Diego de Rivera's murals in Mexico City. The suffused faces of the peasants. The Day of the Dead.

I see, says the blind man, a hole in the wall. You're a liar, says the dummy, you can't see at all.

Words be signs of natural facts; natural facts be emblems of spiritual facts. Who was it died in Paris between brothel and confessional (exact whereabouts of his immortal soul uncertain). Was it Rivera? *Entre la nieve y las flores, ocultaban el Cristo.* Take him away. Condor legions.

I stood beside you under the umbrella. The holy terror came towards us, a religious battering ram, she wept real tears, or seemed to, a huge and heavy throne carried by over a hundred penitentes. Mother of the Bled-White-One, who had gone ahead, laid out naked under chiffon. You asked, May I touch you there? You had your back to me and with your hand you touched me there. Dignitaries of Church, State and the Armed Forces marched past, the soldiers with reversed rifles were goose-stepping. *Tenemos! Tenemos!* They went past us, a line on either side, with two scarlet cardinals. You could see the skull-caps, the *mozettas*, shining like agaric in a wood. *Dos procesiones.*

Later it began to rain. A long narrow awning protected the Youth Front from the unpredictable elements. A band played, pack up your troubles (oddly enough) in your old kit bag, and smile, smile, smile. I sat with Charlotte outside a café in Velez-Malaga. There were dusty orange trees, and opposite us an old church mouldering away. Madre de los Remedios. OYENOS! She wore her gold solar chain and watch hanging down over her bust. Her amulet, solar myth. The Roman numerals were blue. You might feel it ticking over your heart. It suited your golden look. You said: One day shall I model for you in the nude? and laughed. The links of the gold chain dense as grain.

Two carabineros with patent leather Bonaparte hats watched you with their lizards' eyes. They had undone the top buttons of their uniforms. Their automatic weapons were on the table, and you said one of the catches was off. You wore your Empire dress. You looked like Cybele the Phrygian fertility goddess, of whom we know nothing except that she had big breasts.

No morals, you said, absolutely none. Crawling in and out of each other's beds like slugs. Amory had slept with Sandy and an unnamed Spanish wife, and with Nancy Summerbee before shacking up (your expressive term) with Tracey Weddick, having discarded Fay Blair (whom Charlotte had never met), while Casanova Park had slept with an English actress and with Sally Banks and Nancy, and Charlie Vine with Sally before shacking up with Salina, while Lazlo Summerbee had shacked up with the London barmaid somewhere down the coast. Sally Banks had slept with anybody who wanted to go to bed with her, even Adolfo Sanchez. She had arrived with an officer from HMS *Ark Royal* who had complained to Adolfo Sanchez that she was insatiable, needed it eight or nine times a day, a veritable Messalina. And Olivia had slept with nobody, unless Charlie Vine had attempted her, in the intervals between Sally and Salina. And Bob had slept with only you, his unfaithful spouse. And we had been intimate on your spare bed and in the sugar bushes and under a carob tree and in the sea once.

I went around to the Baylesses' place, leaving the plaza to the frightful Falangists. Daisy opened the door. Hullo, she said, I thought you were sick. That was two days ago, I said, now I'm better. I'm glad, the child said. My daddy's working. Mammy's out. Out where? I said.

Visiting, the child said.

She looked at me with her mother's eyes. A blue look.

I've got a new comic, Daisy said. Doya wanna see it? It's real nice.

Let's see it, I said.

I went in. She brought out the comic paper. *El Capitan Trueno y La Lucha con la serpiente*. Goliath. Characters with powerful pectoral muscles and the faces of brutes addressing each other in bubble talk. Super Girl. *Habitante de los grandes abismos oceanicos* (thick fish with bug eyes down in the depths of the sea). 3000 m. *de profundidad! Madre de los Remedios. Le Silence de la Mer*.

Do you like it? Daisy asked.

I do, my dear, I said. I love it.

⁂

Phrases I associate with Charlotte: Whizz-kid, kiss-off, smart ass. Did you ever eat an oyster? It's like eating the sea.

31 DAISY: The other day she painted a bird without a head and then on a separate piece of paper a head without a bird, Charlotte said. She folded the two pieces together, put them in an envelope, sealed it, went out closing the door behind her. Then she knocked. When I opened the door she handed me the envelope and said. Here, some mail for you. And hasn't spoken about it since.

What do you suppose that means? I said.

I guess she knows there's something going on, Charlotte said.

⚭

Stubby finger, coarse skin, big pores, rough texture, shiny. The tips of her may-I-touch-you-there were stubborn pads indicating the practical side of her nature. May I? Thoughts, hands, drugs apt, times fit. Mature willing—else no creature seeing. *Manos de mi corazon.* On Samana Santa in Malaga among the crowd on Avenida Larios, penned in with rain dripping from the points of my umbrella, and the Saviour coming high on the *palos* dragged by two hundred *penitentes*. Her hand on my May-I-touch-you-there. *Fuego lento en el Horno.*

I thought I could defeat my feelings by permanently hiding them, but that made me really ill. It was snowing, she said (it was New York winter), and it looked like a mad dance.

You see how false are those spirits I call high, she said. I go to bed every night full of remorse.

32 DROWNING DREAM: I walk along a corridor very familiar to me, but one that has become narrower and smaller. I have returned to Nullamore. It's like going home in the holidays from college to find the whole place shrunk. It's the long corridor leading from the back door, the lamp-room, by the battery-fed wireless, down by the small room where Wally kept his papers, past the cellar door and its sixteen steps down, to the cold paved flagstones below the line of dusty bells, the stench of the servants' toilet, to the kitchen. It's the corridor my mother cleaned down on her hands and knees, with bucket and brush. I pitied her; when I was older (we had left Nullamore) and I could tell her that, she listened, said: But then I was happy. She was happy down on her knees—a country washerwoman. Later, when I was away in Montreal, she would keep house for an old mad woman, and encounter the humiliations and fears that I had felt then, seeing her on her hands and knees. But I say it again: My old fears—as an adult I'd remembered, and told her that I'd pitied her, a washerwoman's job after all. No, my mother said, no, I did it for preference; it soothed my nerves. I was never happier. So one can be mistaken about intentions, practices, results.

My father is sleeping in the lamp-room where he kept the Aladdin lamps with their long glass funnels, and the coke and wetted slack for the boilers. Sometimes it was the lamp-room, sometimes the furnace-room, called one or the other depending on whether one was thinking of fuel or light. My mother is sleeping in the study. Someone in the house is murdered, not one of the family. An intruder? I cannot say. I am the murderer. My brother Wally appears on the scene. Without speaking, as is habitual with him, he enters the murder-room. Which room? I cannot say. Is the victim man or woman, young or old? I do not know. But soon I will know. He comes out, expressionless, does not look at me, as was habitual with him, walks down towards the kitchen. The victim should have been lying on the bed. I see the bedrail. The bed itself appears to be empty. But someone has lain on it, for the covers are rumpled. The dream ends; another begins.

I am standing on the edge of a deep ravine, deeper even than the gorge at Ronda, below the Puente Nuevo, on that dangerous road where Amory drove like a madman to the *corrida*, to the biggest and therefore most hazardous arena in Spain. Below me the narrow valley is lost in haze. It drops away, bringing to mind the fall to the riverbed by the *tablazo* where we went walking, Charlotte and I: a nightmare fall. I stand on the edge, my backbone and knees turning to water. Gape not into the abyss, lest the abyss gape back into thee, dreamer. The unheard-of depths lure me into them; I experience vertigo.

A great straight tree (Aleppo pine?) stripped of its branches straddles the void. The upper part is burnt flat, a long footbridge of ashes. It narrows in the distance against the precipitous sides of a bluff or escarpment; *scaglia*, burnt hills beyond. Fearfull of that headlong fall, I am nevertheless lured on to this 'bridge'. I step off the precipice. Now I am advancing along it, but dreaming this, mere dream subterfuge. Nevertheless I feel the air on my face and hands, the headlong fall below me; and so, half-dreaming, knowing myself to be dreaming, I find myself three-quarter way across. I stop, seeing the footbridge coming to a dead halt against a solid wall of rock. I must get back again. Below, the abyss. I cannot turn; overcome by vertigo I drop to my hands and knees, facing the rock. If I try to turn I will surely fall. I feel *space is in me*. Down on my hands and knees I cannot move. No sounds rise from below.

It's summer, I know this from the appearance of growth on the tree-bridge, from the appearance of the rock, from the smells of summer in the air. (Are there odours in dreams?) I know a hopeless, nagging fear: fear of total extinction. I try to crawl back. Impossible. I am caught there, unable to go back, useless to go on, fixed in terror. Below the drop waits. No sound. This dream ends; another begins.

I am looking after Daisy Bayless, supposed to be. She is

younger, only learning to crawl. We are in a shallow estuary. She 'rows' herself in a plastic bucket. I watch her. She does not look like Daisy, but I know that children can change, and I see her as Daisy, Charlotte's child. Charlotte is there too.

I look around. The child has disappeared. I wade through the stream. I am 'beside' myself. I come upon her plastic drawers waterlogged in a pool. Clutching these in my hand I hurry on. A small weir splashes into a deeper pool. Moving awkwardly as if in thick treacle I come upon the little body under the surface. I put my hands into the water and lift her up, press her to my chest. Her eyes are closed and she lies coiled in my arms as if peacefully sleeping. Perhaps I can still save her? Ignorant of mouth-to-mouth artificial respiration I merely pat her on the back. She makes no sound, does not breathe. I walk up and down in distress, carrying her, stroking her. In these moments of doubt she dies. I cannot call out, my tongue is leaden. Her mother is there, waving to me cheerfully. She thinks that I am being affectionate, looking after her child, but the child has died 'on me', as they say in Ireland. Died in me I should say. I, her protector, her Irish uncle, have failed her.

From these three close consecutive dreams I woke up drenched in perspiration. I felt that my mother was in the room, counselling me, Go easy. Easy does it, Dan. The window was open. The Levante had started to blow. Wooden frame tapped against wooden frame. I thought that I had betrayed Charlotte; some trust, something implied and recognized; her child—'our' child—was dead, and it was my fault. Frozen, I waited for worse to happen. Nothing happened. I waited, my perspiration dried. Wood tapped against wood. I felt very strongly that my mother was in the room. She stood in the shadows. In the early morning light it was all vapoury blue-grey shadow. I left the bed and went to the window, secured the blind, looked out not on Spain but on North Africa: a moonlit heavily-shadowed white wall.

I had watched you sinking, going out of life. I had measles and you were spooning gruel, I was back again in my childhood laughing at Wally because he was covered in red spots. You said: Wait till you see yourself, and held out a mirror. I was worse than Wally. You nursed us, read Hans Andersen. I was dizzy after weeks in bed, it was like walking on a ship, I vomited. You were laying out quicklime for the slugs. They came out at dusk and left slime trails.

You were young, walking with your own mother in Carrick. My taciturn grandmother Nelly Orr smelled of face-powder, musk and camphor, walking slowly through airless rooms. I heard Lehar, Massenet's *Meditation*.

Whitish matter oozed from the corners of my mother's mouth. She was almost gone. My past was going away with her, she was taking it away, her eyes sunken, features caved-in, drawn. Always short of money in her life and always backing horses. The snow was falling, the punters in the open stands had it on their shoulders, the racegoers were huddled together for warmth, all looking one way. Corrie Vacoul won the Dundrum Steeplechase, a two to one favourite. On the walls of Mooney's bar the blown-up prints of yachts were keeling over in the bay. It was Sunday the 16th. The saddening music came from the tape-recorder. Cybele who carried towers and temples in her head, who was she—the mother of Attis? Another of those dying and resuscitating Mediterranean goddesses. She bought me a Jameson and soda in Doran's of Baggot Street, had come shaken from the bedside of the dying Mrs. Bowden who worked in the Irish Sweep offices at Ballsbridge. The taste of toddy and cloves in my mouth. The double-decker bus went down the hill by the harbour, the Top Hat Ballroom, the cottages of Monkstown, the pond in Blackrock Park. Evening light filled the lower compartment. Schoolchildren, active as bees in clover, sang glees. The whang was that of poorer Dublin, the Coombe. They were coming from the sea.

You were dead. You intimated: *Take heed of what you see, my son; for as you see me now, so will you one day be.* You were Sedna the Earth Mother, the old woman who lives under the ice. White birds flew to unknown lands over your head and the aurora borealis danced in the sky, but you heard nothing except the roaring in your head. You were down among the walrus herds and the seal herds and the big fish. You were a deep fish, half that, half human, little soapstone mother.

They buried her on a grey autumn day, slightly head first (she was always impetuous), put a framework of wreaths on top and left it at that. No thumping of clay on the lid. Not many were there. It was almost nice to be going to earth before the winter.

The grave, *das Grab*; in the old Gaelic poetry it was the 'dark school'. To prop up the earth with a stone. She belonged to the earth, and it belonged to her. And the past too, and not only her own past. It was there. Hands long still in the grave. Look at the clouds. You had existed as a part of the seminal substance of the universe that is always becoming and never is: and now had disappeared into that which produced you. Many grains of frankincense on the same altar: one falls before, another falls after, but it makes no difference. Some things are hurrying into existence, others are hurrying out of it; and of that which is come into existence a part is already extinguished. (I stood in Doran's snug with my mother, and in my Menswear overcoat thought I would never die.) Everything is only for a day, both that which remembers and that which is remembered. Thou art a little soul bearing a corpse, Epictetus said. St. Paul called the human body a seed. It was sown a natural body; it was raised a spiritual body. Persephone. Xochipilli the Lord of Flowers.

⊂☙⊃

Phrases used by my mother: A drop (or let-down), a land (a harder drop: a disappointment), a windfall. The heel of the hunt; I can't fathom it; a queer fish; it never rains but it pours. It dawned on me. A real Yahoo. A black Protestant. Wall-falling (lassitude, inertia, state of will-lessness).

33 I AM IN A CLASSROOM: It is very familiar, from National School days in Sligo and then preparatory school and then college days. It is an amalgamation of three different places and three different times when I had been three different persons. I do not pay much attention to the fittings. The classroom is known to me. The teacher is absent. It is during a recess. An unpopular boy is being baited.

He begins to assert himself a little, unsurely and ineffectively. The tormentors grow bored and show it. They begin to move away. To make some impression he threatens to take off all his clothes. All right, they say, take off your clothes, it makes no difference to us. In a half-hearted way he begins to undress. They ignore him.

The dream continues but the place changes. I am standing in the hall of a big house. The front doors are open into the garden. It's summer in the country somewhere, I seem to know the place. I am not uncomfortable, though I have not seen the place before (dream connivance). The classroom walls have rolled aside to reveal this hall and garden (dream duplicity). What am I doing there? I sit there reading near the steps.

Charlotte Bayless sits on a low chair. Beside her, kneeling and holding both her monkey paws in his, is Amory. He is speaking in a low voice, very persistent, propositioning her. I recall something de Rougemont had said about seducing women, the five approaches. Amory is well past the first obstacle, her indifference. She is leaning forward, her face close to his, flattered and won over by both his words and his persistence. She is agreeing to whatever he is proposing. She could find the time, the opportunity, if he could find the place. I am struck by the tactics used, how he had positioned himself close to her and kept on talking and never letting go, not taking his eyes off her. He is most persuasive and she is disarmed by his methods; tactics which it would never have occurred to me to use, but succeed very well here. I am close to them but cannot hear what he is saying. He is murmuring into her ear. She is laughing. I pretend to read, thinking, *she is not behaving very well*.

Seduced by his arguments, won over by his boldness and persistence, she is agreeing to everything he suggests. *Fuego lento en el Horno*. There are others in the garden. I see McSorley, prizewinner from college days standing there, the prizewinner for mathematics who limped.

It is he who is watching Charlotte and Amory, saying nothing, just watching, pursing up his mouth. I am waiting for them to walk arm-in-arm into the garden. Will I shout out after her? They do not move, but Amory goes on murmuring. McSorley walks past them into the garden. He wears spectacles and has no limp.

I see my brother Wally walking in the garden with a pale girl with light brown hair. She wears a green beret and old-fashioned clothes. Wally looks the same as he has always looked. He wears a heavy Aran jersey (although it is high summer and the garden full of butterflies). They are quite near but do not look at me. I notice long female hairs sticking to the Aran jersey.

To one side of the main hall (which somehow resembles Nullamore) a female figure is undressing behind a plastic semi-transparent shower curtain. The narrow back tapers to narrow hips; I see the cleft of a trim ladylike bum. It's Sally Lester. She turns, draws aside a curtain, steps out rather flushed in the face. I get an eyeful of her long legs, dark triangle, heavy chaumontel pears. She passes me going into the garden, murmuring something to the effect that she will liven up the party. But there is no party.

Amory and Charlotte ignore her, their heads still close together. She smiles at what he dares to say. They could be honeymooning or new lovers infatuated with each other. The bare feet of the Dorset Stripper make no noise on the tiles. She goes out into the sensuous disorder of an untamed garden.

A while later I see her coming towards me along the path clasping to her a bunch of long-stemmed gladioli, not out of prudery you may be sure, but more likely to draw attention to her nudity. She has become the buxom female model in the art class hiding her bush with long-stemmed flowers plucked still damp from some garden: an illustration from *The Artist*. Quite soon she must drop them, pose for art students, listen to the scraping of charcoal and pencils. Venus Aphrodite, the tender dangerous love-goddess of the legends. She clasps the flowers to her, the stems browned a little at the stalks. She walks there, attempting to liven up the party, but there is no party, and my faithless one and Amory ignore her. She only succeeds in scandalizing Wally and his Irish girl friend, who are making for the gate. By the position of their lowered heads I see that neither approve.

McSorley stands in the hallway. He has come in silently from the garden. He stands there without taking his eyes off Amory and Charlotte, the former still holding the latter's hands, the fair head still bent to hear what the bearded lips are murmuring. The nibbling lips of a goat. It is a lesson in seduction. McSorley's eyes are full of tears. He stands there watching them, and I stand observing him. Tableau.

In this dream, I, a non-participant throughout, did not utter one word. But there again does one speak in dreams?

34 THE PICTURES IN THE WAITING-ROOM: The surgery of Dr. Jorge del Bosque is situated above Calle del Arropiero, near the junction of Calle Pintada and Calle de las Angustias where the latter street crosses over to Calle de los Trancos, the waiting-room abutting on the street, and the surgery. In the waiting-room a picture in an antique frame reveals a lady seated in an armchair alongside a bed. She is leaning forward with an anxious expression, one hand pressed to her breast and the other, in a limp and exhausted way, to her forehead. A young bearded doctor dressed in black, with a choker, stands gazing solicitously down at her. The lady gazes up at him in supplication. She wears a full-skirted brocade dress; her face escapes me, I see blonde curls. She has adopted a stilted pose next to a small canopied bed, her elbow rests on this while she gazes fixedly at the doctor. Whatever her ailment he can surely cure it. Perhaps she is pregnant and married and it's not the husband's child? Perhaps it's the doctor's child?

She has come from a party, feeling weak, and summoned him to attend her? She knows she is pregnant. The doctor might be one of the guests, perhaps at her party; this manly, bearded, attentive doctor, both professional and correct, may be her lover. Or else they are lovers at the preliminary stages of an affair? Or perhaps as yet unkissed by him, but finding him attractive, she is attempting to seduce him, feigning some ailment? Or are they lovers at the end of an affair? The embarrassment apparent in their respective poses leaves this open.

Or she is pregnant, and the child she is carrying is his. She has not told him yet, still searching for the right words. He stands by the bed, waiting for her to collect herself. He could be a doctor from Chekhov; the dress and manner would be about right. The protagonists in Chekhov's *The Grasshopper*, which I had seen at the Jewish B'nai Brith Society in Montreal bored by three-quarters of it, but overwhelmed by the end, the husband dying and the floor opening. The errant wife repeated 'Give me your honest Christian hand,' and some of the Jews beside me laughed in a guarded manner into their beards. Chekhov had based the story on fact, antagonizing a real couple, branded them as adulterers. The doctor's wife had some arty-crafty place in a watch-tower or fire-station, and had gone on painting trips with the painter Levitan.

A steep flight of tiled steps leads to the surgery proper. There are more pictures there. In hot weather the blinds are draped over the balcony rail and everything is conducted in a subdued light. The light comes from the street below and the doctor's face is lit accordingly, an actor near footlights. He has a filing cabinet and instrument tray, two bookcases, two chairs for patients, and his own untidy desk. The surgery is somewhat drab, cluttered up with objects, papers and bottles, brown rubber stethoscope. A dim old-fashioned room for receiving patients. The room itself matches Dr. del Bosque's manner: reassuring, quiet-toned, dim, old-fashioned.

One wall is enlivened with a monochrome print of a very bloody operation performed in the olden days, in the old manner. Also, but in colour, yellow mostly (a colour pleasing to God), *Enferma del Amor*, by laughing Jan Steen or Leyden. Genre scenes from the old Dutch masters. A picture (untitled) of a tall girl, with coils of thick ash-blonde hair, big feet and even bigger breasts, subsiding stark naked into the arms of a meaty brown-skinned surgeon who supports her with a hand on her stomach, a typical Shamanistic gesture. She is further supported from below by a skeleton who ardently embraces her hips. Much pubic hair on view.

Behind the doctor a crucifix without even a wasted Saviour is inset in a holy niche near a calendar on the mouldy wall. A small room leads off this. Here he keeps the famous fluoroscope. One of the walls is curtained, a couch stands against it, a shaded wall-light over it, an overhead fan.

The atmosphere. Downstairs in the waiting-room the general atmosphere is good, no feeling or smell of sickness, but many flies. The doctor is slow and methodical, a wait of two hours not being exceptional. He examines the patients one by one, upstairs, seeing one patient off, greeting another on the way up. You could be sitting patiently below, imagining him working in the surgery when he calmly walks in off the street. He is the doctor for the local middle class, the *extranjeros*, not liked by the poor, who prefer to go to Malaga, almost fifty kilometres away. *El Cabron* they call him: The Goat. They say he prescribes only pills.

He works hard, keeping long hours with no assistant or nurse and leaves the surgery without a word if called away on an urgent case, never complaining of the long hours. We have found him reliable, a kind man, his manner calm and reassuring. He murmurs, jokes a little, speaks some English. Olivia was his first English teacher. Sometimes we cannot pay him. He never presents a bill or complains; *No importante*, he says. It is more important that you should be well. Pay when you can. He laughs, one tobacco-stained finger adjusting the bridge of his spectacles, a chain-smoker.

In the surgery there are fewer flies. It is cooler, the ceiling higher. Dr. Jorge del Bosque waits at the top of the stairs.

⟨❦⟩

One night, passing late, I saw horses outside the doctor's door. They were tethered to the window-guards. A scene out of the past: horses at night outside a doctor's door. Some sick person from the *fincas*, the *pueblos* of the sierras. No telegraph wires went there. They had ridden down with the sick one. A patient with a grey face being tended by candle-light; the silent companions watching in the shadows of the room as the doctor, whistling between his teeth, probes and probes. Snake-bite or thrown by a horse; a rupture; a haemorrhage?

Themes of surgeons, operations and autopsies very frequent in Holland, but not so much in Flanders.

35 OLIVIA IS DREAMING: She dreams of a maid-servant, a pale, round-faced girl 'somewhat like myself' with a 'simpering' face (Olivia, who never simpers, has a poor opinion of herself). The maid is tall, wears 'nice clothes': a long white diaphanous dress with wing sleeves that suggest the Brontë sisters, puffed out leg-of-mutton sleeves that fall away from the wrists. When she moves they spread out around her very elegantly. The maid-servant and Olivia are dancing. They are crouching down like dark heathens or fighting cocks, imitating the motions and ritual movements of some Eastern religious dance, crouching close together, hair hanging over their shoulders, moving their heads from side to side in a drugged manner, as if secretly mating. Little by little they raise their voices in a 'kind of gabbling and scandalizing' that is supposed to be humorous, but which isn't at all, their faces close together, crouching, moving their heads up and down, and pretend to be kissing through their hair. 'Why us? I don't know. Certainly I would never have begun it myself. The maid-servant and I are dancing. Why? I don't know. Our arms across our chests, then our hands on each other's shoulders, kissing through the mesh of hair.' It is supposed to be 'flagrantly indecent'; but it wasn't that. I could not see the point of it myself.

Then, raising the pitch of their voices, they indicated that the whole thing was a joke; it was a kind of mime. Three people were watching, a stout, very respectable aunt or mother-figure, not clearly seen, an elegant doctor wearing a black suit, and a 'flower-like' daughter. As they dance, the diaphanous sleeves of the dress spread out around them. Olivia, through this, sees the daughter watching them; she is not well, in some way not specified, in fact she is ill. Very pale, her movements are quick, agitated, she is 'all nerves'.

The other adult figures are 'sinister but extremely elegant'.

All three are laughing at the dance. They are all laughing as if it were the best joke in the world. The doctor holds a pair of spectacles in his hand and is wiping his eyes. They are laughing so hard that tears are running down their cheeks. The aunt-mother shakes all over. She is dressed in a voluminous russet and black outfit, wears a demi-veil which she has pushed back, and laughing so heartily she looks like a tea-cosy with steam coming out of it. The pale, ultra-nervous daughter laughs until she becomes hysterical.

The doctor, now very serious, puts on his spectacles, stares hard at the laughing daughter, and brings out a long narrow plastic tube from an inside pocket while the aunt (mother) figure holds her down very cruelly, he inserts this illegal-looking instrument into her brain. She faces them with her eyes starting out of her head, watching the tube, which is trans-parent. The doctor holds her by the shoulders, and taking a deep breath, begins to pump a yellowish-brown liquid (coming apparently out of his own chest) sluggishly into the tube, and from there into her brain. When the fluid starts to move the daughter's eyes become fixed. The doctor holds his patient to him, one hand clutching her shoulder, and staring into her eyes; with his free hand he seems to be pumping. The liquid appears to be moved along by the doctor's respiration. He takes deep breaths, looking intently into his patient's eyes. It's some modern gadget, Olivia says.

36 OLIVIA PROPOSITIONED: Olivia was in the Marissal one night with the Baylesses. There was a dance under the revolving lights in the hall behind the bar, where formerly Amory and I had played billiards. The smiling barber with the chubby face of MacLiammoir was talking to Olivia, who was sitting at the bar next to a fashionably-dressed Spanish woman. Presently MacLiammoir was dancing with Charlotte and Olivia drawn into conversation by the Spanish woman. They spoke French, the societywoman breathing Rum and Coca Cola.

Je vous ai déjà vu ici, n'est-ce-pas? she said.

Oui, said Olivia. *Nous . . . je viens ici quelquefois. Mon mari prefère l'autre bar.*

Vous habitez dans ce quartier depuis quelque temps? the woman asked.

Oui, said Olivia. *Ça nous plait beaucoup. Je me rapelle vous avoir vu aussi, ici dans le Marissal.*

Non, said the woman, *à vrai dire, je travaille à Malaga, ou je donne des leçons de danse. Je passe le weekend ici quelquefois. Je l'aime bien, cet endroit, il est tellement tranquille.*

They changed the subject; spoke of other things. Then the societywoman said:

Je vous troure ravissante, vous avez surement beaucoup de soupirants—

Olivia thought that she was now dealing with a Lesbian. Never before had she been approached by a Lesbian.

Mon frère, par example. Je crois qu'il voudrait bien coucher avec vous.

Oh! said Olivia.

Il le fait très bien, the woman said brazenly.

Mais, je suis mariée, Olivia protested. *Et, a part ça, je ne connais même pas votre frère.*

Il habite ici, vous le connaissez sans doute de vue. Il est un grand brun, plutôt pale—lui aussi, il est danseur.

Peut-être bien que je le connais, Olivia said—(knowing quite well whom the woman meant). The brother was a pale, constipated-looking fellow who danced Flamenco on occasions at Adolfo Sanchez's hotel. Girls with pale lipstick seem to be either constipated or in the middle of their period—the brother looked like that; stiff-backed and slack-jawed.

Les français font bien l'amour, said the dancing mistress. *Ils sont doués au lit* (insinuatingly, laying a hand on Olivia's arm).

Oh! said Olivia.

⁕

Olivia stood next to the dancing mistress at the bar, the brother between them with his head down, looking vacantly into his beer. You are very attractive, she said to Olivia in Spanish, and must have many admirers. *Beaucoup trop*, Olivia said, being mistrustful of compliments, particularly artful compliments from women.

My brother here, the woman said, would you not like to sleep with him? Taken by this directness—for the brother was listening, not raising his head, or raising it only to look at some men standing at the bar, Olivia said something to the effect that not *all* men were attractive to her, not even all Spaniards. *Gitanos*, she said, now she found them attractive (thinking possibly of the tall dark-faced man from Calle Italia, the dominoes champion of the Balcon de Europa bar). Seeing that Olivia was not interested, the dancing mistress changed the subject. The brother stood between them, the go-between, hang-dog, saying nothing, watching another Sodomite sitting near the door.

The brother was queer all right, had worked in France as a hairdresser, and was connected with MacLiammoir who worked in Frankfurt, cutting women's hair, as a dog-barber too, waiting for some permit that was held up in Spain. Olivia danced with the brother whose sister, the procuress, had solicited for him. He was double-jointed and 'very rubbery', not dancing too close, clicking his fingers, his heart evidently not in it.

Whenever they chanced to meet after that, Olivia and the dancing mistress, they avoided each other's eye, and saluted a point on the road equidistant between each other. I saw her a

few times in the El Molino bar in the company of young fashionably-dressed Spaniards, possible protégés from the disbanded
dancing class.

⊙❧⊙

Dancing with another woman, it's like drowning, Olivia
said. A woman's heart is like a room filled with pitiable stuff.

37 DREAM NEGRESS: I am in a small room. It appears to be the shallow living-room of a narrow bungalow. I am standing by the window. The front door is closed and Olivia has instructions to admit no one. I am working.

I am not working. Someone stands at the door, knocking or ringing but I hear nothing; through the lattice window I see the caller, part of her. A Negress stands there, her waist above my eye-level: I see black thighs and hips, a curve of implacable thighs, the fierce grip of stockings to suspender-belt, panties with a rose design. The suspender-belt clutches like a tourniquet. All in all, a considerable eyeful.

The dream moves on. Now I am in a courtyard. A small group of players, mummers, are about to perform a modern version (perhaps a corruption) of something old and traditional. The Negress moves into the dream. She lies down and is covered with a blanket up to the neck. She closes her eyes, half smiling, and mimes sleep. One of the male members of the troupe, dressed in Shakespearean style with a short cloak, walks away from her. Someone beside me begins to explain the 'mysteries of the ancient rites'. I pay little attention, watching the 'sleeping' Negress. With eyes closed she is still smiling.

The man runs towards her, his cloak flying. He comes up like a footballer attempting a difficult conversion, a field goal. With the full force of his iron-shod boot he kicks her head (her hair is cut short, her skull the shape of a football). The skull emits a dull sound, like a coconut. Has he killed her, addled her brains? The force of the kick should have torn the head off her shoulders.

But she rises, smiling. In deep trance, she felt nothing. That is their secret: they can withstand any pain, since they are removed from it, inert in coma. She is hard and impenetrable, like iron or stone, as if covered in the ointment that Medea smeared over Jason to protect him from the Colchians. The voice continues to give a detailed account of the Ancient Rites. I am not listening. I watch the Negress calmly rising, folding the blanket, brushing her skirt, smiling to herself. She begins to walk away. I watch her go, marvelling, remembering the suspender-belt that clutched like a tourniquet.

38 WHAT'S IT LIKE TO HAVE ONE? Charlotte asked me. It must be wonderful to have one. To feel it there between your legs, the weight of it. To be conscious of it all the time.

You would have me wear a codpiece? I said. In Sir Walter Raleigh's day, the gallants bolstered their doublets with *bombast*, to make the thing look heavier.

Sir Walt in Cork, the butter hairy, his troops strutting on the Mall, the native kerns deceitful, liars by necessity, not a virgin in the land.

Why not? she said, and looked at me, considering me; her eyes with that blueish tinge.

Something I felt: *You are I, and I am you.*

She herself preferred sanitary towls to Tampax because that gave her a feeling, an equivalent, a weight, Why not?

What about a young one's breasts and hair? I said.

She took this quite seriously. Yes, to feel one's breasts, to let one's hair down, feeling it on one's naked back. To lie in bed naked and feel hair on the bare skin, that was something.

Her own hair was long and oily, as long hair tends to be, particularly in hot regions. Oily hair gives a better feeling of abandonment, and a hairless Venus has no power to charm the human heart.

Hairy butter. The bolstered gallants. (That worse devil that's between my thighs.) She'd go for that? Passionate, but envious of the male, the ordained taker. *Que desea usted? Prefiere usted la carne al horno, a la parilla, hervida o guisada?*

She wants you to come for supper, her husband had said, putting his hand on my shoulder. She told me to say a place is laid for you. She's preparing something good. Won't you come?

Your eyes, Charlotte. I see reality in their shades of colour— not aqueous, not vitreous—the deeper parts of Lake Garda on a sunny day.

Maud Gonne at Howth station waiting for a train. The sea-wall by the harbour, the tide coming over the sandbar on Claremont beach. The English actress Lily Elsie standing on Windsor platform waiting for a train. To see the deeps, the aspirations and the vanity of civilizations lost in the wandering depths of an ageing and vain actresses eyes, an ageing ex-beauty waiting at Windsor for a slow local train.

The human body made up of liquid, flesh, bones, humours, chemicals, puff-paste. Its bond, tie, kinship with inorganic matter, that slowly encroaching activity, the waste of the world; and how through the single loved body all that is most appealing in that other person is represented, continually fêted, yet continually being withdrawn. Love, that most despairing grip; the cruel fabled bird that pinches like a crab.

She was all that for me.

39 I'M NOT GOING TO HELP YOU ANY MORE (Bob Bayless told me).

He was half turned away, looking sourly into his Victoria beer, his shoulders hunched up. His cheeks, seen from this angle, bulged like lugs, swelling out as if he suffered from *dolor de muelas*. His lobeless ears gave him a somewhat degenerate look.

I digested this piece of information as best I could.

You were helping me? I said. This is news to me indeed.

(My recent past like a chute, and she and I falling pell mell down.)

Sure, I was, Bob said. I was pimping for you . . . but not any more. Anyway, you wouldn't have gotten very far with her unless she'd strewn a few roses in your path.

And Amory? I said, producing the name stealthily.

Amory? What the fuck has Amory got to do with it? You must be mad. Amory means nothing to her. I know her well enough to say that. You need fear nothing from that quarter.

I said nothing, bought him a beer, stealthily.

Who was Amory? Not Palos, not the one who invented the saw, slept with his mother, not Philoctetes either, but Talus— one of those impetuous and no doubt liverish Mediterranean divinities, the freak fire-giant created by Hephaistos in the story of the Argonauts. He had a mountain forge in Etna, beneath the earth, and Minos as guardian and protector of his preserve, the Cretan coast.

Thrice a day he walked around the island, and never stopped to sleep; and if strangers landed, he ran up the hill and leaped into the furnace; became red-hot; and rushed down upon them. None but Medea could face him. One vein filled with liquid fire.

That was Amory the wild man, climbing outside staircases in Montreal; shinning up the side of a house in Calle Nueva, putting the wind up the Hools.

40 PAST: Surprisingly hairy, Charlotte had said. (Their bedroom floor sank in the middle, it was a cave-like place. His pyjama pants had a deep rent in the groin.)

Enough of that heating sex stuff, Bob said. Enough of that low-down steamy stuff. Romance—that's what we need, romance and lots of it.

I thought: With you I could be happy. And immediately afterwards: With you I'd know true misery. I was old enough to be her father. I could not imagine her ever being old: she was so young, she existed with a certain vehemence about her, yet physical weakness was an essential and very touching part of her nature. Her low blood pressure. She was an American golden bathing girl, the blonde in the red convertible crossing the Golden Gate Bridge in the evening, heading for some assignation in San Francisco, her small and somewhat avaricious hands on the steering column, her eyes out on the bay full of boats. She was moving away from the old Jew father, her Polish past, her mother with the lined face, whom I had never seen yet was so disposed to like. I pictured her as a little plain, a silent and preoccupied woman. Her daughter was a privileged being, free as air.

She said: On the middle of the bridge the temperature changes and you can smell Marin County. The wind blew in from the Gulf. All the suburbs in San Anselmo and San Rafael and Mill Valley felt it, right down to the Golden Gate. (The big open car went through the multiple shadows cast by the arms of the bridge.) She was pursued by a low fellow from Piedmont. He said: My momona is like water. He meant his semen. He was skinny, skinny-minded. They met at a party at Albany. There was a room set aside for necking. In the gloom the bodies were stuck together. They were trying not to make babies. He asked her to join him. He had a cousin in Reuter's, his conversation was dull. He was very avid. Play ball, honey, he said, play ball.

Her whole face glowed as though with light, she had lanterns under her skin. A freckled young fellow from Oakland took her into the hills around Sacramento. His portable played bossa nova—'Desafinado'. He wanted her to dance with him in the nude. He had carroty hair. The hills were deserted (far from the family kitchen, the rotting oilcloth, the smells of cooking vegetables), burnt sepia. The freckled young man swam naked in a stream. The portable played 'Desafinado.' He attempted to get on top of her in the water. I did not love him, she admitted sadly, I did not want it.

One day in an unimaginable place she had come to me. From San Francisco, on the same line of latitude but on the opposite side of the globe, the only wine growing region in the United States, had come to this cold fishing village under different names and disguises, though nothing I can say here can convey what she looked like or what she represented for me. She had a gilded look, and was preceded by a number of avatars.

Greasy cobblestones on a wide boulevard in Aachen. It's raining. I go through the German Customs. A narrow street in Maastricht, over the border. In Holland too it has been raining. The streets are wet. I enter a cakeshop. A Dutch family sits at a table. Stout parents and a pasty-faced son, and your first avatar: a pale-faced sprite with long black hair, aged about fourteen, a face to make the patrons stare. In an umbrella stand the umbrellas were leaking. The place was overheated. I sat near the table and watched you. You never noticed me.

An early afternoon in a wet August, and cold too. I was in a train travelling from Ostende to Cologne. The flat fields and ponds of Belgium went by, peasant women with wooden rakes passing below, not bothering to look up, and all the stations named after battles of World War One. In the early morning I saw a grey river: Old Father Waters, *Vater Rhein*, Europe's open sewer, tumbling away towards Holland. The rain poured down the carriage window, entering the Alps.

Beyond, all changed. It was summer in Austria, with that feeling in the air that the returning heat brings, the lethargy of winter shaken off (it had been no summer). The earth was dry and the sun warm. The train was going on to Greece. Down the corridor the reports of the beer bottles as the wire fasteners came off. Cool in the closeness of the carriage, the limestone taste of the beer, and the seed pods bursting along the track outside. From all the stations the train seemed to retreat backwards. The train waited for half an hour in Spittal-Linz. Across the tracks another local train was getting up a head of steam to continue on up the valley. A young blonde girl was standing at an open carriage window. All her life she had lived in this warm valley. A dust road went alongside a river, a passing car sent dust high into the air, the white butterflies that are called *Kohlweisslinge* flew over the fields. I waited in the close carriage for the line to be cleared, watched the girl across the tracks. Did not my happiness lie there?

I was sketching in Tegel in West Berlin, one of three dull and shabby French districts: Tegel, Reinickendorf, Wedding. I saw your avatar running in the school yard, a girl of perhaps seventeen running at full tilt across a school field on an autumn day in the divided city. The girls were in full cry, the leaves scattering under the trees. Did you notice me? I came back next day and there you were again. I trespassed, entered the school building. In the corridor the stench of collective farting. They must have been given beans for lunch. From the sketches I made oil paintings. I did not try to paint you. Did you notice me there? Probably not.

In Dubrovnik harbour at seven in the morning, the cafés are full of sober citizens taking their coffee before the day's work begins. In a tram going up a hill you are sitting beside me. You speak a language I do not understand. I do not know your name. Dobrila Pantic? You breathe, you are brown-skinned. Heavy-lidded eyes. The tram goes grinding up the hill into the walled city, leaving behind an awkward squad of soldiers, a gesticulating officer. Perhaps he knew you were aboard the little tram, which seemed to be lifting off the rails. You smiled. It was not what one might call a fixed smile, no, it came from several quarters at once. The actress smile of the Frenchwoman Sylvie Selig (seen in *Elle*), and a more guarded and wistful smile

—more in the eyes than in the mouth—of the Bolivian bride *Señorita* Marcia Paz-Pero (a sad sweet smile from La Paz, her name part of a city) whose wedding picture I had seen in the *Irish Times*; and the pulpy lips and bare shoulders of the Ballet Russe dancer Tamara Karsavina, a sepia photograph seen in a book picked up in a Dublin bookshop and never opened again, in Stravinsky's *L'Oiseau de Feu*.

The collective charms of these sirens converge and meet in one: you, Charlotte Bayless-Harlan-Lipski. In dreams you were always moving towards me. And you looked different every time. We had loved each other before we had known each other. We had been unfaithful to each other before we even met.

41 A CONCEALED LETTER: Would you let me see it? I asked her. Okay, if you wish, she said. I'll tell you where I've hidden it. You can get it yourself.

She had hidden it under one of the wooden shelves in the upstairs loo that the artful Con Brodey, playing a loud treacherous Charybdis to Rosa's smooth and slippery Scylla, had caused to be erected, a small closed-off annex with handbasin and w.c. Will you be my man will you carry my can. It's in the upstairs john, Charlotte told me.

The blue-eyed Martin Hansen was infatuated with her. I had not noticed him staring at her in that pointed way with his frantic Danish blue eyes. They were strange eyes, a paler and more washed-out blue than hers and seemed to be fixed in intent, enmarbled, staring. They were both blue-eyed types, and both born in the same month—Hansen made a big issue of this.

Charlotte told me that Hansen, undressing behind a rock one day, had exposed his pale male backside to her. He had written her a love-letter and given it to her surreptitiously as they were dancing up at the Summerbees' place at Torrox. He asked her to destroy it when she read it, and this she had promised to do, but without much intention of keeping her word. She, you may be sure, fairly glittered in his arms; desired now by yet another artist, a handsome fellow with eyes the colour of a blue Scandinavian summer. Married, but what did that matter? So I had another rival.

Martin Hansen followed her about like the infatuated Cohn following Lady Bret Ashley. Tracey Weddick rather modelled herself on the same lady, whom Hemingway had modelled on Lady Twysden. Cohn the Jew was Harold Loeb.

They took to going together to the beaches, the three of them with the child, and sometimes Bob joined them later on in the evening, then going on drinking on the plaza outside the Marissal. And I kept away from her all this time, or for some of it, feeling the wedge, ignorant of the rival there.

But down on Torrecillas one day she told me where the letter was hidden. So she told me that much, wanting to be straight with me. She wanted me to find it myself, making me a party to her deviousness. Behind the attractive wife's secret hidden in the john I detected the adolescent girl, and behind her again a younger and almost innocent Charlotte Lipski. I wanted to go there and read it, see what Hansen had to say for himself. See what made Charlotte glitter.

Martin Hansen's billet-doux: Dear you! I believe you will find this foolish and childish—but I think I may write myself out of the sad mood I am in now, the few more glimpses of you, our departure for maybe forever and all around that (the handsomely infatuated Martin Hansen had written). Forgive my sentimental phrases—but I feel much pain looking back on the hours spent with you—and jealous against those who will put eyes on you from now on.

I believe so many have told you about your beauty and grace —but let me just whisper in your ear that you could have been my muse—I feel a masterpiece taken from you as model. But never?

I remember when you first came into Antonio's—your sweet voice, as I love—your grace—and a warm wave rose in me. I shall not tire you with the list I have made of small events— but it is true, and I take the little shell with me home—and it will keep my secret, my non-spoken words to you, confessions in long night hours. It is in a way the only thing now to do—to depart. I cannot in the long run just make conversation with you weighing the words to be neutral—when I wished to shout to all the world about you! You must throw this away—and I hope you will forget it—but before you do—I want you to know that I love you. Simply!—and so complicated!

Excuses for everything—my behaviour, my feelings for you —my bad spelling.

Martin

⟨❦⟩

Scylla (Rosa) had six heads and lived in a dark cave. She turned her head from side to side, almost reversed it like a bird, nervous of me. From her cave she fished for all things (particularly compliments); hers a rock which no man could climb though he have twenty hands and feet. Treacherous behind her blandishments, the sea-hag with the young whelp's voice.

42 SURPRISINGLY HAIRY, Charlotte said, referring to the limp Dane, Martin Hansen. She spoke through her nose. I saw the rent in the groin, the reciprocity of brutes, and my fever came on again. A little feverish sweating announced the return of my soul. At night now I wore his pyjamas with the tell-tale rent in the groin. My Malta Fever was cured, but I was not cured of her who wore nothing in bed. Where will you be? I'll be wherever I'll find you. Where will you go? Go where I'll find you.

Surprisingly hairy: some male brute out for *pratique* (an afternoon connection, what Amory called 'a good siesta fuck,' in a flat near Kezer Stadium where the ghosts of the immortals still dodged and ran). You know how she turns questions aside when she doesn't want to answer, Olivia said. She doesn't answer you, asks another question, changes the subject. I won't have that. I asked her how was Bob. I was concerned about him. She wouldn't answer me. Well, if she wants my friendship, she must come out and get it. I can't stand this hedging and slyness.

Yes, that was her way, avoiding the questions that she did not wish to answer, deflecting them away from her, turning a question dexterously aside as though she had not heard it, and setting off at a tangent with another. She said: The *Baylesses* did this, did that, in another place, another time; but what she meant (and what she was understood to mean) was: I Dilly Bayless did this, did that, in this or that other place. She had a way of cramping Bob's style, putting him down. Was that the Jewish side of her, that deviousness, or just the woman? She was the Jewish Queen. Passionate, but envious of the male, the taker: that dominance. But wasn't there female dominance too? The privileges that went with youth and beauty. She was out to outman man. The whites of her eyes seen in profile, somewhat bloodshot from the glare or from hair-washing, indicated clearly enough: You please me, didn't you know? And then: But, sir, I am married—hadn't you noticed? And then: But you do please me, all the same. (That which is wished for; that which will not come again.) Humiliations, the crestfallen Bob opening the door said, I've had plenty this morning, I'm getting it like buckshot. Charlotte had found sand in his turn-ups and intuited that he had been down on the beach with the Omagh woman. Sand in his turn-ups, sand in his bleeding turn-ups! Blue bloody murder. She had fairly lit into him. *Move up MacKinerny, make room for Muckinurney!*

I asked her when she'd lost her virginity.

Sixteen, I guess. No, late fifteen. I got laid properly when I was sweet sixteen. I couldn't pass a road-drilling machine then without thinking of my impenetrable hymen. I went once with a girl friend to the theatre. There was this long guy in black tights that we couldn't take our eyes off. I was full of silent admiration. My friend wasn't so silent. She married him later. A guy called Dick Heller. He fucked around.

43 THE FLAT NEAR KEZER STADIUM: One day, in the bar El Cruzero Bob Bayless told me of their first night together.

It happened in his flat in San Francisco, in the days when he had been employed as a pop-corn vendor at the San Francisco Zoo. Charlotte (then merely Miss Harlan) had a well-paid job in Sausalito over the Golden Gate Bridge. They met at a party, got on well together. He said that she had 'gotten to sex very fast'. Talking about it. In those days he was ending a longstanding and unsatisfactory affair with another girl, also Jewish. Nothing he did pleased her. He was losing his nerve, felt his 'knackers shrinking', had 'dry runs', the girl could not come.

There had been nothing casual about Charlotte Harlan. She 'raised the hair on his head with stories of her sex life'. He felt very nervous with her, fearing he would disappoint her. She had 'slept around', never kept her lovers waiting. She agreed to come to his flat.

It was in an old area of the city, near a football stadium. He had come back dead tired from working at the Zoo. Waited for her, feeling 'randy as hell'. But she did not show up. Disappointed, he went to bed alone.

In the early hours of the morning she turned up, full of apologies and smelling of Bourbon, carrying a small parcel of indeterminate shape. She sat on the edge of the bed. Two Jewish lawmen had been buying her drinks in a Sausalito bar. She got away at four in the morning to keep her appointment with Bob. It was something she prided herself on. Her word was her bond, if she gave it she kept it. *Siempre*.

You know what they say of Jewish girls and professional men? Bob asked, cracking his finger-joints, sitting hunched up over his drink. No, I said. Can't resist 'em, Bob said. That's well-known.

He asked her what she was carrying in the small parcel.

Hick, she said. No, but what? Bob said. Wait, she said, I'll show you. She undid the string, showed him a short nightdress (transparent) with the price tag still intact. She took off all her clothes, put on the nightdress, struck a pose. Never put to the blush. A knowing riggish charmer. Mlle de Maupin offering to love's play her dark declivities. You like it? she asked. Oh sure, sure, Bob said. Good, she said, sorry for being late. Then she was throwing off the nightdress and getting into bed with him. He feared that he would fail with her, as with the other Jewish girl. He did not fail with her.

Why does he inflict these poxy details on me? Because he perceives, knows that I am infatuated, and deeply infatuated, with his wife? Perhaps so. Because he sees that she pleases me. Because it pleases him to tell me such painful details.

Olivia and Charlotte at this moment came in with Daisy. They had been buying salted peanuts at the kiosk. Charlotte sat beside me.

She spoke of an onanist on a hill in San Francisco at night, a silhouetted man jerking off. They were below and saw him against the skyline. She spoke of the nudist colony at Martha's Vineyard: a maid going down the path to take orders from the nudists, all thirsty, seriously sunbathing.

The tom-cat's prick had a kind of barb at the end of it, Charlotte said, and withdrawing from the she-cat it drew blood, and so issue. And the hedgehog—for the female it was painful. The she-hedgehog screamed when the buck (did one say buck?) covered her. And bats, she said, how did they do it? In flight? Bob was laughing at her. Can't you talk or think of anything else but penetrations? he said. And ways to do it. Now bats and hedgehogs. Jesus, Dilly!

Charlotte looked away, smiling at her thoughts. Her manner was suggestive, her manner of speaking, the tone of voice inseparable from a certain look in the eye, sentences tending to trail away. She could communicate wishes and desires with her hips, her hands, her thighs, her eyes. Much of what she said was delivered as an aside. She spoke like this in her husband's presence, and it was as if she was speaking behind his back, in his absence. He listened, hunched over the table, watching his wife perform. To me she spoke with the white of her eyes, the strength of her back, her wrists, communicating with more than her voice, expressing more than her voice could say, my lechard mistress with the curved little fingers of a Mongoloid. Her speaking looks admitted more than her words allowed: ours was an acquaintanceship that had soon improved into a friendship without reserve.

> *Que linda manita que tengo yo;*
> *Que blanca, que gorda, que dios me la dio.*

Screwing, Bob said, blowing out cigar smoke, frowning; you bet I know it. He had a sensual wife. He was proud of her. She had Polish and Jewish blood, two extreme forms of racial oppression; but she could not be down-faced. She was a New Yorker through and through. To the Poles optimism is a prime source of strength; throughout their ordeals (and history has supplied them with many) they have always hoped for a better future, and were always ready to fight for it. In gusty Poland.

And New Yorkers? Bronx and Yonkers; had she not emerged from the Lower East Side as the 'toughest kid on the block'; pouting and shivering, rather remote? Now in her nature like all other daughters, she took chances. A ghost girl at an open door, Jewish. A spirit; she had her fling. She worked in her old man's shop. Old Lipski, a Polack. The shop was closed on Saturday, the Jewish Sabbath, when old Harlan (now he was Harlan) made up the books. He was saving to send his girls through college. Charlotte heard heavy traffic passing at night like battle tanks. She knew nothing of nature, the bird on the bough; nature was the filthy East River, the smell of fruit in the stalls. The boys were cat-calling near the fire hydrants, wolf-whistling at the bigger girls. She saw condoms in the dirty river, bobbing out with the tide, life was flowing out with the condoms. She stood at the corner of Orchard and Delancey Streets, grew up in the musty air of her Jewish-Polish home— the Jew's alluring daughter flanked by the castrating father. They ate matzo balls, gefilte fish, kosher salami; the old man read the Talmud; the Polish Ashkenazi. Charlotte knew a few words of Polish. She began to drift; sometimes she felt dead.

She was bitten by a horse in the country. Her aunt Esther Billig found the marks on her bottom, purple weals a handspan apart. She had befriended the animal and then it turned vicious, savaged her with its great seaweed teeth. She went to the ball park and the football stadium, track meets.

As a young thing, walking in the woods, she had seen a 'mad mouse' going in circles. She looked at it, walked on.

She was a young girl, then. A beekeeper with protective mask and gloves beckoned to her. He wore wellington boots and a big hat. He waded through a meadow. She followed him. They came to the beehives. He opened one, beckoned her to come closer. She came up to the hive. The swarm flew up at her. She ran. The beekeeper was making extraordinary sounds. She ran like the wind. A bee, buzzing like electricity, entangled itself in her hair. When it stung her, she felt the pain like fire. The disturbed hive was about her; she could have fallen, been stung to death there. Her head was stung and burning. She never went back there or reported the man. It was an extraordinary thing to do, set the bees on her. She supposed it to be normal in the country. *Zaar ba'ale chayim. Chushem.*

She was growing up, filling out. An admirer by the fire hydrant told her she was a dish. A dicey little Jewish dish. She had a weakness for athletes, trackmen; later on it would be professional men. She was quite free in her ways, having at the age of fifteen lost her virginity; then to Antioch University, and there became beautiful.

Jews, we are Jews, the old man said, never forget that. He showed her an umber snapshot taken in the city of Lvov (or Lemburg), an old bearded Jew in soft white boots, grasping a holy book. Stealthy light in the defiles of the ghetto, the watch-tower with its broken lantern. You are Jewish. The old man mistrusted Goys.

How could she for a moment forget it? She was Lotte Lipski, not Dilly Harlan (or Gittel Mosca), the embodiment of impulse and sexuality. Pinky swears, she said, crooking her little Mongoloid finger. Scout's honour!

There were more Jews in metropolitan New York than in all Israel. More than double the total of European Russia: over

$2\frac{1}{2}$ million in New York alone. Joanovici the subtle calculator who made a fortune out of scrap iron during World War Two. Neiman Marcus and Naum Goldmann. Chanuka candelabra glorifying the Maccabees. Harlem pawnbrokers and Bronx rent-collectors. The richly-left Ida Rubenstein. Silverstein and Goldblatt, Gottlieb and Gundelfinger, Gottfried and Gavronsky, all lived there profitably.

Had she not escaped from two kinds of bondage—her father's European background, and then Orchard Street? Graduated from Antioch and married to Bob Bayless, sailed for Europe, Tangier, with the child, the little girl I felt so disposed to like.

The very worst thing to be, Bob said, was a Polack Jew born about 1900 in Poland. Hitler didn't like Polish Jews. And by the time he'd finished, helped by Himmler, there weren't too many left.

And the very worst thing to be in Czechoslovakia around 1938 was a Sudeten German Social Democratic Jew, which was just what some of Dilly's male relatives, out of pure Jewish cussedness, had to be. The Nazis wiped out the lot.

Sir Thomas Browne kept maggots in boxes, Bob Bayless said. I remembered how he had taken the news about the Nazi Baron, and Charlotte laughing. His face grew longer and longer and he said: So you laugh at that? Then you are a fool, my dear. The traces of gaiety in his wife's face became fainter and fainter and then left it, until her face had the helplessness of someone who is no longer believed in.

Auschwitz, Majdanek, Sobibor, Belsen, Treblinka. Oldrich Lipski the subtle calculator.

> These images in the Great Memory stored,
> Come with a loud cry and panting breast
> To break upon the sleeper's rest.

Charlotte admitted to me that after two years of marriage she had been unfaithful to Bob. The man concerned was a mutual friend. She had not planned it or wanted it. It had just happened.

This was painful for me to hear.

She had been 'very happy' with that nameless and featureless lover. (For some reason, this was less painful to hear). Bob had never known that there was anything going on between them.

It began one winter after a party they gave in San Francisco. Bob had been working as a peanut vendor in the San Francisco Zoo. And Charlotte (so Tracey Weddick had told me) had been 'giving him hell'. Jesus, how low can you get? It was in their flat overlooking Kezer Stadium. The man had left the party early. He forgot his car keys. Charlotte found the plastic ring with his name on it, the keys, and had gone out after him into the streets. He was on his way back when she saw him. A line of cars drew up at the red light, she called his name and waved the key. They went 'into a clinch'. Previous to this he had never tried anything on.

Charlotte did not go to his flat that night. But it was more or less settled between them that she would. About a week later, when Bob was at work, she went. She found that she liked him. He was a good lover, Charlotte said (had 'kinda exotic tastes'). I experienced another, sharper, pang of jealousy. He never returned to their flat near Kezer Stadium. She went to his flat instead. It was all very discreet. Bob, suspecting nothing, asked her why they never saw him anymore. She said she didn't know. Bob 'liked the guy'. A love-letter came which she burnt. She never told Bob about it, and the affair ended. As a love-token, he gave her a silver fruit knife, which Bob later discovered. He asked her where she'd got it. She told him that she had stolen it. He believed her.

For this affair she suffered no remorse. Deceitful by nature, she lied whenever necessary. Lie in your teeth, Charlotte said. Even if found out, lie in your teeth, admit to nothing.

A sin concealed is half forgiven.

She stole compulsively from bars and hotels. A silver fork marked *Los Manueles* was out on a table in Granada, then it was wrapped in a paper serviette, then her handbag was open on her lap (she asked me to cover what she was attempting to do), then the jaw of the handbag snapped shut and the fork had disappeared. Was she a kleptomaniac? Or was it something other than that, some atavistic urge, Jewish trick for survival, putting valuables aside for the calamitous day?

And her attitude, after all, was not all deceit; for had she not been frank with me? You and I are alike, she had said; and I, who had never been told that before, least of all by a good-looking woman, acknowledged it to be true. We were alike. Her hands, those small and rather ugly monkey paws, told me something which her charms tended to conceal: she was avaricious, a perfect little furry beast out of the jungle. Something of that was in her nature. *Yes, I'll take, I'll have that; that I must have,* her small prehensile hands indicated. Eyes sometimes deceive, hands never. All the brilliance of those Gorgon's eyes said, *what I like I see, what I want I take. But do I see thee?*

She said: When my mother was asleep, she saw herself sleeping. She said: My cousin (a graduate from Columbia University Law School) who works as a clerk for a Noo York Judge . . .

The fruit knife given to her by a nameless lover had not been stamped with the name of bar or hotel, and Bob had never seen such a knife in any bar or hotel, yet he believed her when she told him that she had stolen it. Lifted it from 'some bar or other'. O credulous husband! But I knew where she had got it. These lies were bonds between us. She would not deliberately lie to me, or not until I had been ousted by another lover. And in the meantime she lied glibly to Bob.

Because they lived together, slept together, I picked quarrels with her. And because I, like any callow youth, could not live without seeing her, I 'made it up'. I wrote her letters, sent her presents of books through the post. Sybil le Brocquy's book on the Dean's marriage to Stella.

We had quarrelled over nothing. The peace offering was Madame le Brocquy's book on Swift's *supposed* marriage. I called at No. 12, hoping to find her alone. Charlotte answered the door, standing there in Rosa's white sweater and white slacks, barefoot, an apparition of hope and youth. She looked at me with those extraordinary eyes, saying nothing, just watching.

Come to see you, I said miserably, white as a maggot and just as mean.

Come in, maggot, she said smiling, admitting me. Got your

present, she said, and your letter. And that was all she had time to say, for her husband's voice began booming upstairs. Then he was coming down in his broken *alpargatos*, roaring for mail. He had confused me with the mailman; I had arrived at mail delivery time.

No, Charlotte said with a bright look at me, no mail—Dan's here.

Bayless came down with his hands in his pockets.

Expressions used by Charlotte: Step-ins (not corset), all washed out (exhausted). Prat, fanny, butt, can, *Dreck*, *guck*, screwball, ass. Happy as clams, ignorant as monkeys in a tree, high-tail it.

44 FINGERS: Sally Lester had long creepy fingers like the Duccio Madonna and a face so pale at first that she seemed to have greenish cheeks. A long white incredible body. We were standing there in the press of the Balcon bar at two in the morning with Spaniards several deep on either side of us, and she did that, masking it with her mantilla. A sexual sophisticate or goodtime girl. She brought to the game an indecent haste, like a beast committed to the deadline of its brief rutting season. Playing the field. A tall girl with an outsize bust: *mammalia ponderosa* from the girlie magazine, a glistery-lipped mammiferous tease. Amory would not look at her. She watched the effect in the mirror behind the bar. Antonio Tertio was watching us with his heavy eyes. This was straining probability a little far. Are you good in bed? Sally asked in a silky voice. I saw Antonio's eye-brows shoot up. And in walked Olivia (in the mirror).

She was hardly in the village before she posed for Gimpy Guerrero, showing off her 'mean tail' and her 'badly slung' bust (Vine's and Tracey's comments), wearing only a black fan and a whore's smirk. Prints were passed around Antonio secundo's bar. The Dorset Stripper. She used conventional inducements and refused to be deterred, even in the most public places.

She did not exist for Amory. His Fay Blair had borne a passing resemblance to Veronese's Venus in the Prado, in the eyes and mouth and dumpling aspect. The eyes, the blondeness, the amplitude of haunch, the backs of her hands almost dimpled. A cool breeze rustled the leaves, a hound or two, a Cupid, and sated Adonis with his heavy head on her loving lap, the fatty hands protecting. The Golden Age lies behind, not before.

45 OLIVIA DREAMS OF THE RED CARDINAL: I am sitting at a bar with a friend, when an old Cardinal in red comes in with a what-do-you-call-it? (a ciborium, I said).

Yes, a ciborium. To distribute the wafers. He is talking to someone whom I cannot see at the far end of the bar, but I hear his voice, a haughty English accent, very clear authoritative enunciation, '*Oh indeed, did my mother say so?*' In a short while I hear the murmuring of Latin. He is distributing wafers at the back of the bar. Two communicants pass me on the way out, their eyes lowered. They are dressed as Scots lairds. One of the men wears clothes that are a size too small for him; between kilt and shirt the blubbery folds of his hairy belly protrude. They pass out of the bar.

Archbishop Charbonneau, I said. And you don't call them wafers.

46 OLIVIA DREAMS OF THE CROSS: A most extraordinary thing, but very Spanish, said Olivia. I'm standing in the hallway of the house with a number of people, locals, mostly children. I'm talking to someone. Then the sound of the double door opening and closing. I look up. There, against the frame of the door, is the Cross and Christ on it, the crown of thorns on his head and his feet pierced by the nails. He is bearded, has long hair, the Pre-Raphaelite Christ, moves his head slowly from side to side. A loin-cloth? I can't say. Trust you to ask. I didn't notice. He wasn't stark naked or I suppose I'd have noticed. It's the life-size figure you get in churches. No wounds, or if so they do not bleed. He is very white.

The Cross is placed against the doorway, set off by a rich background of fine dark red velvet. On its appearance—and it happens quickly: the door flies open and the apparition appears— there is dead silence. It is not the reverent silence you'd expect, I imagine in churches, no, this apparition causes a feeling like terror. The Man of Sorrows is oblivious to it all with no reaction to anybody there, just this sideways move-ment of the suffering head, coupled with the anguished look. I thought you were going to come downstairs, and wondered what you'd make of this. I felt it would mean something to you. It meant nothing to me. Not in the religious sense anyway. Certainly it was a shock: the Cross there as large as life against the door and Christ moving his head from side to side.

You come trailing downstairs then with nothing on, carrying a towel, *very* tall and with this other thing too, sticking out, *la resurrection de la chair*, which doesn't appear to embarrass you. Well, you've just got up. For a moment you don't catch sight of the Cross, then you do, take it all in, show no surprise. Then you go up and flick at his face with the towel, a quick flick, like this, as if swatting flies. The next thing Bob Bayless is standing there, wagging his head from side to side, and laughing silently, like the Cheshire cat. We all understand then that it was nothing more than a practical joke. This was something you had understood at once. No, I can't say whether you did or not.

47 OLIVIA DREAMS OF THE COURTYARD: I am in a courtyard, said Olivia, the place is held by a terrorist Government. Interrogations are proceeding. I'm being questioned. One of the military tribunal hands me a coin wrapped in paper, murmuring, 'You must shout out what's on it. It carries a light sentence, you won't hang.' He seems to be well disposed towards me. I take the coin, unwrap it, but can't decipher what's stamped on the face in Latin. He urges me, 'Out with it! Shout it out!' But even though my life depends on it I cannot make out the inscription.

All this is done in immoderate haste. Anything could happen. The shootings have started already. Executions are in full swing. A crowd of women come running towards me from one of the huts. A lynching mob! All the horrors, the shootings out of hand, the arbitrary trials, the hangings, are real.

As I examine the coin, one of the lynching party, still running, screams 'Dispatch her!' Now the dream halts. It's as if all were engraved in silver or brass, still trembling from the pressure of the engraver's burin. The kind interrogator, the courtyard, the running women. Only I am made of flesh and blood. Only I will suffer, this I know. The dream runs on. A stout, flushed harpy tickles the soles of my feet with a broom and bursts out laughing. All at once I understand that this is no lynching mob. The terror ends with their laughter, them laughing at me. The inscription is now clear to me. I shout: *Ola podrida!* Shits! Abominable fucking pigs! *Putridus!* But they have all disappeared—the harpies, the kind interrogator, the courtyard. I stand there confused.

48 EQUINE: Olivia and I went walking by La Luna. She wore a pair of blue denim slacks, mine in fact, that fitted her tightly, and washed until the colour was a pleasant lime blue—faded cobalt. She seemed to be painted blue below the waist. There was an orange tree laden with fruit, blazing with yellow oranges. Brown goats grazed nearby, where two elderly patriarchal goat-herds with black cloaks and long staffs stood minding their flock. One of the nanny goats was consuming a bitter orange. Its colourless inimical eyes watched us go by, its jaws moved from side to side in a lateral ruminative manner and juice squirted from between its teeth. The two Biblical herdsmen had no eyes but for Olivia, they gaped at her moving melons, blue moons, as we went by.

Later, on the way home, with the light failing, a horse stood near the sugar factory, in the gloaming, outlined against an olive grove. It stood with its legs splayed apart, stiff as the wooden horse of Troy and between its widely separated legs a long punitive thing swayed like a branch in a breeze—bringing to mind the statue of Colleone's horseman brandishing a naked sword. It was silhouetted there, no mare in sight, dreaming. Do stallions dream? Once in the middle of the night, out walking near Foxrock, I had heard one scream. Freud claims that geese dream of maize. Impossible to verify, unless oneself a goose, but surely probable. The Pueblo Indians call maidens after the colour of maize. Come little Yellow Maize. Come little Red Maize. Come little White Maize. The horse stood there darkly outlined against the olive grove, motionless as a statue.

49 HER POLISH GRANDMOTHER: Do you get it regularly with your nice wife? Charlotte asked me. Hardly at all, I told her. Once in the summer and once in the winter. Like Cato the Elder.

Charlotte considered this. It was a subject that deeply interested her.

No intercourse at night, she said, nothing . . . she must get fed up. What kind of love is that?

She gave me a considered look. I was a poor fish, a pathetic case. The famous side-glance. *Tänzerin* Tamara Karsavina in *Feuervogel*.

Passion is nice, Charlotte said. A wheel going faster and faster.

Sometimes I think you want to eat me, Charlotte said.

Beauty dies earlier, Charlotte said.

When I'm touching your skin I think I'm touching my own, said Charlotte.

(Her fondness for salted peanuts, her monkey paws.)

I have a funny heart, Charlotte said. A displaced heart. It's not on the left side or the right side but more in the middle. Can you feel it there? (I did so, what she said seemed to be true.) It doesn't get enough oxygen and before we came over I had to have many injections for this old misplaced heart of mine. I think it's okay now. Hope so anyway.

Coming out of anaesthetic makes me feel wonderful: this cold wind blowing off snow mountains, Charlotte said.

Did she know that we slept in separate beds in different rooms? Olivia in the front room, I in the airless cell in the middle of the flat. She knew.

Their bedroom was a cave-like place, the floor sank in the middle, her night things hung on a hook. She wore nothing in bed. Once she had woken and discovered him on top of her.

Once, half asleep, she had touched him. He had started to climb on top of her, she had not wanted it. She thought she had touched a different face. I'm getting nothing, thinking of you, she said. I'm only coming by thinking of you.

Once I came up to see you, she said. All the lights were off. I called Olivia's name. I listened. Your clock sounded loud.

I was alone in the studio, I said. If only you had come in. I wasn't sleeping. I was in bed. You could have come.

Charlotte said nothing. She wanted me, I wanted her. I dreamed her. She spoke to me sometimes in the sweetest, softest voice. It was her voice for me. Her voice of voices.

My Polish grandmother, Charlotte said. My mother was the third child among four brothers, Lupold was the first-born, the favourite, the Crown Prince. The fifth child arrived late. He was the homosexual. His health was poor, he spent much time in bed getting injections. It made him very bad-tempered. He'd smash all the tea things because his hands were shaking. Later he married a pharmacist. Another brother shaved his skull, either bald or with a little island on the head.

Lupold was the favourite. My grandmother couldn't stand being contradicted. It could happen then that she'd run after him, cutting with the riding whip. They'd scream at each other. Then she'd lock all of them out. She threw keys at Lupold. She had bad headaches. It wasn't her fault I suppose that she was so short tempered. The house was enormous.

My mother had to stay awake at night because grandfather was out all night boozing with friends. Mother would stand at the window looking into the park. Later she suffered from insomnia. Grandmother was very energetic. She went riding, and would climb to the very tops of mountains. When they lost all their money, they kept students, boarders. Three hairy lads, one dirtier than the other. They brought in fleas. My grandmother got them out, cursed them, washed all the rooms. She had great energy.

I stood at the bar counter of the Bar Coloroa, a most dim

trysting place. It was nine in the morning. There was an advertisement: DANONE! I stared at this sign (what did it signify?), waiting for her. Antonio Molino sat alone at a table by the window, pretending not to see me. Waiting for a cup of coffee to materialize before him. Asses and mules passed, the Poniente blew dust and straw about. More asses and mules in Spain than anywhere else on God's earth. I had coffee and cognac. Outside in the cold the migrant field hands shifted about. People passed in and out of the municipal market opposite. She did not come. Half an hour passed, an hour. The sign said in a low voice: DANONE. I waited there. Olivia had said: I know something you don't know. You're in love with Charlotte. And I know something else: I'm leaving you, buster.

I left that bar and went into the Bar Martin down the way. They were playing chess. The stomach of a very stout man pressed against the table, he was smoking a pipe, considering a move. They were drinking anis. The bar extended into the living quarters, the owner had heavy eyelids and a permanently displeased expression. His wife looked sad. They opened very early. A pendulum clock showed a quarter to the hour. I ordered anis. Half an hour passed. I decided to go back and work. There was nothing else to do. I paid and went out. Charlotte came round the corner from Calle de las Angustias, blown along by the wind. She said she would get *churros* at the market; could I wait? I said I would wait in the Bar Coloroa. A truck was backing, its rear light pulsating redly:

PEPITO Y MARI

Gas   **Oil**

Charlotte was talking to her maid outside the market. Manolo had appeared out of nowhere and was bearing down on her. I went into the dim bar. Presently she came across with *churros* on a ring of reeds. She was glowing. The woman brought the coffee and put it down in front of us. Outside it was blowing dust and straws into Calle del Ingenio, leading to the abattoir.

⟨✵⟩

My grandfather on my mother's side was a Jackson, said Amory, he inherited a snuff-box. We stood in the bar Baleares in a narrow street behind the Credit Bank of Spain hard by the brothel quarter. We were drinking draught beer on this thirsty morning in Malaga.

You can't get too much of a good thing, Amory said sagely. The sign on the wall facing us proclaimed: MUTUAL CYCLOPS.

Que pasa? the Mack Sennett behind the bar asked. He had bushy circumflex eyebrows. Time passes, Amory said. No, you pass, the Mack Sennett character said, moving his circumflex eyebrows. Time stands still.

Si no bebe ha tenido bastante, Amory said.

50 THE KEY: I had thought of asking Charlie Vine for the loan of his key, the use of his place while he was away. From time to time he went off on unannounced trips to Malaga or Gibraltar, to Portugal and Tangier, or to have his passport stamped at La Linea. Sometimes to bullfights in Ronda, Fuengirola, involving a day or more away from base. He had an abrupt way of departing without a word. And his flat would be locked up for a few days. Then he would be back again with some domestic acquisition such as binoculars, an umbrella, pot. Had I the key to his flat, I would have free access to a discreet bedroom, and could take Charlotte there and no one gainsay us. It was very tempting. I had been tempted by the idea off and on (love with me is slow and uninventive), but had done nothing about it, beyond mentioning it to Charlotte. She admitted that the idea had occurred to her too. She was agreeable; that was something I liked about her, her directness: she took what she wanted.

I could ask him for it, she said, say I wanted to sunbathe nude on his roof. But he knows I can do that already in our place . . . and so does Bob. I think your idea is better. You ask him.

I did not ask him. Instead I asked Olivia, to hear how the lie sounded. It sounded well enough. Plausible.

De Rougemont believes that there is an unmistakable connection between passion and lying. Liaisons are fed with lies. Gallantry, in one form or another, compromises half the vices. Beauty and honesty have ever been at odds.

Maison de rendezvous, maison de passe. We needed a discreet place of assignation, and Vine had it, a rooftop flat with stairs leading into a quiet street, and a landlord who lived off the premises. El Commandante José Herrera lived in Malaga. The flat was opposite the post office in Calle Granada in the vicinity of the market. Charlotte visited the market every morning

283

(Alibi No. 1) and letters could only be posted from the Casa de Correos, for there were no postboxes in the town. The post office stood diagonally opposite Vine's place. (Alibi No. 2.) I could meet my love there; physical contact would surely cure me; I could work again.

If anyone were to see Charlotte going in that direction, she need only say she was bound for the post office (choice of one) or the municipal market (choice of two); and if anyone saw us coming out of the flat, well situated with three or four semi-blind approaches leading to and from it, we could very plausibly say that we had been visiting Vine, found him out, or with a note up to say that he had gone away. We would never have been discovered in that lie. Only Olivia or Bob would have seen through that deceit. It was very tempting, and I thought about it, how I would approach Vine. There it was. The rule of desire for realistic passion: to hold a great power within a small volume. To have the key in my hand.

The way Charlotte suggested was the way I would have asked; he need not know the real reason. I could have asked, but never did, and so the opportunity passed. On quite numerous occasions we could have used the empty flat, made love on his Red Indian blanket, discovered the plains where the buffalo roam, perhaps have reached a deeper intimacy, even learnt to trust one another. Vine, a most discreet person, would not have asked questions. If she wanted to sunbathe nude on the roof that was all right by him. If I wanted to work there, that was all right too. He would not have refused me the key, and certainly he would not have refused her, for he was under a certain obligation to Charlotte.

When he first came to Nerka he hadn't much Spanish, soon moved from Rodolfo Sanchez's hotel, on Bob's suggestion, to No. 18 Calle Pintada, where he had the whole house to himself. There he lived in a downstairs room extensive enough to stable a dozen cattle, with a blanket over his shoulder, the doors and windows closed, huddled over the butane heater, with a *brasero* (the Oriental chafing-dish) lit, and still complained of the cold, acclimatized as he was to central heating. He had the butane heater going with the carbon fire and complained all the time, bitterly, of the cold. He could not get the room heated to his satisfaction and was seriously thinking of going back to Canada. The walls leaked and sweated; he needed a sub-tropical climate or a hot girl to warm him up. He had never been so cold and uncomfortable in his life. This was Vine's bad time.

When the chance for a warmer and cheaper apartment came, he asked Charlotte as a favour to negotiate for him with the Commandante, and Charlotte was only too ready to help. She had Yiddish and French and was not finding it too difficult to pick up a third language. She prided herself on her (Jewish) ability to get the best of a bargain, beat the man down; it was a positive pleasure to negotiate. We had waited for her in Antonio's bar, Bob and myself. In an hour's time she and Vine were back. They had a real bargain: the Commandante had been asking two thousand pesetas a month out of season and three thousand a month in season, and Charlotte had beaten him down to a flat one thousand three hundred pesetas per month for the whole year, with an option on another year for the same price and this Vine had paid down in a lump sum. They had had a drink in the Bar Martin to clinch the deal; and Vine had a nice place above the traffic, such as it was, in a quiet street, near the market and the post office. He was in clover. And all thanks to shrewd Mrs. Bayless, whom Charlie had nicknamed Fred C. Dobbs. Well might he feel under obligation to her.

I did not want to compromise Charlotte. I felt that if I were to ask Vine for the key he might guess my real purpose, for he had seen Charlotte and me going around together, might indeed have seen more than we knew of, through his field-glasses. But he would have handed over the key and kept whatever his private opinions were to himself. That was the only way I could have asked for it, advancing crabwise towards my object; and in fact he was the only one I could have asked.

When his old flame Salina Biez arrived on the scene it became more difficult. He had told us that she was due; we had heard a great deal of her, how Charlie had stolen her from Penrose; how she was the queen of the clique, a compulsive talker ('old

Salina could talk the scrotum off the statue of David'), strong on dialectics. We had got to know Vine's circle of friends in absentia: the others were Penrose, Benny Marsh, Furbank, all strong talkers (Marsh came later and was a disappointment. He worked for Reuters, Penrose lectured in philosophy at Liverpool University. Salina and Charlie had ambitions to write high-class fiction), and she was expected to come from Canada. And then one fine day she was due.

Vine went and fetched her from Gibraltar, took her back home into his wigwam. And they stayed there for about a fort-night while Vine thawed out. Even after that they did not go about much, but kept to themselves, circling about the flat. Vine was not drinking in the bars and had gone off pot as soon as Salina arrived. He had been cold and celibate for the best part of three months before the arrival of this *muy recogido* lady, a swarthy blackhaired party who dressed like a Comanche. She had short kinky black hair that looked as if it might be oiled with buffalo grease to make it lie down, dark fierce-looking eyes, the whites very pronounced due to her smoky complexion. She had an impatient manner. Whatever clothes she wore, no matter how concealing, gave one a good idea of how she would look naked. She was talkative. Sliding on her feet—the espadrilles could have been moccasins—glowering, a well-built resourceful girl with three or more abortions behind her, she and Vine became the subject of much local gossip in that part of town.

Vine was dark-complexioned, myopic, wore tinted spectacles, broad in the shoulder and narrow in the hip, his feet dwindling away to nothing. He walked like a plainsman, his toes turned in, with a matter-of-fact manner, hands plunged in his pockets. He dressed like a soldier: levis and reefer jacket were his uni-form, crumpled at the knees, he rarely changed. Ass and shit, Vine said, in the terminology of a buck private.

The night I saw them arriving together at the bar El Molino, glowing as though they had just come from the bath, I knew Charlie wasn't going to be cold much longer and was glad for his sake, as I had grown to like him. Previously I had mis-trusted him, considering him Jewish and ashamed of it, close with his cash. I asked him what he thought of Babel. He had never heard of him, and accepted another drink from Bayless. Singer, then? No, he had never heard of Singer either. Penrose was inclined to belittle him. Charlie the stoic, a good little man. I don't like the way you said that, Olivia said, showing her hostility to Penrose, who only laughed, pointing his long nose.

Young lady! Penrose said, avuncular. Young lady, this is really outrageous!

That first night there in the bar we all got tight and Salina, swallowing one cognac after another, became dogmatic, trying to dominate Olivia, who will not be dominated.

I asked her what her feelings were for Charlie, who was talking with Olivia. She admitted she wasn't 'gone on him', but loved an oboe player in a different country. The second part she confided to Olivia later. She had left her own true love in Italy. Olivia thought her an immodest girl because she wore only bra and panties on the public beach and showed pubic hair. (It turned out she had come without swimming togs.) She said that Charlie knew all this; she had been honest with him, and he was resigned to it. I marvelled at this, myself. Resigned to it! I may have hinted, with too much cognac, about my own feelings, for when I was drunk I had to talk about Charlotte. Salina might have guessed as much; for she must have seen us together from Vine's battlements, and no husband in sight (Bob's skin couldn't take the sun, so he stayed indoors during the day and worked). He too was writing, but not fiction. I told Salina only so much, feeling that if I told her more she might pass it on to Charlie, since they were so intimate; no doubt she was making her own deductions. Then if I were to ask Charlie for the loan of his key, and he handed it over, not guessing anything, Salina might well say 'I think I know why he wants it', and Charlie 'Why?' and she 'To lay Charlotte'. And then the fat would be in the fire. I thought that I could rely on Vine's discretion, but about Salina's discretion I wasn't so sure. And, I didn't want to hurt Olivia.

I would not have her know what others knew before she knew, namely, that I had been unfaithful to her with Charlotte. So finally I never got around to asking Charlie for the loan of his key, the use of his place, which is perhaps just as well. There was no knowing where such rashly undertaken confidences might lead: lead to trouble. I had enough trouble.

Vine himself was not immune to Olivia's charms. She liked him, and made it quite obvious she did, perhaps not as much as she liked Bob Bayless, that rooted man, but she did like him, no question of that. I thought she might, on hearing these developments, go with Vine just to spite me. It's what I might have done in her place: Vine was a close and secretive man. And now that his enforced period of celibacy was over, what might he be inclined to do, given encouragement? He knew that one day Salina intended to leave him; she had told him so. And Olivia would still be there.

Phrases associated with Olivia: From time to time. Drunk as a flying fish.

51 POLNISCHE JUDEN: Dangerous to be Jewish in Europe (that ancient bone-heap) in Hitler's day. Doubly dangerous to be Polish-Jewish. For if he hated all Jews, he had a particular hatred for Polish Jews. *Das Armseliges Volk*. A name scraped out from the end pages of the Pentateuch, from the *Familienstammbuch*. And a life that was once, now is no more. No, not even a trace left—the careful blade, the scraper, has made the record clean. The Jew-taint *Judenblut* like bacteria under a microscope. Scraped from the end pages of the *Familienstammbuch*, from the well-thumbed pages of the Pentateuch.

Dangerous to have a Jewish relative, by blood or intermarriage—even distant relative—in Himmler's day, the Gestapo were digging like weasels into the files. The records were being carefully sifted, Gestapo intelligence tracking back the taint as far back as the Thirty Years War, and only brought to a halt there, the churches pillaged and the records lost.

She might never have come out of Poland, might well have died in Poland: the Lipsky (or Lipski) family only one among many such Polish families perished, the stain wiped out. Jablonski, Handy, Leitgeber, Lilienthal, Kawecki, Morawski, Lipsky (or Lipski) serving only to fertilize Polish earth, by lying dead under it, making it habitable for Germans to live on, walk on. She might have ended her days as a Jewess in Auschwitz. As a child holding on to her mother's skirt, an actress from an old silent movie. A cry of terror, a dismay, a retreat; an appeal, a regret, to say nothing, to beg for life—it's all too late, they had no pity in dealing with the *Untermenschen*. Groping, then the shot, the injection, the canister falling, all begins to be lost. They go to join the great Polish dead, the Jewish dead. Charlotte Monowitz, dead; Charlotte Birkenau, dead; Charlotte Dachau, dead; Charlotte Auschwitz, dead. Lonely sorrowing stations, all lost. A group of victors and vanquished are standing under the shade of spreading limes or oak trees around a Polish manor-house, walking together in some Polish park. A misty scene with the quality of an oleograph, a picture from the past. A lemur-like paw, with shiny digits, pulls aside a half curtain, a little Jewish girl observes them. She had pale Polish eyes. She is there. She is my opposite, yet part of me. She who appears so permanent, is transitory—a souvenir. Lost long ago. I can neither hold her nor let her go.

Somewhere in an apartment in the Jewish sector of Lvov, a child, impervious to all this, too young, moves about. Dangerous to be there; doubly dangerous to be Charlotte Lipsky (or Lipski), one of the Slav *Untermenschen*, Polish or Bulgarian or Pommeranian *Halbaffen* with their polluted blood, Lipski, Lilienthal, Leitgeber, in Hitler's Europe. His agent had sat opposite me, had looked at me out of his troubled bloodshot eyes, had told me that he was his Fuehrer's soldier still, and I believed him.

A blank page, a name scraped out, a life that was once, now is no more. Too late already. Eyes that had looked submissively into Hitler's eyes (full of dead Jewish eyes) had looked into my eyes. In an aloof and surly manner he had indicated that if I were to go too far, say too much, he would tear into me.

But she was fearless (somewhere on the Nida or the Bug a small boat is sailing, Charlotte trails her hand in the water, her father holds the tiller, watching his daughter. I cannot see his face. He does not like Goys, he would have his daughter marry into her own race. The sun is going down. The Bug is the colour of blood. Charlotte Lipski, or Lipsky, trails her in the wake of the boat. It's an evening in Poland in summer, the sun going down. Under the evening clouds a red sail moves; the clouds reach over Poland into Germany, where the preparations are being made).

To flee across the fields and take refuge under the solitary tree where no one has ever died. Kissing in the dry heat, on the track between walls of rock; her glowing face, the urgency and warmth of her embraces. She had come so far; I would take her there. We went away from the river, by caves where livestock were kept. She led the way up the path. Her black slacks unzipped at the back. There, I think, she said, pointing to a kind of wild arbour surrounded by a dry stone wall, a grove of olives and a single carob—like Inishere, but for the trees. We lay down under the carob tree. It's a hardy tree that can grow on top of rock if needs be, in war and famine the people make flour from its seeds (a tree of poor hard countries); otherwise it is used as cattle fodder. Under the carob tree's shade we became one. When I embraced her everything began again. We were on the rough ground. She lay back and smiled. The crickets whirred in the grass. The sun beat on the rock. *Limpia! Limpia!* called the olive picker (who had not stopped singing until then) to someone over the broken wall. When I kissed her there I experienced something comparable to liquification. Her head lay in a small clear area where the earth was a darker colour. Did you ever feel like crying? she asked. When? I asked. After we make love, she said.

Things that a clever girl can find to say.

The tree plain and simple cannot burn away; it cannot resolve itself into its component elements. *Der Apfel fällt nicht weit vom Baum*, the Germans say. Dead trees love the fire. (And on a sudden clear light presented me a face, folded in sorrow.) *Der gute Mann*, Herr Hund, in chamois-tufted (or pheasant feathers) Tyrolean hat, and the stout calves of a resolute killer, slaying deer in the Harz Mountains. The German horn. *Kiefernwald*.

I looked out of the window one morning and saw Daisy Bayless walking on a carpet of morning-glory flowers. The child walked on this incandescent blue. It was not yet eight and the fishing boats were going out. The sound of a donkey-engine meliorated over the water. Daisy called for me to come down. *Morgenschatten in dem Garten. Morgensonne.*

52 BROAD TALK: I heard from the Baylesses that they had been having regular lessons with Dr. Jorge del Bosque on the plaza three or four times a week. He had been dropping in for English conversation. They were seeing a lot of the doctor.

Bob sometimes liked to work or read at night, and then Charlotte would go alone to Antonio's bar, and find the doctor there. Or she would be standing there talking to Antonio, and in would come the doctor.

In cold weather Charlotte suffered from chilblains. During that interminable winter her hands were chapped and scaly. She went to Dr. Jorge del Bosque for medical check-ups once a fortnight, sometimes once a week. To arouse my jealousy, she pretended to find him attractive. He was 'breaking down her resistance', and she was helping him. Recalling what Bob had said about Jewish girls and professional men, I half believed it.

Charlotte suffered from low blood pressure and one night fell unconscious on the Puerta del Mar. Tim Park found her lying on the pavement, out cold. Bob was called out of the bar and gave her artificial respiration. She told me after that she had 'felt wonderful' coming out of the faint. That it was like a cold wind blowing off snow. This faint happened during one of our recurring periods of estrangement when I was not seeing much of her.

The doctor had patiently acquired a little English and was anxious to acquire a little more. Charlotte (who had Yiddish and French and some Spanish) would be teaching him. The second half of the lessons were to be devoted to straight English conversation. For the rest, they spoke in Spanish, the doctor correcting pronunciation and grammar. At first they had the lessons on the plaza, in the Marissal, when the doctor had finished work for the day. Later on the lessons were held at the Baylesses' place. It brought them together, improved his chances with Charlotte, she was seeing him at least once a fort-night with her chapped hands in the surgery, not to mention having drinks together a couple of times a week. Charlotte was quicker than Bob to pick up the language, the doctor only too pleased to help her along. By that time they had begun the lessons and were meeting every other evening at a table outside the Marissal. The doctor, all volubility, leaning close to her. The husband, all jut of jaw and peak of yachting cap, watching them. Then, when I had 'punished' her enough, I made it up with her. When I had punished myself and could not bear to stay away from her another day. The doctor was there, revolving about her. And I, a sour observer of imagined revels, revolving on an outer ring, watching them and the husband scowling at her, wondering (myself) what provoked the scowl. What had the two of them been up to in my absence? It was like a play by Labiche, a comedy *de moeurs*, a sofa comedy. The doctor, very bourgeois, very correctly dressed, with his mid-wife's bag under his arm, his medical hold-all (suppositories?), simmering with suppressed passion for the beautiful Tcharlawt Bay-Lees, rounding his lips for the o, pointing to his lips, then to *her* lips, ready to pounce; and Charlotte, her eyes half-closed, going ah, ah, a bright pupil under her exacting Spanish teacher, who was congratulating her on another good performance. *Mas facil*, the doctor said, wiping his brow, *mas facil*. And Bob, narrowing his eyes, studying both of them, affecting indifference.

It amused Charlotte to set the doctor phrases for translation that were both ambiguous and teasing, skirting indecency, and these the doctor very willingly set himself to translate and read out with the utmost decorum. (This was something men and women did better in an earlier century.) There were the stirrings of prurience and sexual misconduct, there was the itch. The doctor observed her, *Mmmnn, mmmnn*, one nicotine-stained finger brown to the joint, touched the bridge of his spectacles, which flashed a warning at her every so often, and she smiled at him—*he* was making good progress. The doctor was being both wary and discreet. From the evidence of her talk, and from her rather free-and-easy manner, he might have thought that some carefully-aimed innuendos might well serve there, for he heard on all sides, and half-understood, very broad talk. Her eyes may have told of some sort of promise—a promise of something more than friendship. A rumour of bedrooms. When he spoke, she listened, 'all eyes'. Her vague and tender smile, lips slightly parted as if all the better to breathe in life. A moist, intelligent, warm young woman. When she spoke, he listened with eyes half shut, smiling to himself. He was very polite. He came into the room next to their bedroom, was offered something to drink, saw, through the half open door, their bed. Sometimes Charlotte begged to be excused, if she was too tired to concentrate. She said good-night, closed the door. The doctor continued conversing amiably on a wide variety of subjects with the big *muy serioso* American scholar, while Charlotte prepared for bed. Hearing her moving about in the bedroom, a tap running, decking herself out for the conjugal bed. Movements in a bedroom: *mouvements du coeur*. The doctor was improving his English in the most edifying surroundings. When at a loss for a word, one positive tobacco-stained finger thoughtfully adjusting his spectacles, going *Mmn, mm, mn* . . . he was scheming to get Tcharlawt in her panties behind the fluoroscope.

One night I was at the Baylesses' place when he was expected. They urged me to stay. I said no, I could not stay. But I stayed. Could I do otherwise? By this time I was as infatuated with Charlotte Bayless as ever Beyle had been with Melania Louisin. (Like Beyle) I was troubled by certain ambiguities in her dealings with some of her admirers. I observed her with the doctor. Henri Beyle watching Richard Wagner watching Melanie Louisin. They both behaved correctly, impeccably, the doctor formal enough, Charlotte with that gay, sparring manner of hers. And if they behaved perfectly, wasn't it a certain indication that they had something to conceal? I waited for the look that Beyle thought he had seen Wagner give Melanie Louisin: a look *as if he had been intimate with her*. I only caught the corners, the beginnings and endings of this look. They were both experts, after all, at hiding their real feelings. The few nights I spent watching them were so uncomfortable for me that I decided not to repeat the experience.

The doctor came upstairs. The lesson began. Bob Bayless politely enquired how the excavating at the cave was proceeding; had any worthwhile (*importante*) discoveries been made? this in good, firm, slow, reliable Spanish. *Si*, the doctor affirmed, *Si !* (this was a subject very near to his heart and he never tired of speaking of it). *Muy importante*, the doctor said, shooting a look at Charlotte. *Muy, muy* (warmly) *importante*—this with great emphasis.

A lady archaeologist had been summoned from Madrid to supervise the diggings. I wanted you to see it, the Doctor said. I looked into his eyes, dark Spanish eyes, the expression there was guarded and troubled. He had seen Garcia Lorca in Granada. I imagined the eyes of Garcia Lorca, the eyes of someone who is to be taken out of life and destroyed, we will never find the reason.

The subject of primates was mentioned. In *Español primado. Muy similar, si.* The doctor said that if the archaeologists discovered the so-called Missing Link, the jump, then his faith would be shattered, no other word for it. If it was proved conclusively that man had evolved from that pre-human stuff, fungus or spawn, from the most primitive organisms in the sea—that is to say, out of pure dirt, or nothing (the brown primeval soup of nostalgic sepia hue); if Man had evolved from this to build his cathedrals and hold to his faith, which meant everything to him (to Dr Jorge del Bosque), then that faith would mean nothing. It would be shattered.

Bob Bayless gave him a look which expressed quite plainly his feelings; he could scarcely believe his ears. *Por que ?* he asked; *por que ?* Did it matter? As he saw it, it did not matter a fig how Man had evolved—slowly, losing appendages that would make him a relative to beast or even fish, moving slowly from the depths of the equatorial forests and from pure blood ancestry to anthropoid apes, advancing into the light, such as it was; or sprung direct from an all-wise Creator's hand—did it matter, in the long run? To his way of thinking, it did not.

To you, with respect, the doctor said, shaken with emotion, perhaps not for you. But for me it matters very much. (Shaking his head, stirring his coffee, dissolving a lump of sugar. A Spanish

Catholic.) So they went at it hammer and tongs, no holds barred: God and the Father, the Father and the Son, Darwin and the apes, the Descent of Man, the Garden of Eden, *Homo Sapiens*—Charlotte thrusting out her jaw and widening her eyes at me behind the doctor's broad back.

When the good doctor had left with his notebooks under his arm, an exemplary student, Bob Bayless began to talk in a most angry way about St. Francis Xavier, the Basque co-founder of the Society of Jesus. He cursed the absent man. Such credulity! Imagine patients putting their lives into such hands! What could they expect from him, if only one half of his mind believed in the science of medicine, and the other half in such hocus-pocus? His teeth clenched on his cigar, the muscles of his jaw moved as if crunching nuts, his forehead corrugated in anger.

I always associate the Catholic Church with French tropical diseases, Charlotte said.

The strong sunlight of the outer glare made an extraordinary impression in her eyes. The pupils becoming blacker and more noticeable even as they shrank, the blue-eyed look exaggerated; the glare there reflecting some strength of the sunlight and more strength of her own. Power to be, power to be. Tigress-eyed.

She was beautiful but did not trade on it, in spite of what Olivia said.

She wore her hair in a long braid down her back, had a golden tan, darker about the buttress of her shoulders and shoulder-blades. She wore a costume of blue and white horizontal stripes, dark blue trunks. A style popular in the 20's that had come back into fashion in the 60's.

Melonglaze skin, gentian blue eyes. Slight apathy, burning face and hands, whites of the eyes pronounced, pupils dark and enlarged. Colour of a cornfield her braided hair. Boss of her strong shoulders: high-lighted butternut woodwork on her curves.

Her age of discretion, the touch of her hand, the look from her eyes; amber and musk scent, the ardour of her ways. *Liquidis perfusus odoribus.* And then: the pleasure of seeing her running on the damp sand of the shoreline on Torrecillas.

Thudding along, pacing her shadow (a smaller and younger version of herself, Daisy). Disturbances there; she who did not abuse her power. It was that I had collided with; all that packed-in-life hit me. Without her, wanting her, I was nothing. I was weightless. Or I was: Want. Need.

There, that day, with the sun over the ruined tower, Charlotte, running at full gallop, the mane of her hair streaming, struck me with her shoulder, all her young force, in the ribs, solar plexus, and down I went. My soft (soft?) convulsive beauty had all the wind knocked out of me. She had hit me like a ton of bricks. And down I went.

53 BAROGRAPH: It was an instrument for recording weather fluctuations. Behind the glass, the graph moved, the fine tooth of the nib scratching along the drum, the temperature marked off in old Father Time's shaky hand, a patient record of the passing days and weeks.

The tall naked girl still swooned in the handsome surgeon's arms. He wore a white head-band, his white surgical smock reaching to below his knees, the ardent skeleton continuing to embrace the lovely patient's hips. *Don Señor* Humedo Muerte loves *Señorita* Besa Vida. And always did, and always will. *Laus Veneris*. Our Lady of Pain, the obscure virgin of the hollow hill. The doctor taking advantage of an undressed lady patient, in flagrant violation of professional etiquette while the artist is doing the same with a nude model.

Downstairs in the waiting-room a young girl of six or seven waits with her mother. The latter, fanning herself awkwardly, watches the child. Who was sick, mother or child? The child took the fan from her mother's awkward hand and used it naturally and with style, her eyes closed, head lifted, feeling the breeze stirring her curls. The old people behind me did not speak. The younger ones talked to pass the time. Illness is not discussed. It makes a pleasant change from Ireland where one's current illness and the foul weather are forever under discussion.

A girl of about nineteen, attractive but cross-eyed, who had come in with an older woman and gone upstairs ahead of me now uttered a high-pitched scream. Downstairs they shook their heads, not sympathetic, contemptuous of such undignified behaviour. The Andalusians are, and always were, noted for their bravery, valour. *Muy valiente*, they say of bullfighters, the highest praise. Caesar, that bald adulterer, had even remarked upon it. Was it the shock of the fluorescent screen or the touch of the doctor's fingers that caused the scream?

A Civil Guard came in with his small son. Unfastening a button of his uniform, he sat down and took off his shiny *bicorne* Napoleonic hat. Seen from above (the only way to look at it) it is *tricorne*.

It was hot in the waiting-room. When my turn came I went upstairs, slow as an old man. The Doctor sat behind his desk, writing. *Buenas tardes*, Don Jorge, I said. He stood up to greet me, came around the desk to give me a Roman handshake. I was an old man, bent and wheezing.

I am an old man, doctor, I said in Spanish.

I think not, he said, but won't you sit down. I sat down painfully. I am suffering, doctor, I said.

How did this come about? he asked.

An accident, I said, a stupid accident.

His white shirt was open three buttons down, there was a fuzz of man-hair on his pale chest. He prepared to examine me. With the tips of his fingers he ausculated me. There, there, painful yes? Painful, *si*, I admitted, wincing, Oh *Jesu*, most painful. Acute pain on the left side, the doctor murmured, good, good. Now.

Not so good for me, I said (sweating like a horse after a hard gallop). No.

Not so good for you, no, the doctor admitted. His fingers were rather short, round-tipped, sensitive hands, with a growth of black hair on the backs. He was surprisingly hairy.

Please, he said, just one moment please.

He ushered me ceremonially into the darkroom where the fluoroscope was set up, asked me to remove my shirt. With some difficulty I did so. I felt inches of steel under my solar plexus. The room lacked daylight or ventilation. The doctor switched on the fan. A breeze began to blow cold against my chest. I stood half naked before the fluoroscope. Take a series of deep breaths, the doctor said in Spanish. The light came on in the screen. His fingers touched me, three or four inches of cold steel pushed into my side, under the solar plexus.

Again, the doctor murmured, his eye fixed on the viewing aperture, again please. I obliged him. Again the jab of steel. The room turned mauve. The doctor said *Hmmm* and touched his spectacles with his fingers. Again, he said. I took a deep deep breath and this time saw purple fluorescent light. The doctor said *Hmm* again. He switched off the machine and switched on the light above the couch. Now please, the doctor said, leading the way back to the surgery, follow me. I followed him with ribs collapsing, sat.

How did this come about? he asked. You have been fighting?

At my age? I said. Hardly.

I told him of Charlotte's shoulder-charge (all that packed-in-life) and Daisy dry-diving, using my chest as a springboard. The doctor was slightly amused at this; as he had suspected Tcharlawt was at the bottom of it. He laughed in a guarded manner, two nicotine-stained fingers pressed to the bridge of his spectacles.

What is it? I asked.

You have two fractured ribs and another partially fractured, Dr. Jorge del Bosque informed me. And now, with your permission, I must tape you up. If you would be good enough to lift your arm.

He stood beside me armed with a roll of elastoplast and a pair of scissors. I lifted my arm, perspiration flowed. He proceeded to make a good job of taping me up.

Do not play with American girls, he counselled me. It is *unsafe*. Yes?

The doctor laughed to himself.

You may dress, he said.

I did so with difficulty. The doctor told me that I would have to stay in bed three days, to allow the fractures to set. He shook my hand with a good-natured and playful expression on his face.

American girls, he said, shaking his head, they are hard, *muy duro*, yes? You must not play with them. Not on the beach. It is *unwise*.

I went down the steep stairs and out into the street, moving slowly, like an old man.

One night I was at the Bayless' place when the telephone rang. It was a strange sound to hear in the house. Rosa Munsinger had it installed for incoming calls from New York. But this time it was not New York on the line but a local call. It was the doctor phoning from across the street to say he was called out, and could not come for his lesson that night.

Charlotte was holding the receiver, listening to the doctor make a pretty speech in English, and then she spoke in fluent Spanish, and the doctor congratulated her on rapid progress (his tongue in her ear, in her mouth). She had her back to her husband and was smiling at something the doctor was saying, or possibly smiling at something her husband was saying in a loud hectoring tone that was almost certainly audible to the doctor. 'Don't drop 'em, Dilly! Don't drop 'em now. Keep them on!' And then (Charlotte smiling sweetly was again murmuring into the receiver) in a worried aside to me: 'I don't trust her with that smooth bastard. No, Sir, I do not.' Now Charlotte was speaking very confidentially into the mouthpiece, lowering her voice, her back to us. And then she was smiling at something the doctor was saying to her. Then she made a witty reply in Spanish and we could hear the doctor laughing. He was enchanted with her Spanish. When a woman thinks her husband is watching her closely, she will sooner offend, the old book says. Charlotte's lips were close to the doctor's ear. Her hair had come down. Ask him whether his trousers are bothering him, Bob said.

One night the doctor overplayed his hand. Bob told us about it next day. Dr. Jorge del Bosque had arrived late the previous night for a lesson and he (Bob), tired after working all day and not feeling up to it, asked to be excused. The field was left open to the doctor. This was doubtless something long anticipated: he and Charlotte alone at night. In order not to disturb Bob, the lesson was held downstairs. They were drinking wine. The doctor made a pass.

He had taken off his spectacles and was kneeling by her chair —the picture of gallantry. Tcharlawt! *Mirame! Mirame, por favor*, Tcharlawt!

She would not look into his brown bedroom eyes. He pleaded with her. They were caught in their respective poses: he kneeling and pleading, she seated with averted eyes. The doctor asked her to kiss him. She told him, now that the situation had become embarrassing, that he had better go.

Next day, before lunch, two bottles of Malaga dulce were sent across as a peace-offering. Charlotte laughed about it, but Bob was not amused. He said he wasn't going to have any doctor making passes at his wife. As things stood, he could not trust her. She had said the doctor had beautiful eyes. He had taken his spectacles off and begged her on his knees to look at him, but she wouldn't, or so she said. But if she didn't look at him how did she know he had beautiful eyes? Tired out, he himself had gone to sleep as soon as he had got into bed. He knew nothing of what had gone on below, except what Charlotte told him. He made a joke of the peace-offering, the bottles of Malaga dulce. Probably trying to get rid of the stuff, he said.

After this the doctor's attentions wavered, fell away. Then, as abruptly as begun, ceased altogether. He had been choked off. Bob Bayless was polite, but no more than that, when he met the doctor. Who or what had turned him off? The Alcalda? The Falange? Don Pedro? His wife? His own conscience? Or a combination of these? We were never to know. But he stopped pursuing Charlotte, indeed virtually stopped seeing her, avoided Antonio's bar and never called again at No. 12. Charlotte still went to see him in the surgery. But as the summer came in, she would go less. I was just as pleased with this arrangement. And began to see more of her than hitherto.

❀

I told you about the time he had his hand just about on my cunt? Olivia asked. No, I said. He asked me why my heart was beating so, Olivia said. Yes? I said, and . . .

I asked him what could he expect, dammit.

What did he say to that?

Olivia thought about it. 'Madame, you're beautiful,' she hazarded.

Madame, you're wet, I said.

For a month Olivia had a cold and a bad cough. Then an infected finger swelled up. She feared tetanus or worse, amoebic dysentery, caught from the contagious fields. There was human excrement there. The mules, bearing loads to and from the campo, lived under the same roof as the mule-man.

You should go to the doctor, I said.

And wait two hours in the surgery? she wailed.

Yes, if necessary, I said.

Oh all right, Olivia said.

Dr. Jorge del Bosque told her that she had come at the right time with her infected finger. If she had not come, very likely it would have blown up to this size (alarming demonstration) and likely burst, probably that evening. Very serious, he said, and prescribed an antibiotic.

The whole Peninsula was rotten with liver ailments and antibiotics.

For the cough, he examined her behind the fluoroscope. For patients there was a couch against one wall, a shaded light above it always on; the fluoroscope had two screens. Olivia in bra and panties stood between them on a small platform, as the doctor seated himself on a small stool. He could reach behind the screen and touch his patient's hips to move her about if he so desired. Peering into the viewer, he announced dramatically, Your liver is enlarged!

Olivia didn't believe him. He was only trying to justify putting her behind the screen. The room was in darkness except for the shaded light above the couch and the light on the screen. The doctor's fingers were short and round-tipped. He had no assistant or nurse to help him. His manner was calm and reassuring.

They were standing close together, Olivia in her underthings, the doctor with one eye glued to the aperture, his spectacles pushed up to his temples. Then Olivia discovered that *her* hand was close to his crotch. Without saying a word she removed it. The doctor gave no indication that he had noticed. He told her to dress, not to catch cold.

Back in the surgery he invited her to sit down. He seated himself behind the desk, took a pad, confirmed the date, began to write out a prescription. Olivia remarked that in Spain, so she had noticed, one could be quite well in the morning and seriously ill by afternoon; why? The doctor tore off a page and handed it across to her, explaining that everything in Spain was rapid, that was the Spanish nature after all. We take our opportunities quickly, we make love quickly, we forget quickly, he said.

You like talking about love, Olivia remarked amiably.

Oh you know how it is, the doctor said, shrugging his shoulders, for a doctor it is different. (A special sort of approach was needed.) And why was it that each time she came to see him, she looked younger and prettier? He would not forget that she had been his first English teacher. And when was she going to have a child?

I don't know, Olivia said. Perhaps never. The doctor sadly shook his head. And was she happy?

His wife was in Malaga. She had taken a flat in order to be near the children where they were attending school. He was a bachelor again, alone in the house, fending for himself. The implications were obvious enough.

The compliments were flying thick and fast, Olivia said.

When she was taking her leave of him, he enquired again, pointedly, And you are happy? When she was already halfway down the stairs, he asked tenderly, though perhaps tactlessly, after *Tcharlawt*.

Tcharlawt Bay-Lees; how was she?

Oh fine, Olivia said, fine.

Charlotte, knowing how the doctor felt about her, was wary of exposing herself behind the fluoroscope. What would the good doctor see there, in addition to an enlarged female liver? A profane stained-glass window without colours, the bone-structure and hidden organs of my impatient love outstretched like flowers, lovely marine sponges lit from within.

54 VINE: Vine told me stories about the far north of Canada, stories of the Doukhobors, of Manitoba, Saskatchewan, the immense grain-trains coming from the far wheatlands, the endless winters. His father, old Vine, went from room to room slapping his pockets, looking out of the windows, sighing. Charlie begged ('bugged') his older brother to break open Indian graves, three knowles, hoping to find pemmican. But all they found were some arrow-heads and dry bones. It was illegal to desecrate Indian graves.

All the Indian wars were lost, all the tribes extinct, the buffalo herds sadly depleted, the reservations miserable holes. A dark tunnel through which things were continually passing.

Vine resembled Harry Kernoff, the same troubled Jewish eyes, hunched shoulders, evasive manner, the same expression behind the thick corrective lens. He told me of the death of his young sister, who had mumps and got up too soon. A half-tear-shaped snowplough sent a spew of snow a hundred feet high into the freezing air. Her father was with her. She died on the way to hospital, was buried with frozen flowers in cellophane bags, put into the earth. It was in the depths of winter. (I thought of the unsubstantial wastes of snow, the freezing air, no birds, a sister lost in snow. Sadness is something like ice.) *Liquidis perfusus odoribus*. Neither catalpe tree nor scented lime.

My father was a great curler, Vine said.

Red Indians smell of smoke.

It was so cold you could hardly open your mouth, Vine said. The language you express yourself in shapes the mouth that speaks.

Lake Eyrie, Vine said, that big open sewer. Dead water. I like only the bathrooms and toilets of the rich, Vine said.

55 WINSLOW, ARIZONA: They don't keep to the Reservation, Bob Bayless said, just hang around the town, boozing on rotgut liquor, covered in flies, and looking mighty pathetic, when you consider their grand beginnings. The Plains Indians never saw a white man until his white brother was fixing to shoot him, drawing a bead with his Springfield.

The Redmen, the last of the great tribes, Bob said, Iroquois, Nez, Bannock, Cheyenne, Ute, Apache, no more bison hunting for them. Their whole economy was organized around the buffalo herds, like Eskimos around the seals. They made tepis out of the skins, ate the flesh, made ropes and wool from the rest, got their tools from the bones, their thread from the sinews, their fuel from the dung. Jerkee.

56 WHO WAS PADDY KELLY? One evening I called on the Baylesses as they were sitting down to supper. They invited me to join them. I said I had eaten already. Okay, Bob said, amuse yourself. We won't be long. They began their meal. Charlotte picked at the food, watched me, and kept getting up to serve her husband or help Daisy, and then more picking at what was on her own plate. I took a book at random off the shelf and sat down to read. It was one of the Old Ram's *Tropics*.

But I dislike being in a room while others eat. I asked Bob if I could take the book to the Balcon Bar. He said fine, okay. They would join me there.

I sat near the coffee machine and opened the book again. I had read it years before in Shackleton's studio, had not liked it then, and found I liked it less now. I came upon the phrase 'if I am a jackal, I am a lean and hungry one; I go forth to fatten myself'. I remembered it. There was a turf fire, the studio white as a bone. Roger Shackleton lived in Leixlip. Murdered infants had been discovered there, under floorboards. I believed him. I believed anything then. I had no money, few hopes. Little money, no hopes at all. Brigid Egan modelled nude for Roger Shackleton. Her skin had an incandescent glow, sitting on a rug before the turf fire. Her ambition was to live in a castle, with owls. I live in a castle, I told her. (Howth Castle, Kenelm's tower; I could just pay the rent, though I didn't tell her that.)

It was morning. A thin and submarine light leaked through the windows of the studio. Someone knocked on the door. Come in, I said. I was reading Petronius, muffled up. The air was chilly. Is that you, Paddy? a voice asked. No, I said. Who is it then, bejasus? the bowsy voice asked, and in came the homosexual housepainter, his face raw from the morning air off the quays. I thought you were Paddy Kelly, he said. He borrowed something and left. Would Shackleton ever see it again? I laid down Petronius and took up the Rawmás. I began to read. Perhaps an hour passed. A jingle of harness came from the yard below. It was mid-morning. I heard rapid steps on the stairs and the door banged open. I was muffled up like an owl in the blankets. Is that you, Paddy? the same North-side voice asked. Bejasus, no, I said . . . It's still Ruttle. I threw back the bed clothes. I was dressed for the day, but for jacket and shoes. I put on my shoes and began to tie the laces. Who is Paddy Kelly and where is Paddy Kelly? I said.

He's just back from Korea, the homosexual housepainter said. Do I know him to see? I said. What does he look like? Oh the loveliest looking young lad you ever clapped eyes on, he told me. I do shag him in his marriage bed. And how does he like that? I said. He loves it, the housepainter said. Begob he loves it. Belike, I said, belike.

And there I was reading the Old Ram again, and the ex-housepainter was famous and married, and Shackleton was serving behind a bar in London. Presently the Baylesses came in. Daisy was in bed. Charlotte wanted to sit by the window. I ordered drinks. The *gitano* from Calle Italia was defeating all at dominoes at the other table. I sat with my back to them, facing Charlotte. Miguel brought cognac and coffee. *Gracias*, Miguel, Charlotte said. *De nada, Señora*, Miguel said. *Una copita*, Bob said, *para usted?* Miguel said no thanks, it was too early. Later perhaps. *Bueno*, Bob said.

While we were drinking I heard chairs being pushed back and voices raised in anger, then the sound of a blow. It was all reflected in her eyes: aroused men were fighting, there might be bloodshed. She was held by it, the luminous eyes changing, more charged, pupils impinging on the iris, like a cat at night. She sat with her spine very straight, watching.

There was a scuffle behind me, panting, then another blow. She did not flinch, her eyes blazing, all pupil. I half turned in my chair. A big man, his face convulsed with rage, was standing over a youth. The latter's left ear was flaming. The big brown-baked *hombre* wore a black mourning band. He had fetched the impudent youth a buffet on his lughole to teach him a sharp lesson. The youth was sneering silently at him, curling his lip, about to say something truly cutting, and the big man, standing over him with his chest out, gulping air, was challenging him to say it. Next time he would really hit him. He towered over the domino players. They were all standing. The man from the kiosk now intervened as peacemaker. He held the big infuriated man by one arm and talked reasonably to him. The big man rolled his eyes and kept watching the insolent youth. The domino players were no help at all. The big man allowed himself to be mollified by the informer. They all trooped out.

What in hell's name was all that about? Bob asked. A slight difference of opinion, I said, blown over now. I didn't know they went in for fisticuffs in this country, Bob said. Well they don't, I said. A nation of bullfighters; you need trickier footwork for that. Charlotte crossed her legs. I asked her would she like another cognac. I caught Miguel's eye.

Had Charlotte been in the youth's place, she would have waited until the big character was off-guard, then hit him as hard as she could where it would do most damage, and run for it—I'd have slugged him and high-tailed it, she said.

Another image there. She had been that once: a pale young thing with Polish blood standing in the freezing school yard at Samuel Gomper's High, the school named after the founder of the Women's Garment Workers Union, the WGWU, one of the least corrupt in the graft-ridden city. Her hands raw, her eyes streaming in the cold. Put upon and not accepting it, not taking any lip from anybody. A ghost girl running with her face working, hair flying. Quick to take offence, striking and running, the smallest and toughest kid on the block. Dilly Lipski.

My grandfather, dead beyond recall, had hands so hard Bob said, that you'd think you were shaking a stone man's hands. He was a tall, self-made man. A clip on the earhole from fists like those would be no joke, although he never offered to clip me one. His dukes got that way from playing baseball before the mit was invented for catchers. In old Whittier.

I looked at Bob's big shoulders, his lugs, lobeless ears. He had long arms, a long reach. He had worked on the railway, dragging sleepers. Once on an oil rig. His hands were large, impassive, freckled, not the hands of a violent man. The band of gold on one finger indicated: Stand off—she's mine.

Nixon's town, Charlotte said, Whittier.

When I was a young Okie in Whittier, Bob said, my mother used to hand out food to the local poor kids. A regular Ma Joad. They lived from hand to mouth, as you might say. The Bayless family lived high on the hog. Railings oxidizing, worms in the vines, sometimes the poor mothers liked to give something in return. Mustard sandwiches. Jesus! There was this Quaker foot-washing church there. In the Silent Hour you could hear the stomachs of the Quakers rumbling.

We sat there drinking. The domino game had broken up, the players did not come back. Custom was slack. I thought of Charlotte's own background, Manhattan, Lafayette Street, Delancey, Orchard, the garment workers' district, the dirty river that she had told me of.

Far-away Staten Island and the big empty-headed lady on her high pedestal turning green. Holding her torch on high, the empty democratic gesture, France's gift. Tourists gaping from under her high tiara. The pen in the port.

In the dustbowl where my father grew up, if one of the windmills went out of order, granpappy would be called in. He'd climb up into the sails and stop the damn thing with his bare hands. I swear to God he was like that.

Grandmother remembered riding in a covered wagon, Bob said. A dog sitting up beside her with its tongue out. The dust and heat of the track. Never trust a colonist. The history of north and south America is the history of rapacity.

Whittier, Charlotte said, that's where my dear husband grew up. A true Okie.

Sholy, Bob said. His blue thinking eyes looked at the Plaza. Nixon that White drug-store Indian, that detergent salesman.

Tell him more about the Quakers of Whittier, Charlotte said. Tell him of our backward lovely land.

I have a Red Indian uncle, Bob said. His mother was a full-blooded Cherokee and his father before him a Scots farmer who once drove a stage coach in Oklahoma. Owned it and drove it. My uncle James Lafayette McKnight advised my brother and me,

'Do something, boys, even if it's wrong'. Yankee pragmatism. He's still living, resident in Los Angeles. A good man. I wouldn't take his advice too seriously, though. Perhaps he's changed.

The younger brother of Bob Bayless had attended a creative writing class given by Walter van Tilburg Clarke, author of *The Ox-bow Incident*. A movie had been made of it.

We spoke of films. I rarely go to them, I said. I once followed Yeats into the Grand Central in Dublin to see a thing called *The 13th Man*. I sat behind him and heard him sighing. It wasn't very good. Nothing to do with the occult anyway.

Some customers came into the bar. Ever heard of James Coburn? Bob said. He's a star. He and I were in the same club in Junior College. We were buddies. He's made a million in the last two years.

57 ON THE THIGH OF A MIGHTY WAVE: It was Christmas Day. The Baylesses came dressed formally: he in a dark suit, white shirt, slim jim tie, black boots; she in a sort of half-length housecoat and black stockings that reached to the waist, clasped her about the hips. *Strumpfhosen.* They brought presents, a bottle of JJ from Malaga, flowers, oil paints. We sat about and drank the whiskey. When Olivia took her siesta around two we went out. It was a strange day of white light on white walls. The town seemed deserted. We encountered Exley and invited him to dinner; We drank Cuné in Antonio's dim bar. And then back, not sober, to the Christmas dinner. The tougher parts of the chicken were in a paella, the tender parts fried in oil and garlic. Charlie Vine came. Exley did not complain of the toughness of the chicken, but threw the bones about. Adelina had been waiting for us at the top of the stairs, beaming like the Queen Mother. She served up the first course and left. Vine was subdued and left early. We sat around the *brasero* and finished the whiskey. Bob spoke of his time in Korea. You could buy good whiskey tax free at the NCO club. He was second radioman, radar operator and titular gunner on a seaplane. He had enlisted in the navy so as not to be drafted into the infantry, and had spent a good portion of his enlistment in training schools. I'd gone to an electronics school in Memphis, Bob Bayless said. I was assigned to crew nine. I managed to learn the Morse code, was given a chance to fly. It meant extra money and an easy life. Air crewmen stood fewer watches and did less work.

Blues, peacoats, winter hats, fall-ins, fall-outs, leaves, pick-ups, occasional women, fuck-ups, the Korean war, Bob Bayless said. We were enlisted men.

When I was fighting for democracy over there, flying in old PBM's, stubby-winged and heavy, couldn't land on four-foot swells, with none of the grace of the more famous PBY's, we patrolled the east coast of Korea, the Tsushima Strait and the Yellow Sea, in an anti-submarine outfit.

The port of Wonsan, Bob Bayless said. Barber-shop music and college songs. It was Christmas 1952. The sea was icy. If you dropped into it, you wouldn't survive long. One of the seaplanes came down, thirteen officers and men. None survived.

Those Kamikazes, Bob Bayless said, feasted and shaven to the pluck, got into a kind of flying chicken coop made out of fence posts, orange crates, put together around a bomb. And in those things they'd set out looking for an American destroyer. Some of them never made it. They'd explode somewhere off Wonsan. Desperate men. It was generally known that the Chinese used the Korean war as an extension of cadet training.

The seaplane ramp, Bob Bayless said. We flew out over the strait, a short gravy hop during which we photographed shipping. I was not at all prepared to die.

The brothels were paper-thin, Bob Bayless said. The whole joint shook when some of my buddies were hammering a job, polishing their knobs. The bar hostesses were perfect. They were human and gentle, and they needed us. I had never been around a collection of pretty, young, intelligent girls who needed me—not as a civilian and certainly not as a sailor. It was a blessing, a whiff of a dream, and another eloquent argument against worry. I knew I wasn't going to cream it.

Leaning back in his chair, puffing at his cigar, Bob looked at his wife. Her swollen lip was back more or less to normal (what better proof than a cut lip can a woman want that a man has her on his mind?). American service girls seemed a bit coarse in comparison, Bob said. A big perfumed WAVE took me on her capacious thigh and dandled me up and down. Nothing came of it except that I was keenly embarrassed, enough to bring tears to a man's eyes. She explained to me that it was all she could do, it was her 'difficult' time. Period like lava flow, I should imagine. Glad I didn't have to perform. She'd have swallowed me up.

You didn't fuck around with a shipmate's girl or wife, Bob Bayless said. Jim McCracken, Joe Moody, Pat Fanning, Kramer. Fanning laid another man's wife. The husband got wind of it, beat the shit out of her, then got him drunk one night in a bar, laid him out with a bottle and then began kicking and stomping him. Sure as hell ruined his good looks. It was the last time he polished his knob there.

❦

It was cold in the Balcon de Europa bar in the morning. There was snow along the sierras, cloud on the Cuesto del Cielo. We were alone there. Miguel served us, did not see us, did not hear us. She crossed one black-stockinged leg over the other. I saw her brown thigh. I heard a child crying. What was it doing in the *retrete*? It was the stink-sump of Spain. How did women manage, crouching over it, in ammonia-reek powerful as chloroform, and rise up again?

Sometimes she dominated me with her eyes, but more often than not it was her voice that dominated me, but when she sat on the high bar stool at the Balcon bar it was the inner side of her brown thighs that dominated me. She spoke of the past, that time before she had known me. Miguel served us, tactful, did not speak, saw nothing, heard nothing. (Heard all and understood nothing.) I watched her face, her teeth, eyes, mouth. Slight apathy, burning lips. She looked at me without saying anything, her eyes slightly charged.

She was younger then. She was kissing a hairy chest in Chicago. Then that one disappeared out of her life and there was another. He shot squirrels, went about naked with a gun in a wood. He was a theological student, liked Oscar Wilde. Naked in bed together they ate grapes and he read *The Nightingale and the Rose*. Kind of innocent, Charlotte said. He gave her a present of the *Shropshire Lad*, his rose-lip't girl.

Charlotte breathing through her nose, laughed, remembering the theological student going about naked in the woods. Then there was another, there would always be another (her Byzantine nose here became more pronounced, whitening across the bridge), she was attractive to men. Would she remember all her old lovers? Would I too have that immortality? Waves, distant waves, a ghost of you.

I thought of the Albanian wood-cutters white with dust of

314

the road, that I had seen in Sarajevo, come on foot out of Ethiopia carrying Bronze Age saws. And Amory cutting logs in Canada, grunting at each stroke, a true woodsman. Amory burning the road in his Combi, heading for the Laurentians.

That grey period in Montreal. The centre of the city was a cemetery. Mount Royal, where the dead looked down on the living. Ville Marie (a settlement of missionaries), then Place Royal (a fur trading post), and before that again it was Hochelaga (Iroquois Indian village). A girl once seen undressing near a lighted window, later accosted in the street by Amory. The turreted roofs and outside stairways of old Montreal. Stairways useful for assignations since they led directly, in some cases, to bedrooms on upper floors. Amory climbing, a lover set out with all his equipages and appurtenances. His hot amber eyes and intrepid ways. A rose clenched between his teeth would not have been inappropriate. He liked high game on the edge, good sticky salty cod from Newfoundland. He had whom he pleased. That was a strange madness of his—to be forever waking up in a strange bed. A true *carpe diem* type, his days were filled with vital cravings and satisfactions. Consorting with Montreal whores, he had caught a dose of the clap.

He enjoyed life as a cannon ball enjoys space, travelling to its aim blindly (and spreading ruin on the way?). A Scorpio. He had tattooed arms, lime blue shapes of hearts entwined or ships in storm, guns belching fire and smoke. I never looked too closely. His army and forestry background. Puce needle diggings. Amory digging with a rutter in Cumberland, down in an open drain.

A fast river cuts a deep trench, Amory said. A slow river cuts a shallow trench. Munge, Amory said (meaning morning mouth). Ullage. We passed an open drain (the stench was enough to make your hair stand on end). Shit, Amory said, I love it. I can't get enough of it (inhaling deeply as though it were flowers). Not bearing to be quiet, not able to abide still at home. Now abroad, now in the streets, now lying in wait at corners.

You dig the soil to get something out of it, you have a woman for much the same reason. (Amory digging with his wet tool in a trench in Cumberland.) He knew he was finished if he stayed there. A perishing wind blew down from the Grampians. He had to get out. Amory struck with a hatchet, grunting at each blow, sweat poured down his face. The bulge at his crotch was pronounced. A true *carpe diem* type. No more sickness of excessive evacuation. The sun went down over a hill.

He's changed, Olivia said. He was different in Canada, steadier. There he was a man. (With an excreta phobia.)

And now? I said. Here?

Here he has become a chimpanzee, Olivia said.

⟨●⟩

The way she walked away from me that day, heading for the brick works and the cemetery, walking with that aura of hers, that short chopping stride, *paso fino*, with the certainty of being seen and admired. Women feel it in their backs when they are being seen. The road, the *carretera*, bore her along on its back. The conviction of her own power of allure carried her along. She turned without stopping, saw that my eyes still followed her. I was a little below her on a cinder path that went branching off at right-angles. It led over the tableland to the sea. Her lemur paw waved. I waved back. Without breaking her stride she went on.

She was my bit of stuff on the road. Like most women, and all attractive women, she craved the touch of flannel. Was that the last time? If it was, I did not know it then. I was going to establish my alibi. Swimming, dear. Not waving but drowning, dear. Charlotte was returning with her own plausible lies to her waiting husband, though what she would tell him was true enough up to a point. Up to the point of her lies, that is. She would not tell him an outright lie, but her omissions contained falsehoods; her elisions were masterful. Out walking for two whole hours, dear, seeing nobody, speaking to no one, had a beer at La Luna.

So she went jauntily down the road, no doubt still feeling me as I still knew her, being permeated with her. So she knew she was out of her depth, gliding away, knew the wonderful, dangerous intensification of feeling that comes with lying and

316

cheating in love. There is no prescription against voluntary things; it is against form.

She went away from me down the road and I watched her go. The seat of a Jewess? No, not the broad prudent seat (or *pompi*) of rumpy Rosa Munsinger, not the spare flat deflated seat of Sonya Hool. The tresses or hanks of dark hair proper to a Jewess—Rosa's Brillopad hair, Lilly Lowen's orange golliwog locks. The look of a real Jewess, Jewish linen, the Alexandrian effluvia of torpid female Jewish flesh? She was none of these. She was my only spare-time fair, loving, Polish-American-Jewish lure and love.

Unlike Tracey Weddick's incessant spate of talk on that never-to-be-forgotten and never-to-be-diminished-or-thought-of-badly, rich, purse-proud America, the friends one had never met; God had been so good to make them all American. The great steak houses of the great cities, American self-confidence, Yankee push and self-reliance, cities great as New York (capital of conspicuous waste), the parfaits, or was it T-bone steaks, at Rumpelmayer's. San Francisco, sometimes called Queen City for its known high percentage of homosexuals. Charlotte had not that narrowly determinable view of the race and of the places occupied by the race, that spurious and obsessive concept of nationality that so many Americans have. She was American, yes. Jewish too, though she disliked the term 'Jewess'. Negress, Jewess, they were the same.

Was there something that said *Juden* in those eyes of hers? Some knowledge, some sadness, dredged up from God knows where? Or was it merely the power that certain beautiful women have of suggesting and invoking landscapes? Their eyes gaze if not into at least towards a landscape no man has ever seen, much less penetrated. That small woman. That Jewy woman.

Had I not once looked into eyes as heavy-lidded, as expressive, as sad? The brown eyes of Marcia Paz-Pero, youngest and prettiest daughter of the late Bolivian Foreign Minister to Ireland, the small Republic. It was in the Dawson Gallery. The two girls went around together, one blonde, one brunette, one serious, one smiling, both consulting catalogues. Marcia was the dark serious one and her Parisian friend—some name like Monique—was blonde and bright. They kept coming back to one painting. Greene the gallery director introduced them. The girl called Monique—if that was her name—wanted to buy the painting as a present for Marcia Paz-Pero's father, then alive. It was a small oil painting not characteristic of my work.

Later I saw her (Marcia's) photograph in the Social & Personal columns of the *Irish Times*, where it was formally announced that she was to wed a Dr. Brian Goodall of Templeogue, an inter-provincial rugby player. The honeymoon would take place at La Paz. Dr. Goodall practised in Connecticut. He was the only son of Mr. James (Jim) and Mrs. Constance (Conny) Goodall of Templeogue, Co. Dublin. His fiancée was the youngest daughter of the late Don Xavier Paz-Pero of La Paz, former Bolivian Foreign Minister to Ireland, then deceased. The blonde charming friend, Monique or some name like that—had not come back for the painting. Mr. Greene had put it aside for a while. Someone asked for it. He said it was bespoke. But later sold it.

The photograph of *Señorita* Marcia Paz-Pero had caught a certain look at times evident in the eyes of Mrs. Bayless. When she was depressed, she was really down. Her dumps were profoundly Jewishly deep. The look conveyed something of: Now I am neither happy nor sad, I am what I am.

I'd think then of her: *I know you . . . and yet I do not know you.* A sullen wife and a reluctant mother, she sat all day in silence by the fire. I thought then: This is and is not Charlotte. Was it not Jewish, that dolour, and impenetrable gloom? I don't know. Probably it was. Some relative had told her that she had eyes 'just like Uncle Ibn's'. But he ('a loud-mouth with five grown sons in trade') 'definitely had Jewish eyes', according to Charlotte. So she preferred not to believe it.

Look, she said (standing up close to me and opening her eyes wide so that I could study them, smell her Cointreau breath), do you believe that I have Jewish eyes?

Yes, I said.

Do not believe it, she said. I have Italian eyes.

You have Italian eyes, I agreed.

A partial failure some of the time, semi-successful part of the time, that's how it was then. It was very strange. That winter, and the termination of our intimacy in the Spring. Say May Day.

PART IV

Summer 1963

Andalusia

58 BURRIANA BEACH is one kilometre long. At the beginning and again at the end, a cliff runs parallel to it, an ascending ridge of khaki-coloured sandstone and burnt-sienna shale, Spanish brown, broken here and there on the upper levels, under cultivation whenever possible and fenced off with palissades of old dried cane fence or blocked by the uneven character of the land itself, the buff and dun-coloured earth making way for the variegated green of the crops. Sweet potatoes, beans, tomatoes. Below this, a mustard-coloured cliff peppered with holes.

The land climbs into the *campo* and from there by stages into the sierras; ascending ranges scarred by fire-breaks and crowned with lowsized savin and pine. The village of Maro is situated on higher ground up there by the caves. In summer the nearer ranges of the sierras stand out clearly, the back ranges diffused and hazy. In winter this changes and far and near alike all the ranges stand out with an equal and vivid clarity. A windbreak of cane grows on the region lying alongside the narrow shore, its high plumes waving in whatever winds that blow. The terraces descend from the broken table-land (*tablazo*), shale mixed with granite and calcite, where in prehistoric times a great river came down, carrying all before it. Of this all that remains is a small stream that dries up in grass and moraine before it reaches the sea. Sedimentary rock occurs further along, the stains of fishermen's fires and dried human excrement. Where a gulley or ravine comes, gaps open out, there in former times the wide river forced its way past this delta into the sea.

Terraces in chromatic colours, never dull, even on overcast days. Three or four breaks in the cliff, sable and greens, a windbreak of high cane. A couple of long-boats, their fishing days over, disintegrating on the sand. They have, in the prow, the rough outline of the jaw mandibles of gibbons, a design prevailing unchanged since the Phoenicians occupied Malaga.

Fires, then, a plume of cane, a cliff riddled with holes, rock-stains, chemicals, rain, irrigation waters, human excrement—*terra incognita*. A dried-up delta. A special territory, special associations. Up there I can never take you; we will never be alone together there. Where will you be? Where will we go? I'll go wherever I'll find you. In a word, we'll lose ourselves, Charlotte.

⚜

She's never in her life before had such attention, such love, Bob Bayless told Olivia. She doesn't know what to do with it.

Olivia repeated this to me: that never before in her life had Charlotte Bayless received such attention, such love, and that she didn't know what to do with it.

From whom? I asked. From him?

No, Olivia said, from you.

59 DREAM TROUGH: In my dream I am walking you home. Some locals, young men, are watching us. My hand about your waist feels the smooth roll of your thigh through the pocket of your slacks. At the corner on the Puerta del Mar I stop for cigarettes. But you've got cigarettes, you say.

I walk into a poor shop, a shabby place with bolts of poor quality cloth laid out on the counter. No one is serving there, no such shop exists on the Puerta del Mar. It's a pure dream figment, nothing else. Siesta hour, about four in the afternoon; the sun bright and hot, the Poniente blowing papers about. We stand at the counter, Nobody comes. The village boys stand grinning in the doorway.

The dream changes. There is a narrow water trough with a wall directly behind it and you are submerged nude to your neck in the water like Arletty in *Les Enfants du Paradis*. The village boys watch us closely, anticipating impropriety. The word has got around. I want to kiss you. I am wearing black swim trunks. I lift you from the narrow dream trough. You come out wet with your knees up, your face serious. A beautiful gentleness glows from your skin. You are wet but you are on fire. That certain acceleration that only comes from within has always pleased me. Gravely I kiss your wetted lips. Feeling your damp hair, unable to delay any longer, surreptitiously I begin to draw down my trunks with one hand, concealing what I am doing as best I can. (The rule of desire for realistic possession: *to hold a great power within a small volume*.) In a guarded manner the boys cry something that sounds like—*Wotan! Wotan!*

60 ALAMEDA GARDENS: As we walked in Malaga in the Alameda gardens, her hand touched mine. We entered the cathedral, attempted to kiss in the porch where a great leather wind-break hung down like the bark of a rotting tree. A woman, scandalized, walked past us, we broke apart, went out into the sunlight into the city divided in two by a dry river-bed. Stricken with bubonic plague in the seventeenth century, sacked by Napoleon's troops in the nineteenth, it fell to Italian troops in the Civil War. Their war. Public garottings took place on the riverbed. Hans Andersen had stayed there in 1860.

My hand touched hers. Photographers were stooping under their hoods. Stout men like Emil Jannings. They developed the prints while you waited. Charlotte walked there. She was infected with another life. We went past flowering judas, plumbago. I was moving in another century with another woman. Hans Andersen, wearing a smoking cap, a red smoking jacket, and puffing a clay pipe, looked benevolently down from a balcony. Charlotte was confessing to me her secret desires. We walked about Malaga. They had put up at a pension near the market. Pig's blood ran in the drains. It was the site of an old arsenal.

I discovered happiness in her company. She was dressed in blue, wore black stockings. (Hans Andersen, drinking English beer, listened to a band in the Alameda playing fine airs from *Norma* as some Jews in caftans passed below.) We walked past the gardens of flowering judas in Malaga. Every possibility has its equal but opposite alternative, a balanced weighing of values can never end, the dream drags out its own repulse.

She was paid a compliment, a *piropo*, on Avenida Larios. A man whispered: You're a lovely cunt. I wouldn't like to get into bed with a Spaniard, Charlotte admitted. Antonio's sister had threatened to sleep with the first man who asked her in Malaga, but she lacked thirty-five pesetas for panties. She felt she was going mad, thirty years old and life slipping away. She would go with the first man that looked at her. I wouldn't do that, Charlotte said. Look, it may be that love is a kind of curse.

Oh if only I had some of that curse, Tcharlawt! poor deprived Carme Criado cried.

Uncontrollable thoughts, lips, hands, eyes. The game of laugh and lie down. Constraint vanishes with the dark.

⊙❈⊙

Charlotte had the roundest cheeks. As a child she had been a poor eater, not all that much appetite, and so reluctantly to table. Her mother wouldn't take it. Any food left over from one meal appeared again at the next. Matzo balls, vegetables, gefilte fish. I got to hate the stuff, Charlotte said.

No waste, her mother told her. If half the world starves, you eat that now, girl. Charlotte held the food in her cheeks, left the table, spat it out. These hamster tricks of her girlhood gave her round cheeks as an adult, a slightly comical look; but she was not ill-favoured, no.

She had the nose of a person who likes to have her own way. It came straight down from a low hair-line—a Byzantine profile. On the bridge of her nose the skin was a paler colour over a shallow quarter-inch of healed old scar, *Windpocken*. She had small-pox as an infant, itched and scratched all over. Her mother tied her hands to the bed post, as the women in labour in the olden times were tied, so that she would not mark herself permanently by scratching. But she was desperate. She got one arm loose. She scratched, it left a permanent scar like the symbol of the Peace Movement. It merely added to her charms.

I was different, she said. I felt myself to be different from the others. I loved evenings. The end of it—the day. The others played, I didn't care for it, the games they played; it tired me. I had this low blood pressure and sometimes fainted. Once I was given oxygen. It was wonderful coming out of it, this cool breeze blowing, like off the sea. I loved the time just before a storm. I felt it in my body, my blood. A black sun, she said.

I didn't want another day to start, sometimes. This one seemed

327

sufficient. But I really loved the evening. I wanted to keep that feeling, the pity.

(I saw this quiet preoccupied child with her long hair and long jaw, standing alone, watching another East Side day expire. The rough lads were calling by the fire hydrants. Dilly Lipski! Make do with what you can get, that's all there is.)

◖●◗

I got my first kiss at the age of seven, Charlotte said, during school recess. There were eight of us, four fellows and four girls. The boys arranged it. The girls made their choice. The one I wanted was Axel Staudinger. He was the boldest. They waited until dark. The girls lined up. None of them had been kissed before. It was in a yard with a high wall. One of the boys counted to three and then Axel kissed me. When he was kissing me another nasty boy called Buddy Hulke was climbing over the wall and saw us.

The others all got pecks on the cheek but Axel Staudinger kissed me on the mouth. He said, Now I want to marry you, Dilly. Give you a ring and a car. I liked being kissed by him but I didn't want to marry him. The boys were Andy Vita, Ed Walter, Bruno Schultz, Axel Staudinger. The girls were Sabina Klingner, Carol Buck, Mary Henel and me.

And you remember it still? I said.

Oh yes, Charlotte said. Why not?

I saw the scene, the daring group, the darkening school-yard, the lout climbing the wall, Dilly Lipski in the arms of Axel Staudinger. The Jew's daughter all dressed in green. The energetic dream of childhood. Just one boy kissed just one girl. It was like that then.

Why so many Germans? I said.

I guess they were in the neighbourhood, she said. All big hairy fellows. All jerks.

That awful German word for neighbour, Charlotte said. *Nachbar!* God, it must be the ugliest language in the world. NACHBAR! They talk too loudly and too much. And how they love *Ordnung* and *Schunkeln*. Sausages!

At the age of eleven I was kissed more slowly and heavily

328

by a slow, heavy German. I didn't know what he was after, how could I. I didn't like being followed. I wasn't ready, Charlotte said. How could I be?

What is a kiss, why this, as some approve: the sure-fire cement, the this-and-that, quid and pro, lime and glue of love.

Put me down in your notebook and don't forget me, Charlotte said.

She looked at my lips. She wasn't asking me what I thought, she was bearing me away with her. I looked into the lure of those eyes, a glare of sun on water, and there were the shadows of former lovers. I experienced a deep prod of longing love. We were almost there already. The door was closed and she was undressing. I touched the back of her hand with my fingertips. We communicated our intentions without speaking.

Put me down.

What construction could I put on her words? I had attempted some sketches of her Nefertiti head, the long neck, the pull of hair, but the results had not been good. We would find a place somewhere. On Vine's roof or in the Hools' empty flat, or in the *campo*. She would come to me, a naturalist, friend of air and sun. *Wald und Wiesen. Komplexität der menschlichen Natur.* The long braid of corn-coloured hair laid along her spine was her *trenza*, her mane.

⟨⟩

It was a liberal arts college on the east coast with Jewish alumni, near the town of Yellow Springs. Arthur Morgan, an important personage on the TVA governing body gave grants to the university, the Kettering Institute, donations to the chemistry section, chlorophyll, the colouring matter of green parts of plants. What makes the grass grow green. Fels Naphta soap. Research on human teeth. Wright Patterson Field was not far away. All the pollen fell. It was a low-pressure area, bad for asthmatics.

The Talmud, the Polish Ashkenazi, the Haggadah, the Hadassah, the Temple. The roof of the synagogue was blue. Tahoe was an Indian name. Brockway Hotel was on Lake Tahoe. Was Lake Tahoe blue? Second table to the left in the dining-room.

What colour was the dining-room, Charlotte, tell me. What colour—lime green?

The huge water-shitting machines of the gold companies in and around Sacramento, Charlotte said.

It was her country, her past.

By the age of twenty-two she had had nine affairs. Five had been serious. She was in high school. She was in college. Some of the girls had affairs but kept quiet about them. They spoke about boys but not of what they did together. Girls became pregnant. Later some of the couples married. Charlotte and her first boy-friend (faceless track-star covered in acne) went 'steady' for two boring years. He was a quarterback with false teeth, the result of a collision with a hard blocker or tackle. He had a football scholarship, very dull in class, couldn't get proper grades. He was mean-minded ('skinny', Charlotte said, 'skinny-minded too') and sometimes cruel.

61 BULLS: You were sitting under dusty orange trees outside a café in Velez-Malaga opposite a decayed church. You who liked the 'tight asses', of the bullfighters, the *coleta* was 'the bugger's grip'. I sat beside you. You were glowing.

A sword went into a bull with a wedge-shaped death thrust. The bull, weak in the knees, was toppling over, vomiting blood, rolling its bloodshot eyes. 'They look sad,' you said, as one went below at a fast trot. Why not, it had about ten minutes to live. *Domino, descabello.* The crowd. A longing without focus. The severity of the rules. Here's one for Hera. *Puyoza,* deep as it could go. The blood came jerking out. Ritual bleeding. The lance was tearing at the hump of the black bull. Charlotte watched everything. The capes lured the bull away. It went at a trot, its back torn, bleeding.

A young Malaga widow in mourning walking in the back streets, black hair recently washed, black two-piece suit, high heel black shoes, her sadness veiled in crêpe. A Madonna with long dark eyelashes; that tranced look. Seen later drinking lemon tea in a café.

62 HORSE: Smells kinda high in here, Charlie, Charlotte's voice called from Vine's bedroom. Smells of hay in here. Do you stable a horse here?

Grass, Bob said, you mean grass.

Do you, Charlie? Charlotte said.

No, Vine said, only Salina.

I stood by the wall and looked into the empty street below. It was siesta time. The Poniente was blowing dust about. An awning flapped its white letters on a blue ground: *Ultramarinos. La Ina. Domecq. Tel. 116.* Opposite three *casas* had the same number: 77. Charlotte came out of the bedroom.

I wanted to have her on the bed.

Now the tall mute came stalking below, keeping to the shade. The only sound he could make was that of a very faint, distant, but perfect *burro*. He terrified Daisy.

Broken fragments burning all the while and there you are sitting aside all this and more balanced on the tip of your perfect (and you can balance on that, *ah si*, and more) swaggering bottom and all.

Today I shall try a white bed sheet which I have misused before. It is for very tiny work with the advantage of a bit of a bleed. The colour shall be applied literally from the rear. Art from the Bulls of Altamira to the Horrors of War has sought to limit the scope of what is beyond our capacity to order, and comes in the end to be a desperate attempt to disturb the equilibrium of the most harmless objects. A pair of boots. A chair. Or, most intrepid of all, a straight line.

Someone has said: *No se puede vivir sin amor.* In the bars whenever anyone made the toast *Salud y pesetas* (say Antonio), either Bob or Olivia would add *Y amor*, and Charlotte would add the tag, *Y tiempo para gastarlas*, and look at me without appearing to do so, a trick she had.

332

She lay on the sand. The goat-herd was pestering her. They watched me come. The brown hand with the symbolic gold ring made an intensely private gesture. Over the hot sand the beach was roasting. She watched, enigmatic behind sunglasses. Close to her, I said: Come into the shade.

Okay, she said.

I helped her collect her stuff. We went across and sat in the shade of the cane branches that I had rigged against the sun. The goat-herd crouched in the shade of the cane plantation with another sepia man who had appeared out of nowhere. They observed us in no friendly fashion. The herd of goats, some black rams with trailing bullybags and ewes in shades of brown and khaki, grazed on the beach. She said: I thought I'd be doing you a favour by keeping away. I read secret hostilities and judgments in her smallest gestures, in the inflections of her voice, and in her silences. She was most unreasonable. She could tear off my shirt, land on my bare back with her sharp heels, pierce my chest. It was difficult to have her physically present before me. It was a question of rearranging my feelings about her, keeping them in decent bounds. She was all about me. To sit in silence opposite her, as I often did, was not enough, thinking: The more she talks, explains, the less she is (although her stories, her past, charmed me). When she was present, I froze; when she was absent, my desire was hot. We moved from bar to bar, always forgetting the earlier version, I not able to keep up with the moods of the adult woman. she needed to be entertained; in other words, wanted me to draw off a little in my infatuation, let her breathe. And now what was left?

The dust of goats returning hanging in the evening sun.

63 TOLLUND MAN: They lay in the shade of the rocks, face down, their heads on their forearms, as though sleeping, heels crossed, worn out by the drudgery of pulling in nets. In this position with their faces close to the ground, they waited for the girls to come down and start undressing.

Pointed like retrievers, eyes mere slits between sand and hair saw pale underdone English flesh being squeezed into, or out of, the cups of a bra, the ample curve of a French bottom being forced into (or out of) a tight bikini, saw a German girl's pubic parts. The long imagined could at last be seen. Not all the masturbators were found in a horizontal and prone position, all prepuce and grit, no, some hid themselves behind the boulders on either side of Carabeo beach, had a quick eyeful and then down, shy climbing animals with long brown hands. Long-legged girls wearing nothing much in the way of clothes came down the path and undressed openly by the sea, while the onanists crawled around in the shade. Each his own, the longer known the more alone. Thus one may observe the ways of the world and the varieties of fortune. The foreign girls splashed in the water or lay prone on floating air-mattresses, paddling with their hands. The beach was marked as though a pack of horses had trampled it (from the pulling-in of the long nets).

Charlotte swam far out in a motionless blue sea where long wakes of bubbles showed her progress. A single boat rowed near. Tired, she held the stern and asked in Spanish, Can you take me? Not here, the Spaniard (an impudent waiter) said, choosing to misunderstand her, over there (pointing to behind a boulder). He towed her in.

She went to Torrecillas beach alone, protected herself with a ring of stones (for throwing), heard the *voyeur* creeping through the cane, but was not molested. A great dark mahogany-coloured face stared down on Playa de Carabeo from his coign of vantage by the wall. I saw dark eyes and the slanted nipples of a gorilla.

On the edge of the table-land above Burriana beach the old man squatted, gazing down on half-naked foreign women stretched out at their ease on the sand below. The Tollund Man moved from prostrate form to prostrate form, seeking whom he might devour. All the males of the village, young and old, were obsessed with women; some of the summer visitors gave themselves to the local studs. Don Pedro thundered at the women from the pulpit. The men kept away.

The Tollund Man was small-set, sinewy, not more than five feet five inches. His hay-coloured hair was cut short, his skin beige: beige body and beige trunks (I never actually saw him in clothes) virilia much in evidence, purposeful bulge of his manhood. His eyes were the colour of over-ripe gooseberries, slack and set close together and so fixed in their regard that they might have been endowed with a dog's double vision; a kind of snouted face, a small nose, the general air of a simpleton, but a corrupted one; this semi-simpleton with his squashed face and chest looked like the thing dug up in The Hague, throttled and thrown naked into a Dutch bog when Christ was young, to ensure that the sown seed would come up.

He walked in a stiff manner, rocking a little on his heels, conscious of his hands, a dog on its hind legs, a little beige-coloured manikin full of lust. What else but lust would have carried him from beach to beach through all the long days of summer? He was seeking a foreign bitch on heat, some careless young thing whom he could cover and none be the wiser. I had seen him frightening women who were by no means young, suddenly appearing in their midst and sitting down, more canine than human, but alarming, the dog face fixed and set permanently in one expression and on its lips a wistful dog-smile. He patrolled the five beaches as effectively as any beach guard, the eyes watchful, expressionless, the pointed muzzle with the half-smile, the dog-smile. He went from one end of Burriana to the other, then over by the rocks on to Carabeo, spent time there only if there were females about;

then over the rocks and rubbish to the coves below Calle Italia, good hunting grounds there, then on to Calahonda, from there around the old Bastion on to Salon, back up the ramp and down Calle Alemania and Calle Malaga, past the convent to Torrecillas. I had seen him near the tower there, and again at the far end of Burriana, three or more kilometres away. I had never seen him fully dressed, never seen him in the winter, this stiffly moving young *voyeur* who covered the beaches as though condemned to it. I had never seen him pick up a girl. In him was revived my own vacantly-gazing puberty at Bundoran and elsewhere. The *Amadán*. An old woman in Galway, who had some knowledge of Queen Maeve, would tell that the *Amadán-na-Breena* changed shape every two days.

Had he double-vision too, like a dog? Bull, whale, bird, rabbit, hen, each eye seeing quite a different picture. In a dog, the face is situated mainly in advance of the cranium; whereas in Man it has withdrawn below it. And the mind? What picture does the animal mind see or remember? The shrinking brain-case of our nearest animal relatives, the anthropoid apes. He walked through the beaches full of women, through his dog-brain the flesh paraded back and forth, shedding its inhibitions with its clothes. Heedless of results, uncalculating of contingencies, a passive victim of sudden impulse, and the most subservient dupe in the world (just like a dog), he was ageless, perhaps twenty.

I saw him 'pointing' at a near nude girl. The bathing costume she wore was the same colour as her skin. She seemed naked. She was alone. He sank to his knees by the edge of her beach towel, in an undertone addressed her, drugged with her, muted and grounded in longing. She stared at him but his expression did not change.

It is like that in *le pays de l'imprévu* in the summer, with the *voyeurs*.

64 HANDS: Weeds grew by the roadside. The hot mid-morning sun shone on the bakery. Flies crawled over the pine table and got into our beer. The warmish Victoria *cerveza* left a viscid scum on the palate. It was too hot for beer-drinking. Too early. I asked the woman in the *taberna* for Fanta lemonade. It was more *del tiempo* than *frio*. I made lukewarm shandies. We sat outside the bar. The place reminded me of summers long past in Dromore West. The proliferating weeds of summer. I was a nipper going to school. Time stood still. *En busca del tiempo perdido.*

No roadside hedges here, or ditch. The ground fell away to tilled fields, olive and almond groves, patterns of cultivated land. Two ragged children, one with finger in her mouth, one with shaven scalp, both drawerless, stared at us. Charlotte wore a thin lilac blouse with half-length sleeves and buff corduroy slacks very tight in the fit. She wore sandals and her skin was brown. The eyes of the children never left us; *estranjeros* were rare up Frigiliana way. What were we doing there in the hot mid-morning outside the bar at La Molinetta? I heard the noise of farm animals at the back of the *taberna* and the sound of the irrigation stream going down into the valley. I looked at her and thought of bed. But it was too hot for bed. The sound of running water put me in mind of her naked, swimming, laved by the sea. It had been too hot in the bar. The flies had driven us out. Flies inside; outside, the watchful eyes of children. They wore thin frocks and nothing else, their faces dirty, hair matted like gypsy kids, and they stared, stared at us, drinking beer and lemonade.

We had come up the dirt road the six kilometres from Nerka. I had waited on the bridge there, near the abattoir and she had come on the Lambretta down past the Costa del Sol café-bar. Six kilometres to La Molinetta, another three to

Frigiliana, past the Guardia Civil station and the timber yards where once on a wet winter day, buying wood, I had seen a soldier blowing a bugle under a red sky. A blind man's conception of scarlet. The mansion looking down on the valley had been the last domestic dwelling-place of the Moriscoes in Spain, country-side of Turdetania, El Dorado, *Ultima Tierra* of the Ancients. The Egyptian Screw, Moorish engineers, Iberian coins stamped with figures of horses and bulls. Six waves of invaders, centuries of occupation, then expulsion, then Civil War, in Catholic Ireland and Catholic Spain. One cut off from Europe by the Pyrenees, the other by the Irish Sea. Both on the outer fringes of Europe, both saved from two world wars by their long-nosed leaders; neither part of Europe. Both troubles started by women. Patricius first Bishop of Malaga, Catholic missionaries at Gaudix.

The road was rough. No bus service reached Frigiliana. The *pueblos* of the *Sierra*. We had come on the Lambretta for peace and quiet. Mules were tied up by the wall. The valley fell away towards the sea. *Fincas*, small and white and diminished, were scattered along the sable and burnt sienna sides of the valleys. The *Sierra* stretched away towards Torrox, Competa, Granada, Turdetania. The old Nerka fish-trail to Granada.

I have too much blood in me, Charlotte said, sometimes I think I hear it roaring like the sea.

Her face was much alive, from the exertion of the ride up. She looked down at her hands, her lemur paws.

I have an old woman's hands, she said.

We were sitting there when the Nerka-Frigiliana taxi went past La Molinetta. The passengers were singing. The car was well down on its springs, an old-fashioned and handsome Rolls-Royce, the engine smoking as though fuelled with lignite coal. The gradient was one in four. Smoke curled from the exhaust vent. This old car with its diesel engine carried passengers between Nerka and Frigiliana. The driver hung about Calle de Granada waiting for a capacity load before pulling away. The coach-maker's steel plaque was still in place, untarnished and grand above the running board. He liked to show it off, but it was a little embarrassing, because he was obliged to open the driver's door and once unlatched it fell off. A Silver Cloud, Silver Ghost, or Silver Wraith. Old Lady Royce—or was it Rolls?—was sometimes seen in Nerka. And the brother of the man who had invented penicillin—Fleming. English Amory had called him 'Sir'.

Those long low-slung black jobs always look to me as if they were made to order for 1929 gangsters, Charlotte said, watching the Rolls-Royce smoking up the steep gradient grinding its gear, by the Englishman's place where Phoenician remains had been unearthed. The earth was full of Phoenician remnants. The Rolls-Royce disappeared over the hill, smoking and shuddering, well down on its springs, the passengers silent. Joads go West.

A sign on the blue and white tiles of the old bakery:

PANIFICADORA
NUEVA ROSARIO

(Charlotte was crossing the Golden Gate Bridge in a red convertible.) Then who should come riding up the track but the squat fish-dealer from Nerka, all of two hundred and thirty pounds and drenched in sweat, his unshaven face blazing, his denim pants bursting open at the flies, a Basque beret stuck to his head like a cow-pad on a hillside. Sancho Panza himself. The face and figure were familiar to both of us. The match-stick legs of the donkey looked too fragile for that gross and dead weight athwart its spine. He was sitting back behind the panniers. I watched the delicate feet picking their way, stopping for him to dismount. Sancho Panza's feet were purple and bloated, tortured in *alpargatas*. The matchstick legs fidgeted by the wall. The *burro* had no feed bag. Six kilometres in the heat of the morning to La Molinetta under that load, it was no joke. I saw Cervantes in chains. The explorers who had served their Queens had ended badly. Stout Hernando Cortes from Extramadura, Columbus the opener of the New World had landed up in chains, Raleigh in the Tower. Trajan, Seneca, both had ended poorly, women or no women behind them. Trujillo looking at the face of a corpse. Mucus of life. The brown spongy interior of ancient bones. The sandalwood ceiling of the Capillo Real in Granada still gave off an agreeable odour after the lapse

339

of three centuries. Phoenician remains dug up in a garden. The fifteen-hour fish-trail to old Granada.

Charlotte spoke again of her married sister in Brooklyn. She gassed away for hours on the telephone. Wasn't it bad enough to live dully, without talking about it? Yes, I said, yes (thinking of Charlotte as a young thing, the telephone dragged into the cupboard under the stairs, a four-hour dialogue with her first boy-friend. The Lipski line). *Panificadora. Nuevo Rosario.* Mrs. Ruth Soblotsky sounded as Jewish as gefilte fish or the blue stars on the Synagogue roof. Flies crawled over my bare ankles and arms, and got into the shandy. Weeds grew along the roadside. Hens crossed the roadway. There was no more traffic. The children stared. It was like Ireland, the country I had never left. Green induces travel sickness.

We had come on the Lambretta which Bob had bought second-hand from Sonny Hool who had bought it new in Rome. Draw a line at Rome and below that thirty per cent of Europe is illiterate. Tell it to Trajan.

Something was happening to Sancho Panza's pack-animal. Between its twitching hind legs a dark thing had begun to appear, a thick serpent emerging from its old hiding-place. It continued to come out in a slow burdensome but resolute way (old as water, plain as an eel) until it was the dimension of a man's extended arm, but dark and club-shaped at its extremity. It had the hue and hair of an elephant's trunk; its sloth, coarseness, determination, its all too apparent strength suggested that. A darksome probiscus endowed with life of its own; a shy drop of urine shone at its tip; it flicked up at the belly, blowing flies. I watched this gross manifestation of desire behind Charlotte who was staring at the children. How far must this punitive thing penetrate into the she-ass?

In a while it began to retract itself in a slow vertical movement upwards. And this hydraulic movement continued until it had shrunk back to its natural size and position, more or less out of sight between the animal's hind legs. It grew short and stubby until its shape just protruded from the beast's crutch. Apuleius saw a woman and a donkey copulating in a circus. But Charlotte had not noticed. She was attempting to light a match.

Spanish matches were as poor in performance as Spanish anchors and cannon balls at the time of the Armada. Single matches burnt your fingers when the sulphur stuck, whole boxes were useless or else ignited in your pocket. I lit a match for her. Our boxes had beasts on them. The legend on the back of her's went: '*Meloncillo.—Especie de Mangosta que vive en los bosques de Andalusia y Extremadura.*' And on mine: '*La Piel.—La Piel se vende en peleteria. Animal de experimentacíon en medicina.*'

I listened to her voice and was charmed by it. An accent that took short-cuts and spoke generally of another world where I had never been and where I would probably never go. Senner, she said (centre), winner (winter), twenny (twenty), a voice dreaming away in broad daylight. Drugged with Victoria beer and heat, lulled by that voice, I thought how she must fill the day for him, full of her nakedness so close to him when he woke—her bare back, her tangled hair. He must go into sleep full of her and come awake again in the morning and be full of her. Close as lauthanium and didymium, or Spix and Martius, or Singer and Bandermann, inseparable as a couple of partridges, her kisses sweeter than persimmons. And then go through the day, if she was not with him, full of her. I wanted what I would never have: her night-form.

The eyes of a certain old man pursue me into sleep, Charlotte said (as though she could mind-read). He comes into my dreams and talks a lot but mainly in Yiddish. That's okay, but he speaks indistinctly as if he had his dentures in and with his head half turned away, as though he was afraid of me and yet had come to accuse. What he is accusing me of I don't know. I understand little of what he says, although he talks a lot. It's about something he lost, a holy object. He doesn't seem over-anxious to recover it, only wants to talk about it. He certainly does that all right and sometimes threateningly, as if it was my fault or as though he was expecting something from me. Don't ask me what. I was afraid of him at first but now I'm getting used to him. Who could he be, do you suppose?

It was very quiet. The flies crawled over her bare arms and along the cracks of the pine table. I stared over the roadway at the white *fincas* dotted along the hills. In the distance, across there in the blue dreaming air, they were like mushrooms of the valley. I looked back at the sign in blue and white—*Panificadora, Nueva Rosario*—and wondered was Rosario dead? A little boy was watching us from the steps of the bakery. He looked quickly away, hiding his face with his hand. The hand was heavily bandaged.

The Chassidims speak of Dybbuks, ghosts of dead ones who are able to subdue time and space and try to live in some other person, or die or else finish something, Charlotte said. That's extremely important for them, their soul. He might be one of those characters.

I could make nothing of this, I knew nothing of Chassidims or Dybbuks, so I said nothing. The little boy under the sign PANIFICADORA continued to watch us. His face was like hers. Charlotte as an unlettered lad in Andalusia, born without privileges. Never to attend school but just to sit out on a step in the sun and watch the mules and the mule-men going on the road. Watch the weeds grow, her (his) mind a blank. I looked again, caught the boy looking away, a fair-haired male child with her colouring and profile, her sulky mouth. A male Charlotte.

The boy was watching me.

I did not want to look at him, be found staring at him, for now I saw that the unbandaged hand was also deformed. He looked at me looking at him, as a woman looks at you without her clothes for the first time, a look of curiosity, modesty, defiance, and something of shame. All the fingers of the unbandaged hand were swollen to three times their natural size and weight, rather like the growths on cacti or potatoes, thick as another limb. The whole hand was swollen and curved and heavy, a shiny brown (the great lethal blisters of mustard gas). Both his hands were affected, one bandaged and one not; he had two appendages that could lift nothing. He tried to hide his face behind the bandaged hand, that swollen potato-blight hand, when he saw me looking. It was a sadly shapeless thing to look at, and I felt ashamed, looked away. These were extremities indeed.

Let's go back, Charlotte said.

342

I went into the bar to pay for the beer. Sancho Panza sat on a bench with his legs apart, his shirt open, his pants bursting at the flies, sweat pouring off him, sound asleep. Two empty Victoria *cerveza* bottles stood by the shambles of his feet. I asked the woman what disease the boy was suffering from, and she told me that it was an unknown sickness. He had been born that way, ten years ago, with both hands affected, and now one leg. The disease was spreading. The doctor had given him up, a sad and hopeless case. I gave her some money for the boy. We left the *taberna*. I rolled the Lambretta out of the shade on to the dirt road. The children stared. Sancho Panza's pack-animal stood by the wall, its head buried in a sack. From under the blue and white sign the boy with deformed hands watched Charlotte mount the pillion. He had Charlotte's face. We set off. She held on to me.

I stopped about a kilometre short of the bridge. When will I see you again? I said.

Whenever you like, she said sweetly, working me over with her eyes. I had been sorry company. Tonight? I said.

Okay if you wish, she said. We'll be on the *paseo*. Behind her I saw something move in the ditch. A black object in the cutting, where the land fell away to a ploughed field and one almond tree, old eyes observed us. An old fellow dressed in black corduroy was rooting around for herbs, love potions, bent over, poking in the ditch. His antique *esposa* was there.

Spanish girls consider rosemary an aphrodisiac. Romero in its natural state in the soil detects homosexuality, since it remains invisible to the eye of the Greek lover. Basil detects adultery, drying too quickly in the hands of adulterers. German girls sprinkle endive in the food of their lovers. Strindberg associated celery with lasciviousness. Schiller kept rotting apples in a drawer of his writing desk. For him it was the odour of the sweetest corruption, and an aphrodisiac.

The root-man held up a knife and a bunch of something which he had got from the earth. Good in stews! he called out brandishing fennel. *Muy bueno!* They were gathering fennel, he and his doxy. Road-verge weed-cutting for the indigent old (a brainwave of the War-on-Poverty Generalissimos?), not here, they were ancient fennel-pickers. I remembered something Bob Bayless had said about Yankee pig poverty in the Kentucky uplands, hardly supported by US expenditure of 88 cents per week per capita on public assistance schemes. Jes sittin an spittin. We gotta chase them bums out of them hills. *Potajes!* the voice cried. *Garbanzos!* (bunched fingers to puckered-up lips and rolling his eyes). *Muy bueno para comer*, the root-man said with great emphasis.

We began walking down the hill, Charlotte pushing the Lambretta. *Morcilla!* the root-man called in a breaking voice. Blood sausages. Good! *SI!*

Ajo! the voice called from the ditch. *Arroz! Judias secas!*

Ah si, Charlotte said. We left the root-man behind us. Charlotte rode away. I walked after her. No traffic passed me going in either direction. I crossed the bridge. To the left-hand were the marvellous mountains, range upon range. I saw Frigiliana like something observed through glass, the redoubts of a medieval fortress meandering over a hill, a vision of an earlier happiness. Rosemary for remembrance.

All the good things of life belong to others, time alone is ours.

65 AGAPEMONE: The Roman aqueduct straddled the gorge. Without girders, brick interlocked with brick in an ingenious system of supports and counter-supports. Lofty as a cathedral but with nothing behind it, just a brown brick façade, most strange to see out there in La Aguila valley. On the top tier—the fourth—an irrigation channel crossed, cold water from the sierras channelled down into the land below. Off-centre there was a kind of bell-tower. A two-headed castiron bird (eagle? merlin?) hung head down there, motionless, a sign. La Aguila. A bronze weathervane from Roman times? The riverbed was dry.

Coming into the curve with her hips surging away from me, my hands felt her warmth under the thin summer frock and the noise of the Lambretta's engine volleyed off the cement guards. Her young hair smelled of hay, the thin dress clung to her body. The bridge exits were narrow. Our shadows mingled on the parapets as we drove across the bridge in high style under the hot mid-morning sun. Her blonde hair blew in my face.

She was the headstrong young bride galloping sense-drunk over the hard New Mexican earth, into Tularose Valley (if that was the name), through the yucca, the heated air on her face and hands, riding off with the groom. She rode a bay mare, her unbound hair streaming in the wind, her fingers in the mane and her knees bare, all covered with sweat. Land of gila monster and yucca, sagebush and cacti. She knew it. I saw her going not where, her mouth open, her teeth bared.

Travelling from another continent, was it still a game? Had it ever been a game? But she was not riding away from me now. She was riding with me. It had ceased to be a game, if it had ever been that, in the sugar bushes. She had been pro-vocative certainly, had encouraged me and allowed my hopes to rise.

345

My hands felt her warmth under the thin frock. Could I hold her. I cannot say. When a woman thinks her husband watcheth, she will sooner offend. What she does with no witness to it, she may often be found to do it, the old books say. What do the old books know? I can't say.

We parked the Lambretta on the Maro side and began the climb down. The gorge led out to the sea. One could swim nude, Amory said. I had never been there. I carried a towel. Bob was working, Daisy was with the Hools, Olivia had taken a picnic lunch to Torrecillas beach on the other side of town; for the first time in more than a month we were together. Charlotte had told her husband that she was taking a ride towards Maro. I had told my wife that I was sketching in the *campo*. Beyond La Luna I'd waited by the roadside. She arrived at the hour she said she would. She was Cora with the bitten lip escaping from the oily Greek husband, her custodian, the past. I was Nick, set on a downward course of damned adultery. We began the climb down.

The terraced fields were as elongated and stony as the walled plots of Inishere, *my Tir na nÓg*, dropping down terrace by terrace towards the riverbed. Thorns caught at her skirt and marked her legs, and I wondered would Bob notice. We climbed a wall, I went over, reached back to help her. She jumped, came hard against me, I kissed her sweet and shuddering lips. Part of the wall crumbled and earth and loose stones fell away. I heard a weary male voice calling a name. *Adolfo!* the voice said distinctly. I heard other voices calling below, on the far side.

Creepers grew along a makeshift fence, the ground broke, we continued on over a series of walls. A large wasp or bee buzzed angrily in the cane. Charlotte was making a droning sound in her throat. I asked what was the matter. Oh she said, her face streaming with sweat, we have so little time. As soon as we get there I'll have to start thinking of getting back.

Tie yourself with your impossible voice, the only hope in this vile despair! She from the depth of herself giving out murmurings and virtual groans. I kissed her again. Being with you makes me light-headed, she said. So we continued down through the little walled fields, Charlotte droning away. The American bombers were patrolling over the peninsula, laying their long vapoury trails, Hank and Herb the *xopilotes* who await only the ratification of death. Over us another bird flew, the cruel fabled one, the winged wanton, the *Sceleratus*. Inamorata, let be, let be, let no one see; give secretly if you give at all. Hab or nab. Long ago I had desired her, this sun-darkened creature of wind and sea verge. Behind us traffic began passing over the bridge, a motor horn sounding stridently —a blare of klaxon; the impatient rich were crossing the bridge. Presently the ground began to level off.

We were leaving the sounds from the bridge behind us. My hand touched her arm, closed on it, felt the honey. The path meandered on through weeds and thorn. I felt elated; my youth was returning. She went before me, she who had my recovered youth in her hands, the switch of long hair bobbing, my bay mare with her *pasa fina* short stride. She stopped her droning to say, I was looking for you last night. We were in the Marissal until two. I didn't go out, I said. She offered no comment to this but went on before me, moving in her proud, contained way—a nervy beauty. She had delicate ways, ever gliding and labile, *de bonne aire*. A beautiful woman at odds with herself adds to life; a prey to moods and tidal changes. And again the arabesque of her strong spine. A switch of life, of spirit; the strong roots which came down from the body into a tree of potent beauty. She had that high-colour look of glowing good health. She was the most beautiful woman I'd ever had, possibly the most beautiful I'd ever known. Then we were progressing through sugar-cane that rose twenty feet high. She went, barred with sunlight and shadow, her eyes on the path, close to me in a dream. I was soon to penetrate one of her disguises, in an atmosphere extraordinarily vivid and suggestive. I pulled aside thorns to let her through, she murmuring in her throat, soaking with perspiration that ran down her face in great golden drops. She lifted her arm and perspiration gleamed in her armpit where dark hair lay like wetted fern—a sharp, delicate plant-like odour. Around us the insects were emitting a high-pitched electric buzzing, a gunmetal blue fly remained intensely in one place. A ditch sank down into a moat and rose up to a rampart topped with weeds; on the other side the vegetation closed in and the path appeared to end. A most inaccessible place. There was an odour of mimosa, flowering wattle, tang of pollen, the clinging flavour of the illicit. The blossoms were thick enough to hide you. I had left a damp country where the cold girls said no, and come to the *Tierra Caliente* where the girls were beautiful and hot and said yes. Charlotte had stopped droning. She was bathed in perspiration. This must be an Irish form of seduction, she said, taking my thought. You take girls into the thickest bushes you can find. It's nice and private, if a bit hot. And we can't even lie down.

She laughed, a vixen's bark. Wait, I said, wait. Okay, she said. I descended into the ditch where oleanders grew soft as molasses. I climbed the rampart surrounded in vapour and insects, my shirt sticking to my back. Beyond the bank, the path, more defined now, went on. The plantation had begun to thin out, and the sea could not be far away. There was fresh mule-dung on the path. It goes on, I said. Good, she said. Swallows came down low making that rending sound they make, a jubilance that curls and breaks in the air.

We moved along the track and wild flowers and ligneous odours. Presently, below the thick wall of weeds, on a track that went parallel but lower than the one we were on, moving in Indian file, I saw something that I had hoped not to find there. A mule with red trappings was tethered to a banana tree. I said nothing and we left it behind. Then brown boulders hove into sight and there was the Mediterranean, the closed sea. Is it much further? she called. It's just in front of us, I said. Good, she said. Christ I'm hot.

A little shingle beach lay before us. The calm blue sea was unwrinkled by not the slightest breath. The swell, as thin as gauze, rolled over the shingle. Above us hung the astonishing Andalusian sky. But to every Eden its serpent: a squat Guardia Civil observation hut stood its ground on the mound. We had come this far to be caught by the Guardia. Perhaps it was their mule I had seen? I had never seen them riding mules, although perhaps to reach this out-of-the-way place they were obliged to ride. We climbed down to the water's edge. I turned and examined the hut. The door was off its hinges, no water jug stood on the window, it looked deserted. I could not see the owner of the mule. From the cliffs on either side no *voyeur* could spy on us, no centaur of lower Andalusia gape down at Charlotte undressing. I had hoped for privacy, the shingle was hard, I'd expected sand. Grass grew before the hut.

Look over there, Charlotte said, pointing (very little escaped her). There's an old buff up there in a cave. I looked, and sure enough there was the mouth of a cave with a Neanderthal Man the same colour as the rocks (sepia and burnt sienna) patching ragged clothes the same colour as himself under the overhang, and paying no attention to anything else. He did not look the type to spy on a foreign woman swimming nude, he seemed to be wrapped up in his patching. Charlotte sat down on a rock and the monkey paws removed *alpargatas* and then she stood and her briefs were off; she began to arrange her hair, a touch of perspiration gleamed in her armpit. God I'm hot, she said. Let's go in. He can't see me down here. With an extraordinary frenzy she pulled off her dress. She unhooked herself, threw me a look as if lifting a veil. The candour of her eyes said: If you want me, take me, for I am yours today. Put the wild clematis in my hair. Our trip to Cythera had brought us together here, to this deserted beach. It was an improvement on the great murky fishing-grounds of the far north. The sun beat down on her nakedness, a Paleolithic Venus with a big bottom and a narrow head. My little votive figurine. Her skin was beige about hips and bust, the rest the colour of seasoned wood. A sort of fluid glow emanated from her, very feminine, very fully formed. Take care you do not mistake my person. Let the fasting part alone till I grow old. *Tu tienes cuerpo preciosa*, I said. Oh you are nice, she said. Let him look if he wants, now, I'm going in. Are you coming? Yes, I said. I made myself naked.

She swam over submerged boulders and great undulant marine rockeries of brown stuff that resembled submerged yucca, the glistening sheaths lolling this way and that, then between spurs of rock out into the open sea, until we were out of sight of the old man. Charlotte was Marie Boursin, the midinette 'Martha de Meligny' of *Nu Fond Verdu*; she too was water-addicted.

We went out over moss agates, star-like villi and the so-called Trophoblast which looks like a hedgehog that has rolled up, with all the points sticking out. Red dots appeared below us, sea-urchins more apparent than real, blood islands pulsating.

Kissing her again, touching her with nothing on and with nothing but water below us, I experienced a sensation comparable to liquification. I received a serious stare from eyes of unparallel depth. She was trembling, and I was trembling far worse than she. I saw the observation hut again as we swam in—the Agapemone. It should have been covered in flowers, ivy and vine, emblems of cleaving and clinging. And not far off—only visible from the sea—stood a temple or grotto dedicated to the Marine Venus of Cadiz; a love-bower arousing in the beholder the notion of a place of assignation for violent and dangerous love-making.

Look, Charlotte said. (Love, whose notice nothing can escape, had spied something.) My eyes followed her pointing arm. The old one was leaving his shelter, carrying off a sack with his head down. He was leaving. The place was now ours. We swam back to the beach, the open hut, the Agapemone.

She came to me flower-shod and swaying, each step a fragrance, lost in remembered delights, to lay her clothes by mine. Drops of water rolled down between her breasts. She was saline; a beautiful woman: a crest of eyelids, breasts and hair. The finest lady in the whole world or within the lagoons. The golden wards of life. We lay side by side on the sea-grass before the police hut. The charm of her voice did not fail her even in whispering, sounding over a new depth with vibrations as though her throat were an echoing place, of sounds hardly released. I was to occupy her husband's place. She was free of any moral scruples. How familiar was her sea-cold skin to my touch again! She soon warmed in the sun. Her lips were grapes that tasted of resurrection. She spoke to me in her voice-of-voices. I was hidden in her eyes, dazzled under the liquid ardour of her quietness. Her hair was long again, her eyes were wild, her swimming, imagining eyes. One blonde touch set us both on fire. I can't stand this much longer, she said.

And then, murmuring in the back of the throat, don't bite me now . . . Oh don't bite me, or he'll beat me for sure this time . . . The hair on her nape was damp, a marine odour clung to her fingertips, her eyes were closed, her legs were being attacked by flies. Soon she was roused to a seismic pitch of excitement, down on the grass the colour of a lion's mane. Give it to me, she whispered, oh give it to me now! I lay on her directly below the window of the observation hut. She stretched out her legs, her eyes shut fast. She returned my grave kisses and I was lost. Naked she lay, clasped in my longing arms, I filled with love, and she all over charms. But Pan was sleeping, not alert, in the hut. Oh, Charlotte murmured, oh, oh, as if she were dying. A shadow lay across me. I was a dull spirit indeed, inert and settled as alluvial matter, a torpid deposit, a sediment. I was failing because of the shadows on my exposed and craven back. Automatic rifles were trained on me. (It was as if the scene were engraved on metal, still trembling from the engraver's burin.) The rightful husband was standing there denouncing me to two leering Guardia. Never had they seen such *extranjero* behaviour. A couple glued together on a beach in broad daylight. Olivia was observing it all coldly from the window and the hut had ceased on the instant to be the Agapemone; no withered flowers or dead ivy hung limply from it; it was what it had always been—a disused hut, a decoy, with old human excrement in it. There would be a fine to pay certainly. I made myself as small as possible. Officer, it is not us. You dream us, *Señor* Guardia. Dream us. I waited for the touch of the gun barrel on my back, the ribald laughter.

Charlotte felt me changing, I stared into the depthless blue of her eyes. They were extraordinary, not aqueous, not vitreous, no, but the deeper parts of Lake Como on a summer's day. What is it? she whispered. Someone there, I said. Oh no, she said, not that, please! I looked then.

There was no one there. Only a rusty tuna tin with its lid curled back. Isabel *atún*. A curved fish biting its tail. No can-opener in sight. Nothing, and yet we tremble. Why? Wrong, Charlotte, I said, sorry. There's no one there.

And now a stranger with no clothes on sat by me on the grass, her lips thrust forward in a sort of pout, she was looking out at a grey-white ship sailing on the horizon, leaving behind it a spreading pall of smoke from its stack; this was slowly spreading out, smearing the blue. It doesn't matter, she said, taking my hand. Don't worry. Sit by me on the grass. It was as if we were holding hands in silence and everything had been said long ago. I fished out a packet of Celtas.

Look at those clouds, she said. I looked up. Like animals coming out of the sky, she said, and running away. But I could see no such animals.

There are no fixtures in nature. The universe is fluid and volatile. Permanence is but a word of degrees. Our globe seen by God is a transparent law, not a mass of facts. *Mon âme d'affreux naufrages appareille.* The soul that (allegedly) adores swimming.

She sat with her chin on her knees, looking at the false clouds. Before she had half smoked the cigarette she threw it away. It began to extinguish itself of its own accord. She sighed and said that she had to be getting back. She had to go—I felt the words as one feels the touch of hands on one's forehead when there is nothing more to say. It is nothing. I am here. I'm still here. (Dressed in her naked simplicities.) It's over. I must get dressed, she said. She began to pull on her clothes again there on the rough grass by the empty hut.

66 I DUG A SHALLOW TRENCH. The sand was cooler. I brought cane branches and stuck them in a row. The sand was burning hot. I wore *alpargatas*. You had to wear them crossing the sand. I dug sand again, piled it against the cane, propping the cane up with stones. Then I put down a beach towel in the shade and lay on it. It was now tolerably cool.

She came down the path onto the beach, advanced towards me about a hundred yards, stopped fifty yards off, put down her beach gear, stepped out of her dress, lay down, presenting to me her fare-you-well behind.

The goat-herd was dun-coloured like the earth, baked brown by sun and exposure. He had a crook. He stopped, stared at her. He crouched down on his hunkers a pace away from her, spoke to her. She answered him in Spanish. He began to edge up closer. Now she could either continue talking to him or get up and leave the beach. The dun-coloured goats came all around them. The rams were black with trailing bullybags.

⦅✿⦆

We were in the cane-brake together. Her period was over. I looked at her; my whole being was concentrated upon her. We undressed and lay together. It was painful for me, taped up as I was. What could I do for this hot angel burning at my left side, whose appeal for me was dangerous, primitive, a late touch of spring in my blood? While her touches burned (she was experimenting with me), the earth was our bed, the world at an end. Stage by stage she shed herself, gave herself to me as she would to no other man. We were Paolo and Francesca in the whirlwind being hurled about.

When would we meet again? (she was dressing). When would the earth taste of our lips again, touch my anxious spirit? I heard the crackling of the cane like the rending of a nearby membrane. I drew away, watched her buckle on her Mary Janes. Would my sensations be forever intellectual? Life scooped up, ahead of us the pit of all the caresses that somehow we missed. There was the rending sound of the jets at their supersonic back-firing and above us a small tanker plane was falling away from one of the bombers, now recharged. Silver objects in the illimitable blue. The empyrean. *Feuerhimmel*.

That's how it was with me the last time I delivered my body to it, and that instrument which is called the mind.

⊂€✦꒱

Her unbound hair is streaming. She is in Mexico with Bob, the smell of the sweating horses, the leather, the sensation of galloping, excites her. What the groom shouts excites her, although she does not understand him, she gets the drift. *Schwanz*. Wild tail. The groom from the livery stables is galloping alongside her. The flying manes are standing straight out, Bob lies far behind, the distance between her horse and the groom's (the impudent fellow coming hard on her tail) diminished as they put more distance between themselves and Bob. The groom is shouting something, shouting and showing his teeth. He is not bad-looking. He is pointing urgently ahead. *Culo?*

(Enveloped in dust you ride together with this Mexican desperado into a secret place. A bluff hides you both from view. Your husband is out of sight. Out of sight is out of mind. Are you out of your mind? You say you cannot stand it, but I wonder, Charlotte. I wonder.)

Later, they ride demurely out. Bob has ridden in a circle; he catches up with them. They are flushed. (Bob Bayless admitted to me that hard riding gave him little pleasure, only 'aching balls'.) Charlotte said that galloping excited *her*. Bob, with a sneer on his face, threatened to horse-whip the impudent groom. Charlotte admitted nothing. They had galloped into a small canyon and out again. Had he not seen them? no, he said, he had not, trying to calculate the time they had been trapped inside, looking at her blouse for buttons undone, looking at

354

the zip of her slacks, keeping his thought to himself. Nothing would change her. She gave him a challenging stare. Well?

By Jesus, Bob said, had I not a perfect right to horse-whip that little Mex fucker!

Help, I said weakly, help. Your wife has broken all my ribs.

Serve the fucker right! Bob said.

(I *love* horses, she had said. Not old hacks, dray-horses. But racing horses. I like their eyes, their legs, their necks, their *smell* [this very nasal]. I don't like cows. When I was with my silly sister in Connecticut I'd go into this field of cows. There was one cow there that watched me. I did not like it, the way she stared at me. That awful bovine empty look they have. But horses—they're different. They're *wild*.)

Charlotte brushed her hair away from her face, looked quickly at me, laughed.

Don't give me that horse-eye look. Wild equine eye, always open.

⁘

I had a dream about a white horse, she said to me. Going where? I asked. Galloping? Grazing? Standing still?

O just going, she said, going through the dream. A messenger from God—Hermes. It was sweating so much it seemed to be smoking, as if about to burst into flames.

A spider was weaving, with a slow retiring action, its web among the blue flanged arms of a yucca plant. Charlotte's web. Nature's realm. Why is the spider considered a sexual symbol? Its sloth and patience weaves in the morning hours, lovers of dampness, saturated vegetation.

Slugs!

(Sometimes I was not the man for her. And at times she indicated that plainly enough.)

67 THE WOMAN IN THE BIKINI: We passed the shallow cave littered with human excrement and then a single rubber boot upended among thorns and weeds (had a drunk gone down?), and beyond that again thick clusters of cacti hanging over the path, mottled as toadskin or the back of an old man's hand. Burriana beach was deserted, the late afternoon sky clear except over the sierras. We undressed near the rocks, left our clothes there and waded in. With her unbleached hair and daily deepening tan, Olivia had never looked lovelier.

She swam out a little way, said, Curse it! stopped, pulled off her bathing cap, grimacing, threw it back towards the beach. It fell short, filled at once and sank. I retrieved it and threw it up on the beach. Olivia swam out ahead of me, her brown shoulders out of the water, our shadows following us below until we lost them in deeper water; she kept on swimming out and I following. After five hundred yards she stopped and looked back. There was the narrow valley that led to La Luna, and there on the summit, above the olive trees, the white Cortijo with three green blinds over the window balconies. Beyond stretched the sierras of unknown name, unknown altitude, range upon range. All that resounding landscape. A mountain-girt valley, pylons, the whole burning scene. Two loaded bombers were coming up silently, laying a long condensation trail back towards Gibraltar (among the notable beauties of our times—vapour trails). An erubescent sun was going down, day declining, evening coming on. Mountains older than Marathon when the world was young, older than the first battles in Europe, Salamis, Plataea, older than Sparta or Jericho. Boulders the size of modern tenements had rolled down the incline into the sea among the detritus of a great river that had flowed out into the Mediterranean in prehistoric times. River of unknown name, river older than Garavogue. Each evening now bats the size of small umbrellas flew out of the boulder-strewn recesses below the *Mirador* at No. 68. One boulder there, over on its side, had at some unspecified time begun to split asunder, a gap at first quite narrow widening over the centuries. A boulder bigger than the Split Rock from the ice age on the roadside near Easkey on Sligo Bay. Older than Thermopylae, the Persian War, the Peloponnesian, the hundred-and-twenty-year-old war between Carthage and Rome. A third of the way up the fissure a fig tree had begun to grow. In spring it was covered with marguerites.

The debris of the centuries. Celtiberians, Romans, Visigoths, Moriscos, until today; monarchies and republics, until today. A lost ducado, an Agaric dagger, neolithic flints, a votive axe of diorite, the bones of a darker race, the carbonized remains of black paste used for painting the body. A well-polished tear-shaped pebble, coloured black, two centimetres long, a snailshell neck pendant: ornaments of the long-dead in the great cave. A shale bracelet broken in the making, here as on the Ligurian Coast. And of all that, what remains (all the prospects flattering to human pride)? A real estate dream on the *tablazo*, a silent bed of dry boulders under the long summer's drought.

The American bombers were now directly over the Cortijo de Maro, their wakes still running out. Their supersonic thunder rumbled in the hills. *L'an mil neuf nonanthe neuf sept mois du ciel viendra le grand Roy d'effrayeur.* Olivia, all naked quick and panting, surfaced beside me, wet hair about her shoulders, a Venus so enchanting, showing off her bare dimpled back. Remember, she said as soon as she had caught her breath, remember the goings-on up there with Amory? (pointing to the green house with the green blinds). And to be sure I did remember the times there with Amory and blonde, freckled Fay Blair from Lachine, Quebec, the evening party on the back terrace and the table on fire and Fay calling, Piss on it, treasure! Piss on it! I had never cared much for Fay Blair, nor indeed for any of Amory's women: not for ailing Milly Mayne whom I had known in Montreal, nor Fay Blair who followed her, nor Tracey Weddick who followed *her*. Fay tittered; it set my teeth on edge. She had the biggest studio in Spain above the bodega but hardly the talent to match those grandiose quarters, commodious enough for El Greco. She had a retarded palette, an atricious colour-sense, subject matter that resembled Old Silurian doused in animal blood and vegetable carbon, an ooze of yellow, a smear of raw sienna, tar-black, rough as a Bronze Age pictograph, thoroughly 'modern', in intention at least, in accordance with the best standards of the going taste. The paintings had no depth to them and were painful for me to look at, doubly painful to comment on. Wilkie called Spain the Timbuctoo of artists. Fay Blair, one of the Corn-Bean-and-Squash girls of Old Quebec.

I would not dance with her at the Maro *feria*. While Amory danced with Sally Lester, Fay Blair and I sat alone, turned to stone. Deciding the fate of nations? she asked, tittering, and I felt a pompous ass. On the rostrum behind us a *compère* introduced the singer, a bold-faced girl with bare shoulders. The orchestra played *Moliendo Café*. It was the rage all that year, bawled out by Paquito Jerez. Sally Lester danced past with Roger Amory. The bold girl on the rostrum behind us sang at the full pitch of her lungs. Lucky nations! Fay Blair tittered into her gin and tonic, thyroid, bitter.

That's how it was between Fay Blair and myself. Amory was finishing with her after four or five years not of faithfulness but of a kind of constancy. Love's a vapour, pretty soon you're through it. Or not, as the case may be; but when the evening mists of Elysium had cleared away—odd that they should have turned up in old Nerka of all places—Amory had departed with the willowy Blair girl and the fire was out. They had gone through some of her capital and had to find work; Fay in the London Telephone Exchange and Amory in advertising—that was the price. Four months later Amory came back alone. Then Fay Blair left for Greece, so we heard.

I had the feeling, very unsettling, that I was disappearing; or rather that the person who experienced these fine feelings was not I, not Ruttle at all. Taking a deep breath I dived. The wrinkled and blurred sand was down below me, ridged and wrinkled with reflections from the surface, tessera stippled with light away from the blue air and all the brilliance above the surface. And, swimming down, the curious feeling persisted, that I was disappearing.

It is not true, not true any longer, that we come to live on the earth; we come only to sleep, only to dream bad dreams. I touched sand, suddenly there before me, clawed at it, the interior of my head crackling like an aluminium basin, then up with bursting lungs. Above me on the surface there was a confused shape, Olivia minding her own business. Coming up in a rush I caught her about the waist, surfaced alongside her. I tried the dead-man's carry, drawing her along, treading water, until she pulled back her hair and brought up her knees. Enough! said Olivia. I drew down the top of her costume, caught her about the upper part of her body and kissed her salty lips, reflecting that I did kiss a queen. She was rolling her eyes, saying something into my mouth. *Fornications avec l'eau.* For are there not as many lustful as continent fish deep down in the chambers of the sea? Aye, and more. I brought her costume down about her waist, and then about her thighs, saw her *chaud-froid* posteriors and shadow zone. Our shadows merged on the bevelled sea-bed; ferocious male Hornos Llopis grappling with submissive female. Up tip! I said. Tip forever! Hands off, Olivia said, disentangling herself. That's a bit much. That's a bit thick. Aren't you a great one for nature?

She swam away from me on her back, her feet kicking in my face, pulling up her costume with both hands. I dived again, saw above me the costume, the trend of the female downward slope.

I followed her in. A gang of young lads were running down the path, one carrying a white beach ball with black markings. We came in and lay down on the towels. The footballers threw off their clothes and began kicking the ball about. They had five beaches to kick a football on and had to come to this one, and from a whole kilometre of shore to pick this sunlit corner to pester us on. Spain had entered the World Cup and they were young male Spaniards who could no more resist chasing a ball than gundogs resist going after fallen game. Some of the younger ones were stark naked, most pre-pubescent. One was not, very obviously, and he controlled the game by virtue of seniority and size.

They played close to us, mauling each other, breaking, falling and wailing from foul tackles, scrambling after the ball, shouting all the time as only Spaniards can, calling for quick passes, 'Manolo! Manolo! Manolo!' And Manolo, a regular Puskas, lunged, lost his balance and sprawled before us, his ape's legs spread wide and covered in hair, scapular bouncing on his chest. His hat, a kind of slouch but in straw, with the brim rolled back cow-boy fashion, flew off. Then he was up again, dashing sand from his straw hat, jamming it on his head, the ball at his feet, dribbling it, shooting at goal, down on one knee, his hands spread wide.

'Manolo!' they all cried, and the small goalie was running back. And then the ball was back in play again and the attack began all over. 'Manolo! Manolo!' as if their lives depended on having the ball at their feet. Then Puskas had it again and was bouncing it on his knees, and then on his head, and then he kicked it far out on to the water and they all cried in dismay. In he charged, holding on to his hat, and went under. The white ball with its hexagonal black markings bobbed on the surface and some of the smaller nudes were after it, but Puskas came up spewing water from his mouth, his hat still on, like Baron Corvo in a Venice canal, and he swam back and waded in twirling it on one finger. These antics were for Olivia's sole benefit, but she was not interested and had her back to him. Puskas threw out his chest and posed with the ball trapped under one foot, arms folded across his chest, hat at a rakish angle, so that drops of water fell from his straw hat and from his arms and phenomenally hirsute legs: but Olivia paid him no attention. She lay on her stomach, reading *The Good Soldier*, borrowed from Bob Bayless. She was going steadily through his books. Now she was reading Ford Madox Ford, alias Ford Madox Hueffer, said to be a great liar.

When Puskas saw this, he lost heart, turned away, sauntered over to the rocks and lay down, using the beach ball as a head-rest. 'Manolo! Manolo!' the young ones cried; but he ignored them. They lay down on their stomachs on the sand and began creeping towards us. I watched them coming on, and Puskas watched them too, from under the brim of his wet hat. They came on, undaunted by my watching them, for we represented a new species whom they wanted to get a good close look at, burying their faces in the sand and then coming on.

Andad, niños! I said. *Andad!* They stopped, pushing their simian fingers through the sand, throwing it over their shaven heads, squirming with their backsides. This was better than the Ciné: the new species spoke Spanish just like El Menuillo. Puskas stretched out his hairy legs and yawned prodigiously as if he were in bed.

This is no good, I told Olivia. Let's move. Move? Olivia said, but we've just come here. Let's move away from these playmates, I said. Do they bother you? Olivia said. They don't bother me. They surely do, I said. All right, Olivia said. Let's move then.

So we moved away from them and spread our towels out in the last of the sun and lay down again. They stared at the wet imprint of a woman's behind on the sand, the damp imprint of a man, and at a sign from one of them began creeping after us. I stared at them, they stopped, I waited, I looked away, they came on; and in this way they insinuated themselves up close to us, as before, forming a half circle around us, their fingers pushing into the sand, drawing rings, taking up stones, breaking pieces of driftwood, glancing at us furtively, sniggering, putting their heads down, moving their brown bums.

Don't you pay any attention to them, Olivia said, turning a page. They've got no ball. That fellow over there has it. Hairy Legs. Look at them. Poor dears they are bored, she said, and went back to her book.

God's curse on them, I said, can't they be bored somewhere else? Their skulls were shaved to the quick and their bodies as thin and brown as the driftwood they lay among. I could almost touch the nearest with my foot. He was staring at my toes as if he had never seen such palely deformed human extremities before. *Niños*, I cried. *Por favor. El mundo es muy grande!* But they only stared through me. It was not me they were interested in, nor in Olivia reading, but in a point somewhere just behind us. For God's sake, I said, will you look at them.

Fifteen of them were staring at us as if we were inanimate objects that might be stared at for a long time with impunity; we too were strange animals in a zoo, with heads on long necks and eyes that stare right through you, as if they had no sense of you, standing there behind the bars. Ignore them, Olivia said, with her back to them, showing them her dimples. I swore at them. Crusoe amid fractious livestock. Get to hell out of here and leave us in peace! I cried. They did not move or hear me, least of all understand me. I stared at them, and they stared indifferently back at me. I gave up then, lay back and looked up at the sky.

The sun, low now, was sinking behind the *canavera* on the upper path where the night bull Manolo had a plot of land. *La nature t'attend dans un silence austère l'herbe élevé.* The silence of the weeds, the wild flowers at Howth; along the damp margin of the drive the tall white-flowering weeds, like celery, were wincing in the breeze. I tried to paint their silence, their stoic presence, a child's Secret Place, *secreta loca*; I could not. Small blue wild flower growing on the seawall above Claremont Beach. Doris Jameson, Gladys Hale, names from a seed and flower catalogue. I saw the tide coming in over Claremont strand, advancing over the sand bar. How many days had I lain in the dunes there with Doris or Gladys, looking at Ireland's Eye. From the turret on Kenelm's Tower of Howth Castle you could see the pale Lilliputians running on Claremont Beach and the diesel train coming from Sutton Station, and passengers hanging out the carriage windows, waving. I swore at them. I wore a black suit, a Latin Quarter hat: Stephen Dedalus. I stared at the male swimmers at Balscadden bathing place. A big man with an awkward style swam out half a mile, rounded a moored tar barrel, swam back, set out again. A wit called down, *For Jesus' sake, Jack, come in owa that an leave us a supa whether!* A dark, blubbery face, bald as a walrus, stared at me from the tide. For God's sake, will you look at him the wit beside me pleaded. The dark face in the sea spat out water and shook his head just like a walrus.

The sun struck at an angle into the top of the plantation, its weakening rays went through. The vegetation was lighter from beneath, ochre shadows between the stalks, the heads, forming blankets of light along the ground. *A tes pieds son nuage des soirs.* I walked with Exley, who wanted to be a writer, but who did not see or feel, by Piper's Gut and Fox Hole and Highroom Bed and Gaskin's Leap down to the Millionaire's Cove, down to the sea-caves. He saw nothing, observed no world at all: a man who had to bring himself through the greatest tedium to act. A speechless protagonist. A petrified man. He wants to write; is that, after all, possible, compatible with what Exley is?—a kind of ghost. I do not know. He shows me typed pages. Has he hidden talents? I don't know, tell him what I think; he accepts that, goes away. He will be back. I know that. Exley does not speak either. We swim in the cove, hear some young ones singing on a rock. The sun goes down. I am uncomfortable with Exley. We go back to Kenelm's Tower and drink Guinness. Calm down, calm down. He begins to speak. He shows me what he has written. He cycles here. Twenty miles. He lives like a mediaeval monk on wheels.

The grass and flowers are becoming damp as if the water were rising, Gainsford St. Lawrence is walking in the grounds of his estate. I speak to him, my landlord. He answers curtly as always (descendant of Lawrence O'Toole, first Archbishop of Dublin). He shows me Bindon's dyspeptic portrait of Swift the Drapier in Howth Castle. The mown lawn comes up to the castle walls, the castle appears to float in the air; from near the pavilion on the upper field it seems to be inundated by the sea, there before Bull Island. I paint it. Rhododendrons seem to go with crenellated walls, Olivia says.

Small blue flowers, that Olivia informs me are plumbago, grow above the tiled walls at the Limonar and Caleta suburbs of Malaga, whose first bishop was St. Patricius. Flowering Judas grows in Malaga gardens in the Spring, near the English Cemetery, by the Gardens of the Dark Door. The cemetery is also a nursery garden, for the chemicals that the dead give out are good for living flowers. Lord Talbot de Malahide, specialist in Tasmanian plants and gardens, importer of rare rhododendrons, walks in the grounds of his estate, where I am permitted to cut dead wood. He has a clipped manner of speaking. He bids me good evening. I smell nettles, wet weeds, cut grass, compost for the silo, ullage; the broad-leaf hairy weed that is used for pigs' fodder. The odour of the beech hedge after rain, evening chorus of frogs croaking in the sunken pond at Howth, the noise of a car's tyres on the gravel drive at night, the smell of her on my fingers. I do not know the names of the weeds caught in the last light like this. Something touched my arm.

Stop snoring, Olivia said. You are making a holy show. I sat up. The *niños* were covering their faces and sniggering. Had I been day-dreaming again? Shore-dreams.

It was difficult to see anybody moving on the upper path where it looped around the eucalyptus tree. A broken-down cottage stood on the point; beyond it, a long, low building was under construction: Guardia Civil living quarters. A couple whom I had never seen before were coming down onto the beach. They carried beach gear. I watched them come down.

They took up a position midway between us and Hairy Legs, who appeared to be asleep, one leg crossed over the other, his straw hat tilted down over his nose. I saw fifteen brown slits crawling away from me. Now it was the turn of the new couple to be stared at from point-blank range.

The woman was plump and short, with blonde hair and practical Gallic legs, well-fleshed and endowed with those globed compacted things over which thought lingers and love plays. This became apparent when she removed her dress, undoing it at the back and stepping free. She wore a meagre bikini. Her husband or companion was thin, pale, with black trunks, caught in the act of removing his trousers. He lay down on the sand, resting his weary head on his arms. The woman began dolloping *Ambre Solaire* on her arms and legs. She was no beauty, but well-fleshed. Puskas now woke up and with both hands behind his head began showing off his hairy armpits. The woman sat down, crossed her legs, dried her hands, took out a paperback from her beach-bag. She sat reading there as coolly as if she were in the *Bibliothèque Nationale*, not raising her dark glasses from the printed page, though her ripe charms were hardly contained in decent bounds by two thin strips of cloth.

This nubile *tableau vivant* lay in the sun with all the indolent calm of a naked woman sunning herself on the sand; a privileged body on which the light fell to perfection. Puskas, in shorts, a holy medallion about his neck, finely built, a satyr's head and narrow in the hip, his legs surprisingly heavy, brutish even, covered with dense black hair (particularly below the knee), stared with unabashed Latin frankness, his legs now slightly parted with one hand resting casually on his member. Come lust for women on him, his weary eyelids closed, the sun had dried his chest and forearms, but water still sparkled in the hair of his heavy centaur's legs. He lay horizontal but part of him at least had become semi-vertical (his hand was now quite blatantly inside his briefs and his eyes were shining immodestly under lowered lashes); he had passed almost imperceptibly from the caress intermittent to the caress contiguous, working away with patience, encouraged by both a memory and a hope (Priapus in the shrubbery gaping at the Lady on the Swing).

As the swing rose higher and higher the lady became divinely flushed, her voluminous skirts and numerous petticoats ballooning out about her, and she was leaning back, one court shoe in the act of falling off. Priapus had been walking in the woods alone, had known secret places, was trying to get his eyes in true alignment with the upsoaring thighs; moaning, clasping himself in a fever of lechery, his sap rising. The Centaur Nessus carrying the wife of Hercules over the river, losing control of himself, was preparing to ravish her on the far river-bank, with husband Hercules looking on. He had gone too far and could not desist. No. He would have her at all costs, even with Hercules bellowing.

But the woman in the bikini wore less clothes than the wife of Hercules, at least before the centaur interfered with her; and as for the husband or protector, he still slept with his head on his arms.

The sun had by now reached the top plumes of the plantation and had begun to send its long last rays over the beach. The centaur lay labouring away in the lengthening shadows by the rocks. Some of the brown sandboys were creeping back to us, still faithful, dragging what Bob Bayless called their dicks through the sand, whispering among themselves, about us and our dirty lives. The Frenchwoman turned a page, dried her hand, did not look up. I wondered where Charlotte might be; probably over on Torrecillas.

I went in for a last swim, tired of looking at the lure and the lured which went on all summer and on probably all the beaches up to Port Bou, and beyond, to Gibraltar, where the apes came from. No end to it. I swam slowly out until I was tired, turned about, lay on my back in the water. There was the valley opening out, there the Cortijo de Maro with its green blinds down, there the groups on the beach looking like lumps of sandstone. Were the sierras higher than the Knockmealdown Mountains, higher than Knockalongy in the Ox Mountains? were Hannibal's towers older than the sea-forts of the O'Dowds and McSweeneys on the headlands of Killala Bay? I didn't know. Older than Ballymote, older than Ardnaglass in Skreen? I didn't know, but very likely they were. I turned away from the beach.

A small red sail was tacking off the point, far out off the Maro headland, the ruined towers repaired by the last Bourbon king, against Barbarossa. Laz Summerbee, the lecher, born under the sign of the Ram, looking for secluded sites along the coast. Had he some fresh young thing aboard? Beer in his lockers and probably something stronger: bourbon. He wanted to get Mrs. Bayless aboard the *Venu*. They might go in for a dip over the side. *Desnuda*, Laz had said. He had a way of playing with his mouth, like a greyhound, little bubbles of boredom and suspicion, little wrinkles (various memories, indecent certainly) and agitations (not to be found out by Nancy); he sucked in his breath, perspiring, nervous as a whippet. *Desnuda*, Laz said. After the warmth of bourbon, how the little yacht would rock!

When I came out again, Olivia was closing her book and sitting up. The *niños* had drawn off again. Look who's coming, I said. For the Baylesses were already down on the beach and making their way towards us over the rocks.

366

68 THE LADY ON THE SWING: Charlotte sat opposite me on a rock. She wore a low-cut dress that left her shoulders bare. Her hair hung down her back *à la négligence*. She could have come from bath or bed, a long *siesta*. She had washed her hair and they had waited until it dried before coming out. They had not expected to find us on Burriana. Daisy was with the Hools. Charlotte had been sunbathing in the nude under the new *cana* erected by Eduardo, last of the Noble Savages, who was by way of being infatuated with her. They had come out for a walk, had not troubled to bring their togs. How was the water?

Where Charlotte's skirt rode up I saw her brown thigh. A small woman with no impression of frailty, a broad child-bearing pelvis. From regular sunbathing her skin had turned the colour of a tree trunk.

Bob sat on a rock near her, so that now both were in profile, facing each other, one below the other. Charlotte wore dark glasses, her unbound hair over one shoulder. She touched her cheek, sensing me watching her; adjusting a strand of fair hair, her wedding ring shone dull gold. Bob chewed on his Rumbo cigar, the muscles of his jaw working, his Okie ridge very pronounced now that he had his hair cut. A royal pair; Queen Nefertiti and King Akhnaton. Oh the power of paternity, the strength and purpose of fathers! The very ground seems to shake under their feet, that firm and assured tread. You too, Bob Bayless, you too.

A big stoop-shouldered man, solid and troubled. Niggery nostrils, wide Numidian lips, crustaceous Negro lips. Each night the bourbon bottle sank half a finger, a whole finger, or to nothing, and he drank beer as he worked, puffing on fat cigars and frowning at the pages that he would not show me, would under no circumstances show me. He had said: I hesitate always to show you things. Judge them in context, Sire. Bear in mind that I am a lad of the working classes, an Okie, a Methodist, a Californian, an illiterate, unlettered, humpbacked horse's ass. Proceed from there. He was writing of the friendship between Shelley and Byron, that was all he would tell me. Could I see some of it? No. Superciliary ridges and glebellar regions both strongly marked, prominent chin under the piebald beard, wide mandibular rama, slightly sloping. They went horse-riding in Mexico, Charlotte's hair streaming like a mane as she went galloping off with the Mexican groom from the livery stables. Bob had wanted to horse-whip him. Charlotte had just laughed, denying nothing.

Admit to nothing, she had told me. Never, never. Lie in your teeth. And I loved her all the more. Her solid monolithic husband was staring through his dark glasses at something at his feet, eyeballs bulging a little. Drowning in bourbon, the hard stuff, given to verbal pyrotechnics, sometimes exasperated. No joke to be caught fooling around with his wife, no. (Had he not threatened to personally horse-whip the obstreperous groom?)

Ants were crawling over his *alpagatas*. The rock he sat on was alive with them, the hard-working insects that lose their wings after copulation. The contemplation of insects provokes a certain shuffling of the feet. They are almost older than the mountains; the same termites that existed for two hundred million years, ants and bees for forty million; older than *homo sapiens*. (And what had I lost?)

Take a look at them bastards, Bob Bayless said. Ever see an idle ant? Move, bloody pismires, he said, his head down, watching them. They were travelling this way and that frantically over the face of the ochre-coloured rock. Will you just look at those buckos move!

I watched a group, some pushing, some pulling, carrying off a relatively large mud-coloured insect, feebly waving its pincers (I did not know the name of the insect caught in the last light like this). They bore him calmly down into the earth, through a crack in the reddish rock, a diminished Jesus descending into Limbo. (Santa Via-Crucis de las Ilustre y Venerable Cofradia de Nuestro Padre Jesus de la Pasion y Maria Santisima del Amor Doloroso, closely followed by the Real Hermanidad de Nuestro Padre Jesus del Santo Sepulcro y Nuestra Señora de la Soledad.) Calmly down, calmly down, lay me calmly down, my mourners. What great Emperor of Tollan turned himself into an ant and dived into the bowels of the earth after food for his people? His image, the plumed serpent, as potent a symbol for those dead people as the Cross for the Christians today, all under eight metres of lava. The last of the insect, a pincer waved (it was dead, it only seemed to wave), a leg moved, all vanished. The Spanish waning light does sometimes show these felicities, unexpectedly producing this sombre illumination of grime.

Behind Charlotte and petrified in an indecent pose, lay the Centaur, a stone garden-god. By the rock on which she sat I saw an oar broken in two and nails driven crookedly into it, spliced with another newer piece of wood and secured by wire. It had broken again, the wire and nails were rusted and the rust had spread, staining the wood like dried blood. But, on closer examination, that which at first appeared to be the broken halves of one oar, were in fact sections from a third, different oar, used as a splice. The end of one, the handle of another, the blade of a third.

I closed my eyes. From afar their voices seemed to say:

The ant never sleeps (his voice) . . .

Never sleep (Olivia's voice).

They have something like an ideal state, a Roman state (Bob) . . . a slave state. Yes, something on those lines you know.

They have cows (her voice) . . .

And funerals (Bob). They don't have the drones like bees do. No, they don't. The male bees are useless . . .

Only the *cream* of the bees (Olivia) . . .?

A few are quite enough to fertilize the Queen (Bob). (See them build their fine white sugar palaces, every handful of sand starts into life! How high will a mountain be, piled from the bones of all past animals and humans?) I opened my eyes. How many days does an ant live?

Charlotte, hugging her knees and smoking a Bisonte in a

composed way, turned to smile at me. Swimming and constant sunbathing had given her this glow. I thought: *Perhaps it is necessary to begin not once but many times?* Do you know who you look like sitting there? I said. A model from Opiz. (They wore their hair in cornet fashion, those high-busted ladies with hour-glass figures pinched in cruelly at the waist, walking in an arcade on the arms of Napoleon's officers, conquistadores in dazzling uniforms with the rapacious little faces of weasels under the high shakos, their eyes bulging a little, supercilious, keen; one could imagine them claiming the rights to their possessions—the pay they had earned, their women—sabre-rattling, heels tapping in an echoing arcade.) This is my Empire dress, Charlotte said. You like it? I do, I said, it suits you well. Behind her the voyeur had his legs wide apart as callipers, and appeared to be in immoderate tumescence. Jerkee. Do you ever listen to vespers on the radio? Olivia asked. It comes over really nice in Latin on Radio Malaga. I love to listen to it.

I hear it when Bob's working, Charlotte said. Sounds okay to me . . . kinda 1935. (Behind her, a stone garden deity, horned Pan petrified in stone at the extremity of his lust. Priap in full rut. I wondered who would see him first.)

But no one had been able to see with the eyes that someone accustomed to seeing such things now perceived. We are dealing with a protuberance less than a metre above the sand. The protuberance referred to is seven metres high, and juts out for six centimetres. The edge seen from the front, is round or oval, and looks like a club with the thick part uppermost.

Sounds more like 1790 to me, Olivia said. It's the sound of old Europe. Listening to music gives one the illusion that there's a higher purpose after all. The dirt seems to drop off, she added a little pompously. (The voyeur's feet were now planted blatantly wide apart as stretched compass points straining at the cross-heads, and his bare feet dug into the soft sand; ants might have been crawling over him, he was fidgeting so.)

Boy, has he got a boner! Bob said. Got his hand over it, I said. Doesn't seem to mind us watching anyway, Olivia said. Gone too far to mind, Bob said. We stared at him. Charlotte said nothing. Has he got his thingamajig out? Olivia asked.

Charlotte watched him but without appearing to do so, her hieratic face outlined against the rock, her lemur paws carried a Bisonte casually to her lips (an imperceptible blush, a faintly outlined curving of the lips?); masturbators were nothing new to her. Was she staring at him? One lens of her sunglasses had a thin crooked crack down the centre, as I had noticed already in Granada. She had been staring at him and thinking of something, but when she saw me watching her, she turned her head indifferently away as though her thoughts were elsewhere, still smiling.

Bob claimed that she showed an excessive interest in *virilia*, spoke and thought of nothing else. High heels tapping in an arcade, dazzling uniforms, severe mouths under trimmed moustaches, a male hand on the slack of a rounded female arm, a hand caressing, a hidden hand, agreeable gestures, and all dilated, all dilated. Long ago I had seen an old movie in London's Bayswater, a careful elderly hand arranging objects on a bedside table, the ferrule of an umbrella crushing an insect crawling on a terrace, an ageing bridegroom faced with a young wife, the bride swimming nude in a Czech lake. Ants, bees, worms, symbolize what? Flies, the tremulous senses, insects. We can assume they have no consciousness; it shows. And man? . . . a questing hand, a language. The human hand that has gained something in dexterity from the lapse of ages. *Ecstasy*.

The voyeur's reverie, like the caveman's before him, was wholly sexual, his thoughts filled to overflowing with the so desirable possibilities so close to hand (Miss Vita Chouiseul seated nude on a swing in a leafy glade proudly exposing to best advantage the rich rounded beauty of her buttocks, banksides beddamped with dew, huge cloudy symbols of high romance, the revolutions of a pseudo-French pocket-Venus on a swing): a garden swing, a flushed lady recklessly rising with it, studious to display pudgy pale French legs, rounded knees, unprotected thighs, one court shoe in the act of coming off. He had one knee raised and one hand inside his briefs: a potent image of transfixed desire. Charlotte removed her sunglasses and stared boldly at him, her oceanic eyes somewhat bloodshot from the glare or recent hair washing.

The eyes speak, say: 'That's the past, for what it's worth, it's over, will not come again,' but the memory of those days, those old loves, brought to her lips a smile of amiable complicity, and her eyes were full of a veiled sweetness. Her made-up eyes, glances, said: 'Undress me, you excite me, bestir yourself, sir. Know me, stir me.' A beautiful gentleness glowed from her as if she had lanterns under her skin (a restless lady conspiring at home); her beauty made me disconsolate. But I am of the present, and you are of the present, and we are together and isn't that good? or so her eyes seemed to say. Her reflective blue eyes said: I am aware of a world, spread out in space endlessly, and in time becoming and become, without end. Animal beings also, perhaps men, are immediately there for me; I look up, I see them, I hear them coming towards me, I grasp them by the hand; speaking with them I understand immediately what they are sensing and thinking, the feelings that stir them, what they wish or will. They too are present as realities in my field of intuition, even when (as now) I seem to pay them no attention. (Was it distraction, or close attention? I could not tell.) A man catches her eye and she returns his glance. How she blossoms under male attention! Sometimes I thought she wanted nothing less than an uncontestable brutishness to satisfy her; and then I felt ashamed of feeling that. Sometimes she railed at Bob (as, in the periods after our intimacy, she had felt entitled to rail at me) for being too staid and cautious; his cautiousness and overt concern for her got on her nerves at times. Five years her senior, he had qualities befitting a man much older; a disgruntled, staid old man apprehensive of all that might threaten his present and future, his comfort, his hold on her. She found, no doubt, those anxieties oppressive, burdensome; became embittered, wanting to break out of the traces; she 'therefore' tended to become vulnerable, in given situations, to the attentions of other admirers, even anxious ones such as myself. Bob's old man's fears and apprehensiveness, his avoidance of any kind of trouble or aggressiveness in other men (the mean Texan fleecing him at poker, and Bob refusing to play poker with him again; being 'put out' changing flats—even if it only involved moving a few hundred yards up the road)—against this staidness Charlotte revolted, preferring the other Bob Bayless, the young man who had courted her; the rakehell, the wit, the breaker-up of dull parties. This uncertainty of his I thought a very un-American trait, certainly a trait in Americans I had not encountered before, and it was a trait that I liked. It was something Olivia liked too. Bob's moral nature. Olivia admitted that she could have fallen for him; she admitted that at once. A burly somewhat reserved man of the America of La Salle, Booth singing to himself in a clearing where no white man had trod before; Parkman, Thoreau. The Puritan Oligarchy. The Great Plain. Walter Prescott Webb.

In the meantime, Priapus, lost in the undergrowth, was groaning to himself, deep heartfelt groans. The lady, discretion thrown to the winds, and quite giddy, was rising higher and higher, one leg outstretched, going at it recklessly. The Centaur was trembling, standing there ramrod stiff, buck-naked, holding up to his slack prurient eyes a thick bunch of grapes. The lady on the swing was showing more than her pudgy knees and fully fleshed white thighs, driving down hard above the prurient eyes. There was a whiff of something (the ochre boulder was now fairly teeming with ants) as with glazed eyes the goat in the shrubbery began scattering his seed on the leaves.

Passionate, but envious of the male. Thirsting to snatch a fit and inwardly harbour it. She had confessed to two three-act affairs in four years of marriage, I the unlucky third. And before that? I dared not inquire too closely. She'd had many lovers, no concern of mine.

It's Pepe's daughter's new *novio*, Charlotte said, the one he doesn't like.

Bob stared at the shameless one. His come-and-go finally down, all deflated, he had drawn his hairy legs together, his hat over where his hand had been, his hands behind his head. It's him right enough, Bob said. Trust Dilly to notice a thing like that.

The sun was now gone off the beach; the woman in the fuchsia bikini was pulling on her dress, tugging it over her hips. The protector or husband had not stirred; she touched him with her bare foot, he looked up. The other, the Centaur of Lower Andalusia, sated with her person, was now sleeping. Olivia retired behind a rock to dress. She held out her wet costume and called to Charlotte, Can I lend you mine? And then, to me, Why not lend Bob yours? But Charlotte didn't want to go in with her hair washed and Bob said that anyway it was too late. It was time to go.

⊂€✿⊃

Charlotte and I climbed the path ahead of the others. We passed the groups. The husband was dressing, the wife or girl friend was quite plain. Above the cave a stream of brownish water was splashing over the bed of rocks. The irrigation canals were running; the dams had been lifted in the *campo*. I took her out of earshot of the others who were coming behind, talking. She walked ahead of me.

As we came onto the path I had seen Charlotte give the centaur a quick, calculating look, and there was the upended rubber boot again. Where the path ended above the cave we had to climb a narrow gulley in the rocks to reach the upper path, and here the brown stream was coming down as a small waterfall. I took her arm and felt a honeycomb of sensuality. In her there was this itch: the itch to do something inadvisable. I helped her up. The others dawdled behind.

My trousers were wet to the knees and her Empire dress clung to her hips. Tell me, I asked, did it excite you . . . that fellow back there? What do you think? she answered. I don't know, I said. Women are different. Are they excited by male exhibitionism? I don't know.

Well, *I* was, she said, giving me a limpid look, her face a little flushed from climbing.

The path went in a loop and we followed it. I looked back. The others were out of sight below. I took her arm, squeezed it. Was that her nature, then: a sexual sophisticate, a good-time girl, giving herself to any who took her fancy? Where shall we have a drink? I said. I'm tired of the plaza. I saw the top of Bob's head.

374

An object was shining like a jewel some way out at sea, marking the division between darkish water and the still opalescent marine fields in the sun. A lone swimmer was breast-stroking out to have a closer look. Let's go to our place then, Charlotte said. We have some *tequila*. All right, I said.

Below us the *niños* had recovered their ball; their high excited cries came up to us. The swimmer had reached the shining object and was triumphantly holding it aloft, an empty biscuit tin. Puskas, the randy centaur, was staring out to sea.

Memoria. Practica. Repeticion.

69 WATERBED: We were swimming far out off Burriana in a rolling sea. The ranges of the sierras rose and fell, rose and fell, at the whim of the waves. They broke further in, collapsing like ten-feet walls. The sea was soft as blue satin and in it she was naked.

The small pink object Charlotte held in her fist was all her bikini, her long hair contained in a white bathing cap covered in coin-like sequins the size of pesetas. Her face looked different, pulled by the cap. I wore my bathing trunks on my head. We did not touch or kiss above the water. Her eyes were extraordinary. Then a great wave carried her up and she cried out and I saw nudeness somewhat magnified as in glass.

I shall drown with you, laughing for love, and you mix with me, lips and eyes. *Manchmal eine Stunde, Du bist Du, der Rest ist das Geschehene; manchmal schlagen die beiden Fluten hoch zu einem Traum.* The big waves came on, gripping and releasing, taking us a little way with them, then rolling grandly off towards the distant beach where Olivia and Bob were fooling about with Daisy. Charlotte was pushing farther and farther out and I had to follow. For a time we would be hidden down in the hollows and the beach disappear, as we were drawing together towards each other in the water. The waves, by a kind dispensation of nature, hid us from the shore. I took her hips and entered her in one movement, so that we were joined together under the surface in the closest possible way. We were drifting away, Venus brimming, Leander toiling to his death, until a great wave took us from behind and I flooded her. The ardour of that watery embrace—nothing ever so tart, soft, determined and sensual. I felt the grip below release me and felt nothing but the going forward (I was all prow).

I came out of her as the wave went away and we drifted apart. I saw the bell-tower far away. We were certainly far out, perhaps caught in a current that would not let us return. I feel your hands on my breasts, Charlotte said, even when they are not there. She turned in the water, brought up her knees, began pulling on the lower part of her bikini, as the ranges of the sierras rose and fell, rose and fell, at the whim of the waves. Voluptuous waves. It was May.

Immortal water, alive even in the superficies.

70

KAMPEN NACKT-STRAND: You should see Brigitte Winkler in a bikini, Olivia said. She wore a red one down on Torrecillas today. There was a young German with her and he looked as if he wanted to eat her.

You'd think you had the whole picture when you see her in a bikini, but not at all. She was showing us some photos of herself taken in the buff on Sylt, where the Berlin nudist girls go. There was a hairy naked fellow crouching in the shallows, described as a 'good friend'. She really is startling nude. The female shape undressed is so blatantly sexual, so hungry-looking. I wouldn't like to be a man.

The odours of inlets and creeks. Brigitte Winkler had great simple eyes that stared appealingly. Medea, wife of Jason, leader of the Argonauts, stood in all her beauty alone on the Cretan shore. The ship Argo waited some way off, the Argonauts in it, tired and hungry from following the Golden Fleece.

71 ON THE OLD BASTION: One night, after dinner at La Luna, returning home, Charlotte and I walked ahead. There were dark clouds threatening rain, an overcast and cold night with nothing possible. We walked fast, fifty and then a hundred yards ahead of Bob and Olivia. When we reached the village I took her in by one of the side streets, hoping to shake the others off. But when we reached the plaza they were there before us, sitting at a table outside the Balcon. Charlotte and I ordered drinks and walked to the end of the *paseo*. As we reached the barrier all the lights of the town went out.

Through a break in dark fast-moving clouds an improbable harvest moon looked down. I stood close to Charlotte on the old Bastion where King Alfonso had stood, and found it good. *Quelle reichlichen Wassers*; *source d'eau abondante*; it had formerly been a Phoenicean settlement, famous for its fine silks under the Moors. The King on the Bastion names it *Balcon de Europa*.

I saw her face outlined against a huge blown moon. There was no one about. We retired behind a palm tree. She generated heat, this lightly-clad lady, this passionate piece. She was all atremble. Her Cointreau breath. Propitious moments, explicit gestures; conjunctions, impossible conjunctions. She had a very taking manner: the manner of a woman who knows she is being spoiled and loves it. What she liked (and took) had made her what she was: a knowing, riggish charmer. After a while we sat on the wall, it was as warm as flesh. The lights came on again. I let go of her hand. Her eyes were glittering.

I saw Bob leaning forward to say something to Olivia, and Miguel was coming out with our drinks. We went back. The others had moved. Now they were sitting on a bench opposite. As we sat down the lights went out again, and a great groan went up. Children began shouting outside the Ciné Olympia. Miguel had lit candles along the bar.

Then the lights came slowly on again. After a while the others came over and joined us. Bob was in boisterous form and raged away. Listen, he said, hear this. Emergencies of the heart. This is the authentic stuff. He began cranking up an imaginary victrola, and sang:

> Emergencies of the heart,
> Let me be!
> Alien moon, alien moon,

I can't go on, he said. It's too beautiful. Gilda Grey sure as hell sang it better in that hotel room in Alabama overlooking the Gulf.

What is it? I asked.

The story of a great silent screen star who falls on evil days, Bob said. *The Death Scene of Gilda Grey* on the Magnavox— by God it's my favourite movie-star operetta! You can keep your *Magic Flute*.

72 TWO FALSE WITNESSES: One day I saw them coming on to Torrecillas beach with Jesso Wall. I did not pay much attention to the man. The woman came picking her way in elegant high-heel shoes hardly suitable for the beach. Her hair was bleached white and cut short, with a high sheen, cut in a bang across the forehead, and clung to her head like feathers. She had a sharp little bird face, very delicate, with a pointed nose (the nostrils would appear to dilate when the eyes caught fire), a strong jawline; eyes heavily made up. Thin, submerged nun's lips were outlined in a dark lipstick. Over an embroidered white silk shirt and black silk slacks she wore a fringed Mexican stole. A black straw sunhat with chimney-pot crown and a white silk drape down the back completed the outfit. She dressed singularly. The painted black straw glistened like plumage. Her face and hands were pale and she wore mysterious rings, the eyes grey as glass with flecks of blue in them.

She thrust out her hand and jaw at the same time when introduced to me and spoke in a low voice, her neck stretched out. The made-up eyes glittered in the shadow of the sun-hat, observed me, and was apparently amused. Her hand was cool.

The cut-glass voice said something which I did not catch. She had ascetic features: those severe and fastidious lips, the little uncial face shaped for the coif. When she removed the widebrim sunhat I saw a sybillic skull, evoking a beautiful young postulant's shaven head. She had a mineral strangeness about her, a certain remoteness, as if she lived precariously in some high altitude; those nostrils sensed snow. Was she a nun of some extinct order, a house suppressed for some irregularity, perhaps even heresy? There was something both fantastic and fastidious in her bearing (some rare tropical bird bored with captivity, a neurotic macaw with a cage assigned to itself)—a certain freakishness, the irresponsibility of some non-human creature, its heartlessness and its charm. I trembled in her company.

Later I came to know them a little better. One never got close to them. I never felt comfortable with them. Viva van Velde-Soutes, born Nordlinger of Syracuse, New York, wrote poetry. She had once met Lowry. She studied geology then. Claude had known José Luis Cuevas in Mexico City. They had run into Jesso Wall in Mexico. Claude had been a successful painter in Paris, where they had lived for three years after their return from Mexico. Now they had given up Paris, given up art, and were travelling again. They spoke of a community of like minds in India.

They rented a house near the convent there by Torrecillas beach, lived behind the wall next to the two cycling ladies. They did not go out much, just a few drinks on the plaza at night, not needing company. Viva knew Tomalin, Parian, Quahnhuac—Cuernavaca, the Mexican background of *Under the Volcano*. She had lived ten years in Mexico and liked it. She had not cared for Paris. They had a place 'somewhere in the centre.' She mentioned a tower, an open fireplace, the poetry of John Clare, Mallarmé, Gaston Bachelard.

Paw-riss, she said disdainfully, thrusting out her nun's jaw, no, they had not much cared for Paris. They seldom went out there. The river was okay. They wished to visit India.

Indea-h the submerged lips articulated. The old wisdom. The face that should have been powdered, the enigmatic eyes, observed me, took account. Who was this dense Irish person? She sat opposite me, invited to do so, to take a drink, shaking with an unknown emotion. Pallor of an ivory face, its lofty dissolute air. She took short choppy steps like a Chinese lady.

Her age? It would be hard to say; age did not much enter into it. Early to middle thirties, but she could have been fifty. Nina Foch. Mistinguette. *Rara avis*.

Viva van Velde-Soutes rarely laughed, it was a tinkle of broken glass. Nervous, fidgety, thin-boned, pale, rather *sunken* in manner at times, when she would not address one, she was a strange one, *très soignée*. Formerly married to the San Francisco 'surreal' poet Hugo Latimer III. Latimer, praised by André

Breton at the age of sixteen, had had his head turned. He knew Ginsberg, he said. He came later.

They were 'heads,' Bob Bayless said. Without hash they might have died of boredom. They were not fitted by temperament to endure, much less describe, this gross world we inhabit. Viva had turned aside to meditate. On what? I do not know. Eternity. The Beyond. All is vanity, nothing but vanity; smoke now, smoke and dream.

You write poetry? I asked her. My huge farmer's hands rested on the table, my breath was foul, my feet stank, I tore a cigarette to shreds. Viva told me that she had a small volume published at her own expense, but it was a kind of poetry that would not now satisfy her, and in any case the entire stock had been destroyed. How? By an act of God. (Fire? Water?) What she was attempting now pleased her better, and she would perhaps type up some of it to show me some day. Did I know John Clare? She promised to lend me some of his poetry; it was one of the few promises she kept. I said I preferred Robert Herrick, who had taught a pig to drink like any gentleman. Viva gave me a long considered look. She was translating Bachelard's *Psychoanalysis of Fire*, but was not entirely happy with her version. *C'est difficile*, she said in her white, cut-glass voice. I saw the turn of an enigmatic eye, delicate blue of the iris, a speck of gold, in the shadow of the black straw sunhat. She smoked Charlotte's brand. An even whiteness of small perfect teeth against the darkness of lipstick, and the table trembled a little. Their place was perfect; she slept alone in a small curtained four-poster. A face seen by Pepys through the white curtains of a coach—the Duchess. It was Viva's high style. A gigantic dictionary, Bird Parker, someone's *Missa Brevis*, geological specimens from four continents, a long-stemmed hash pipe, stones from the beach. Claude wore a Phrygian skullcap on the beach, had a concavity in his chest, spoke in a deep voice, was evasive. Their life was all promises and dreams, much sensibility (perhaps too much), much talk. Exquisite in detail but in volume disappointing. There was nothing much but smoke behind that beguiling façade.

73 HUEFFER AGAIN: We went down to Torrecillas. The foreshore was damp to above the sun shelters and a big sea running, a full moon dragging the tide, such as it was, the waves washing the shore. Perhaps I would remember it like that: the Levante blowing, awnings flapping, lit in monochrome like an old photograph taken under a hood and developed in cheap and diluted chemicals. Dampened sand in strange sunlight, it was like coming out after weeks in bed with fever as a child, or a Rumanian or Russian resort on the Black Sea or the Sea of Marmara, the Bosphorus. This reality had begun to resemble the old print that Pepe Gomez had hung in the bar: a poor, bleak, windy place, quite deserted.

Olivia and I sat away from the sea, on dry sand in the wind. I had pulled the adhesive tapes off and was tormented with a heat rash that would take months to go. I was finishing *The Good Soldier* (*A Tale of Passion*). I was finishing with her too. I had not seen her for eight days. They had gone to Madrid, seeing off Tracey Weddick and Jesso Wall, who were flying back to the States. The last time I had seen her sitting at a table on the plaza, she had looked miserable, pregnant and displeased. Varicose veins had come up on her legs and she visited the *retrete* often. I had not spoken to them. Spite after tenderness, close all the traps, if you cannot be magnanimous, be mean. Olivia and I were leaving for Greece. Nancy Summerbee could give us a lift as far as Paris. I wanted it to end as badly as possible.

Then Bob Bayless came down alone.

He approached us with some diffidence and asked if he could sit with us, as if we hardly knew him.

Of course, Olivia said.

They had driven back on the previous day, he said. His eyes were red-rimmed, his nose was peeling, his manner

384

nervous. He thought that Tracey was not too happy with her psychologist. She and Amory had been better suited, but Amory had left Spain. Charlotte was down with a cold and feeling sorry for herself. She had gone to bed as soon as they arrived, but might come out later in the evening.

I said nothing to that. It was the end of my bondage and slinking about, I would leave her to her sullen moods, pregnancy and varicose veins, I had no wish to see her or speak to her again.

There were long silences now; a coolness had developed between the three of us. Bayless felt awkward and showed it, avoiding my eye. He went in for a swim. I watched him, a big-boned man pushing himself resentfully through the water.

What's wrong with you? Olivia said.

Nothing, I said.

Bayless came out of the water, stooped, looking defenceless without his spectacles. He stood some way off on the damp shore, drying himself. Dressed again, he folded his wet togs into his towel. Olivia had gone into one of the cabins. We waited for her to come out. She came out. Bayless said he was going back. The waves were slamming the shore, the awnings cut by the rising wind, the place was reeling. Olivia sat on the wet sand adjusting her cap.

Well, see you this evening on the plaza! Bob Bayless cried into Olivia's face as though she were far away from him.

Yes, Olivia said faintly, I suppose so.

He went off the beach, his shoulders hunched. I lay back on the dampened sand of a beach I hardly recognized. There is only peevishness and disordered affections. The stream of the world had changed its course once again. *Schwimme, wer schwimmen kann, und wer zu plump ist, geht unter.*

We did not go out that night. Olivia retired early. I half expected them to call, but they did not. I went to bed after midnight. The next day would be our last in Nerka.

Don't you want to see her? Olivia said.

No, I said.

Instead we went to Salon beach, where we had not been all

summer. The Baylesses never went there; it was behind the church and the Puerta Rican Ambassador's summer residence. Once in the winter I had gone there with Charlotte and been pestered by the niños. A poor fisherman's cottage before the sea, just a single room with the ruins of a bed.

Olivia and I went down the cemented ramp. Three *merenderos* stood there with their cane shelters facing the sea, and behind them a mean row of fishermen's cottages with naked children crawling about amid lean cats and scrawny fowl. When the children saw us coming down, they left whatever they were doing to come and gape at us. Olivia bought a ticket and disappeared into one of the cabins. The *niños*, naked and brown, whispered, pointed below the half door at Olivia changing.

The waves were pounding the shore and sending spray over the *merenderos*. It was the second day of the Levante; on the third day it would be finished. There came a low roar with each wave and, far off, a rather constant surging. Another primitive one-room cottage made of mud and stone stood under the overhang, the cliff forming the back wall. Within was a low bed, wide as a field, with a tattered cover of muddy colours, brass knobs and bed-rails, a woman's soiled and faded shift. A pig was tethered to one side of this lowly edifice. It kept dragging on the rope that held its foot, grunting and sour-tempered. Olivia lay down beside me. The *merenderos* were deserted. The little enclosed beach reeled in the heat. It was less exposed than Torrecillas, farther on. The *niños* stared at us, their shaven heads close to the sand. The pig—a sow, its belly heavy with udders—kept hauling at the tether, pushing with its snout and grunting, all its energy concentrated on breaking free. With only half attention I read Ford Madox Ford on the two couples united in intricate connivance. Nobody swam in the disturbed sea. I was sick and tired of being stared at by children. The waves kept pounding the beach, the wind sending the spray over us, an irrigation stream spewed from a high rock, the sow was almost free, Olivia was sleeping.

I watched a young woman with a bandaged leg going up the ramp; she carried an urn on her hip, which jutted out to receive its weight, a poor dress clung to her sweat-soaked backside. I watched her go up towards the Plaza de los Martires. It was tiring work. She had a strong spine. I gave up Ford Madox Ford and lay supine, without any will, in the all-pervading stupor of the sun. It was our last day. I was tired. The illustration on the front showed a couple locked in an embrace under the eyes of a third party, a featureless female who stood close by, her right hand grasping her left wrist, the face a pale blob in a cowl of dark hair. The lovers appeared to be embracing on a highway. The land stretched away into the distance. A scene though perhaps not Spanish, yet in its particular manifestation it was purely Spanish. The couple went on kissing and ignoring the watcher. Was it the sea in the background? The middle ground certainly looked like *tablado*. Why did the woman watch so closely? Was it to give herself more pain? Were the others unaware of being overlooked? Or were they taunting? The tall madame being kissed so ardently was giving at the knees; she favoured a 1920 style tight dress that hung in awkward folds about her legs. She was his bit of stuff on the road. *Beati Immaculati*, one dollar and twenty-five cents in the States, ten cents more in Canada. A tale without moral point told by a narrator suffering from moral inertia.

Half asleep, I heard the irate high-pitched squeals of the sow clamouring to be free, and felt someone watching. I looked up as the beast broke loose. It came trotting down on to the beach, its ears and tail going. Now you would see rooting. On the ramp, about midway down and pointed in our direction, stood the Bayless ménage. My heart jumped in my chest but I affected not to see them: I was reading. Daisy waved and called. I observed them furtively through my sunglasses, heard my name being shouted. Daisy then called 'Livia!' 'Livia!' but Olivia did not hear. I said nothing, heard nothing. They were discussing whether to come down or not, fearing a rebuff. Then they decided. To hell with it. They were coming down.

Charlotte sat beside me and nothing had changed. The *niños* had taken Daisy away to see the liberated pig. Bob and Olivia were swimming in a dangerous sea. I felt the heated metal of the key under my hand. Charlotte would not enter the water because of her cold. Soon it became too hot on the sand and we moved to the nearest *merendero* and sat in the shade, ordered Cruz Campo. It wasn't *frio*, the boy said, it was *del tiempo*. All right, I said, bring it anyway. So we sat at one of the empty tables and drank the beer that wasn't *frio* and watched the others swimming up the near-side of a mountainous wave, just as Daisy appeared to be drowning with an anxious expression in the wild surf. Jesus, look at the child, I said, and saw the key on the towel and the Vintage paperback folding up in the heat. She'll be okay, Charlotte said calmly.

I saw her face against the disturbed sea, the braid pulling the temples back, a face 'washed with all waters' as the Germans say, and thought: One day I shall be old, but will always have had this (but would it matter, then?). This impossibility. Is it possible that I had ever meant anything to this young beauty? It was unlikely, but nevertheless was so.

Isn't it a pity, Charlotte said.

What? I said.

That we couldn't, Charlotte said, one last time . . . (her ellipsis were masterly). Do you remember the last time? she said, fixing me with a vatic stare.

I thought about it. No, I admitted.

May fifth, she said.

So she had remembered. I had meant something to her.

I thought you'd gone off me, Charlotte said. The sun filtering through the intricacies of cane made submarine patterns on the table, on her face and bare arms.

No, I said.

I'm glad, she said. I would have liked to have gone to bed with you one more time. It's a pity.

A blue plastic bucket was carried out. I saw Olivia's face in the middle of the sea. They were surfing. Two young fellows were riding the waves with them; they were dark as mahogany with the sun shining on their arms. We watched the swimmers. Presently the waves hid them from view. Bob and Olivia stayed within reach of the beach, while the others went on out to where the waves broke beyond the Bastion.

Are they not too far out? Charlotte said. Could you reach them if they got into difficulties?

I thought not; I would not reach them in time. It was stupid to go out so far. Wave after wave came in, pounding the beach.

Bob and Olivia came in after a while. Daisy was running on the beach; she hadn't drowned after all. I ordered more beer, big beers for heroes. Bob was in boisterous form. We sat there pleasantly. Then they were for inviting us to dinner at La Luna. It would be a farewell party for us. And would they ask the van Velde-Soutes and Nancy Summerbee? We could all meet at Antonio's for drinks before dinner. Laz was said to be in Leningrad, looking at yachts.

⸎

I stood next to her at the bar. The van Velde-Soutes could not come at such short notice: they were high on pot, Bob said, both had a 'glazed' look. They had the kind of vacantly dreaming smoky look that you see in Persian cats; it went with the privileged life. Their thoughts were hazy as ranges of far-off mountains (the misty horizon that can never be completely outlined remains necessarily there). Another time, they said. Any other time: they would be delighted.

Nancy Summerbee came twittering in, very brown, with a long string of cold-coloured beads over an incandescent pink dress. We stood along the bar and Bob called for gin, the cerebral alcohol. Booth's dry. Soon the ladies became gay. Bob drove Nancy's car to La Luna, with all of them singing.

Of that night I do not recall much. Olivia's mocking 'I'll buy you one more drink, Robert Bayless. If I buy it, will you drink it?'

The party ended at three next morning. Olivia had left at one o'clock. Nancy too had retired. Bob was sleeping, and Charlotte sat on my lap with her arms about my neck. So it ended as it had begun, with her sitting on my knee, myself none too sober.

I'll give you this rotten cold, she said.

Give it to me, I said, I'll take it from you.

If you want it, if you don't care—okay.

I kissed her pulpy lips. Then I put a question that had been troubling me for some little time: namely, whose child was she carrying? She looked at me with her blue eyes.

His or yours, she said. I'm not sure.

Our child. Fertilized by the wind, like a tree, or the mares of folklore. And I had supposed that distinctions would have been made. Where did his conjugal rights end and where did mine begin? In that narrow space, one wet absent-minded Sunday afternoon, the child had been conceived. Half of her, the mother, belonged to him, father and husband, half to me, the intruder, one might suppose. Unless, of course, she was portioned out in thirds: one-third to him, one-third to me, one-third belonged to her past (Jewish past). And then again there was time for any opportunity that came her way, as I had. Or had she no fixed point that I could call mine?

She had come an hour before our first assignation, walked out on to the little balcony, going out into the blue air to tell me (not troubling to lower her voice, with Olivia slicing oranges in the kitchen) that she couldn't go through with it: she didn't know what face to wear.

I had fed on her, she had obsessed me, my mind full of her. I dreamed her as she dreamed me, we had discovered strange affinities. I loved her but had never told her so, although I suppose she knew.

I'll miss you, she said, her voice glottal, as if she had tinfoil in her throat, and the tone pitched over that, making it vibrate; she pronounced her words with a shallow breathing blended with the sound of h. I'll be seeing you in Dublin, though.

The fantasy was kept up that we would all meet in Dublin. Her face was hot, glowing. I kissed her on the cheek and on her closed eyes, feeling her fever close to me.

> Here's to the man who kisses his wife,
> And kisses his wife alone;
> For there's many a man kissed another man's wife
> When he thought he kissed his own.

Two and a half hours later, at seven in the morning, Olivia and I left with Nancy Summerbee for Paris. Adelina, looking more than ever like the Queen Mother, came to see us off with jasmine in her hair. Olivia wept. We were all set to go, and Nancy climbed in behind the wheel of the Volkswagen. A

Spanish chest was roped to the luggage rack. Then the Baylesses came. A collective hangover made us gay. I kissed Charlotte for the last time, in Spain, in life, not on the lips in company, but chastely on the cheek again; she was my lost sister, my unconceived daughter, and her young skin felt cool. Nancy turned the ignition key and the engine fired.

See you in Dublin! they called, standing outside No. 14 and waving. See you in Dublino!

The car began moving. We drove out of Nerka on to the *carretera*, taking the rocky road to Granada.

> Here's to the man who rocks his child,
> And rocks his child alone;
> For there's many a man rocked another man's child
> When he thought he rocked his own.

PART V

Autumn 1963
and after

74 YOUR AVERAGE MALE GREEK seems abstemious in his drinking habits—at least compared to the Irish. On the other hand they have brought grand old meditative nose-picking to a fine art: up to the elbow with eyes half closed, worry-beads going in the free hand. The women keep to the background. The sun will come up again each morning and sink again, says the poet, so that we experience violently every day two worlds.

It was too hot in Athens at 90 degrees in the shade, so we moved to the coast. The Vardari wind blows across the Aegean and is felt as far away as the Dodecanese Islands. A difficult sea to cross in winter, they say. It comes from Poland, blowing through the Iron Gates there below Belgrade. *Portas de Hierro*, a fighting place at the junction of rivers.

In Greece, I ask you, is Charon's obol still placed on the lips of the dead, as the Aztecs placed a precious stone on the mouths of their dead, to represent the heart emerging brilliant and pure from the fire-consumed body? When their lords and nobles died, they placed a green stone on their mouths to represent the dead man's heart.

Green, *verde*, do I love you? Colour of mildew and mould. A curious love of that septic colour, which in individuals is always the sign of a subtle artistic temperament, and in nations is said to denote a laxity, if not a decadence of morals.

EPISTOLARY (2)

I

A Spanish postcard from Bayless addressed to us at Od. Heracliton 191, Kolonaki, Grecia, undated.

Dear Dan,

Did you get that card from me? A little while back and rather idiotic. We had two from you, one very odd thing that arrived recently. I like your postage stamps.

Send cigarette wrappers, labels off Greek bottles, scraps of sketches, old Dawson Gallery catalogs, and I'll send you fouled Kleenex and discarded baby shoes. It will be a true communication of souls.

Grecia sounds nice, if a bit far-fetched. And the language . . . well, just take a look at the alphabet. There's something wrong with them bastards. How do you manage? You are remembered here. Miguel and Antonio ask after you. The *extranjeros* too. Was it a good summer or a bad one? Torments of the *paseo*, babble of the plaza, Nancy's shiner. We met you pair. That's sufficient to be going on with.

In a week's time we take a brief trip to Paris. Stay a week or so. Write. Love,

BOB

II

A French postcard from Bayless, addressed to us from the Hotel Racine, Rue Racine, Paris, 8th September 1963.

Dear Ruttles,

Our trip here was hazardous. We reached Benidorm after a day of vomiting (Daisy) and half-fainting (Dilly), because of too much heat, too little sleep, hungover. The landscape was great but it was too damn hot to enjoy it. Benidorm's a city from a horror movie. It had Otto von Hapsburg, who made (destroyed?) it, Marbella had some Hohenlohe prince, and rest assured that in good time some of the remaining German royal families will put their aristocratic blue noses into old Nerka, and then Adios!

From Benidorm up north it's no longer Spain but hell, especially after Barcelona. I never saw so many accidents, so many road deaths, smashed cars, stout and hot-tempered Northern and Middle Europeans killing each other en route to the overcrowded beaches.

The wayside taverns (we visited a few) full of bellowing Belgians, certainly the most swinish of people, even worse than the Germans. I have met only one Belgian whom I liked, and he was a man of the world. In the evening we decided to drive on because we couldn't find a hotel, and after twenty-eight hours nonstop driving reached Port Bou more dead than alive. Daisy had earache.

Now we are in Frogland. Everything seems very expensive after Spain. And the citizens a mite curt after amiable Andalusians. But the colours are clean (Dufy?). Charlotte, who just went to the store, said she will write soon. 'Tell them I *will*!' she shouted, herding daughter downstairs. So I tell you. C. will be writing.

BOB

III

Towards the end of September we were back again in Dublin. About a month later Charlotte wrote.

First Letter from Mrs. Bayless:

Calle Pintada 12
Nerka (Malaga)

October 30th 1963

Dear Ruttles,

I have dreamt of a thousand poetic lines to write to you. They sounded dull in the morning. Although my epistolary style has been much admired in the past, I am timid now, recalling Dan's severe strictures on old correspondence from certain presumptive Madame de Sévigné's—that damn tiresome old bitch—and so have decided to write you a newsy letter and fuck the style. I am four months pregnant but hardly notice the swelling. I am not with child. My stomach swells from a lifetime of laughter. I miss you both, can't seem to make new friends. Not here anyway. And the Spaniards only want to talk about my condition. I run a great deal in public to give the impression that I am still light-footed and hope no one notices the protuberance. August was very hot.

Nerka sweltered. Was *muy demente* most of the time. For the first time in my life I was tired of so much sunshine, longing for an overcast day when you could open your eyes fully and not have to squint into that unbelievably powerful sun. It freckled me at the age of twenty-five and I was furious. I perspired most of the time. Bob said 'Don't it smell in here?' (his filthy study). He smelled strange but I didn't know how to tell him. (I'm bad to *everyone*).

Paris was nice enough. Bob worked at the Bibliothèque de Club d'Anglais and Centre de Culture Américain, seated between Shelley and Lord Byron. I spent my time in the open air at the Luxembourg Gardens with Daisy trying not to get accosted. City being ruined by foreigners. Too many streams coming in, and the heart somewhere else. Don't tell a native that, though. Paris is all mirrors. In a room you walk into yourself. It's another mirror.

I am busy getting drunk on a bottle of Valdepeñas as I type this. I opened a bottle and am trying to finish it before Bob comes back into the kitchen. According to your card to Bob, received ages ago, good things were happening. I am glad. Was the Dawson thing a sell out? Excuse what may have seemed a disinterested silence and let us know. Your letter was very short and, forgive the expression, very dry. We really think of you but must weed our way through much trivia to find a chance to write. We spend many hours just staring angrily at each other. Gossip follows. Don't read on.

We heard from Tracey. She and Roger are still in cahoots. Miss Nancy Summerbee is in Los Angeles (subsidy) getting her PhD. Doctorate. She perseveres. Her never-loving Laz is remarried and having his 93rd child by his 64th wife—a dark-haired Swede, according to Tracey. He is avid for easy money and Scandinavian sex, that myth. Do you suppose he's a satyr? I sometimes wonder. The abominable Spicer and his girl Eila are wedded. He is writing a simplified history of the Civil War (ours) from the Confederate point of view. I believe the Parks are assisting in research. Rosa Munsinger is in New York playing a clavichord put together by the resourceful Mr Spicer.

We often talk of you pair. Those five months in your old barn of a place were the most lady-of-the-Manorish of my whole life. Imagine—seven bedrooms! Daisy spent most of her time tormenting the next-door hens. There is no saner occupation. I went in for it myself at her age, with my silly sister in Connecticut, and I knew 106 different ways of upsetting them.

This morning one hour after table tennis with Bob I saw three white balls circling around a blue sky. Found myself on the beach grabbing for all three of them. Strange. Low b.p. kind of substitute for drugs. Magnificent half-sleep dreams all the day. Am too tired to eat; kind of boring in the long run.

Forgive this uninvolved letter. I was drunk when I started it. I am not now. In the interval I had no peace.

Much love,
C.

Postscript in Bob's hand: Meant to tell you, your cat ran off within a sennight of your departure Greecewards. It was a fine animal, spirited without the attendant rudeness you come to expect from the lower forms.

IV

Letter from Robert Bayless.
Undated, like all his letters, typed, employing single spacing, the text on the obverse side being presented upside down, as if he had let it go over the roller. He wrote as he spoke.

No. 12 Calle Pintada,
Nerka (Malaga)

Dear Olivia & Dan,

Charlotte steps a little less briskly into pregnancy, tires in the afternoon, sleeps long hours, is given to staring into the sea for long periods, and is overheard muttering odd questions—What is life? What is Time to outraged flesh?

(sounds like a Jewish W. Faulkner). We have never felt so much like vacationers as we do now, with you all gone and time using itself up uselessly. The weather has been poor of late, failed to come up as it did last year. We are already colder, the *merenderos* come down; it becomes Fall. There are clouds. There have been early rains. The wind roars in one day from the Gib and is answered the next from the other side. Boiling irregular surf, spray as harsh as spit, and you know it's over. I apply tonight to Frankfurt for a job and have inquired in Seville and Puerto Rico. But this is a hoax. I'll go back, become a magnate, and found a Grant.

The van Velde-Soutes have gone. They are exceeding strange, as you may recall. They called uninvited one evening around six and stayed until exactly two next morning, going on about immortality. Remind me of the Lamed Wufniks of Jewish belief—vague righteous beings who die if they realize who they are. Ominous to meet oneself. Particularly if one isn't quite sure who one is. Claude practises for two hours every day on the guitar, and then sets himself four hours for mathematics. Do you suppose he's attempting to match Bach fugues with the tango? Three or four years back, he had this inspiration—and remember he was a painter, selling his stuff, and in Paris at that—it came to him one day, like to Saul of Patmos that the real thing was math. So he quit, took up math. He discovered the Egyptians, the early ones, and started this text. He's mad about their state, social arrangement, religion. Talked about them as if they had just shut down last week. Malraux has written somewhere: 'I am as profoundly ignorant of ancient Egypt as a man would be of love, if he had not experienced it, however much he might have read; as profoundly as each of us is ignorant of death. All I know of it are those figures which I contemplate as I pass by. Europe has made them a race of corpses.' Europe, Malraux says, means first of all shop windows.

Möllberg with the pointed ears and the damning view of history used to say that Egypt had invented the soul. But what would we know about that, in our times? Theban tombs and over the dust of nothingness hovers the gesture, at once attentive and hesitant, of mothers putting toys into the tombs of children.

His wife is a Beat version of that kind of woman who presses flowers. Recently from San Francisco came their old amigo, her former husband Hugo Latimer III, a poet quite famous in those parts, Claude assured me. The city on hills is full of phonies—and I ought to know, coming from there myself. Anyway he appeared on the scene. Rarely ventures out of doors, is putting down flowers. A delicate little man with nervous blotches on his hands and some weird yarns about his recent 'moon thoughts'. My friends, stay away from them fucking moon thoughts. He has long feet and hands, which are the signs of class; was nosing out places he thought, or said he thought, that Byron and Shelley had nosed out before. Don't think they would have recognized them but he seemed to. Of course, it could be that we're just living in different worlds. How how it was is. Buddy of Paul (*Let It Come Down*) Bowles, Burroughs, the self-promoting Ginsberg. Self-seekers to a man. He's stopped being quite human.

Grass no good for writers if used in excess. Develops too much confidence in ones 'creativity'. Every high a little autobiographical improvement on what is sometimes slightingly referred to as the real. But it is good sometimes, for the development of appreciation and concentration. I don't think any of those drugs expand, but they do allow you to refine your focus on objects, music, sensory taps.

They are keen on these things, difficult to get them off the subject, want to talk about nothing else, and it gets boring. All mad about a pretentiously bad novel put out by a Persian (no less) disciple of Sartre—*The Blind Owl*. One night Dilly and I listened while HO III read about ten pages aloud in a *white* voice while the others were hooting and writhing about like kids at a Tom & Jerry cartoon. It was all so much hot air to me, but Claude, who had read ten or fifteen pages that afternoon—the *same* pages—said it was even better the second time round. Now what kind of shit is that from a pub? Now I ask you. But they are damned serious about it.

For myself I haven't read anything new. Symbolic gestures, games of political consequences—at sixes and sevens here as elsewhere, as always—govern the art of the day, and it is an art of the day, with a scramble for pertinence obvious. The movies are dead of course. My children will have it easier, being somewhat in the minority (one of them not even born); if Daisy turns queer, marries a coon, or becomes a junkie, she'll probably survive, though some sort of extra combination will be necessary by then if she is to survive. Any kid born in this great democracy in the last fifteen or twenty years is in for a rough go-round, no matter what. Still, it's nonsense to foster neurosis. I too am a WASP, of course. A low form of life.

Read the disguised homosexual fanaticism of J. Baldwin Esquire now being sold as clearly reasoned prose and bought and read by the Wasp minority. He'd be tolerable, maybe even good, if he got out of the intolerable habit of blaming things on things, this reason on that cause. He approaches Genet (the Saint) in his muddled references, but the Frenchman makes everything sound like his own invention; whereas Baldwin can't transmit beer into piss without borrowing some theorist's pipes.

His punching-partner Ninbad the Nailer (Xinbed the Phtailer to his *close* friends) is seldom out of the news, one way or another, and has a new novel being serialized in *Esquire*. Produced I understand by a one-handed typing method he has been perfecting in secret. It leaves the other one free to leap on the lap. Who spoke or wrote of books designed to be read with one hand, onanistic fantasies? Mirabeau? Now we have books being written with one hand; that's progress, boy, Yankee pig style.

Looking back on old things. Read once more Joyce's P of A the other day. A brazen man wrote that. Hemingway was sixty before he could make such a fuss about his youth, and even then it came off like a plea for sainthood. 'The instant wherein that supreme quality of beauty, the clear radiance of the esthetic image is apprehended luminously by the mind which has been arrested by its wholeness and fascinated by its harmony is the luminous, silent stasis of esthetic pleasure . . .' Try that on, Sir, and if it fits loose in the arse we'll take it up in a jiffy.

A minister of the church—denomination shall be nameless —told me when I was but a lad that the Jesuits turn out boys with fine minds but not one of them can shit into a barrel without hitting the sides—this because of filthy tutorial techniques. Is it true? Bloom/Joyce's interest in anal matters makes one suspicious. Molly's brown and those shy Hellenic female divinities that Poldy was trying to probe in the Museum. If it is true, I can write a book about it. Sure I can. It'll be a bestseller, and a musical comedy will be made of the story.

I want to know the PhDs. I want to talk to them. About important things. None of the old kitchen chat for the young Prof. What was Milton really up to? Was Dickens in love with his mother's maid? And Keats' commas, are they symbolic? On and on. A thesis later: 'The Function of Christianity in World Literature Since the Thirty Years War.' Ten thick volumes, seven devoted to footnotes. After that a lifetime—or what's left of it—spent developing a new grammar, which excludes the article from formal prose and introduces a new full stop or period. Honorary degrees from Clyde State Normal and Monroe A. & M. I see myself as emeritus, a doddering old chap with a strange odor, salivating on coeds in seminars, ionizing slowly like cheap paper.

Talking of shit: I'm all that for a typist, speller, often mix words—here for hear—also shorten by dropping whole syllables and employ mystical ellipses. This is not to be confused with carelessness but is technique. At the time of writing a man named Gilbert is preparing a chart which will explain three of the levels of meaning. Remember: no matter how much you think you are getting, you are not getting it all.

Some of this spelling and typing and punctuation belongs to my forthcoming handbook: 'How to Write Fast Without Knowing: A Layman's Guide to Mediocrity.' By God if the Jesuits had got hold of me as a youth I'd have been great. Ruttle, my name in lights! Bayless! He's your only man.

Smart, Jesus, but what a heart. Loves the little people. Gives gold away. But what a thinker!

Will probably write again before we leave for Bavaria, give you our thoughts, such as they are. When? Going to a dark bed there was a square round Sinbad the Sailor roc's auk's egg in the night of the bed of all the auks of the rocs of Darkinbed the Brightindayler. Where?

This prescription was written of a country I have never visited, referring to a people I hardly know. Except your good self. Charlie is fine, would like to hear from you. Nerka droops. Keep in touch. Love,

BOB

V

A Letter from Alemania.
Early in December, Charlotte wrote from Munich:

Haus Nord
423 Isabella str. 26
Munich

(undated)

Dear Ruttles,

Snowed about a foot today. City very startled, quiet. People look pale and grey. They say it's been a bad fall in Alemania all over. Munich under snow is very cold. I don't mind it. Daisy wild. In the morning it is glittering and fresh and new but around noon the city dust and traffic has turned it all grey, like the people.

The air is heavy, the buildings, the thoughts of the citizens. They like a soggy reddish plum-cake called *Zwetschgen-Datschi* with their morning coffee. Bavarians wear green Tyrolean hats, some with fancy plumes, pheasant feathers. The men have great calves. The girls are very pretty. The Isar is a deep detergent flood, flowing very fast between high walls.

Outside the city it's white. Then the *Föhn* blows from the Alps and the snow and ice melt and you walk around snuffling and feeling extremely miserable. A strange emotional state created by early rising, snow, sunrise, and lights in

Baroque places. Next day it's freezing again. Then more snow, and again *Föhn* and only good luck saves you from one cold after another. It's a thin, warm wind and in it you can see double, *twice* as far as usual—like the visionary Shelley, my scholar-husband informs me, so we have Shelley-vision, and that's nice. One can see the Austrian as well as the Swiss Alps from the top of the Franenkirche where I have never been.

I'm sleeping half the time—getting pale again. In a few weeks I'll be as white as the bellies of hundreds of frogs we saw on the road to Poligny at night. They wanted to cross but only some of them made it. Most of them were killed. Hours later we ran across some animal, I think already dead. It made a different sound to the frogs getting it (you could barely feel them, except in thick clusters), the tires made a hollow sound going over it—first the front—then the back wheels. Don't ask me what we were doing in Poligny. We passed through Queve en Brie and Sucy, the cheesy part of France that Napoleon gave to his generals, Marshal Lefèbre and old Colonel Aversin, Colonel of the Guard. And I must say I loved it. But we didn't delay as Bob wanted to get to Paris and the reference libraries.

When we reached here, Daisy spent the first few days weeping, until I put our 'remembrance tree' (a dried-up palm branch) over her bed. That stopped her, I don't know why. We stayed outside Munich at first, at the Gasthof Lidl in Tutzing am Ammersee and then at Gasthof Huber at Ambach am Starnbergersee. Formidable Alpsview in former place when *Föhn* blew. We slept at night under feather quilts of blue and white gingham. All the furniture was pine, the boards were bare, and colossal red-faced hunters wearing little feathered Tyrolean hats came puffing in, in top boots, clicking their fat heels very properly, throwing out their chests to say *Grüss Gott!* Nice old building with panelled walls, furniture Bavarian style, painted closets and so on, only a few yards from the lake, where you can fish for Renken, a special fish of all these lakes. But you could just as well leave the fishing alone and eat a roasted Renken with a salad and a bottle of wine or beer.

Do you know München? *Rumpelkammer*, old suitcases, played-out fiddles, discotheque dancing in very dark cellars, listening to very ugly people sing very rude songs. We visited Bürgerbräu-Keller, famous beer hall where Hitler began the Munich Putsch in 1923, a little before my time.

There are many canals from the river Isar and a temple known as Monopteros, as well as a Chinese pavilion and in the distance across the English Garden the two west-facing towers of the Frauenkirche. The chestnut trees are out. I like walking there. Many *Fusswege*. We found the pavilion among the trees. I thought it was part of the Zoo but there is no Zoo: it was a carousel. You pay 40 pfg. and have a choice of mounts, little wooden horses or storks pulled around to traditional music. Yesterday, *Donnerstag*, a bridge fell down in Zürich.

So it goes. A surprise every day. And just when I think I can't get a bigger surprise, along comes one that is *much* bigger.

We visited the English Garden and Nymphenburger Schloss. Daisy came away very addicted to 'tree-trunk' cakes (Baumkuchen). We took her to a Puppentheater for a great *Midsummer Night's Dream*. Went to Le Calvados—'jewel of French gastronomy'. Toulouse-Lautrec posters and a great wine list at La Bonne Auberge. Café Luitpold. Genuine Slivovic at a Bosnian joint, real Russian vodka at Romanoff. And jazz hot at the Domicile.

At the Bar Ascona was Rio Gregory in person—the well-fed guests (I quote the guide book) 'gazed in wonderment at his nimble fingers'. Jesso Wall and Claude of *Blind Owl* fame would have been in raptures. The legendary German over-eating in evidence everywhere—the stout citizens methodically stuffing themselves with oysters, pepper steaks, flambée, Porterhouse steaks wide as the hind legs of elephants, Chateaubriands and Hamburgers prepared 'by hand', washed down with beer, Mosel, Burgundy, topped up with white sausages and warm pickled lung. God, but the Bavarians love to put it away. How they must have suffered after the war when they couldn't get enough of it. And, of course, during the war it must have been unspeakable.

Filet à la Viaekönig Gun Boa sounds rather dangerous.

Italian pizzas broad as today and tomorrow, Hungarian Goulash. The great steaks of Chesa Ruegg. Hofbräuhaus, Ba-ba-lu. Under the former chambers of the former Pacelli-Villa you will find a crowd of well-behaved people dancing to the sound of a well-run discotheque (the guide book jargon is catching) in the Cosy George Club—not so well behaved at Schwabing, which on the whole we preferred. Bob put away many Halbes at Gastställe Leopold, bemoaned your absence. Bar Simpl, Pasta ascivta at Café am Siegestor, Heuboden (Hay-loft) with cow-bells, halters and farm implements, a kind of Bavarian El Molino. I looked around for Antonio Molinos Campos and his eternal stones, but he wasn't there.

Old clocks, pewter, odd shoes, faded books, beer stains, medals and coins, ikons, local customs gone wrong, the chattels of times long past, wooden peasant furniture, wooden peasants uncomfortable in Stadtmitte, Baroque cherubs with genuine worm-made holes.

Now you know München.

Hope this won't be the last letter from my other self, because in a short time it will be the only self there is, and I want to keep in touch. I miss you. Much love.

Yours,
C.

Bob had added a postscript:

We go on from here to Amsterdam, where the frows come from, and will write from there regarding Dublin leg of journey. Stay well. Best.

Bob

VI

News from Grand Central.
Cablegram from Amory about this time. Posted in hot haste in Grand Central Station, New York.

CAN YOU BILLET ME STOP SAILING 24TH DUBLINWARD
FROM NEW YORK REPLY AMORY.

VII

Dutch Postcard from Robert Bayless.

Hotel Grace
Michelangelostraat 31
Amsterdam
Holland

15th December 1963

Dan & Olivia—This is just the handy card. All well but suffering from saddle sores. We dine cheap at Indonisian restaurant, served by waitress who, going on her flawless accent, might have come from Akron, Ohio. Signs of the American Occupation. Seagulls shit all along the HEINEKEN beer sign on rooftop over Leidseplein. The beer itself tastes mighty like Amstel canal water, and indeed there is a brand brazenly so named. Amstel lager-beer. Dutch courage? Avoid it. Whores very thick underfoot. They call after you —'Nackyball'. Avoid 'em.

We have this tentative plan: Leave Hook 20/21; London for one day thereafter. Get out on 23rd (we'll look around London on the way back, neither of us very keen on travelling like this), so we should show up by Xmas-eve, if that's okay.

It would be better if we stayed in a hotel your end. I need mornings to contemplate suicide and Dilly to perfect her growling. We are tired of travelling, folks, and look forward to some rest(?) in Dublin. But will we get it? Daisy will stay with C's globe-trotting aunt Esther Billig in London's Camberwell. Can you read me?

Love,
BOB, C. & D.

Letter from Roger Amory:

186 Second Avenue, 4F.
New York 3, NY

19th December 1963

Dear Dan,

On with the Bacchanalia. I think of you home in Dublin. The year on its way out. I recall the sourness of my last days in Spain—disaffection, disquiet, straw-clutching, preparing to run before the wind again. Scandinavia was a fiasco, Barcelona a disenchantment, London—as ever—misery. New York, in some ways the most exciting city on earth, a nut that won't yield to the tools I possess. Tracey marrying her shrink later this month. Broke, but not broken. Moments of extreme buoyancy. Unjustified perhaps.

I wired you because I needed to see you. I've cancelled the trip, however. For the present at least. Met an oceanographer last week in a bar, who invited me to the Caribbean on a research trip for one year ('For twelve months we will be free in the world'), beginning in new year. There's a chance of scripting a film for the universities involved. If I can hold out until then I should have some hard news. Then I'll earn, then return to Spain.

Splice the mainbrace steadfastly.

ROGER

75 THE PRICK OF THE CYPRIOT: We went under the archway and there was the gate of the night club. Then I pressed the bell. Bob and Olivia were following but out of sight. Will you ever come to the States? you asked. No, I said, I don't suppose so. Will you go back to Spain? I said. No, you said, probably not.

I heard a piano playing upstairs. Will we ever see each other again? you said. I don't know, I said, probably not. You can write to me, you said, special delivery in whatever city I am in. I will, I said, though I knew I would not.

I turned back to the gate, rang the bell again. Over the gravelled forecourt the night-club door opened and Jan Kimpinsky the stout young Polish owner looked out. You were falling slowly away from me with a look of petrified reproach on your face. You looked as though you were going to faint. I lifted you up and you were glaring at me. You said nothing. Lot's wife. You were laid back against the bonnet of a car with your eyes closed and Bob was stroking your hips, whispering to you. You were in pain. One high-heeled shoe was stuck in the narrow drain conduit. The Polish owner unbolted the gate and admitted us. You were brought in, half-carried between us, your ankle twisted. You asked for lemon tea. You would be okay, you said. There were some Dutch sailors at the bar. A Cypriot asked Olivia to dance with him. She said all right. The Cypriot had beady eyes. I went upstairs and watched them dancing. An orchestra of two (piano and saxophone) played for them. No one else danced. I went down below to the bar. I could hear the music and the scuffle of their feet.

You were sitting at a table drinking lemon tea. Some drunks were arguing, some serious men playing poker for moderate stakes. Then the music stopped and there was some applause and Olivia came down followed by the Cypriot. I can't get rid of this fellow, she said, buy me a drink. I was drinking Mateus. The Cypriot watched the poker players. He dances quite well, Olivia said, if only he would keep that hard little prick of his to himself.

He was small, he sweated.

You were very pale. I watched you. I did not speak to you. The Cypriot hovered around Olivia. We drank more Mateus Rose. Tell you what, I overheard the persuasive Cypriot say, I'll make a bargain with you. Oh no you won't, Olivia said, that's my husband standing over there.

⁊⊛⊱

It was the Baggot Mews club. The Baylesses had stayed ten days in Dublin before returning to London. I had found them a flat in Belgrave Square (unlikely Irish address) with a Mrs. Maloney; a fine Georgian square around a sports-field for adolescent school-girls. We lived nearby, beyond a brown-stone Baptist Church. I took Charlotte one day to the Dropping Well pub on the river.

They left; sailed from England for New York. Not long after that Charlie Vine arrived. In the unheated flat in Belgrave Square he suffered from the cold, in that useless summer. Then Vine left for Canada. A chapter closed. I decided to take Olivia to the Aran Islands, where she had never been, in the following autumn.

76 BITCH GODDESS: He was in Davy's cocktail lounge with a red-headed American woman, a poetess from Rapid Falls, Minnesota. Or Grand Falls, Michigan. She was known to me in the sense that I had spent a certain amount of time avoiding her.

They were stuck together, oyster kissing. A wrinkled suit hung loosely on that barrel-shaped torso of his, a soiled white shirt stuck out at his paunch and erupted again around the collar of the jacket. Hatless and tieless, he looked as though he had been fighting. An intoxicated Roman Emperor in the days of its decline, a Caesar with boorish and foul ways. He needed a shave, his Tiberian jowls shook, he had a bruised look.

And she? *La Blanche Biche* was as she always was. The lurking eyes, the lips parted in anticipation, the tip of the tongue showing, the nostrils slightly dilated, here the passion that excites the game. The right hand lay open with a nervous twitching, while one of the legs was disposed to advance. One could see that she was full of designs and coquetry. I knew it was all for effect, this White Nun was no Messalina.

It was a slack hour of the day in the bar. The playwright looked about ready to befoul himself—a thick-set, broad-shouldered, bull-necked, foul-mouthed, low-born famous man, raconteur, tosspot, living legend. His ordinary life and talents lay in ruins about him, money he had frittered away like water. Drink, the ruin of many a good man, had brought him low. Now there was no impetus (except the destructive impulse for hard alcohol) and no redress. He earned his fees in the States, but the life was destroying him; to be so much in the public eye was confusing. Not far away, in the window of the Aer Lingus office in Grafton Street, caught off-guard by a news-camera, and more rumpled than ever, he strode purposefully across wet tarmac, shirt open to the navel, sporting a black eye. Off a London flight.

He did not notice me standing at the bar when he went to empty his bladder. He looked bad—par-boiled with booze. The urinals began flushing as the door opened and closed behind him. A hand forced coppers into the slot, four pennies dropped, and an invert began whispering something earnest and consequential into the mouth-piece. I moved back so that his doxy could not see me. The deathly-pale lady with the Titian-red hair—a languid one who wrote lapidary verse—had for some months been hounding me for a book I'd most unwisely borrowed and later lost. She claimed that it was a rare edition, irreplaceable and demanded a painting in return. When I refused that, she threatened to impound a raincoat that I had left behind in her flat. I could have the raincoat when I handed over a painting. So I went around coatless.

But she was watching me through the black wrought-iron gate now, giving me a horse-eyed look. Before I could make a move (like paying for my drink and leaving) she came out, smirking. You rat, Ruttle! she breathed, and I smelt good liqueur off her. Benedictine. The lady was rich and paying. I, who had an embarrassing overdraft in the bank and wore neither headgear nor raincoat, since the bitch had impounded it, hoped that she would at least have the tact not to mention the missing book or the painting she wanted for it, and decided that I would be rude to her if she did. But she was all affability. Messalina, she of the positions and procedures. The face, the anxious eyes, the tightened lips, the active chin, nervous and full of misgivings. Nobody prises any secrets from *me*. The hand you reach me in the dark.

I had to be careful in my movements around Baggot Street and Leeson Street, avoiding Ely Place, where she holed up. There were a few areas where I could feel safe from her. Entering the Arts Club in Fitzwilliam Street I would find her dining alone, and be invited to join her for the pleasure of hearing more about the rare Synge copy lost, take the chit. I thought I was bribing my way free. I was not. She had no sense of humour and could be venomous. Like all acquisitive persons, she had an unpleasant side.

But we were talking at the counter there easily enough,

until she picked an injudicious moment to clutch my arm, whereupon the playwright appeared suddenly behind her, his untimely arrival announced by the persistent flushing of urinals. The invert glided away from the telephone, wiping his palm with a handkerchief, a rolled *Irish Times* tucked under one arm.

She touched my wrist with moist fingers, a moist possessive touch from a disdainful lady. *La naturelle température des femmes est fort humide.* Young ones at their first flowers attract dogs. Bitches on heat. Like to like. Blood and flowers. Geranium? poppies? A queer vein of prudery. Lady, lay off touching.

Whassit you've got there, Ruttle? the playwright demanded truculently. His chest stuck out, his cock feathers ruffled, a great oppressed eyeball glared at me. I had been making up to his moth while he was out for a piss: that was offensive enough. Confronting deceit and double-dealing, he breathed his hound's breath over us. His intention was to be as offensive as possible, short of actual blows (there seemed to be none of his henchmen present). There is a kind of success that is indistinguishable from panic; such was his nature now; he was suspicious, hating. The poetess caught her breath. I love this man, she said insincerely, clutching his arm. This proved nothing. The playwright, rocking on the balls of his feet, glared at me. Whassinnit? he asked. Gin, I said, *solamente*.

Giss us that here, he said, his chest out like a diva's, or a man diving. I pushed the glass towards him, a double gin waiting for Indian tonic water. His hand trembled as he took it up, and down it went in one long swallow; the unshaven bullfrog throat bulged. He wiped his mouth with the back of his hand. The poetess looked the contrary of delighted. This was no way to drink gin. Her right eye closed with a nervous twitching while one of her legs was disposed to retreat. She had had just about enough of this. I caught one of her enigmatic looks. She took a step backwards, said (to him) Let's go, honey. This is no good.

She walked back into the cocktail lounge. The nettled playwright shouldered me somewhat in turning to go. Watch it, Ruttle, he said. Don't press your luck.

He would set his bully boys on me, his hatchet men, he would so. Brehon Law. He followed the poetess back into the cocktail lounge, where an affected male voice was now braying inanities. The barman Billy watched him go. The poetess was sipping her drink as if she had never moved. Some pages were spread out before her on the table. She handed a sheet to the playwright who stared at it with a glassy eye. Whaw kinda fuckin cock is this?

I looked away. When I looked through the grille again they were back at the oyster kissing. The hands of the clock stood at ten minutes to five, Dublin time. I ordered another drink. A glass of Spatenbräu.

How's it going, Dan? a confidential Northern voice murmured close to my ear. I looked into the Manager's cod's eye. Badly, Billy, I said, poorly enough.

He had the look of a person suffering from liver trouble. Upstairs he had been going over the books. Now he was down to empty the tills and cater for the select evening trade. The Campbells were coming. At more difficult times he had accepted post-dated cheques, even advanced me loans. A quiet-spoken unruffled manager running a decent bar.

Your man is here, the discreet voice murmured, *sotto voce*. I know, I said, he's been through. The Manager shook his head, his mouth pursed up. Bad business, he said, a sad business (looking at neither the bad business nor at me). He's putting it back all right, the conspiratorial voice spoke close to my ear so that none might overhear.

Funny place to look for pussy, I said.

The Manager did not reply immediately, but confined himself to rolling his cod's eyes in a deeply sceptical manner to indicate that he had heard. It's always those who can't who try, he said out of the corner of his mouth.

I heard the newsboys calling in the street outside. They didn't say *Heggle-the-Male* anymore. Now it was the *Evening Press*, a *Daily Mirror* for all Ireland. A lady with an eyeguard whom I knew by sight now came in and sat alone at a table near the door. She opened her handbag and began to rummage in it. Paddy went to serve her. A newsboy came quickly into the bar, slapped an *Evening Press* down on the counter, and was out again through the swinging door. They were calling at Combridge's corner. The playwright at times had been their news—dancing jigs on the stage, roistering, contemptuously drunk.

Paddy the barman, a tall, blond, curly-headed man such as you would expect to find pucking a ball on a hurley field or shoulder-charging at a GAA match—now served Eye Patch a glass of JJ and Vartry water. He had a specially concerned way of serving those who drank to their perdition. At that early hour there were already two in the bar. The Manager put on his spectacles and opened the newspaper. I read:

'YOUTHFUL TRIO PLAY WITH ZEST.'

Mr. Rigby-Jones, of Irish Ropes, photographed at his factory in Newbridge. T. P. Kilfeather Visits Ghost Town. Rain was falling on the ghost town. Newbridge. A battle of sorts had been fought there by pike-men in the olden times; a skirmish. Let your manhood be seen by your push of pike. I had once passed through it on a bicycle.

That old fart, what does he know about it? an irascible male voice demanded. Sweet damn all! A barman like a priest wearing grey bicycle clips crept through the Ulysses Lounge, as more customers entered through the front door, bringing cold air off the street. Be seeing you, the Manager said civilly, moving away. I looked towards the back lounge. She was staring at me, pale-faced, tight-lipped. *L'antique Venus la superbe fantôme.* The Lady from the Sea who had no Father. *La Blanche Biche.* Resentful, watchful eyes saw me, judged me, disapproved of me. The playwright was in an awkward cantilevered position with his great Roman head out of sight below the table, upon which one pudgy and rather defenceless hand rested. The pose was pure Dying Gladiator. The poetess looked down at him and then back at me, as if begging me to do something, restore order. Contrast the sensual charms of the one and the *impudic* head of the other. But I knew well enough it was useless to attempt that. I looked away instead.

The main doors were opening and coming together now like
a concertina as more customers came in. The newsboys were
calling out in Duke Street outside the Bailey. T. P. Kilfeather
had visited the ghost town of Newbridge. Chairman Rigby-
Jones had sat on a board meeting of Irish Ropes Ltd.

When I looked again she was half-kneeling by him, supporting him, whispering good advice into his ear. His deaf
ear. It was a little late for good advice. I could see the big
shoulders and the Tiberian jowls; soon he would be up and
roaring abuse. Or down and horribly spewing. A fawning fellow in a tweed suit with double vents was standing before him,
declaiming in a loud, bluff, bantering, jocular, Irish way:
Ah the hard man! And how's it going? (His name was a byword
and this was his bar, a famous bar.) But the poetess was signalling with a pale frantic hand for this fellow to stand off and
give the man room to breathe. A taxi was summoned, a radio
cab to take the playwright home.

The eyes still watched me, judging me. Hard eyes that grow
soft for an hour. White limbs, and a cruel red mouth like a
venomous flower.

When I looked again they had gone. I heard a hectoring
voice going on and on: Mr. Double Vents. She must have
taken him out by the back door into the lane. They had beaten
a retreat. The newsboys knew him, a North Dubliner born
and bred like themselves; famous like Shaw or Sean O'Casey,
one of themselves. They saw him, in an advanced stage of the
jigs, being pushed into a taxi. That was nothing new. Man born
of woman hath but a short spell to abide and is full of misery.
Similarly for women.

At this hour of this day in Dublin a seated woman waits
for someone. In the background, quiet figures. She drinks,
watches the clock. (The sad lady with the eye-patch with a
circumspect gesture now lifted the glass to her lips, but put
it down again without tasting it. She diluted it carefully with
water.) Paddy hooked on his wire-rim spectacles and with a
sceptical look at me turned to the racing news. I found four
coppers and went to the telephone, dialled a Sandycove number. Nobody answered. It was ringing in an empty house,

somewhere there beyond Maiden Rock and Clare Rock and Lamb Island, feeble but persistent. Nobody would ever lift the receiver again. Bottle-green waves beyond Frazer Bank obscured the sound. I felt I was drowning. The mouth-piece of the instrument was beaded with sweat, the secrets of inverts, the commonplaces of common men. I listened; the urinals were flushing again. All broken glass looks green.

⚜

One night not long after the events just described, I encountered him again. He was alone this time and in a worse condition than before. It was in the wooden atmosphere of the Arts Club, after closing time in the Dublin bars. He was in one of the toilets.

Quick taken, he had fallen into the ladies' W.C., the womens' midden. I feared that her Ladyship would go in and find him there, and then there would be hell to pay. I waited near the door, hearing sounds of human distress within. Presently he reappeared, trousers down about the ankles, hair on end, eyes bloodshot, shaking like an aspen. He begged me, in the name of our dear crucified Redeemer, to do him the small charitable service of doing up his flies, seeing he was beyond it himself. He was uncertain of where he was and what he was supposed to be doing there, having reached the distressing stage in drinking beyond polite behaviour. It was no longer possible to say whether he recognized anyone or not and there was no point in taking offence at anything he said or did. He was like a child again, soiling himself.

Feeling pity for him, I tidied him as best I could, and took him upstairs. He fell onto the bed and began snoring at once. He looked bloated, worn-out, done-in.

He was in and out of hospital after that for treatment. I never saw him again. Singing, or rather roaring:

> *I'm proud of all the Irish blood that's in me*
> *There's not a man can say a word agin me . . .*

His blasphemy and foul-mouthed ways not to mention public buffoonery (a disguised form of sadism) were not to everyone's taste.

77 THE DUMMIES IN THE WINDOWS: On the afternoon of that tiring day, Creation Arcade was empty and the door of the Ulysses Lounge closed against the cold. I looked at the dummies in the windows. The Italian travel agency had mounted an enlarged photograph in colour of Lake Como on a summer's day: On the surface floated a paper hat put together from sheets of an Italian newspaper, biretta-shaped, out of all proportion to the rest. It gave perspective the lie, indeed resembled more a deep boat, a coracle or ark, than a priest's biretta. All the details of sky and lake were correct, as were the details of the paper hat, but together they were not correct, and the effect was as unsettling as the four-eyed man in the old advertisement (a cure for indigestion), clean-shaven with staring eyes and thick hair, who, reversed, became bald-headed and bearded.

The water moved, the swallows were trapped in flight, the outsize paper hat rode motionless, my forehead touched the glass. I looked down at my unpolished and broken shoes and was struck by the distance from my eyes of those remote feet, an exorbitant distance, it seemed to me.

Footsteps were approaching. Quick and decisive, echoing in the arcade, the step of a girl who had made up her mind and was set on her course. High heels came on in a hurry, something more than a walk and less than a trot, but truly sedate. *Paso fino.* Above the water in a cloudless blue Italian sky the swallows drifted over on the Lecco side, the faint and exquisite landscape of Ronsard and du Bellay, the scent of myrtles and everlasting spring. A perfume of lavender pre-vailed. The air did not move, nor the water, nor the swallows, the paper hat floated away. The footsteps came to an abrupt halt before the outspread lake, the great biretta. Providence had interfered to put a stop to her gallop. She made a sound, half murmur, half sigh, staring at the lake, the paper hat riding on the surface and from the corner of my eye I saw a cyclamen outfit, dark hair worn long, thoroughbred legs in stylish shoes, an Italian handbag.

The cyclamen and lavender took a series of short steps, high heels fidgeted on the *terraza*, and again silence. Then the murmur, half sigh. I glanced at her as the cyclamen lady glanced at me, caught a flash of eyes that were all pupil, black, strange eyes. A frank, direct and open look, most unexpected from an unknown woman. Lost at an amazing depth I was no longer moving. Still in this stupor, several seconds passed before she looked away. I thought to accost her, but not then and there; the moment did not seem propitious. She wore a tweed two-piece outfit with no jewellery; her dark brown hair had a high gloss. And again the murmur, half sigh. I decided to follow her when she moved, shifted her ground. The dark eyes, in a face imperfectly outlined, watched me in the plate-glass of the display window. I received it then, the prod of Eros, a touch behind the cloth. The mounting of amorous desire at that most inappropriate place and time filled me so fully that I imagined she must feel it too. Being alone with her there I felt charged; anything was possible. The eyes now shifted their focus, studied the lake.

But, if she sensed anything, she offered no sign. Moving behind me (again the scent of lavender), the steel tips of her shoes clattered impatiently on the *terraza*, indefatigable hoof taps. Somewhere in the city a man waited for her, in the Shelbourne or Hibernian Hotel. She was in a hurry to get to him, and had wasted time. She was very beautiful, a type that wrings the heart. Would not every man, with justifiable emotion, retrace his steps in order to follow her? She had the daintiness of a pretty woman, her amber perfume, the purest essence of that other mysterious thing which charms, excites, makes you want to smile. Moreover, it seemed to me that I had met her somewhere before. Somewhere in the city a man waited for her, a car stood parked outside a hotel. I followed her with my eyes (observation, the most exquisite form of pursuit); and then I was walking after her, following the moving lines of her somewhat thin body beneath the cloth (it wasn't tweed). And then, without trying to remember it, her name occurred to me, and without thinking I called *Marcia*!

She stopped. I approached her, putting on as bold a face as I could, though her manner was frosty, far from encouraging. You may not remember me, but I remember you, I began lamely enough. You were at one of my exhibitions. At the Dawson Gallery. My name is Dan Ruttle.

Ye—es, she said, considering me.

You do not remember me, I said.

I remember you quite well. As a matter of fact I was at your last opening, with McKenna.

I said nothing to this.

Don't you know T.P.? He knows you.

Yes, I know McKenna, I said. I saw him there, but I didn't see you.

Well, I was there all the same, she said smiling. Her tone of voice was low, a voice that implored protection. We were standing in the exit of the arcade. The entrance to the cocktail lounge of Davy Byrne's was down the way. I suggested a drink. She hesitated just long enough for me to think that she would refuse. But she did not refuse, after all. She said she had an appointment (glance at an expensive wristwatch) but had a little time to spare. It would have to be a quick drink, and not in the Davy Byrne's. Her reserved manner, wary eye and downturned mouth indicated, *I do not know you, I do not care to go too far with you, you are a complete stranger, please respect that fact. You are going too fast.*

Anywhere else, she said, but not there. Which began to confirm my feeling that somewhere in the city a man was waiting for her. I considered the Sign of the Zodiac, or upstairs in Rice's. I walked outside her. She moved in the way that had first attracted my attention, a kind of high-stepping, fractious *pasa Castellana*. I had certainly met her somewhere before, but where? In Spain? The Lippizaner Riding School of old Vienna? My feelings? An evanescent sensation of overlap, of a transposition, of a marked inversion of relationship, which however I was unable to define. In a vague but insistent manner I linked this feminine image with a knot of intense feelings: of a humble and distant gratitude, frustration, fear, even an abstract desire; but above all of a deep and indeterminate anguish. I knew her calves, the shape of her body better than the lover (hardly husband), and those high-heeled shoes with their thin straps were already ripping my dreams. I took her by Dawson Street and across a tangent of the Green to Rice's. The upstairs Lounge was open and deserted at that hour. Her maiden name and her married name then occurred to me: Marcia Paz-Pero, only daughter of the former Bolivian Foreign Minister to Ireland: the late Don Xavier Paz-Pero of La Paz. She had married the rugby international Dr. Brian Goodall. She was Mrs. Goodall.

We sat at a table by the window from where I could see the flags on the roof of the Shelbourne Hotel and on into the hazy canyons of Baggot Street. She crossed those thoroughbred legs, the Italian shoes with steel-tipped stiletto heels. I was with a strange woman and wondered how far I could go with her. Her accessories were expensive, the small leather bag might be Italian. She had most beautiful hands. The gold wedding ring would be from Dr Goodall. An emerald shone on another finger of the same hand, which rested on the cyclamen-clad thigh. Half an inch of black shift showed below; her skin was very brown. I tried to study her, to isolate elements of that stirring sexuality, but it was like memorizing the reflections of a diamond. I knew quite well the source of her power (I am trying to identify it by the most commonplace details). Behind her, a blown-up print of Dublin under the Georges took one wall, a city of open squares where high-busted ladies sailed beside cravatted and bewhiskered males through woody surroundings, leading thin-shanked little dogs.

She spoke of La Paz, her birth-place. She had grown up there, gone to University there, left Bolivia to live with her parents in the Dublin embassy, had met Dr. Goodall, became engaged, married him. They had gone back to La Paz for their honeymoon, now lived in Richmond, Virginia, was on holiday.

I am married now, you know, she said.

Yes, I know, I said.

How would you know? she asked, 'the ghost of a smile' on her lips.

I know, I said.

Seasons in Bolivia are the opposite to yours. Our summer is your winter, your autumn our spring, she said. Summers at La Paz are windy and the families of professional people and the embassy crowd go to the seaside, where the children fly kites.

The fascination of Bolivia, and indeed of all Latin America, is that it is a place of incomparable grandeur, geographically, historically and architecturally, while at the same time a piteous place. Public monuments celebrate defeats suffered in wars against Peru and Paraguay. Absurd! Tell that to Victor Pas Estenssoro. Bolivia always won.

I studied the down-turned mouth, listened to that quiet voice that implored protection. (*La Paz, frustracion y destino*). The sad eyes, the down-turned mouth said, *too much! It is too much!* She asked for dry Vermouth.

We have our 'Day of Freedom', she said. What does it look like, that shadowy and elusive thing, Bolivian freedom? A pretty girl on a float flanked by soldiers lunging forward with Tommy guns, looking very fierce, symbolises what we haven't got. I was fined once for not attending one of those functions. If you have any connection with the Embassy you are expected to go.

It is saddening to see the poverty of our beautiful city. The population today is half what it was at the time of the Incas. The Americans won't allow the Soviets to sell us foundries and they sell us weapons. Six years of American aid to support a regime of flour and butter. And the country stays poor. The Indians sell the cheapest food, a few potatoes, bananas and oranges. Hundreds of poor Indians all over the city sitting before the same miserable offerings. In the poorer sector the houses are thrown up anywhere the fancy takes the owner, until the weather breaks and the rain sweeps it away. A few more dead

Indians do not matter. They speak Aymara, a guttural tongue difficult to understand. Government aid is ninety-eight per cent paper promises and two per cent cash. The Indians chew coca leaves mixed with ashes, a bitter chew that numbs the mouth but deadens the cold. Children with cracked skins sit in the doorways, developing sores. The babies' cheeks and lips crack. The blunt-featured women are treated like dirt by the men. Human excrement flows in the central drains. Nothing smells at that height. Marcia Paz-Pero-Goodall said.

Once I was ill, in bed with a fever. I walked through the house in the middle of the night. It was most strange. You look at the stars and wonder where you are, who you are. A mountain hangs above the city. You come out after work, and there it is with its perpetual snow. Higher up you get a double vivid whiteness. La Paz looks marvellous on moonlit nights. There's salt in the ground—you can actually see it. In that silent house in the middle of the silent city, with the whole sky blazing over my head, I thought I heard the ground cracking. My head seemed to be cracking and the sky too.

Her face had changed several times as she spoke. I saw her ill, walking through that house high up in that remote cold city, and felt hollowed out, filled with signs and symbols. I wanted her the more, though now by taking me into her confidence she had pushed me further away. She sipped Vermouth, the emerald flashed (Lot's wife turned to salt). I saw her moving through the livingroom at night, a rolled *Presencia* in one hand. It must have been like the Berliner Zimmer, pre-1939. I saw her dead father smoking a cigar, speaking to the hanged President, the stars of the southern hemisphere burning over their heads and under their feet the firmament burned. *Zona de los gaseo en disaciacion*. That was her home, a strange home, below the *nieves perpetuas*.

Being with her, this young Bolivian wife whose beauty was so striking, set up vibrations in me. An unknown woman possesses a unique charm. Her beauty, so striking, could arouse in me only sadness, only feelings of partings and forsakenness. Hers was a face from the past, a face from another world, a face set apart. I could never touch her. She had the power of beautiful women to invoke landscapes. A sense of rueful distance seemed to accompany her, as if her eyes had come to rest on a horizon that had never been seen by any man. Her voice softened and the pupils of her eyes dilated. She seemed to be recollecting some long voyage over distant waters to a walled island where she was committed by the nature of her mind and organs to secret rites that would refresh her charming and creative stores of sadness.

Behind the narrow bar counter the pale-faced Mr. Rice spoke to the dark-haired Mrs. Rice. The television screen was a snowstorm of blackish dots raining down; the sound issuing from it was *nada*, the vacancy of outer space. Marcia Paz-Pero's brown hand rested on her lap, the delicate pulsations of the blood showing in its bluish veins. Behind her, the little well-bred dogs of a dead Dublin paraded at the heels of dead citizens, high-busted ladies and their formally-attired escorts.

I saw the other city, in my mind's eye. It lay in a bowl a thousand feet below the level of the *Altoplane*. The freezing Pampero blew off the Andes down to the Atlantic, the population only half what it had been at the time of the Incas, like Ireland before and after the Great Famine. It lay between Lakes Titicaca and Poopo. The Andes belonged to Peru. The wars against Peru were fought in high places. A President was hung from a lamp post. Military acts done in a military manner by military men. (All successful revolutions are alike in their success, each unsuccessful revolution failing in its own way). Guevara and his merry men roamed the forests.

Wind blew dust and papers into Creation Arcade and beyond the tunnels, the newsboys, pinched with cold, were calling outside the Bailey. The Rices had gone below. The television screen continued to shower down teeming matter in a manifold state of flux. Double-decker buses passed into Grafton Street, like logs down a narrow river.

The very poor ride on the tops of autobuses, she said. I have done it. You must travel in a sleeping-bag. The roads are terrible. Bad accidents occur when incompetent drivers encounter worse roads and then the buses overturn.

I saw a girl of seventeen lying on the roadside, I suppose badly broken up inside, a pink froth coming out of her mouth. Her parents were there wringing their hands, watching their daughter die. A doctor could do nothing for her. She was in better hands—the hands of God. I watched her die on the roadside. The people are fatalistic and no wonder, for there is much to be fatalistic about in Bolivia. The bus was pulverized. *Estrelló* as we say.

Fatal accidents like that keep recurring while the stoical Bolivians shrug their shoulders, resigned to it. *Es la vida!* What they mean is: It's death. I think it must be something like Spain. You've been to Spain?

Yes.

You liked it . . . or perhaps no?

Yes, I like backward countries.

Oh then you must get to Bolivia. My country is *very* backward. But look at the time. *Dios*, I must fly!

From the window I watched her cross the street. She passed through the gates into the Green. She moved by people, not touching them, walking rather fast. Those legs, that back, that containment, that present walking past (density times duration) moved me strangely. She walked under the motto (I had forgotten it again) FORTITER ET PECTE. *Impavidum ferient ruinae*—Horace?—chiselled over the open gate, and disappeared among the trees.

On the opposite pavement a crowd of idlers stood before the display windows of an electrical appliances shop. A shadowy manic form gesticulated wildly on a television screen, but no sound came up to me.

78 JACKALS: We had sat in the Dropping Well pub on the Dodder river, down from the weir. Reflections of sky and clouds were moving in the vinyl table-top. Vine stood at the bar. A little bell rang below somewhere. Below the weir no youths were swimming, as I had seen naked young men swimming, or rather carried in the flood below the bridge at Mostar. Was it the Drina? When Charlie carried back two pints of Guinness, I brought the conversation cleverly around to the Baylesses.

Unaware of what he was doing to me, Vine said that Charlotte had tinted hair (I hadn't noticed), spoke with an affected accent (I hadn't known) and had gone with Amory. She had come to him, Amory said, on the plaza one morning and said 'Let's fuck!' Vine said, and I believed him.

I literally felt an internal weakness and (white sky and blue clouds moved across the glass table-top and the Guinness on Vine's breath was bitter, old Charon rowing off Lethe wharf) my stomach turned. Vine imparted some information that I could have done without. She had tinted hair, an affected voice, Miguel was dead.

He, the great Dun Beast, had been sitting on the Calahonda beach wall, minding his business, reading a book. On the spur of the moment she, Queen of Old Nile, had approached him. He did not notice her coming submissive, heeding only the need. About them the fumes of the morning. She touched his arm, said nothing. He looked at her. It was the little shepherd hour. They went to the Hools' flat. Their excuse was that they were looking for books. She had the key. They went up.

That stud had mounted her, and she had wanted it. Engulfed with irresistible force. The nibbling lips of the goat. Stretched out on their backs, sated, exchanging a few words, smoking.

She had sat opposite me at the same table, had drunk the same drink, taking off her gloves. And I took her hands in mine, looked into her deceitful eyes. Dross of dreams, shapeless muck left behind by the Nile of sleep. Had it ever been blue, the Nile? Coffee-brown, excremental flood. Neville Orgle the Dublin antique dealer had felt some other effluvia along its banks—hope. Hope for himself? Hope for the Jews? Hope for Europe. Egypt? That ancient Egypt that figured in Claude van Velde-Soutes' foolish fancies. The shafts of the pyramids. Along its banks jackals prowled, persistent as gypsies. Haunt of young depraved Queens, themselves half-jackal. Jackals of the Nile drink as they run so as not to be bitten by the fish. At night their eyes shone and they cried with raucous human voices.

Hot land. Land of double-dealing. A sun on wand in knoll of sand she showed, clad in her cramoisy-hued chemisette. Or nothing at all. In the desert where the dung-fed camp-smoke curled . . .

Fall into the Nile today, swallow any of that yellow flood and you need fourteen injections. Beasts of antiquity bred on the run, their glans encrusted with blood and excrement. The word Amory was so fond of using: 'ecrement' he called it. Amber is known to be the dung of the three-legged ass. Munge.

They came into the Hools' living-room with their tongues out for it, threw off their clothes like all-in wrestlers. He put his lion's tongue into her mouth, her yin took his fierce yang, and down they went like tyros. Amory being a low sort of fellow with a dirty mind. His consumption of women was notable.

So she had done that to me. How many times? It must have been like that, or along those lines, something of that nature. Her nature? His? Who knows.

Oh Queenie!

I had a pocketful of letters from the Baylesses. They both wrote a good letter, wrote rather as they spoke. I re-read these on the *Naom Aoinne*, the S.S. *St. Edna* out of Galway, city of the tribes, bound for the Islands. Aran, the last landfall before America.

A little chain of islands, an amulet of three islands. On my first visit there I had spoken to an old man who had known John Synge. These were the letters.

EPISTOLARY (3)

I

512 East 13th Street
Apr. 4D., New York, NY

(undated)

Dear Ruttles,

Laughs and things from the States. Briefly, the voyage was rough, the book is finished, Charlotte enlarges prodigiously. It rains.

We got into the tail-end of one of the lady storms. D &D did four full days in their cabin. Deck D. Cabin 425—bed D. The dining-rooms were often deserted and people rushed from the films, palms pressed to their mouths. *SS Seven Seas* wanted stapability. It had been an American merchantman, a supply ship during the war, and then the Germans converted her. There were tea dances and concerts and a snorting, fart-ridden beer hall filled with naturalised Yankees weepily essaying drinking songs. Also Irish, for we called at Cobh and picked up seventy-odd. They sang of Kevin this and Mary that and bemoaned the lack of wine of the country. Pure immolation. Emigrants lured by the wealth of the New World, young men with scorched faces and sideburns, women with pale, hairless legs in flowered dresses. It was a rough crossing if rough crossings are judged by the amount of regurgitated food about the decks. Except for those overwhelmed to the extent that they could not utter an oath between retching, everyone seemed to take it very well. A young man staggered in from the deck, the front of his person moist and sticky, ganzy and gob both a sad shade of green, sat down beside me and looked at me puffing my Schimmelpennick Duet and watching the curtains swaying out from the walls (bulkheads to us *real* sailors) and said, 'Sure an' it's a man that's not right in the head that wouldn't be sick in one of these things'. I agreed. I wasn't sick.

Roger and Tracey met us dockside and we spent the afternoon with them, drinking Piper Heidsieck. He left for Rhode Island that night. He attends diving school there, in preparation for his Caribbean trip ('another string to my bow'). He continues in his personal beatification. People rush to him, he has luck, he gathers to himself acolytes, admirers, lovers, buddies. He and Tracey are still in cahoots.

A week after we arrived, we visited him in Rhode Island. He was sharing a cabin on a river with all of New England at the front door. At eight o'clock one morning, after a rousing night, he was in the stream, digging up oysters from the mud, happy as all hell. Hippocrates laid down the rule that one should always keep the head cool. Total immersion in water good for introspection. Swift bathing his head in the Thames at Chelsea. Compulsive early rising is a form of insanity. I could never do it myself. And it is wise for men of action occasionally to do nothing. Democritus devoured by lice.

If he gets the papers he'll stay here for a while, a year, unless he likes the islands. He wants funds to get back to Europe and his writing. I see something of Boswell in him, not the attender-upon-Johnson but the more lickerish side of the great biographer, putting his armour on to screw the whore on London bridge, getting his member in. He has Boswell's gross appetite and great heart. A sinner out for a good lay. What he likes, he likes to excess. What (and whom) he does, he does to excess. It's impossible to dislike such a man—though he can be trying at times. Gongtormented Amory.

With his gladiator's legs and bursting bullybag, he appears

to best advantage in Mediterranean light, wine-bag and speargun slung, slithering down a goat trail to an unknown beach. Out for the day with a 'good book', let us say something as trite as *Last Year at Marienbad* in his grip, with his toke, his almighty-happiness-grass-that-makes-all-men-equal.

New York is a mighty tricky town, no place for the novice or the man without proper credentials. I can see how it would be enticing for him; for if you've worked out your ideas of freedom, if you've lived your version of it as he has, then this city affords you good shelter for the cold periods; a nice place to hibernate, stock up with money and dis-comforture, before trotting back into the sunlight. It's very dirty and there clings an aura of jauntiness, rather like that affected by petty criminals and pimps. And there's money for the moneymakers. So we may leave soon. As I see it, we may continue on across the country. California, the legendary coast, offers no relief aside from the weather. New York would be miserable enough this winter, unbear-able if I were sweeping streets. We've already been as cold as we were last year in Spain, and people praise this season. Here they are finishing up a strike of subway and buses. Everyone in New York has a dog, and every dog in NY shits in the street, and the strike made sweeping impossible. Because of the cold (17 degrees the day we got back) the shit had frozen. You could not smell it, but you could break your neck tripping over it.

Dilly is approaching the period when every part is preg-nant; the earlobes thin out and the toes curl. She looks thinner than ever. She got her hair cut, so it bounces just off her shoulders. It takes time getting used to her with-out the old hair. We carry the trimmings about in an urn. She has been told the new do looks younger. That pleases her, I think, though she never looked very old. She never looked younger than when I saw that long hair spread first, which seemed like a very great invention of mine, so I miss it. But she got bored with the upkeep.

My own feeling is that it had better be a boy or off it

goes to the slave trade in N. Africa. If I have to live with another woman I'm done for. With Bayless in *Labia Pudendi*—title for his biographer.

(unsigned)

Postscript in Charlotte's hand:

Dear Dan & Olivia—This note is added weeks later. I will be brief because I want to get this off to you. No sign of life yet from the old pelvic floor. I wish I could spout it with the delicacy of the sea-horse. Instead Bob and I practise a method called the 'Psychoprophylactic Method of Painless Childbirth' (used in Red China & the USSR & France).

Love
C.

II

**512 East 13th Street
Apr. 4D., New York, NY**

(undated)

Dear Ruttles,

Charlotte had a girl two weeks ago tonight. It was no ski-jump for her. She took dope of course and came out proclaiming her mastery. 'Do you realise I've had another baby? Do you—sorry it wasn't a boy—realise?' She looked very wracked after the delivery, a wild woman with dilated eyes and damp hair. New addition bigger than Daisy at that age; Daisy asked this morning when is it going home. Still, for God's sake, *three* women!

Dilly's delivery no fun, neither was it painless. Went on for 35 or 40 hours. We'd been excellent students of the method which worked briefly as a diversion. Thinking, later on, that had the child been born in Nerka, there might have been serious trouble. Infant's heartbeats slowed down during labour and they had to adjust it. Cord knotted around her in some way. (It refers to the speed, which was tampered with, and they had C. set up for the knife if the beats got any slower.)

It snowed that day and night, and from her hospital window I could see the old East River, the world's least enchanting greasy flood, slobber by six floors below. Cars on the freeway, headlights playing into the snow and the furrowed pavement, blue-white street-lights below and the hospital lights from rooms in an adjacent wing. Taking stock out that window between Dilly's contractions, when she was so dopey it was impossible to comfort her. Then the same whimpered, piped pitch-setter for the next two minutes of screams. They say the dope relieves pain and induces amnesia. It only does the latter, but that's enough.

Afterwards I came into the small room where she lay, dried blood and bruises on her arms, and her lips chapped and swollen. 'What happened? I had it? ... When?' She couldn't remember anything. I sat by the bed and held the infant for about an hour while she talked, beginning sentences, then drowsing off, then picking them up again. We are calling the babe Livia Ann, after a very famous river and a well-known Irish painter's wife.

Sun shine upon you.
Love,
BOB

III

512 East 13th St.
Apr 4D. New York, N.Y.

(undated)

Dear Dan & Olivia,

We are arse-deep in debt. Presents an economic challenge. In fact, isn't that the reality people admonish us to face? What do you owe, to whom, and how do you propose to pay? Answer quickly, for this is a moral matter.

I knocked off a warm and moving letter when the Dawson Gallery catalog came and Olivia's note. Moving and all as it was I did not send it, because I couldn't finish it in one sitting—couldn't maintain the warmth. And such efforts exhaust me anyway. Hence the silence.

Presidential cortège along 2nd Avenue. Flash of a famous smile, wave of a famous hand—5,500 cops line the way. Twelve degrees below. Wind cuts mohair summer suits. Saw Rosa. She looked a bit miffed. Christmas coming. Relax stages. God rest ye merry etc., etc. To Royal Hotel, Jersey. Talk about Mississippi delta. Good. Outspoken. Adult. Tracey there with Amory. She spoke of her puberty in the woods.

I cannot write today because I cannot quite see. A wasted day then. As a home-saving act of selflessness I now turn all Sunday afternoon over to C. Whatever she wishes to do we do. Hopefully she will want to nap. It is a good day for napping.

Recently I reworked our apartment. It's fairly clean and looks ok but the floors slope, and the neighbourhood is rough. Amory, back from sea and gainfully employed, lives around the corner with his Chameleon. Jesso Wall seems to have retired from the picture. Rosa's ritzy black and red apartment is situated in downtown NY. We sometimes see her, though it's a strain. She doesn't send you her love or anything like that. She rarely refers to Brodey, who is lying low, still wanted by FBI. Rosa speaks of him as if he were someone with whom she had sat once in a train, staring across the aisle, as an impressionable young girl.

Later Charlotte's father died. The mean man had been troubled with heart disease for the last three or four years, and suffered attacks, leaking lungs, skin disorders. Yet he continued to work, was at it a few days before they took him to the hospital. One of the causes, it is thought, of the death was his dissatisfaction with the results registered after taking his medicine. So he revised the dose, and it was potent stuff.

Turns out he had $80,000 in various bank accounts. That's not bad. He lived, and had lived, modestly. C's mother who is very sick had been attended by an 83 year old cousin whose medical qualifications would not stand close scrutiny. The old man made generous provisions for the other sisters, Dilly still paying for her apostasy. The mother finally going to get proper care, but she's slid badly now, can't work up interest for the old man's passing, if she's even taken in his dying.

The world is spinning here.

I walk to work, come home for lunch often enough, and will until the weather worsens, which can't be far off. We will be within seven or eight degrees of freezing tonight, but the days are still clear. Windy football weather for about another month, and then all goes grey, and we're locked down for three or four months. Jesus, people suffer in these northern climes.

Some days have passed since I typed above horseshit. I will not change a line. Meant to tell you that when Behan died the country mourned him somewhat. He was a celeb. New York radio gave hourly reports on his condition. Charlotte copied some down for you, I've kept it. 'Just a few minutes ago peace came to Brendan Behan'—this from a Rock 'n Roll station broadcast, a station that lists among its supporters an anti-pimple salve manufacturer: 'Don't treat pimples like a girl, fight 'em like a man'— 'who died a few minutes ago in Dublin.' And then: 'He suffered from jaundice, a liver ailment, and self-admitted alcoholism.' Self-admitted alcoholism is a good deal more severe, if you follow my thought, being a bastard on the conscience as well. So it goes.

Is it really more than a year since we saw you last, slipping deeper and deeper into Ireland and the train station, standing and waving at Westland Row? Long as that since we found our seats, stowed our gear, and began feeling awful.

Best,
BOB

512 E. 13th St.
New York 9, NY.
Apt. 4D.

(undated)

Dear Dan & Olivia,

Our weather is changing. We have warm overcast days and rain, then some cold, but the green has started in the parks. Springs are short in New York. There are warm days in early June, and midway through the month we'll be in summer. It is pure hell. If we stick it out, Dilly and the babe and Daisy will go out of town for a while in July, to her sister's house in New Jersey, some sixty miles away. They live on the shore in a big barn of a place, once a posh settlement, handsome *fin de* houses now being converted into apartments. Hundred-year-old trees and inlets of water, lakes, grazing land. We were there once before we met you.

They go to the park daily and I meet them. LA weighs twice what she did at birth, remains bald, raw veal, spills sounds which can only be interpreted by the lovingly attuned ear, seems to enjoy living. We lunch together. The park is full of drunks sleeping off the endless gala. And mothers, of course. Charlotte wears my old stretch sweater. When we part I picture them rolling off through this grubby town, going carefully over the curb with the carriage, minding the traffic. Dilly's short stride. Liv's wary eye. She wears a bonnet, looks like Mother Macree. Thank Christ it finally turned up spring. Season of skin rash, and the air cluttered with baseballs. Daisy in kindergarten.

Charlotte is afraid you'll think she's all circumference and no centre. That's why she never writes. She will one day. Several drafts proceeding. She thinks she has to be seen. Amory and his *amourette* called, seems none too content in NY. His divorce is final. Saving is a strain for him. Also working here is hard. He has a good job but is still illegally in the country and very calm about it. No visa at all, no permit, would be shipped out if discovered. Spain is holding up some character reference. He aches for an opening, harps on life's absurdities, and those worn strings have been frayed by more noteworthy hands. He should have been rich—royalty in fact—and provided with an ambition which required some sort of physical exertion.

The temperature is around seventy-three degrees. Livvy, who cried for an hour from five-thirty this morning, is at tears again. We leave in two days on a little 3,000 mile jaunt. These are assorted facts, all of them relatively true, which, if committed to memory, could provide diversion for one year, three calendar months *at maximum*. Check me on this. Go ahead. Yours until I'm less groggy.

Bob

Postscript in Charlotte's hand:

A footnote from the little mother. I miss you both. Surprisingly, miss the old times—good or bad? Isn't that the way it always is? There are many days you just want to be someone else—somewhere else; preferably in Spain. Bob showers to go to a party. I drink alone, reading a fascinating tale called *Rats, Lice and History*. We hope to see you some day.

Much love,
C.

V

Apt. 4F.
186 Second Av.
New York 3, NY.

(undated)

Dear Olivia & Dan,

We came back to your (O's) letter. You both sound fine, a bit tight and miserable, but fine. Why does the lad never write? I haven't written since our Californian trip, though numerous letters of merit were started. I always feel I'm sitting down to unpack an old suitcase.

We went to California; we shifted flats. The trip was dull, costly, unenlightening. Went to Mexico once and saw a bullfight, but failed even to get drunk, God knows why. Mexico is kinda grey and mouldy, specially when you get into it there at first. You leave affluence behind and come to a region where the poor tend to stay poor. The tips of a number of states are touching it, or trying to. When you come back it's worse. The first thing that hits you are super marts, Yankee pig prosperity, and you know you're home. After that it's just a bunch of New Jersey turnpikes and the long drag back. Female relatives with doughy arms held up Livia and cooed. Charlotte breast-fed before my father's averted gaze. And my mother inspected the kid for family traits (she has my eyes, Uncle Woodrow's ears, Charlotte's hands; God make permanent our blood). She has only two teeth and very little hair, can't walk. We are four breathtaking floors above teeming 2nd Avenue and across the street from a burlesque house, the only one in NY, largely supported by sailors and single men who sit with their hats on their laps.

Charlotte's mother had a stroke while we were in Europe, another within the last few weeks. I visited her in hospital —an old Jewish woman hidden behind a curtain, gurgling and wheezing her way out of life. Though not paralysed completely, the decline accelerates daily, and there is nothing that can be done. She suffers from hardening of the arteries as well, a continual blitz of the brain. Old age, that abscess.

Down the street I went into a bar I like, an *Irish* bar for Christ's sake, quiet except for the quarrelling Irishmen and a juke box that plays nothing but ethnic airs: *Did Your Mother?* and *The Harp That Once or Twice*. And I in the midst of it, sniggering into my beer, unable to tear myself away. And Paddy the curate, that decent man, fills my glass again on the house. My old friend Hare, whom I may have mentioned, is now among the walking mad and dead.

We may not have the poets but we do have the Gross National Product, cheap cigarettes, and Henry Miller. LSD, protests, marches, a great to-do still about Who-Killed-Kennedy. Television would make you weep, the deodorant ad replacing the sonnet as a precise literary form.

Here we are all prone to sotty-sentimental Spanish aches. I can remember being miserable there myself, but it was a sort of dynamic misery. And for every itch there's a scratch. I think I should like to go back and drink, ambition-free, for once, without feeling time click off—with all due respects to Mr. Shelley and Lord Byron. How can we get rich and cease working? That's the rub.

Last night we had guests for dinner, drank considerably, then went off to see the State Department's movie on JFK—*Years of Lightning*, *Day of Drums*. Propaganda of the most distressing sort. Kennedy disguised to his admirers as a politician, the one role we resented most. His death remains unpurged: we would have him be a Hamlet and for some reason his murder (by Oswald alone) means Hamlet died slipping on a banana peel. After the movie, returned here for too many drinks, which kept us up until 3 a.m. (Day of hangover after night of rum).

Charlie wrote to us from Montreal. He sounded dispirited in this letter. It seems generally to have been a glum year for all the veterans. Children flourishing but the rest of the time going nowhere. Friends, forgive us. Up to the hackles in dung, snow, sleet, holidays, and home economics. Received your handdrawn card. It was very good. Charlotte wishes to add something down below.

BOB

Postscript in Charlotte's hand.

Rosa Munsinger is in New York and *still* playing her homemade spinet. She crept up behind Bob at a party and whispered in his ear: Well, am I any different here in New York? She does not change. How is Dublin? Who do you see? Did you get to the Theater Festival this year? I thought of you during that time. I think today is your birthday. Happy birthday.

I am surprised our longing for Europe has not ceased. I would dearly like to go back to Spain. If some of this money I am supposed to get ever comes through we may invest it in property there. Perhaps in two years. We miss you but wonder sometimes what would we say if we saw you both again. I'm sure Dan would find the right words. And we could always talk of Spain. Love, C.

VI

A year passed. Bob Bayless wrote again. His last letter.

186 2nd Av., Apt 4F.
New York 3, NY.

(undated)

Dear Friends,

God knows time passes, if He gives it a thought, and communications are bad. We think about you often enough, but have such a tight circle of activities, and are generally —we hope—so unsuited to our present circumstances that we glide (yes!) rearward, to the past.

Nothing changes, except the child. That's pure action, I should think: bearing. Daisy is of the type American-Spoiled-Jocular. The new one has a mind like a steel trap. She has sixteen months, seems slight, is good-natured, no beauty. Her crying! But she laughs a lot too. They are too easily loved, the lot of them.

Charlotte's mother died a couple of weeks ago. She (C.) left at nine the following morning, was back at four the next. The Jews stick them in the ground. For a life relatively free of clear-cut oppression, I think she had the toughest, least pleasant I have ever heard of; there was not a whiff of glory in the coming or in the going or what passed between; and when, at the end, she could rest for the first time in her life, she was mentally incapable of knowing that she was free of drudgery. She died on the 16th; Charlotte asks that I tell you this.

When Daisy was born my father died. Livia was sixteen months old when this happened. They are good replacements. I hope they avoid some of the crap.

California, where we spent three wasteful weeks, was just dull, and done primarily for my parents and Livia. She was spoiled and coddled and gifted and over-fed. Doused in blood and love she came out with a bit of vanity and self-assurance, qualities she'll need.

We visited Los Angeles. It's quite a pretty city, but you've got to overlook the smog and the pansies. Fruit of every description—and quite a few specimens you've never heard of, leastways come across—very thick on the ground in L.A. Some rotten, all cynically or creatively inclined, designers and the like, anxious to lay or get laid. Does the imagination dwell the most on woman won or woman lost? The smog is a real son-of-a-bitch. But when it's clear it's really fine. The drive through the city is a perpetual experience of looking down on valley bottoms or up to houses on the hills, not unlike San Francisco's own gridded sprawl. There the hills are mainly limited to one small peninsula, and the well-heeled citizens tend to vote Republican.

As to the Baylesses, we are kicking it along. Nothing more from here. Write sometime when the good spirit moves you; if not, not. Pray, eat sparingly.

BOB

'All my hopes now terminate in being made bishop of Virginia.' (Dean Swift to Gov. Robert Hunter of N.Y. 1709.) As an early Spanish writer noted: 'There is not a nation so stupid, so weak in body and mind as the unhappy Californian.' *Joyeuse Californie*, star-strangled-Banners.

Below this, Charlotte's last postscript, dashed down in her impetuous hand (she wrote just like the Chameleon):

Bob (she wrote) had his first (advance) review on the last day of Tishri, the beginning of the Jewish New Year— surely a good omen—so I thought I should write a note to you. Why have we never heard from you? Do you not write letters, Sir? I have written to you many times. Please write us and tell us of your lives in Dublin. Do you remember Nerka? I wonder how Miguel is; I had an odd dream about him. Was walking again on the moonstreet to Africa, when a big ship with black sails came very fast towards me. I ran and ran, and at the last moment someone fired and the ship sank. Looking up I saw Miguel standing near one of the cannons on the old Bastion, smiling and nodding. If you ever see him again, tell him I thank him.

How are you and Olivia? It's cold over here. And grey.

Love ever,
C.

From the *New York Times Book Review*: 'He (Shelley?) exalted the idea of human love; yet to almost everyone he loved he did some serious damage. Harriet he destroyed. Was his liking for women completely genuine? Certainly his willingness to share the young Mary Godwin with his amorous friend Hogg (as, from their letters, it is clear that he did) suggests a profoundly homosexual tendency. Some such suspicion . . .'

It was a fair review.

That Christmas she sent me a postcard of snow and stars, old Yugoslav art on glass. (That Jewy wife.) The card was blank. As I hadn't answered her letters or her headlong postscripts on her husband's longer letters, she was not going to trouble her mind by writing to me again, this the blank with only my address on it indicated plainly. Her silence was eloquent. And there, as far as I was concerned, it ended; torn across.

VII

Last Word from Roger Amory. A postcard, New York postmark.

338 E. 19th St.
New York City

30 Sept. 1965

Dear Dan,

I just walked back from Greenwich Village to my home via 14th Street, reflecting, if you can call it that, upon the passing of the years. In the centre of the street a subway vent gave up a cloud of steam; a single sorrowful bell tolled from the clapboard belfry of a Lutheran church to the right; one of those ponderous iron trash elevators silently sank into its kerbside slot and pigeons clattered just above it. All so neat. The heavy iron doors came together like hands on the last stroke of the bell, the pigeons soared up with the steam and away. A few leaves tiptoed past. I followed them. So how's life, old son?

ROGER

79 BAY: Ahead of us somewhere in the Atlantic lay the three islands. A fine rainy mist was blowing in from the west. I felt the pounding of the diesels under my feet. Presently it began to rain. We stood on the sheltered side and watched the rain falling on the sea. It rained as it can only rain in Ireland. The sky was overcast and grey, the vessel grey, the sea grey and smelling of Atlantic brine. Under the waters that we were sailing over a squadron of the defeated Armada rotted away. Three gulls were following the wake. The wake led away from the land. The diesels pounded. I felt the decks shuddering under my feet.

Presently the rain stopped, the grey clouds broke and there was blue. Then the sun came out. The sea began to change its drab colour, becoming the colours of the sky. I went below and called for two Smithwick's blue bass at the bar. Olivia and I sat on one of the forward hatches and drank it in the sun. Gulls floated at different heights in the warm air that issued from the stack. On the distant islands and on the sea the warm sun shone. Someone threw a bottle into the sea. The thought crossed my mind that the Baylesses would have enjoyed the sea trip to the islands. With the warmth of the sun on my face and the bass warming me I thought of her. Our trip to Cythera. I drank the good bass, the sun warm on my face and shoulders. I took off my raincoat and jacket. Mildly intoxicated. I felt benevolently disposed towards one and all. All the plain women I forgave for not being her; and her I forgave for doing what she had done with that stud. It was the course of nature: solacing one's existence with a woman one found agreeable. It was nature. I forgave them. In five years it would mean less, in ten, less again. In twenty years it would be forgotten. I thought of Goethe meeting his old flame Charlotte Kestner (née Buff) after forty-four

444

years. All mankind I forgave. I felt magnanimous, sitting there on the moving hatch in the weak sun, feeling the islands, my *Tir na nÓg* approaching. I wondered if any of the O'Donnells had died in the interval. Near the stern the Aranmen and their shawled women stood silent or sat on their baggage. One of the young islandmen took out a gunney sack, untied it, and showed furtively to his friends the stock of a .22 rifle. Possibly for shooting rabbits on Inishere. He tied it up again and put it away. They spoke together in undertones. Olivia put down the *Irish Press*. She said: Voting for the Irish Parliament must be like voting for some disreputable underground organization.

Dáil, I said. Dawl—the Assembly of Ireland. Up in the bow, risen out of the past, Fr Brendan Diffely S.J. spoke to a circle of women, urging them to sing in Gaelic. Two Gaelic speakers, perhaps school inspectors, stood by the companionway, with dandruff scattered like snow on their shoulders. Then a horse broke out in the hold and a Galway T.D. went below to calm him. We looked down. Fresh dung steamed on the boards. In makeshift stalls, cattle and sheep were restless. The horse backed, stepping into its own dung, rolling its eyes. The T.D. moved slowly in to try and calm it. What is that look in the eye that subdues horses? The ex-blacksmith had it. His thick hand moved up the animal's spine. Good man yourself, a Western voice breathed.

Slower and slower between the islands, greater and greater slackening of speed, calmer too.

80 ATLANTIC: The Atlantic was cold, seizing my member in its old freezing grasp. I came out and sun-bathed on the rocks, until the sun went in. It was a grey day on Inishere. The limestone retained little of the sun's heat, not warm like Andalusian rock.

I'm going back in, Olivia said, taking off her wet costume. Can I go like this?

Why not, I said, there's nobody about.

Olivia stood arranging her hair; the Aran sun had given her a delicate colouring. Far away near Clare a hooker with a brown sail was beating between the islands and the mainland. Holding her nose and with her free hand raised like a Civic Guard on point duty, Olivia dropped into ten feet of clear water. Her shadow rushed up to meet her. The sun shone on the sea-bed. Hear Neptune's horn! Somewhere at the back of the island a donkey began braying.

Then its brother appeared on the path above us, weighed down with a load of kelp. A young islander came behind, touching the animal's flanks with a switch. I held a towel about my waist, Kronos covering his privities. Should he take it into his head to sit down on a rock and smoke a pipe? From his position he must have had a good view of Venus in the sea, flutter-kicking along, her posteriors rolling like porpoises. *El sol rompío su envoltura, las mujeres se miraban asustadas.* O lady, when the sea caressed you, you were a marble of foam. He called out a greeting in Gaelic invoking the Mother of God. The donkey passed sedately out of sight. The young man followed, not looking back.

A beautiful Aran day, a shameless coleen in the sea, old Nick Adams sunning himself on a rock. Aran, it is said, is the strangest place on earth. Sometimes for an hour you *are*, the rest is history; sometimes the two floods culminate in a dream.

Olivia went at a leisurely crawl; her style in the water was rather like her manner on land. Turning on her back, without breaking the steady ongoing progress, she began back-stroking, showing off her valleys, dark declivities, arbutus ways. Signalling to me, *Vale, vale.* Does not our earthly life consist of four pristine elements? The solid, the liquid, the heat-conducting, the vibratory (calorific happiness).

It was the time of the autumn equinox, the sun crossing the equator for the billionth time, the sea as unchilly as it would ever be, with its burden of September jellyfish. Olivia, apparently immune to cold, waved to me from three hundred yards out. Beyond her in a haze rose the cliffs of Moher. And where was Mutton Island?

I remembered swimming in a warmer sea. We had gone in below Madame Olga's house one night. The lights of Dubrovnik, jewel of the Adriatic, were down on the horizon, a distant glow. We swam naked in depthless black water. Olivia sat on a warm rock and appeared to be wearing a white costume, so dark was her Adriatic sun-tan. The rocks retained the heat of day all night. She dived deep, and I feared would never surface again, swimming underwater like a white seal.

On a small pier somewhere between Rijeka and Dubrovnik, in the middle of nowhere, a young woman stood and watched. Brown as the earth on which she stood with one good leg and a wooden stump; a kind of sarong about her hips and nothing else, barefoot, she observed me. She was breast-feeding a small brown male infant covered with flies. The steamer was off-loading melons and machinery. I watched her move, her strong shape showing through the sweat-soaked cloth. It was very close and humid. I thought of her as unmarried, the infant the product of some wild night, the father (not caring) passing on. She spoke to the infant, her gums the colour of yew bark when opened. Giorgione's moon-faced Mary. She watched me, a pale northern face under an improbable Panama hat, a white hand moving a paint brush before an easel. Then she set the child down among the water melons, took one up, tested it with her hand, cut it in two with a sort of panga and came over, as blooming as health itself. She looked as if she had been rolling in dust, or been tumbled. Streaks of sweat ran down her face and torso. She offered the fruit, lactating freely, saying something which I did not understand, and I had a near whiff of her, reaching up, ancillary tufts drenched, feeling as if I were away in Paradise. View my breasts! Treat them like melons.

She was chewing some nut that stained her teeth and lips. *Gurra meal a mah agut*, I said, hoping that perhaps the old Gaelic sounded kinder to Slav ears than cold English. She went back to the child again, picked him up, put him to one of her bursting pomegranates. She watched me eating the water melon. When the steamer cast off, she stood on the pier and watched it go.

We had come from Ostend by train, watching pilgrims embarking for Lourdes. A heavy woman was carried aboard from an ambulance. Her face turned purple with embarrassment when the wind lifted her skirt and exposed unsightly bloomers to the gaping crowd at the ship's rail.

We passed from winter and rain in Belgium (stations with names from World War I, hard rain on the restaurant-car window in Köln) into high summer after the Alps, and the white butterflies *Kohlweisslinge* dipped over the shallow river where Austrian cattle waded, changed trains at Ljubljana and reached Rijeka in the early hours of the morning. The tourist office was open. It was not yet seven and they were selling steamship tickets near the harbour. A brown skeletal porter in a loincloth took our baggage away. Shabby privates in baggy uniforms were being drilled by a furious little officer. Olivia wept. I bought tickets and we went on board, eating tomato sandwiches on deck. After interminable hours of heat and sea the sun sank, Olivia went below, the moon appeared, the Dinaric Alps looked like a mountain of ashes. Olivia shared a cabin with two huge German women. I dozed in a canvas chair on the open deck, listening to the pleasant sound of the prow cutting through the water. The passengers sat silent as ghosts all about me. The air was clammy. I smelled pine forests. In the middle of the night a storm came up and raged for an hour. Then all became still again. We entered Dubrovnik, old Ragusa, around six next morning. We were going on to Cavtat and Mlini. Epidarus in the old dispensation.

⑤⑥⑤

Olivia stood below me holding out her hand for a towel. Her nipples stood out. I handed her the towel I wore. What's that you've got there? she said.

Codling or shark. A seagull flew over us, a shadow on Olivia's face, its predatory yellow eye looked down.

C'est moi, silent et mystérieux, I said.

O, Olivia said. So that's it. Here, dry me.

We slept at night in the deserted home of the retired light-house keeper. Downstairs during the day the island women were engaged at remedial work, making sanforized stockings. The mattress was of straw. Hard to sleep on shuck. We told Sarah O'Donnell. After that we slept well on a floating feather mattress. We spent most of the day in the open, the weather keeping fine for us.

449

81 MOGENS STENICKE stood once more in the house where, half a century before, he had first seen the light of day, Danish day in woody Humlebaek. He had been through the war, all the time confident of his immunity to German lead, as confident as Baamonde, at the other end of Europe behind the Pyrenees, had been confident that he was immune to Republican lead. Three years he spent in an English monastery looking for an austerity that was not there.

I was not three minutes in the place, he told me, when I knew it wasn't right for me.

And you came out again, I asked, after three minutes?

No, Mogens said, I stayed in three years.

Then he spent eight years in the Star of the Sea church on the Dublin quays. There by Butt Bridge the Liffey stank of ammonia, old men, lost hopes, diarrhoea. Life there was hard enough, looking after the needs of the destitute. He left, searching for a barer existence, landed on Aran with little money and no trade, slept under curraghs on Inishere, watched the island-women weaving on hand-looms, took eels from the black lake by night and sold the catch in Galway, ate little, listening to Wagner on his pick-up, the *Liebestod*: Isolde hampered by her veils, the yellowish obsession of the fevered. Then he set up two looms of his own and became as accomplished a weaver as the best of the women. He lived in a small cottage near the beach, did without fire or help, staring at the formations of cloud rising over the Clare coast. He made a living where a less resolute man would have starved, lived alone, thinking little of his fellow-men and nothing at all of his fellow-women.

You don't need a fire in winter, he said, observing me with washed-out blue eyes. The limestone retains the heat of the sun.

What sun? I said.

Mogens Stenicke loved to study the clouds, never the same at any hour of the day over the coast. He told Olivia that he knew where he was going to die. She had met him before I did. He spoke reluctantly, not mixing with the islanders, but when he opened up to Olivia in the bar one night, his tongue loosened by pints of black draught Guinness, he could not be stopped. He told her where he was going to die. It was a place called Humlebaek outside Copenhagen. If he never left Aran, would he not be immortal, live forever, watching the generations come and go, playing Wagner? Where better could he take refuge? Where better?

You cannot break wind on the island, he told me, but they know of it.

Hours do not suspend their flight. It is not man that stops time, it is time that stops man.

It was in the library of the house where he had been born. The sun shone through the long windows and pierced a glass paperweight on the desk before him. It turned crimson and the contents stood out clear as anemones in a pool. He saw clearly in it, and his heart almost stopped beating, the spot where he would die. He felt his death; one day the world would go on without him. Somewhere in the house a door closed, the light was extinguished in the paperweight and a sheet of blank paper drifted off the desk.

He sat there in the dim retreating afternoon light, until all the light left the desk, the carpet, lit up a grove of pines outside. Then the darkness came down. He sat in the dark, unable to move, feeling as Lazarus must have felt, not dead though buried in the tomb.

We walked around Inishere one afternoon, by the lake, the tall lighthouse, the long rusted hulk gone aground on the rocks (a cargo of Vat 69). Kelp, rocks, wreck, a rabbit or two, gulls: all progress, all human history, was reduced to that. Olivia told me what Mogens Stenicke had confided to her on the previous night in the bar. It was my third visit to the islands spread over twenty years; my first time with Olivia on Inishere, the smallest of the group. We followed the path leading to the ruined tower of the O'Briens, the wind was blowing in off the sea, like scarves, coming in over the prospective harbour (island dreams of affluence). Children in knickerbockers, Gaelic-speakers, straggled ahead of us on the path to school, an illustration from an old *Strand Magazine*. The yard of the school was silted up to the windows in sand, fine and persistent as snow. I thought of my mother at Salt Hill, that most forlorn of seaside resorts, photographed on a public bench, squinting into the camera lens. She had sat there watching the old *Dun Aengus* ploughing out to the islands, and wrote a postcard to me in remotest Canada. Dear Dan. My sweet dead mother.

Fish were drying on the roofs of the cottages, as on Neolithic lakeside dwellings of the Lower Danube, in the uplands of Anatalia, in Karanova in Bulgaria, Barkaer in Denmark. New Grange in the Boyne Valley. A passive civilization of scattered huts and villages. Homes of the 5th millennium B.C. The smoke that gathers blue and sinks, stench of burning fur. Our precarious beginnings.

In a small walled field at the back of the island I had re-read *Gulliver's Travels*. The ground I lay on was the nearest landfall to America, the Yahoos. A trawler moved between Inishere and Inishman, only its masts visible in a white press of gulls. Above their cries I heard the panting of the engine and saw sandy beaches and paths on Inishman where on the day of our arrival a young girl had drowned. The islanders rarely undressed or swam in the sea; the men seldom seen in the daytime and the females never at night. A shy fringe of Celtic society perpetuated there, hardly exposing their bodies to the air. The sea ended in a sad blueness beyond time.

What does it mean when a girl runs three times around the island? Once, on St. John's Night, I had seen them dancing about a bonfire. Pretty colleens I'd never laid eyes on in the daytime; and pin-points of the fires all along the Clare coast. *Beltane*, or was it later? the summer solstice when the sun is farthest from the equator and appears to pause before returning. Rites of the earth. Peasants of the Vendée play the violin and accordian and the donkeys get erections and mount the she-asses. Wild-eyed island beauties dancing in red petti-coats about the fires. In Andalusia, hidden away in dark little rooms, sewing-girls using up their youth and patience waiting for a *novia*. Plaza de los Martires.

Why are excrements, children and lice works of art? When a girl jumps three times backwards and forwards over a fire, they say she will soon be married, be happy and have a great many children. But when a young man and woman jump together over the fire without being touched by the smoke, they say she will not be a mother during the year, for the flames have neither touched her nor made her fertile. In other words, she has shown that she has the skill to play with fire without being burnt.

Fire festivals of India: songs and gestures, licentious to the point of indecency. On the day of the solstice the Estonians go in for debauchery. August. My night. The flames in the dark and the wind blowing sparks along the shore. Where are the red petticoats jumping in the darkness?

Martin O'Donnell had told me of the kind Dr. Beck, the German who loved the islands and the islanders and had landed in a helicopter with provisions when Aran was cut off from the mainland in a storm. For twenty years he had been coming on research. Then there was another man, also called Beck but no relation. He had gone back to Germany. The older Beck lived in Dublin. The Dane had not got on too well with the good doctor, so they informed me on Inishere. I had never met either of the Becks, then or later. Mogens Stenicke showed me his paintings and brass rubbings from the old church up to its headstones in sand, but when I was tactless enough to bring up the name of Beck, he cut me short.

I believe you didn't get on too well with the old one, I ventured to say.

The young one was worse, the Dane said, closing the subject.

Mogens Stenicke was stout, had white hair, wore a kris. His manner was evasive. He had met Behan on the island. We drank at night with the Dane in the bar near the slip. The other bar was run by a portly publican who had the manners of a Bishop.

The aired sheets smelled of lavender, stronger than the odour of horses or courage. The bedroom was bare and clean as a shell scoured by the sea. It was early and Olivia not yet stirring, sleeping with her arms by her side. In the outside jax I used pages of the *Irish Independent* for what it was intended and 'flushed' with sand. I stood in the cabbage garden. There was an abundance of hen shit on the low wall. I went down to the beach. Martin O'Donnell was there. We pushed the curragh out, while he pulled I waited to put out the lures for mackerel. There was a slick of their oil on the surface. Rings appeared on the water where the oars dipped and the curragh sped over the surface of the sea. It was one of those coral and pearl days that you get on the Atlantic in autumn. Dolphins jump, or sometimes roll. You see them in herds in the sea.

At the end of my first visit to Inishere, the two O'Donnells had not rowed me out to where the *Dun Aengus* rode at anchor, no, but a relative of theirs, McHale. When the old steamship began to draw away from the anchorage, blowing off steam, the two Martins rowed after her. They rowed with their profiles to me keeping on a course two hundred yards astern, pulling hard while the steamship drew away. Then they stopped rowing, and sat there with the oars in their hands, staring after the ship, but at such a remove that I could not see their expressions. Young Martin's peaked cap with the clip button gone, the old man's white hair. The son waved to me, the old man just sat and stared, wrapped in his own thoughts, like Hudson marooned by his own crew in the bay that would bear his name. Was that shyness or island reserve? I had got on well with the old man, reading the *Irish Times* there in the inglenook.

The men were out fishing for mackerel under the cliffs of Moher, the seven-hundred feet drop into which 'Pinkey' Domenech had fallen or been pushed wearing only American black panties. The body had drifted up among the rocks on Doolin beach in County Clare. Romolo Imundi of the homicide squad and women detective Julia McNamara drew back and the Irish police closed the Domenech file. The mother had been murdered about the same time, four thousand miles away in her

New York flat. And the escort of the twenty-eight-year-old American beauty queen swallowed an overdose of barbiturates in a Florida motel. Elsewhere 'Bubbles' Schroder the high-priced Montreal whore had been choked performing fellatio with a Jewish businessman, her last customer. So many rings on the water.

Hidden in the walled fields where the skinning Atlantic winds had left no trees, the men were spraying the potato crop with hand-manipulated German pumps slung on their backs, the copper gone the colour of duck eggs or the dome of the Four Courts. And masturbating with mute melancholy lust in the Neolithic trenches, their minds a riot of obscene images. The sun shone on the meadows, the walled paddocks, a land worked by men; nothing much had changed there since I had first visited the island, three visits past, a third of a lifetime away. I thought of the time in Spain: those transient friends which events bring and events take away.

82 AUTUMN: Fall. All the leaves are turning different colours and all the fruit is grown. Everything is pretty on the ground. The sky is grey and overcast with thin, grainy clouds. The sea grey too, smelling of kelpy wastes, always in movement. The neap tides rise and fall. It makes all patterns, the wind does, with leaves and waves.

We stay here in Lennane through winter. Connemara winter. I am working a little. All the houses of Lennane face the sea, and a small island out in the estuary thick with vegetation. 'Renvyle', Oliver Gogarty's mansion (often spoken of by my mother) is not far away.

It's very grey and peaceful. The pure air moves above the estuary and makes its stir where there are leaves and branches. Benign buss of air: lavender-and-kelp scented air. *Pecata Hibernia: la divisa dal mondo ultima Irlanda*. Odours from my youth; soft verbena-scented evenings. We share a double bed, a feather mattress. One cannot live in the depths of the country and have time for foolishness. Curlew and plover fly over the estuary. We hear their high cries.

In the morning the cool air coming through the open window gives us hope. She lifts her arms. A box of her autumnal face, her pierced beauty. A woman's bruised morning-face without make-up. She raises her arms. A shape immutably fixed yet doomed to change.

Oh this air, Olivia says, it's like Raglan! Raglan where I have never been. Greymouth on the Tasman Sea. Wanganui on Tasman Bay—many times she has mentioned these places of her youth, and of her parents whom I have never seen. Old man Grieve with his set Scot Presbyterian ways, austere regimen ('soup from the bones'). His 'Billy': Olivia being Billy. He had wanted a son.

∽❦∾

456

A village of houses with their faces to the water. Seven o'clock on this July evening, a few children among the rocks and an offshore breeze flattening the sea, driving grey clouds over its surface, the sun striking them from behind, its rays horizontal as it goes down. Everything points over the water. All away! The people too.

Down in a narrow channel between the rocks, waving shreds of seaweed (brown-yellow, transpicuous) stretch and stir with the drag of the tide. The colour of the hills, distant hills, is Paul Henry colour. I've seen it also in the *Schwarzwald*, the Black Forest, where that morbid and melancholy man John Synge played his fiddle to the listening peasantry at the turn of the century. The colour of the grapes in the best wine hills of all Germany. The wine there is golden and tastes of the earth. The woods empty except for an occasional rustic walking with hands behind his back, cogitating vacantly, going on the rides. The fir trees a blue-black mass. Todtmoos. Todtnau. Titisee. Schluchsee. Bühlerhöhe, *eine Insel der Ruhe*, eighteen thousand metres up.

In May a marriage in the woods. Flowering yew. Marjoram, thyme, lovage. Larva, pupa, imago. It is in the mountains that most apparitions of angels and saints occur, and God talks to his own.

Freudenstadt. (But where have all the people gone?)

The upper surfaces of the rocks are exposed as the water recedes. The tide is going out. Down in the narrow channel between the rocks I see darker islands of clouds and a speckled veil of light moving quickly into the shadows. The light remains motionless, water withdrawing on either side. Then it too slips away, a narrow shoot of light. Hue of illusion in the vegetable glass of nature. All the light drains out of the pool.

Little by little the tidewater is leaving the pool, the channel and the estuary. All the houses face one way. And the people, where are they? I send you this extraordinarily empty landscape.

It is late evening of the same long summer's day, a day like any other day, a day like today. Nothing essential has changed, yet all has changed. An old woman, or something like that, with hands on knees, all wrinkled grey and old, sits among the rocks. I have half a mind to go and see; but will leave her (or it) be. The light begins to go, leaving first the land, then the water, then the sky. Soon it will be dark.

No tidal flats, rock, reek of ammonia, kelpy wastes, sulphuric acid stench of foul eggs. Pouring matter, pouring waste, *Vergiss mein nicht!*

The light sets in a new quarter, the tide is turning; it will be full tide again in the early hours of the morning. Pockets of boulders along the estuary opening towards the Atlantic. The level of the tidal water rising against the smooth limestone. Manes of dense brown seaweed wave under the surface over polished stones. The light begins to go. The light is going. Are you asleep? Answer me.

Y SU EPITAFIO: Nerja cemetery.

```
┌─────────────────────────────────┐
│                                 │
│           D.O.M.                │
│     MIGUEL LOPEZ ROJAS          │
│    3 Deciembre 1964             │
│       a los 58 anos             │
│            RIP                  │
│    Tu Esposa e hijos            │
│     No te olvidan               │
│                                 │
└─────────────────────────────────┘
```

We go on loving those we have loved in other forms, or else we begin to cherish in other forms those we should have cherished in the past. Nothing changes. Everything is transformed.

Violette Leduc
La Bâtarde

Man is born as he dies, rebuking cleanliness; and there is its middle condition, the slovenliness that is usually an accompaniment of the 'attractive body,' a sort of earth on which love feeds.

Djuna Barnes
Nightwood

The organic individual presents two problems, the problem of pattern, and the problem of material.

Gordon Childe
*The Origin and Development
of the Nervous System*

This world now present to me, and every waking 'now' obviously so, has its temporal horizon, infinite in both directions, its known and unknown, its intimately alive and its unalive past and future. Moving freely within the movement of experience which brings what is present into my intuitional grasp, I can follow up these connections of the reality which immediately surrounds me, I can shift my standpoint in space and time, look this way and that, turn temporarily forward and backwards; I can provide for myself constantly new and more or less clear and meaningful perceptions and representations, and images more or less clear, in which I make intuitable to myself whatever can possibly exist really or supposedly in the steadfast order of space and time.

In this way, when consciously awake, I find myself at all times, and without ever being able to change this, set in relation to a world which, though its constants change, remains one and ever the same.

Edmund Husserl
Ideas

It is not so long ago—a matter of about a hundred years only—that most decent people still accepted the opinion of Bishop Usher that man was created in 4004 B.C., and that Adam was the first representative of humanity on earth.

L. S. B. Leaky, F.B.A.
Adam's Ancestors

Nothing is granted to me, everything has to be earned, not only the present and the future, but the past too—something after all which perhaps every human being has inherited, this too must be earned, and it is perhaps the hardest work. When the Earth turns to the right—

I'm not sure that it does—I would have to turn
to the left to make up for the past.

Franz Kafka
Letters to Milena

There are men and women hidden in a solid
tower, others under a glass cup, and others
simply amusing themselves near a garden by
eating and pulling up fruit. Under these a couple
with their backs covered by a sort of red egg
shell, madly dancing with large cherries in their
hands. In spite of this we have not yet arrived
at the end of the confounding surprises offered
to us in this gallery of enigmatic scenes. One
fellow carries an enormous mollusc on his back.
This creature busies himself by guarding two
human beings and three pearls, symbols of
the vanity of earthly richness. Another man
bows to a large marble globe which also
imprisons two men. Their heads and legs
extended by both breaches and opposite and
bowing to the same globe are three other men.
One has a big red strawberry on his back showing a wide cut adorned by a flower of evil.
Several groups press themselves around other
enormous strawberries and bunches of red,
violet and blue currants. Finally, a woman, that
the painter has located in a very visible place,
shows the posterior part of her body adorned by
flowers symbolizing the vanity of man's pleasures.

Cardinal Iracheta

I begin to see things double—doubled in history,
world history, personal history.

W. B. Yeats
Letters to Dorothy Wellesley

Look round at the courses of the stars, as if thou wert going along with them; and constantly consider the changes of the elements into one another; for such thoughts purge away the filth of the terrene life.

This is a fine saying of Plato:* That he who is discoursing about men should look also at earthly things as if he viewed them in their assemblies, armies, agricultural labours, marriages, treaties, births, deaths, noise of the courts of justice, desert places, various nations of barbarians, feasts, lamentations, markets, a mixture of all things and an orderly combination of contraries.

Consider the past; such great changes of political supremacies. Thou mayest foresee also the things which will be. For they will certainly be of like form, and it is not possible that they should deviate from the order of things which take place now: accordingly to have contemplated human life for forty years is the same as to have contemplated it for ten thousand years. For what more wilt thou see?

Marcus Aurelius
Meditations

A picture of a picture, by Magritte
Wherein a landscape on an easel stands
Below a window opening on a landscape, and
The pair of them a perfect fit,
Silent and mad.

Howard Nemerov

Purity of race does not exist. Europe is a continent of energetic mongrels.

H. A. L. Fisher
A History of Europe

* It is not in the extant writings of Plato.